Tony White is the autho[...] *Shackleton's Man Goes South*, a[...] published in journals, exhibition catalogues, and anthologies. White was creative entrepreneur in residence in the French department of King's College London, and has been writer in residence at London's Science Museum and the UCL School of Slavonic and East European Studies. He recently collaborated with artists Blast Theory on the libraries live-streaming project *A Place Free of Judgement*, and until 2018 chaired the board of London's award-winning arts radio station Resonance 104.4fm. Follow Tony on Twitter @tony_white_

Further praise for *A Fountain in the Forest*:

'White is always convivial company . . . His books are characterised by stylistic innovation, a feeling for place, a love of rogues and rebels. *The Fountain in the Forest* is no different. It's also the opening salvo in a trilogy. I'm already awaiting the next.' Sukhdev Sandhu, *Guardian* Book of the Day

'A formally daring novel . . . That all these stylistic fireworks can illuminate several rich plot lines, each with multiple twists, which an attentive reader will enjoy disentangling, is the best vindication of experimental prose.' Anna Aslanyan, *Financial Times*

'A truly intriguing venture into the crime genre by the talented White who had hitherto been seen as a lauded mainstream experimentalist . . . There is more to the novel than the actual plot, as White unveils a series of literary challenges which throw the whole story a softball curve, while never slowing the plot down. Engaging and at the same time a chal[...] [di]vertimento, and all rath[...]

'It can be enjoyed at the level of a thriller, and yet it does all these other fascinating things, and best of all it's the first in a trilogy . . . It's such a good book.' Andy Miller, *Backlisted Podcast*

'A complex and twisting plot with a genuinely shocking and satisfying dénouement . . . an extraordinary novel where our sympathies are for a cop who as a cop represents the very forces of repression the gut of the novel abhors . . . An astonishing achievement.' Richard Marshall, *3:AM Magazine*

'A detective thriller of unique calibre . . . intellectually stimulating, yet never elitist.' *Helsinki Book Review*

'White cleverly manages the suspense of the investigation, while showing his characters from multiple viewpoints, presenting their double lives without credulity-stretching plot twists. Any cop? Yes – this is innovative storytelling, at once serious and playful, and White addresses serious social issues in his work with a compelling, very readable style.' *Bookmunch*

'A knowledgeably detailed, intriguing and compelling police procedural . . . Yet for those who feel like delving deeper, an examination of White's methods and motives will reveal new layers, extra nuances and a background atmosphere that lends the novel an added eeriness and potency . . . A book well made: language expertly deployed, place wonderfully evoked, ideas, characters, memories, theories, political subtext brought vibrantly to life, a good story well told . . . Read and enjoy.' Nina Allen

by the same author
FOXY-T
SHACKLETON'S MAN GOES SOUTH

TONY WHITE

The Fountain in the Forest

FABER & FABER

First published in 2018
by Faber & Faber Ltd
Bloomsbury House
74–77 Great Russell Street
London WC1B 3DA
This paperback edition published in 2019

Typeset by Faber & Faber Ltd
Printed in the UK by CPI Group (UK) Ltd, Croydon, CR0 4YY

A CIP record for this book
is available from the British Library

ISBN 978-0-571-33619-7

FSC
www.fsc.org
MIX
Paper from
responsible sources
FSC® C020471

2 4 6 8 10 9 7 5 3 1

For Sarah

PREFACE

During the period leading up to the French Revolution at the end of the eighteenth century, a new kind of calendar was developed by the playwright Sylvain Maréchal and others, and adopted as the official calendar of the *République française* in 1793 before being abandoned on 1 January 1806. The French Revolutionary (or Republican) Calendar created a new way of measuring time from Year I of the Revolution (which was retrospectively designated as having begun on 22 September 1792): a non-hierarchical and secular system of ten-day weeks (or *décades*) in thirty-day months, without days of religious or royal significance. Instead, each day of the week was merely designated 'first day', 'second day', etc. In what became the dominant version of the Revolutionary Calendar, each day of the year also celebrated a different item of everyday rural life (although their precise distribution can vary), whether a herb, a foodstuff, a livestock animal, a tool or a utility: wild thyme, rhubarb, goat and beehive are just a handful of examples. Further, seasonal characteristics were drawn upon in the naming of each of the twelve months. Thus – to take the two best-known examples – *Brumaire* (roughly late-October to late-November) is derived from the French word for mist, and *Thermidor* (roughly mid-July to mid-August) from the Greek for summer heat. Of course, these few notes can scarcely do justice to such a rich subject, and readers wishing to find out more about the calendar are directed to Sanja Perovic's wonderful book (see Author's Notes), as well as to a multitude of online resources.

The Revolutionary Calendar was notably resurrected by the Paris Commune in 1871. It has been satirised – including by Alfred Jarry and the pataphysicians, whose thirteen-month Pataphysical Calendar includes the months of *Haha*, *Merdre* and *Phalle* – and been a source of inspiration to writers and artists. The French Revolutionary Calendar is still maintained and observed by enthusiasts.

Conversions to and from the Gregorian and other calendars are possible, although imprecise, since they depend upon the variant of the Revolutionary Calendar being utilised, and the method for calculating leap years. I therefore make no apology for any inconsistencies or liberties that I may have taken in the pages that follow.

Tony White
London,
21 Prairial 225

CONTENTS

Preface vii

I

1: Fumeterre (Common fumitory) 3
2: Vélar (Hedge mustard) 26
3: Chèvre (Goat) 37
4: Épinard (Spinach) 51
5: Doronic (Leopard's bane) 55
6: Mouron (Pimpernel) 66
7: Cerfeuil (Chervil) 73
8: Cordeau (Twine) 77
9: Mandragore (Mandrake) 89
10: Persil (Parsley) 96
11: Cochléaria (Scurvy grass) 102
12: Pâquerette (Daisy) 108
13: Thon (Tuna) 113

II

14: Pissenlit (Dandelion) 133
15: Sylvie (Anemone) 142
16: Capillaire (Maidenhair fern) 159
17: Frêne (Ash) 170
18: Plantoir (Dibble) 178
19: Primevère (Primrose) 182

20: Platane (Plane tree)   189
21: Asperges (Asparagus)   202
22: Tulipe (Tulip)   208
23: Poule (Chicken)   214

III
24: Bette (Chard)   229
25: Bouleau (Birch)   233
26: Jonquille (Jonquil)   245
27: Aulne (Alder)   250
28: Couvoir (Hatchery)   256
29: Pervenche (Periwinkle)   285
30: Charme (Hornbeam)   292

Author's Notes   302
Acknowledgements   309

I

1: FUMETERRE (COMMON FUMITORY)

Like any British policeman who had been brought up on the true-crime stories of the early twentieth century, Detective Sergeant Rex King recognised the jagged, hairy leaves and the sickly-looking yellowish and purple-veined five-pointed flowers immediately. It was **henbane** – *Hyoscyamus niger* – source of the deadly alkaloid scopolamine. This was the poison that, in 1910, the notorious 'Doctor' Hawley Harvey Crippen had used to kill Cora Turner, the music-hall entertainer who had had the misfortune to become his second wife. But what was a substantial and tall-stemmed henbane doing thriving here in the window box of a Bloomsbury pub, rather than in a **cabinet** of forensic medical curiosities, where it belonged? King made a mental note to let **Emma** at the Safer Neighbourhood Team know, so they could at **least** send one of the Police Community Support Officers, or PCSOs, round to have a friendly word.

With no real powers and little training, PCSOs were sometimes seen as little better than 'cardboard cut-outs' by many of their uniform colleagues. They were the butt of seemingly endless variations on the old joke about 'impersonating a police officer' and the subject of many a petty **cavil**, as well as more serious and justifiable resentments. This was perhaps understandable, given the negative impact on pay and conditions, let alone collective bargaining, that the creation of the post had engendered across the force. But the way King saw it, policing wasn't all blues and twos. Someone had to be out there on dog-shit duty, taking up the slack and covering all the

3

prosaic crap, because there certainly weren't enough real police to do it any more. And if most PCSOs couldn't fill out an MG11 to save their lives, it wasn't really their fault. King knew plenty who would have made good PCs, given half the chance and a bit of training, while conversely he'd had the misfortune to 'work' – he used the term advisedly – with plenty of PCs who were little more than 'coat hangers' or 'uniform-carriers' themselves. PCSOs might not exactly be **indispensable**, but King reckoned that if the Met or whoever did a **Gallup** poll, most of the public would rather have them around than not.

But lethally poisonous plants and PCSOs weren't the **reason** that DS Rex King was walking in a half-trot down Lamb's Conduit Street on this particular **Tuesday** morning at the end of May. Five foot ten with a forty-four chest, and fit for his age in a pair of khaki Dockers and a white Fred Perry, Rex had unzipped his black Harrington for the first time since before Christmas. The appearance of the sun was usually enough to have him paying an early visit to the barber's over in Lamb's Conduit Passage for his usual six-weekly number two, but it wasn't that kind of day. Response had received a call a couple of hours earlier, when a cleaner at the Royal Palace Theatre on Drury Lane had been alerted to a carrion scent by Tom the **night-watchman**, who had been meaning to mention what he had presumed was a dead rat in the theatre's scenery store since yesterday. The cleaner in question was Gertrude Bisika, a grandmother of Malawian heritage who had been granted asylum and indefinite leave to remain in the UK in 1983. She and her now late husband had fled the regime of Malawi's then self-anointed President for Life, the late tyrant Dr Hastings **Banda**. Gertrude's husband had worked in the Malawian capital, Lilongwe, as a private secretary to David Chiwanga, the then MP for the southern district of Chikwawa and one of the politicians killed by Banda in the so-called 'Mwanza Four' incident. Hearing news of Chiwanga's death, supposedly in a car crash on the border with Mozambique, and fearing the imminent arrival on their own doorstep of the dreaded MYP – the paramilitary wing of Banda's Malawi Congress Party – the pregnant Gertrude and her husband had packed a small bag each and fled.

'A dead rat, hmm?' she had said. 'Well, that don't smell like no rat to me.' Having worked as a cleaner backstage and front every morning for most of the thirty-odd years since they had arrived in London, Gertrude Bisika had other ideas. She had encountered more than her share of carrion, from mice and rats to cats and foxes and even – in the early days – the body of a nameless meths drinker who'd somehow got into the basement seeking warmth and shelter during the blizzard of February 1991, when a foot of snow had fallen on London in a few hours and **icicles** had hung along the length of the Russell Street colonnade. When the snow had thawed, so had he. And, oh boy, hadn't they known about it.

This time the smell had seemed to be emanating from somewhere along the so-called Long Dock, a corridor that traced the route of a former alleyway linking Russell Street and **Vinegar** Yard that had once marked the rear perimeter of the Royal Palace Theatre site, but around and over which the theatre had expanded. First when it was rebuilt for the third time and with a larger stage following a fire in 1809, and a century later, when the backstage area was restored again following the stage-house fire of 1908. This expansion saw the theatre annexing neighbouring buildings, yards and tenements around what had formerly been Marquis Court, and roofing over the intervening streets and alleys to create a backstage warren of workshops and storage spaces, dressing rooms and wardrobes, that was almost as large as the auditorium itself.

One part of the stage house that had needed to be almost completely rebuilt following the 1908 fire was the 'paint frame', a workshop where theatrical scrims or gauzes had been hand-painted for centuries, and which – following theatrical tradition – took its name from the frames upon which the gauzes were stretched. Recently it had fallen into relative disuse and now seemed to have been locked up for a few weeks. Gertrude Bisika had wondered if the smell wasn't coming from there, so she had gone and got the keys from Jane who did earlies on the stage door, and opened it up.

She was right. And this is where it got personal, and why Rex King might well have seemed more worried by this call-out than he usually would be. Rex King knew the paint frame at the Royal Palace very well, and had visited many times, because for as long as he'd known him the studio had been sublet by his old mate Terry Hobbs. And come to think of it, Terry hadn't been around for a while.

As Rex had said to Lollo when the call had come in, he was telling himself not to worry, but it didn't help much. After all, if you were called to an incident in your mate's kitchen, it was probably not unreasonable to wonder if he might not be involved. And the paint frame *was* like Terry's kitchen.

He was salt of the earth and a bit of a bon viveur of the old school, was Terry Hobbs, and a drinking buddy of a couple of decades' standing. They'd met in the early nineties in the Coach & Horses pub on Wellington Street, when Rex had been new to the area and had just started working out of Holborn Police Station. He'd wandered into the Coach by chance, looking for a swift whisky at the end of a tough day, and got talking to some bloke at the bar. That one whisky had turned into a few pints, and since then they had somehow stayed in touch. Not only that, but they'd even managed to meet up every now and then, which was not something you could say about all of Rex's friends. Sometimes they would meet for last orders at the Coach, if Tel was in his workshop, or at the Duke on John's Mews when Rex was working late. More rarely this might be preceded by a quick meal, usually to further their ongoing debate about the relative merits of two great London fish-and-chip shops: The Rock & Sole Plaice on Endell Street versus The Fryer's Delight on Theobalds Road. Each would defend the chippy on his own manor, though Rex did have to concede that The Fryer's was usually full of plod. If Rex was eating on his own or fancied getting away from police talk for an hour, he'd usually go for something with a bit more **spice**. Chilli Cool, a Szechuan place on Leigh Street, was a regular lunchtime haunt at the moment, but Rex's love of Chinese food was not shared by Terry, who, given the choice, liked few things better than to stroll through the streets with a bag of vinegary chips.

Terence Hobbs had a good memory too, which, coupled with his raconteur's knack for spinning out epic tales involving local names and faces long forgotten by the rest of the world, made him very entertaining company. A **Mark Twain** of the Thames, you could buy him a pint or two and Terry would pick up this Aldwych *Iliad* where he'd left off last time, whether that had been a week ago or a couple of years. 'Now, where was I, Rex,' he'd say, pointedly raising his voice as he picked up the pint, 'before I was so rudely interrupted by that tosspot behind the bar?'

'Yeah, fuck you too, Terence,' they might say, with a wink; or words to that effect.

'Sorry, love,' Terry might say, whoever it was. 'Not **my type**.'

Terry's stories conjured up a pre-regeneration Covent Garden that, if they were to be believed, must have been populated almost exclusively by legendary drunks, entertainers and artistes both celebrated and forgotten. It was different now. Gone were the days when you'd more than likely bump into Danny La Rue walking his golden-palomino chihuahua in the Phoenix Garden of a morning. The props men, the wig-makers and costumiers, the makers of fake noses and other prosthetics, had all left. Some of them, Terry Hobbs included, had lasted a few decades longer than the market traders, but even now many of them were moving out at best, or simply dying off. Blame the money men, Terry would say, because the question driving this change was the one they were continually asking, which went – for example – something like this: Why should my budget shoulder the overheads of having Maury handmake me a wig in the West End, if I can get it shipped from China and pocket the difference? This was a question that didn't just apply to wigs, of course, but to every **aspect** of the business, theatrical gauze-painting included. And it was a question to which everyone knew the answer.

It was why Terry's business had not been going so well lately either. At least, that's what he had told Rex when last they'd met a month or two ago. He'd said that he was thinking he might have to let the studio go, that things had been on the slide for a while. Rex had been sorry to hear this, of course. Sorry for his friend, but also sorry for the apparent passing of a bit of showbiz history and magic. Getting to know Terry's work had been a revelation to him. Visiting the paint frame that first time had been like stepping back to another age, and Rex had suddenly seen the theatre not just as a building or a place, but also as a kind of machine for telling stories.

The paint frame itself was a narrow space, longer than the theatre's proscenium arch was wide and stretching up beyond the full height of the stage to a gantried roof and skylights far above. Down the middle of the room, if you could call it that, ran a long line of paint tables, crudely built workbenches that were laden with tins and rags and brushes of all shapes and sizes, and around which the floor was a

Jackson Pollock-like accretion of splashes and drips. Running down either side of the space were the frames themselves, enormous wooden constructions that must each have weighed a couple of tons or more, grids of blackened and paint-spattered beams and struts across which would be stretched the gauzes themselves, ready for painting. On Rex's first visit, Terry and the crew were knocking off at the end of a long few days working on a familiar, romantic view of Istanbul for a staging of the pirate ballet *Le Corsaire*. It was exquisite work. There were boats and raftsmen in the foreground, a royal barge and a distant Hagia Sophia rising through the mist in the centre of the painting.

Mug of tea in one hand, Terry picked up a photo from the table, the reproduction they had been working from. 'Thomas Allom,' he said. 'Londoner. Barnes man. Better known as a minor architect and illustrator, but I love these great paintings of his. Been dying to do one for donkey's years. Sometimes it's only when you rework it like this, get into the nitty-gritty of it, that you realise just how good they are.'

The small reproduction of Allom's painting that he was holding had been gridded off so it could be copied on the larger scale of the gauze. It seemed miraculous to Rex, unfathomable even, that such a faithful copy could have been produced by hand and eye alone, and yet still succeed in conjuring the full richness and dynamism of the original. He looked up at the top of the gauze, twenty feet or more above them, and Terry must have guessed what he was thinking, because he reached for the right-hand edge of the frame and with what seemed a mere flick of the wrist sent the whole contraption plummeting down. Rex suddenly understood why there were no ladders. This wasn't just a trough running along the floor beneath each frame to catch the paint, but an enormous drop into which they could be lowered at will. His vertigo tweaked by the realisation that he was standing on the brink, Rex instinctively took a step back. 'Blimey,' he said.

But that wasn't all. More than mere visual **wallpaper**, or simple backdrop, theatrical gauzes had almost magical-seeming properties, which – completing the tour – Terry illustrated by means of a powerful lamp. Lit obliquely from above, the gauze was opaque and the image of Hagia Sophia and the various barges and rafts on the waters of the Golden Horn seemed so dark and substantial that it might have been painted on to board or canvas.

'Now you see it,' Terry said, before taking the lamp and turning it so that it shone directly at the image, 'now you don't.'

Rex was astonished. Within the pool of light projected by the lamp's bright beam, the painting had effectively disappeared, the gauze had become translucent, revealing the wooden struts and the brick wall behind it. Looked at one way, the image was there. Looked at another way, it disappeared to reveal the action taking place on the stage behind it.

'Bloody hell, Terry,' he burst out. 'That's amazing.'

Rex had been right: it was incredible – magical, even. But latterly it had begun to seem that the demand for this kind of theatrical illusion was passing. Projection of an image had never been a substitute for a painting on gauze; the quality just hadn't been there. But more recent developments in digital technology meant that an image could now be projected on to an unpainted gauze from two sources and synchronised perfectly. And there was something quite intangible about this, the light from two sources, that would be enough to give it the necessary lift and vibrancy, to offer a quality of brightness and detail that a single projector could not. The result may not quite have matched the visual **thrill** of what Terry with a wink would call 'a handjob' – a hand-painted scrim – but it cost a fraction of the money to achieve. Once Terry had needed to employ three or four scene-painters to keep up with demand, working around the clock and painting two enormous gauzes at a time, one on each frame. More recently he had been lucky to get half a dozen a year, he'd said, and even that was dropping off. Now – or the last time they'd met – he'd said he wished he could get one or two, just so he wouldn't have to get rid of the place.

Rex told Lollo that he didn't quite know what to think. Had business really taken a turn for the worse for Terry since that last sombre pint? He had tried calling his mate's mobile as soon as they found out the incident was at the Royal Palace Theatre. And then again when it became clear that it was in the paint frame. But both calls had gone straight to message.

It wasn't just Covent Garden that had been regenerated. The Lamb's Conduit Street that Rex himself worked in now bore little resemblance to the one he'd got to know a couple of decades earlier. Holborn Police Station hadn't changed, but apart from one or two other survivors in the area – the aforementioned Fryer's Delight – there was barely a shopfront or an eatery that hadn't undergone at least a couple of transformations. From tobacconist to copy shop to nail bar, say. Hairdressers and estate agents were the other current fads. Further out, of course, and it would be payday loan merchants and bookmakers. Stick around for long enough and you could see the process in action. Businesses that had closed during the financial **ebb-tide** of whichever recession would lie empty for a while, post piling up on their respective doormats. Then the premises would play host to a flicker of pop-ups and fly-by-nights, nothing sticking, until suddenly the machine stops, the money comes back for a while, and for a decade or so you've got an Argentinian steakhouse, a blow-dry bar or an upmarket greetings-card shop. King had the feeling that around here that process, whatever you'd call it – 'boom and bust' didn't seem adequate – might have gone a bit too far, that they were heading for another high-water mark. The idea that a single street could sustain half a dozen near-identical upmarket men's designer clothes and footwear shops, however good they might be, would have been unimaginable when he'd arrived here. Let alone shops that displayed little more than a single handmade leather bag and a scattering of kitsch cufflinks. Or the one that only sold retro-styled reproduction French crockery, of all things. It had gone way beyond any normal cycle of urban renewal.

The Conduit Coffee House, affectionately known as Sid's, a better-than-average greasy spoon where Rex had enjoyed countless all-day breakfasts 'plus two extra hash browns', as well as his more recent 'usual', the rather healthier two poached egg on two brown toast, was now far outnumbered by artisan coffee shops with a side-line in organic this and wheatgrass that. Even the old clock-mender's around the corner was now an upmarket **tea-shop** specialising in cupcakes. Rex had gone in there once looking for a decent coffee, and they'd asked him if he had a fucking reservation. What had used to be The Sun, a great real-ale pub on the corner, had gone through several changes of name and theme, and was currently, and without irony, called The Perseverance.

Over those same years, most of King's colleagues had done the usual and drifted out of town to their various respective domestic idylls, commuting in from Essex or Hertfordshire, but King had lived in the same Holborn flat since 1989. All these years later he still got a kick out of the fact that, living where he did, almost everywhere in central London was within walking distance. Once upon a time, that boast would have meant nights out in the West End, strolling to Camden or Clerkenwell, meeting mates for pints in Bradley's or

Chinese food in Wong Kei. Then afterwards a coffee in Bar Italia before strolling home and walking in through his own front door at more or less the same moment when, for others, the hunt for night buses would only just be beginning. Now he probably hadn't been to any of those pubs – The Pillars, The French House, The Blue Posts – for a decade or more, and walking anywhere was usually associated with the job. Like now. Given the chance, King would generally walk to all but the most serious of grade-A calls, and even those he could generally reach more quickly on foot than in a car. He had stopped asking, 'What took you so long?' years ago.

As he crossed at the lights, King checked his phone, but there was still no word from Tel. Seeing the blue-and-white incident tape that stretched across both ends of Russell Street, the police cars and the ambulance, he quickened his pace. A thin wisp of blue smoke hugged the ground, twisting and curling along the pavement from a discarded cigarette end on the kerb.

'Alright?' he said to the PCSO who was standing at the stage dock door. 'Do they know who it is?'

'Don't know, skip,' came the slightly rueful reply. 'They don't tell me nothing.'

You should be thankful for that, you doughnut, King thought to himself.

'Who's here?' he asked. 'Socks?'

'Yeah, Socks and Fuck Me.'

'Fuck Me?'

'Yeah. Bit of a mess. I know that much.'

Oh shit. Taking a deep breath, Rex was aware that this could be the last lungful of fresh air he would enjoy for a while. He might also be about to see what was left of a good mate. Steeling himself for whatever was in there, and mentally preparing for a potential ID, he

13

didn't need anyone to show him the way to the paint frame.

'What have we got?' he asked the PC who met him on the inside and handed over a paper suit and slippers.

'Alright, skip? Unidentified male, we think. It's been here two or three days. Don't know any more than that at the moment.'

Rex sighed. Good old Terry. It – he – wouldn't be unidentified for long. 'Where is he?' Rex asked.

'Down there,' said the PC, leaning around the doorway and pointing towards one of the drops. Now scrim-free, the topmost black timbers of one of the painting frames were about waist high, which meant that most of the structure was down below. Two rubber-gloved and paper-suited Socks – Scenes of Crime Officers, to give them their full title – were shining handheld fluorescents down the shaft.

It would be easy enough to get pissed and fall down there, thought Rex. Tel could certainly put it away, but Rex had never seen him that drunk.

The next few hours went past in a blur of paper suits and flash photography. These were well-practised procedures that had evolved over the decades to secure any scene and to ensure everyone's safety. The aim was to prevent the loss or contamination of any evidence, whether trace or forensic, that might help to build an information profile. A picture of where, when and how the death – in this case – might have occurred. Whether it even was a crime scene. All of this had to be done before you could determine whether any formal evaluation or investigative strategy needed to be developed. And all of this too, here and now, amid the utter mess and chaos and the teeming unfamiliarity, to most of those present at least, of an artist's studio. 'What a fucking mess,' the photographer said. 'I don't fucking know where to start.'

Webster was over in the corner chatting to a Sock. Taller than Rex, with dark hair and a double chin, in his open-necked shirt and crumpled brown suit, Webbo's substantial spare tyre spoke of a long commute in a comfy car and a fondness for social drinking, but what else was there to do out in the sticks?

Rex was glad not to be in charge. At any death scene, everyone knew their job and their level and got on with it. Training kicked in, whether that was basic work like note-taking and doing measurements or sketches, or more specialist functions such as photography, or collecting swabs and scrapings from whatever **geyser** of bodily fluids might have sprayed across floors or walls, to see if they might yield some DNA. All done by habit as much as anything, with individuals of whatever rank methodically following procedures and training. That was the theory, anyway, but there was always scope for a fuck-up. So all of this activity also had to be planned and coordinated by a qualified CSM, or Crime Scene Manager. Rex had worked his way up the PIPs training – the Professionalising Investigation Programme – hoovering up the National Occupational Standard qualifications, so he had done his share of CSM, and done it well. But when the call had come in and his personal connection with the possible victim became apparent, Lollo – Detective Chief Inspector Jethro Lawrence – had given CSM to DS Edward Webster, with the expectation that Webster would be well placed to take on Deputy Senior Investigating Officer, or DSIO, as well. Deputy, that is, to Lollo's nominal role as SIO.

Detective Sergeants Webster and King had trained and come up through the ranks together, and they got on well enough despite a bit of form in their personal lives. Actually, that was 'the understatement of the year', as people had once been fond of saying, but, as Rex had told Lollo, he wasn't about to let any past differences get in the way of finding out what had happened to poor old Terry Hobbs.

'Right,' said DS Webster, several hours later, when a lull in activity suggested that the initial response phase was coming to an end. 'Let's get him up, shall we?' He looked around, as if searching for something. 'How does this thing work? Got to be a handle or something somewhere. Anyone know? Rex? With respect, he's your mate.'

'No problem.' Rex reached out to rest his hand on the upright, gripping the smooth, blackened wood of the frame before giving it a gentle upward shove. 'It's all counterweights, Eddie,' he said, looking up at the pulleys with their S-shaped spokes turning high above their heads as the great wooden frame slowly rose to his touch. 'Amazing bit of machinery, isn't it?'

There was not much time for those assembled to admire the Georgian engineering. Looking down the drop they had seen rope, so they all had an idea of what to expect. Rex wondered aloud whether the weight of Terry's body might have been enough to lower the frame a metre or two with the sudden jerk of its fall.

As the huge structure rolled up into the light, Rex saw the top of a familiar and nearly bald head. Then the rest of the body emerged, its head lolling to one side and from the waist down its clothes soiled with foul liquid putrefaction. It stank, and no wonder. With a nightly audience next door of – what? – three and a half thousand, perhaps, Rex couldn't believe it had taken this long for anyone to complain about the smell.

In his quarter-century on the force, Rex had seen plenty of dead bodies. He was used to the various transformations that betrayed the dead's steady march through the inevitable stages of decay. But the features of this body – because Rex knew that, whatever this was, it wasn't his pal any longer – were far more grotesquely disfigured by bloating and the other processes of decomposition than Rex might have expected. More discoloured too. What with the mottled greenish tinge and the fact that the nose appeared to be missing, his former mate's features were rendered almost unrecognisable.

'Ouch,' said Rex, reaching protectively for his own nose. 'Scraped off in the drop, do you think?'

'Male deceased,' Webster was dictating. 'IC1. Height: five-eleven or six? Age?' He turned to Rex.

'Terry? Oh, I don't know. Maybe my age; bit older? Fifty-five-ish? Not sure,' was the best Rex could do.

'Suicide?' asked DS Webster.

'Hard to say,' said Dr Sue Stanza.

'Shit!' said Rex, pointing at the shoes: light-tan slip-ons with a rounded and highly polished toe. 'That's not Terry Hobbs, Eddie. The bald fucker had me going for a minute there. Similar build, but I don't think Tel ever polished a shoe in his life.' He stepped forward to look at one of the hands.

'You're kidding,' said Webster.

'No. It's not him. One hundred per cent. Tel's got artist's hands, from all the chemicals or whatever. There'd be paint under his fingernails. These are clean.'

'Well, who the fuck is it, then?'

'Christ knows,' said Rex.

But they all knew what this meant.

If that wasn't Terry Hobbs's body in the frame, as it were, then Terry could be in another kind of frame for killing whoever the fuck it really was.

Webster turned to the duty Forensic Medical Examiner – a.k.a. the FME, or Fuck Me for short – with a wink: 'What do you reckon, Dr Stanza? Is he dead?'

'Well, if he's not,' Sue Stanza played along, 'I'm not doing CPR.'

She went in for a closer look at the gaping wound on his face. 'No sign of scraping there,' she said. 'Even with the bloating and the decomposition, it looks like a clean incision.'

'What does that mean?' Eddie Webster asked.

'That it might well be a hanging,' said Stanza, 'but it's not your open-and-shut suicide.'

When they had been in training, King and Webster had been close, like a double act. Testing each other on the manual and each acting as a sounding board for the other. You had to. There was a lot to take in; you couldn't just absorb these tactical and strategic processes overnight.

Back then, faced with a crime scene, they would have had to verbally go through the checklist just to work out what type of homicide this was. 'Domestic?' Rex might have asked.

'Current or former spouse?' Webster would continue, listing off the subcategories. 'Sexual rival? Parent–child or child–parent? Nope, doesn't look like it.'

Starting out, there was a reason you had to actually enumerate the options. You had to say it out loud so that it would sink in: Homicide in the course of other crime? Robbery or burglary gone wrong? Sexual attack? Gang-related killing? Racially motivated? Unspecified and unrelated? Serial murder, mass homicide or terrorism? HAC – homicide among children? Now they just sort of knew the list, and made a decision without even thinking about it. They didn't actually have to cross all the options off any more. This one was easy to categorise: Context and motive unknown. Which is to say that it was the most difficult kind of investigation.

Once the photographer was done, DS Webster began appointing roles for the wider trawl. Some of this was obvious stuff. Putting a few bodies on house-to-house enquiries and community reassurance, getting hold of all the CCTV, checking the description against missing persons on CATCHEM, obtaining statements from the staff who'd reported it, checking the signing-in sheets on the stage door.

It wasn't just the muffin man who lived on Drury Lane. Dozens of windows overlooked the stage house on the corner with Russell Street. There were mansion blocks, Peabody flats, a school. There was no saying whether anyone in those various windows would have seen anything, but you could never tell what a house-to-house might turn up.

Following up with everyone else at the scene might be a bit more challenging when there were tens of thousands of people – the population of a small town – passing through a big theatre like this every week.

There was a long way to go before anyone would be making any kind of hypothesis about what had happened here, but given the split between front of house and backstage, and anxious to get his foot on the ball and control the play as quickly as possible, Webster decided to reduce the size of the pitch, as it were. They were to obtain what ticketing records they could, but to do nothing with that data beyond a preliminary search for known offenders. The more complicated aspect of the job was making sure the paperwork was not only in order, but also auditable. Everyone from detective upwards knew that was the key to a conviction, and that the better a case was documented, the more chance it would have of standing up in court.

With all of this, DS Eddie Webster was following the Murder Investigation Manual to the letter, but in one respect he decided to do something different. Given Rex King's prior relationship with Hobbs, a man who in the space of a few seconds had been transformed from potential victim to main suspect, Webster had checked with Lollo and they'd asked King to stay on as Second Deputy SIO 'at large'. This was unorthodox, but the looser attachment was designed to give the investigation, and Webster, access to King's background knowledge and expertise, but without overcommitting him or taking him off other current or impending investigations.

At midnight, Rex King was still at his desk in Holborn Police Station. He could have gone home hours ago but hadn't been able to face it, he'd said – not with his friend missing and now possibly wanted for murder. He'd given up trying to think through the conversations they'd had the last few times they had met up. Instead he had been scrolling through the hundreds of crime-scene photographs of Hobbs's studio that had already gone up on to the investigation's shared drive. He didn't exactly know what he was looking for. Perhaps he was just waiting for something to jump out at him. That was a hard enough job at the best of times, but ten times more difficult when you were looking at such a visually busy space. Rex had seen it all before, of course, on his many visits over the years. So he could see through much of what, to most people, might look like generalised chaos – and yet the paint frame suddenly looked strange and unfamiliar. Right now, no single detail was more important than anything else. It was as if the photographer's gaze and the very act of taking these photographs, functional images devoid of any of the usual aesthetic impulses, had broken everything down to the same level. As if only then, by looking at the scene and its constituent parts afresh, but without the usual hierarchies and imperatives of subject or theme, could some new order be constructed from it. In this case, hopefully, the gradual assembly of a persuasive story about how and why someone had been murdered. But the lack of visual artistry, the absence of an imposed vision, always made crime-scene pictures hard to look at. And Christ knows, thought Rex, it was difficult enough already, given what had gone on in there. One obvious thing, as he scrolled through the images, was that – apart from the body – the actual frames themselves were empty. There were no works in progress, no jobs on the go.

One of the last photos in the file showed the back of one of the paint frame doors. Like all the other doors backstage, the entrance to the paint frame was full stage height, in order that scenery flats could be moved around freely. They always reminded Rex of the giraffe house at London Zoo. The double doors that opened on to the paint frame were also thickly padded for soundproofing, so that you could shut them and carry on working during a performance. Most of the crime-scene photos seemed to show these two doors fully opened into the space, but one of them, and only one, showed the left-hand door closed. The photo must have been taken after Rex had left, and the odd thing about it was that there were some marks on the back of the door.

He nearly missed it.

As Rex would tell Webbo later, it was only after he'd scrolled past the photo that he realised there was something about it that niggled at him, and he had gone back to it. It wasn't that there was anything particularly unusual about writing on the walls per se. Generations of painters had been chalking up jobs and specs, or calculating costings, on the walls of studios just like this one, and Terence was no exception. You could see it in some of the other photos – quick sums or phone numbers scribbled here and there – but this was new. He zoomed in until that part of the photo filled his screen. In a loose but sinuous hand the name 'Trudi B' had been chalked on to the black-painted wooden panelling of the door, and followed by a big tick:

Trudi B ✓

He made a screen grab of the detail and quickly typed himself and Eddie an email – 'Just seen this on the back of doors at scene.

Definitely new, not seen it before. Who the hell is "Trudi B" and why has she been ticked off?' – but there was not much more he could do about it now. It would have to wait for the morning. He pressed 'Send', then closed the window and shut down. Picked up his Harrington off the floor, where he'd thrown it a couple of hours earlier.

'G'night,' said **Eric** Jinks, the Enquiry Desk Officer, as Rex King walked past, one arm halfway into the sleeve of his jacket and his body half-turned ready to shoulder through the door and leave the building. 'Or good morning. Oh, but skip? You'll like this. You're still SD cover, right?'

'For my sins, yeah,' said King warily, stopping in his tracks and turning back to face the desk. ''Less you fancy it?'

The EDO was quick to politely decline: 'No, you're alright.'

'Sorry. Long day,' King said. 'What about it?'

After a decade working with the London-wide murder investigation team on the Homicide and Serious Crime Command – and with a particular responsibility for a loosely defined patch that skirted the city, west to east, from somewhere around the Drury Lane end of Shaftesbury Avenue all the way to Shoreditch High Street – DS King had found himself saddled with being temporary lead on Safe Detention and Handling of Persons, SD for short. 'Temporary' in this case meaning two years and counting. The role had come up when Spoony took early retirement in the last restructure, and none of the remaining uniform sergeants at Holborn was up to it. At least, that was how Detective Chief Inspector Lawrence had put it. So they were having to go wider. Then, 'Come on, Rex, mate. Help me out, for fuck's sake.'

The tone was convivial, but that had been an order, of course. Barnsley lad that he was, and for all his rank, Lollo had a kind of no-nonsense Yorkshire informality about him, a gruff non-conformity. It was part of why he was so popular. But in all of their years of working together, Rex had learned that there was no question of ever being able to say no to Lollo. So he hadn't. And in so not doing, DS King had added to what was already more paperwork than he could reasonably get through in a full shift and still do his actual fucking job. But then, if you want something done, as they say, find someone busy.

Still, it had given him a bit more of a toe-in here at Holborn, and, to be fair, the SD role was not so bad. Piece of piss, really. It was mostly about skimming data from other people's paperwork, and the occasional one-to-one with Lollo in the run-up to liaison with the programme team at directorate level. Hop on the tube to St James's Park once a year for flip charts and biscuits with some MPS or MOPAC twats in an airtight conference room that still smelled of the farts of whoever had been in the previous meeting, then back here to cascade down a 'lessons learned' bulletin and circulate the updated manual to a bunch of Dodos – officially, Dedicated Detention Officers – who, earlies, lates or nights, it didn't matter, could always be guaranteed to claim never to have received the group email.

'Inspection date is fixed, or so I hear,' said the EDO.

'ICV?' asked Rex. It was a long shot and he knew it, but Independent Custody Visitors he could handle.

'Yeah, you wish. No: SiC' – he pronounced it 'ess-eye-sea' – 'the works. Inspectorates, Care Quality mob, Custody Directorate. Full document audit, detainee questionnaires, the lot. Bastards'll be here for weeks. Reckon they'll call all the team leads in on Monday for a briefing: Gnat's Piss, Fuck Me, PACE, SD. That's probably why Webbo got Deputy SIO today. Lollo must have known this was coming. What d'you reckon?'

If the EDO was visibly enjoying this, and he was, it was because he knew that he wouldn't have to be stuck in a room with that lot for an hour. The Fuck Me lot, Forensic Medical Examiners, were great people to have with you on the job, but you wouldn't want to spend too much time in their riveting company if you could help it. King wasn't even sure who the lead on NSPIS – National Strategy for Police Information Systems, or Gnat's Piss for short – was these days. What a cock-up! Someone had probably got Chief Inspector for that, leading the development teams and the rollout on what had once, King remembered, seemed an impossibly futuristic online data-entry system. A couple of years down the line and Gnat's Piss had turned your basic ten-minute booking procedure into a frustrating hour of micro-tasks, pointing and clicking at frozen computer screens.

'It's like the Olympics, innit,' said Jinks, interrupting his train of thought.

'Eh?'

'Team GB, skip. International obligations, mate.'

That was true. SiC went all the way up, way beyond Scotland Yard and MOPAC, past the Home Office and up through the Foreign and Commonwealth Office to the UN, the United bloody Nations. The fact that they had all known that an SiC was coming did nothing to soften a blow the impact of which was now written all over Rex King's face, and the fact that he hadn't moved and was still standing in reception with one arm in his jacket and the other reaching blindly behind his back for his left sleeve. The EDO waited a beat and a half more to let the full reality of it all sink in, before following up with the punchline: 'Working this weekend?'

That woke Rex up. 'Sod off, Jinksy,' he said. 'You'll be shitting it like the rest of them. Better hope your own house is in order, eh?' Then, sotto voce, 'Twat!'

'Steady on. Don't shoot the messenger,' said Jinksy. 'I'm not the **enemy**! I hadn't finished yet. I was going to say be careful, because word upstairs is there's been another leak. Looks like we've been hacked again, mate.'

'What's out there?'

'Nothing yet, but I hear it could be one of yours, Rex. Sorry, pal.'

'Eh?'

'Tennyson.'

'Oh, great!' said Rex. 'That's a name I hoped I'd never hear again.'

Christ! Tennyson was the last thing you wanted hitting the fan on the eve of a Safety in Custody inspection. First Terry, and now this pair of nightmares? What was it they said about shitstorms?

That they were like London buses.

You could wait for ages and then three come at once.

As DS Rex King pulled on his Harrington, the jacket's ribbed waistband snagged on the Hiatts and the radio on his belt, just like it always did. After reaching down to unhook it, he smiled and did a two-handed Vs-up to the EDO, then turned and pushed through the double doors, letting them swing shut noisily behind him.

2: VÉLAR (HEDGE MUSTARD)

Sometimes – on mornings like this, perhaps, when it would have been nice not to have to start work until 3 p.m. – Rex King missed the **old** days of shift work, and envied the uniform ranks their two-two-twos and four days off: two earlies, two lates and two nights. Sure, spend a few years with that shift pattern rolling through your life and you might forget your own name, let alone what day of the week it was. Plus it played havoc with your relationships and social life, having to forgo those little things that other people took for granted, like weekends. But still, even if it hadn't seemed so at the time, life was certainly simpler when all of that was decided for you. You might get a bit **crabby** when there was only a six-hour gap between finishing a night shift and starting a late, but truth be told that had never been such an issue with Rex, since he lived locally.

Since going Detective, and now DS, he'd been on the basic eight-to-four, which sounded good, almost like a normal job, but you quickly found out that it was no such thing. In reality you worked all hours: 'as required' was how they put it in the small print. It had taken a bit of getting used to, always being swamped with work, but Rex figured that it was part of the **bargain**. Investigations were often a matter of life and death, and when there was that much **riding** on your actions, you could hardly clock off at four. You didn't join the force for a **free and easy** life, even if you had joined by accident.

When asked, that's what Rex always said. That he had joined by accident, but had discovered that he liked police work. After college, he had been staying on the sofa of a shared house on Coptic Street, close to the British Museum, signing on and scraping by. Coptic Street had been a shithole but, since his friends were renting it from a short-life housing co-op, it was cheap. The only catch – albeit a big one – was that you could be evicted at any time, with less than a month's notice and with no guarantee of anywhere to move to. They'd all been looking for work and one of his mates had seen an ad in the *Camden New Journal*, which had been placed as part of what Rex later realised had been a temporary initiative, a pilot scheme to recruit graduate policemen. Much to his housemates' amusement, Rex had written off for the form. Within a month or two he had been for an interview, passed an entrance exam and had a letter from the Metropolitan Police saying they would **assign** him a place on training.

By this time, Rex's friends had been kicked out of Coptic Street, so throughout the interview process and the run-up to his start date he had been sleeping on sofas all over London. He continued to attend the monthly short-life housing co-op meetings down at Seven Dials, just in case any other places came up. But they never did.

Finally someone from the co-op's management committee had taken pity on Rex, pulled him aside and told him not to bother. The co-op already had more members than places. But he had sweetened this home truth with a timely bit of advice: 'Now,' he had said, 'and I mean right now, might be the last opportunity for a homeless – no offence – young man like you to get on the waiting list for a council place.'

His housemates had laughed and ignored the tip, none wanting to be tied down to anything so humdrum as a council flat. But in spite of their collective incredulity, which had only increased since he'd applied to join the police, Rex had acted on it right away. He had gone to the Camden Housing Office, quite truthfully pleading homelessness, and got his name on the list. Rex couldn't know for certain, but he'd felt sure that it was the promise in writing of a job in an essential occupation in the borough that had clinched it. He had moved into the one-bed flat in the Falcon building on Old Gloucester Street in the summer of 1989, and – sign of the times – was offered it as a right-to-buy early the following year for what at the time had seemed like the exorbitant sum of £45,000. In the intervening period, of course, he had started on the job, and the way Rex would usually tell the story was that he'd thought he might stick it for a year or two, clear some debts, then move on.

Now here he was, how many years later, still living in Falcon. He did have a washing machine but there was no room for a tumble dryer in his tiny kitchen, so he still dried his shirts and **underwear** out on the balcony. He also still used the letterbox to pull the door to behind him when he left the flat, and still jogged down the stairs, as he was doing right now. He still picked up the newspaper from Golding's every morning, and did the crossword when he had a minute; still enjoyed this ten-minute stroll to work.

'The scenic route' was what he called it, along Great Ormond Street, site of the famous children's hospital – the jewel in **Nye** Bevan's crown – with its attendant twenty-four-hour traffic of doctors and nurses, carers and service users.

Later in the morning, to a soundtrack of sliding car doors and wheelchair ramps, doctors and consultants would hold pavement conferences as they walked from round to round and building to building in twos and threes. Taxi drivers were rendered more solicitous than usual by their frail cargoes, but would leave the **motor** running for a quick getaway and a sigh of relief nonetheless. Waves of parental anxiety breaking against the calm acceptance of their various charges. 'Patients' was about right. The pun always struck him: the patience of the sick. Even now, at just gone 7 a.m., there were families arriving for their 8 o'clock appointments. Porters in their uniform polo shirts and blue polyester overalls stood and smoked under the old carriage-works arch opposite.

King didn't have to walk this way. Theobalds Road was a minute or so quicker, and he had once even taken a 55 **bus** that single stop, but coming the back way was a habit he'd picked up in his first days on Borough Crime, and it had stuck. At first he had found it calming to go via the leafy expanse of Queen Square. He had been pretty green himself too, at the time, and had only just discovered that you saw things as a detective that other ranks didn't need to engage with. At the end of what had seemed a particularly grim week managing the exhibits relating to the death of a fifteen-year-old schoolboy, King had found himself on Great Ormond Street. The scenes of suffering that confronted him on the steps of the hospital were redolent of the Passion, or a pietà on some grimly rendered Gothic **reredos**: every mother in the eternal role of Mary; every father **gaunt** and red-eyed, standing with head bent like some beseeching **apostle**.

It had put Rex's own squeamishness firmly into perspective, and he had taken this route ever since. It still grounded him that, however bad he thought he might have had it, these kids were going through far worse, and facing it down with ten times more courage than any copper. However tough a case might seem, for Rex this was just a job, he could walk away, where for some of these kids that struggle was the burden of their whole short life.

Some colleagues couldn't handle it. There were a couple of supposedly hardened coppers he knew who would do almost anything rather than walk down Great Ormond Street. They just couldn't hack it. But having this on his doorstep was part of who Rex King was. He was proud of it. He even rattled the collection tins and sold a few books of raffle tickets at Christmas.

When he was very drunk or maybe looking for a sympathy fuck, King had sometimes spoken about the twin brother he had never known, who had died without gaining consciousness a few days after being born. When Rex was a child, he had overheard hushed conversations between his mother and grandmother, and learned that his brother had been strangled by Rex's umbilicus. If they hadn't gone in to get his twin out, Rex might have died too.

Sometimes, if Rex looked in the mirror when he was particularly tired, he thought he could see his brother looking back at him. Other times he wondered what life would have been like if there had been no problems with the delivery and he had had a brother all these years; a twin brother at that. Or what might have happened if his severely brain-damaged twin had survived more than a few days. Perhaps he would have ended up like one of these Great Ormond Street kids.

Right now, though – today – Rex King had other things on his mind, and top of the list was coffee. Having got home after midnight and 'wound down' for longer than he had planned, Rex had awoken with a hangover that was roughly commensurate – emphasis on rough – with the bottle of industrial Australian Shiraz he had finished at one thirty in the morning. He had just about had time for a shit and a shower, but not enough to load up the stove-top pot and make his usual espresso.

There were plenty of cafes and restaurants to choose from around here, but Rex liked to put his money, such as it was, the way of local businesses who paid their taxes, rather than filling the non-dom coffers of the more ubiquitous chains that didn't. He wasn't an unreconstructed food philistine like some of his colleagues, but, given the choice, Rex would go for a good fillet steak and chips over confit of onglet on a salad of wild hedge mustard every time. For even simpler fare – bacon-sandwich simple – Sid's was hard to beat. It opened early too. Situated where they were, between a hospital and a cop shop, the staff at Sid's were ready to cater to those clocking off nights or on to early shifts, and they had a sizeable menu. They also did good coffee, unlike the majority of builders'-type caffs in London, where 'coffee' **often** meant a spoonful of Nescafé dissolved in boiling water and topped up with milk.

The late-spring air was fresh enough to cut through his hangover a little, but the headache was only compounded by lack of sleep. He had been too drunk to seriously practise any of the relaxation techniques that Helen had once taught him – Imagine that the in-breath is a wave! Breathe out quickly through your teeth! – so had been unable to stop his mind from racing, replaying and dissecting the events of the day. At three in the morning he had realised he was still awake and listening to the steady, **duple** beat – usually inaudible – of the kitchen clock.

Sitting outside Sid's with the *Guardian* on the table in front of him, folded up and unread – crossword not even started – and his coffee and a bacon sandwich on white toast on the way, there was plenty to think about. Three conflicting narratives that would be competing for his attention in the coming days, if not weeks and months. Firstly there was his old friend Terry Hobbs, who was suddenly, astonishingly, **front runner** to be the lead suspect in a murder investigation. Then there was the news of the Safety in Custody inspection. Now – cherry on the cake – Tennyson was about to be dumped in the public domain all over again.

The first of these was puzzling, but Rex had been loudly relieved when it became apparent that at least it wasn't Hobbs's body they had found the previous day. The missing friend still hadn't returned Rex's call, but, knowing Terry as he did, Rex had told Eddie that he was as confident as a bent bookie at **Newmarket** that Hobbs couldn't have done it, that he'd be willing to bet a year's salary that there would be no forensic evidence – not a single **finger-print** – to link Tel to whoever it was that had been killed in the Royal Palace Theatre paint frame.

The second? Rex was less worried about the outcome of any inspection than about the rigours and the burden of the SiC itself. Like he didn't already have enough to do, without having to accommodate a bunch of apparatchiks with clipboards crawling all over everything. He knew that he had kept a tight ship on SD, so it was just a matter of putting his head down and submitting to the **forthcoming** process, speaking when spoken to, framing every response within the relevant regulation, and not obstructing them in any way. Easier said than done, but not impossible.

That just left Tennyson.

Rex felt his forehead **tighten**. Later he would tell Lollo that he felt almost as **indignant** as he had in the run-up to the trial. Why would someone want to drag all that up again? It sometimes felt as if there was a part of the population that was at **war** with the police. Yes, Trevor Tennyson had died on Rex's watch. The otherwise fit thirty-year-old postman had asphyxiated while being restrained following a scuffle as he was escorted to the custody suite, having been booked for throwing an egg at some minor-league **banker** during the Occupy protests. The incident had been complicated by a gap in the CCTV record, but the reason for this was well documented – power cables in Richbell Place had been severed by BT engineers looking for a junction box, and half the building was dark – and Fuck Me's evidence and the toxicology test results had demonstrated beyond doubt that Tennyson's asthma had made this an accident that was waiting to happen.

As the station lead on SD, Rex had given evidence on chain-of-command and booking procedures, and both Gnat's Piss and his own paperwork had backed up the medical evidence. It was a matter of record that no asthma inhaler had been found among Tennyson's effects. Medical records confirmed that Tennyson had a repeat prescription for both a long-acting reliever and the more familiar short-acting relief inhaler, the type that is usually colour-coded blue. Traces of tiotropium bromide in tissue samples were consistent with daily use of the long-acting reliever, but, as the defence had pointed out, this should have been supplemented by the shorter-acting drug as and when needed. But no trace of albuterol sulfate, a.k.a. Ventolin, had been found in the samples, giving a degree of certainty that this had not been used within the previous however-many hours.

According to Gnat's Piss, asthma had not been mentioned by Tennyson during booking, even though the system contained fields for entering known medical conditions, and the booking-procedure script included verbal prompts on medical history and current prescribed medications. If this information had been offered, or if an inhaler had been found among his personal effects during the booking process, a less kinetic approach might have been adopted once things had got out of hand.

The judge's summing-up had reinforced the defence case by strongly suggesting that if – and only if – Trevor Tennyson had had a short-acting reliever inhaler in his possession when he left the house that morning, the balance of probabilities was that he had lost it while travelling to, or in the excitement of, the protest. Alternatively, or perhaps additionally, with his symptoms largely controlled by daily use of the long-acting reliever, there was a persuasive suggestion that Tennyson might even have become blasé about keeping his short-acting Ventolin inhaler to hand, a complacent attitude that was only reinforced by his not mentioning the condition when prompted during his arrest. This carelessness seemed to have been confirmed by a Post Office colleague, a character witness who, while giving evidence, had been forced to admit that he had seen Tennyson borrowing a friend's inhaler at work on at least one occasion. In other words, Tennyson hadn't always carried his own inhaler with him as he was supposed to do.

Rex knew from experience that, when you are watching a trial, whether as a participant of some kind or from the public gallery, you can sometimes recognise the moment when the case is won or lost. This had been that moment. The witness, Tennyson's colleague, had known it too, judging by the expression of dismay on his face.

That had been enough. The four officers who had been escorting Trevor Tennyson to the custody suite at the time of his death were all acquitted.

'Bacon on white toast?'

'Thanks.'

Rex took a bite, savouring the crunch of toast and the crisp, salty bacon, the vinegar trace of the tomato ketchup. As he ate, he continued to roll these three things around in his mind: the current investigation, the impending SiC, and Tennyson. Rex had a fairly good idea of how these conflicting imperatives would be prioritised by Lollo and upwards, and even though Rex himself was firmly implicated within all three, he retained sufficient detachment to have a professional interest in whether his theory would be proved correct.

Of course, given the choice, King would have dropped everything for his mate. Who wouldn't? He would run the case to ground and not stop until he could put Terry one hundred per cent in the clear, but since when had a DS had any choice? Let alone one who was only 'attached' to an investigation.

Knowing Lollo, Rex figured that Tennyson would dominate the day. Where some might see a renewed focus on such a controversial UFO – 'Use of Force' incident – as a bad thing, especially when it was one of the few deaths in custody in the country to have gone to trial, Lollo would probably already be talking about using it as a springboard to demonstrate best practice and transparency. That way, the borough would have a positive and public-facing benchmark in place that could be part of the Met's story when the Safety in Custody inspection started, not to mention be used as part of a counter-narrative if the inspection turned up any negatives. Rex also knew that Lollo could be unsentimental at the best of times – ruthless, even. So if any bodies had to be sacrificed in the telling of whatever story needed to be told in order to set the scene, so be it.

Although Tennyson had happened on Rex's watch, he thought – hoped – that he had been too far away from any real action on this one to be in the firing line, but he knew that he would still have to watch his back. Rex had managed to keep a lowish profile during the trial, using 'bureaucrat mode', as he called it – calmly describing the various relevant procedures – to deflect attention, offering those basic procedural truths to cover the much larger lie, so he didn't want to undo all that and become the focus of too much attention now. He certainly didn't want to become 'the face of the case', as sometimes happened. You were fucked then.

He wondered how long it might be this morning before he'd get the call to go upstairs, whether the lawyers would be there from the get-go. He could guess. It was frustrating, to say the least. For a start, Rex wanted to go back to Covent Garden and have a closer look at that writing on the back of the paint frame door: Trudi B. But if Tennyson dominated the day as he thought it would do, there was no way he'd be able to get to whatever investigation-team meetings

Webster might have lined up, let alone go back to the scene. He'd have no choice but to simply email Webster about the photo again, and hope for the best.

Right now, as he relished the last mouthful of bacon sandwich and drained his cup, Rex had a sudden flash: he knew this feeling. The moment when you recognise that you might be enjoying yourself too much, that your world might be about to change. That all this was too good to last. There was no such thing as a simple pleasure in this game. It was always an illusion, or at best the calm before a storm. Well, it wouldn't be the first storm of his career, he thought to himself. Bring it on. And at least he could see this one coming. Not like when Helen had blindsided him with Webster.

Walking down Lamb's Conduit Street towards the station, Rex knew that the legal teams at New Scotland Yard, and at every newspaper in the country, would already have spent hours poring over whatever Tennyson material it was that had been leaked. Both sides would be doing the same thing, which was looking for something nobody had noticed before. A new angle or something concrete that might have been overlooked last time around. A reason why this had been leaked. They'd be conducting a fine-grained analysis – a 'fingertip search' – for anything that might qualify as new evidence, while also getting updates and steers from their respective libel lawyers about what, if anything, in all of this might actually be **printable**. Rex knew he would find out soon enough what they had each decided, but then, as he turned down towards the staff entrance on Richbell Place, it struck him: Trudi B.

What was the name of the cleaner at the Royal Palace Theatre who had reported it in the first place?

Gertrude?

Could Trudi be a nickname?

3: CHÈVRE (GOAT)

When he got up to the office, Rex sat down and logged in, but not for long. Lollo had evidently been keeping an ear out for him. 'Alright, Kingsy?'

'Morning, sir.'

'Bloody Tennyson!'

'So I hear. How bad is it, do we know?'

'Not sure, Rex. Only just got here myself, so I'm just getting on top of it now, mate. Upstairs were going to try and **schedule** a meeting for ten. Lawyers are a-kip at the moment. Why don't you give Webbo a couple of hours till then, eh? Help him find your mate.'

'Is he in?'

'No, he phoned five minutes ago. M11's fucked, in't it, so he's stuck on North Circular.'

'Be a while yet, then,' Rex laughed. 'I need to go and check something out at the scene. See you at ten, sir.'

'Don't be late.'

Enjoying this unexpected reprieve, Rex went back outside. As he stepped through the main doors, he was confronted by the sight of a man in a tweed jacket and plus fours wheeling a **penny-farthing** bicycle up the **ramp** into the disability access lift, but he didn't give it a second glance. He made a mental note – as he always did – to cancel his membership to the gym opposite. He'd been giving them about a thousand a year in direct debits for the past too-many years, but never even had the induction. If he was relatively fit right now

– and he was – it was nothing to do with his gym membership, but because of a casual decision to always use the stairs in this place instead of the sodding lift. He had stuck to it too. And when you're up and down a twelve-storey building most days, that's a lot of stairs.

Ten minutes later he was at the Royal Palace's stage door, showing his badge. 'I'd like to have a quick word with one of your cleaners,' he said. 'Gertrude Bisika? Can you point me in the right direction, please.'

'Sorry, she's not in today,' said the stage door keeper, a pleasant, bohemian-looking woman with lots of rings on both hands. She was holding one hand over the telephone mouthpiece. 'Hang on, pet, let me just finish this call.' She sounded bunged up. 'Sorry, no, love. You can't just come and work here – you have to send a CV. Send us your CV with a covering letter saying why you want to work here, and someone will get back to you. Alright, poppet. Thanks for calling.'

While she spoke, Rex looked around. In the cramped, cubicle-style office, rows of keys jostled for space with an old-fashioned telephone switchboard, a first aid box, CCTV monitors and filing cabinets, a bottle of **sherry** with a glittery gift tag tied around the neck, a multi-gang plug adapter crowded with phone chargers . . . You name it. The jumble of office equipment, fire blankets, wire in-and out-trays and pigeonholes looked as if it had been here for years, as did she. How could **she bear** to work in such a tiny space, he wondered, but he knew the answer: the bonhomie, the relationships, and knowing this place inside out. Theatre folk were good, tolerant people on the whole. It would be rewarding work, and one of those jobs that you'd get better at the longer you did it.

'Ah, bless!' she said. 'Must think it's the early bird that catches the worm.'

'When in fact it's the early bird with a CV?' said Rex.

'Well, exactly. Excuse me—' She blew her nose, threw the tissue in the bin.

'Nasty cold,' said Rex.

'Ah, I wish. No: **sinus**,' she said. 'It's about yesterday, right?'

Rex nodded and smiled.

She took a ring binder from the shelf, flipped through, ran her finger down a list. 'Ah, no. That's it. She's got a hospital appointment this morning. **Physiotherapy** up at UCH. But you'll probably catch her if you go round there now.'

'UCH?'

'No. She lives around the corner, in the Peabody flats over the road. Tell her I sent you. Jane.'

'Okay, will do. Thank you.' Rex decided that he would have to come back another time to examine the paint frame door. 'Have you got the number?'

As he knocked on the door, Rex could smell curry goat cooking down the hall. 'Mrs Bisika?' he asked. 'DS King from Holborn Police. Jane on the stage door said to tell you sorry, but she thought you wouldn't mind. It's about yesterday. I know you're in a rush, but have you got five minutes, please?'

'Yes, Jane just telephoned me. I was expecting you. Please come in.'

It was a neat flat, with patterned rugs on the floor and antimacassars on the backs of the chairs. Family photos of weddings and children were arranged along the mantelpiece. A larger framed photo of a handsome, grey-haired man was set on top of the TV, and next to it a tulip in a small china vase that sat on a coaster-sized lace doily. He could see from clothing and architecture that some pictures had not been taken in London. He thought he recognised Gertrude Bisika in one of the photos: a young, slim woman, smartly dressed

39

in a beige skirt and cream blouse, squinting in the bright light, but looking quizzically beyond the photographer as if trying to **discern** something outside the frame of the photograph. 'Is that you?' he asked, pointing at the photo. 'You were a looker, weren't you? If you don't mind me saying.'

'Well, my late husband seemed to think so,' she said. 'He took that photo. In 1979. I had just graduated from university in Lilongwe—'

'. . .'

'That's Malawi, where I'm from.'

'What did you study?' Rex asked, genuinely interested.

'Organic chemistry,' Gertrude said. 'I wanted to work in the oil industry.' She must have noticed some giveaway in Rex's expression. 'Excuse me? Do you think I wanted to be a **drudge**?'

'Sorry,' said Rex. 'Of course not.'

'Listen,' she said, 'I'm not complaining – that place has been like a family to me – but when we arrived here in eighty-three I had practically never seen a **skyscraper**. I grew up in the north of Malawi and my father was a newspaper editor in Mzuzu. I met my husband at university in Lilongwe. He was a journalist and a party worker. He wanted to be an MP at home, serving our country, not a postman in London! Believe me, I tried to get work in the petrochemical industry, work that I was more than qualified to do, but it turns out that, in Great Britain, international qualifications are **subjective** things. Or they were in those days. At least, if you didn't have white skin. That was the most important qualification of all. Anyway' – she glanced at the clock on the mantelpiece – 'how can I help you? I'm sorry to rush you, but I am afraid that I will have to leave in a few minutes.'

'Yes, of course. I'm sorry. Physiotherapy for your . . .'

'My shoulder,' she said. 'Whatever you might think, women's bodies were not built for buckets and brooms.'

He asked her to run through the events of the previous morning, which were pretty much as he had already heard: the smell, getting the keys, calling 999.

'So you'll know Terry?' he asked. 'Who usually works in there.'

'Mr Hobbs? Of course! Everyone knows everyone in that place. Mr Hobbs always starts work early when he is busy, and he always says hello to us ladies. A very egalitarian gentleman. Not like some.'

Sounds like Terry, Rex thought. 'Can you remember when you last saw Mr Hobbs?'

'That is difficult to say.' She frowned, and something in her expression reminded Rex of that photo, the promising young graduate. 'Perhaps a month or two. He said he was sorry to hear about Benedick.' She looked at the photo on the TV. 'That was my husband. God rest his soul. Mr Hobbs offered his condolences. Very sweet. So that would have been the beginning of March, when I went back to work.'

So she had been widowed very recently. 'Forgive me,' Rex said. 'I'm sorry for your loss.' He paused for a second or two. 'Just one more thing.' He showed her the photo on his phone. 'I just saw this and wondered if Trudi B was you? Do they call you Trudi? Do you have to tick it off once you've cleaned the room or something?'

'Trudi with an "i"? No,' she said, and laughed. 'Everyone has always called me Gertrude, or Gertie for short, even my husband. That or Mrs Bisika.'

'And the tick?'

'Well, as I say, I have no idea about that,' she said. 'We never clean the paint frame because it's always been sublet to Mr Hobbs for as long as I've known it. And you've seen the place. It's a mess! Where would you start?' She laughed again. 'Yes, we do have to sign off, but we do that on a time sheet that is hung up by the stage door. Anyway'

– she looked again at the phone – 'are you sure that's a "B"? It looks like the number thirteen to me.'

'Thank you, Mrs Bisika,' said Rex, reciting the script and reaching for the wallet in his back pocket, wondering if she didn't have a point. 'You've been very helpful. Here's my card. Do feel free to call me if you remember something unusual, or if anything else comes to mind.'

At 10 o'clock sharp, Rex walked into the tenth-floor conference room, where Lollo and various others were drinking coffee from pump-action beverage dispensers that Building Services had placed on a table at one end of the room. Rex was glad he had already had a decent cup. The projector was plugged in, but at that moment all that was showing on the screen was a bouncing-ball graphic bearing the phrase 'No Signal'. All of the venetian blinds lining the windows along the conference room's long external wall were down, slats closed, but someone had opened a window at the refreshments end of the room so one of the blinds rattled erratically as it was repeatedly but irregularly lifted and then dropped by the breeze. Closing all the window blinds when one or more senior policemen were in the room was a long-standing legacy of Operation **Erin**, imaginative Met code for the investigation into the IRA's London bombing campaign of the early 1990s. The measure, which had been designed to neutralise a sniper threat that was never realised, had been unofficially dropped in the spring of 1998, following the Good Friday Agreement, but then reinstated in 2000, after the rocket attack on the MI6 building in Vauxhall by so-called 'dissident republican' group the Real IRA.

Half a dozen archive boxes were stacked on top of a low wooden cupboard to the left of the door. From where he sat, Rex couldn't read everything on the box labels, but he could see the important bit:

TENNYSON I, TENNYSON II, and so on. He had seen these boxes before, at meetings with the QC who had headed up the defence team. They were the case files from the trial.

He recognised some of those present: the original defence team, couple of Fuck Me, three or four suits from St James's Park – Head of External Relations and Chair of the Audit Committee among them – plus a couple of ranks over Lollo's head: the Borough Commander and the Deputy Assistant Commissioner. Others he was not so sure, but it was safe to say that, with a line-up like this – just the ones he recognised – if the Commissioner himself wasn't here, Rex knew he would be waiting to be briefed immediately the meeting ended.

At a certain moment, everyone sat down and the low murmur of conversation stopped.

'Morning, everyone,' said Lollo. 'Welcome to Holborn. If you don't know me, I'm Detective Chief Inspector Jethro Lawrence, and in a moment or two I'm going to hand over to Tabitha, but I just have a couple of bits of housekeeping, and then I'll explain what the various papers are in front of each of you . . .'

Rex zoned out while Lollo explained where the bogs were. He had managed to get back to the paint frame after leaving Gertrude Bisika, albeit too briefly. The doorway had been left open, but was cordoned off by a mesh of hazard tapes of the blue-and-white POLICE DO NOT CROSS and the yellow-and-black varieties. Lifting them, Rex had bent and entered the space. The frame had been raised, and looked clean. The body had been removed and there was no sign of anything untoward other than an irregular area in front of the frame, where blood had spattered before the body had been dropped. The extent of this spatter was now marked with small fluorescent tags, beyond which a perimeter had been outlined in orange aerosol marking chalk. Right now, scrapings of that spatter would

43

be in solution in the lab at St James's Park, awaiting the attention of some white coat who would pipette out the **sediment** – or whatever it was they did – and extract any DNA.

The rope that had been used as a ligature and to tie the victim to the frame had been removed. The whole thing could have been set up in readiness for Hobbs to walk in this morning and stretch another scrim; start a new painting.

When Rex had closed the doors, there it was: Trudi B – well, it could be Trudi B, or perhaps that was a 13 – followed by a tick.

He had taken a couple of photos with his phone, closer up, so he could see the texture of the chalk against the matt black-painted surface.

So it wasn't a tick, it was a 'V'.

'Trudi B Ventox', it had said, or 'Trudi 13 Ventox' – or was that 'Ventose'? It had been hard to tell. This was a chalk scrawl, not neat block capitals. Beneath that was what looked like algebra, or a tally of some kind: 'C x C III'.

C x C?

C times C equals one, two, three?

Standing in front of it, and reminded of the Tennyson case, he wondered if Ventox or Ventose was like Ventolin; just another brand of asthma medication.

Before leaving, he had snatched another few photos on his phone and then carefully opened both doors again, to leave them as he had found them, before ducking back under the tape.

As he walked briskly back through Holborn for the 10 o'clock, Rex had reflected that, for one thing, Webbo would need to get the photographer down there pronto. For another, whether this was relevant or not – and odds were it wouldn't be – he had wondered how the fuck no one had noticed it on the day.

'I think most of you know each other,' Lollo now said, 'but why don't we start by going around the room, then I'll hand over to Tabitha.'

Sitting to Lollo's left, the Chief nodded and smiled. 'Thank you, Jethro. Yes, let's get the intros out of the way. I'm Tabitha Churchill, as you all know. I've been Detective Chief Superintendent here for four years now, and before that I met many of you when I was Superintendent at Ealing.' She turned to the man on her left.

As DS, Rex was glad that he didn't get to come to that many meetings at this level. It sometimes felt as if you all simply had to agree to hold your noses and collectively immerse yourself in the murky **pond** of jargon and circumlocution. Once you were down there, you might occasionally catch a distorted flash of normal life, the real world, refracted through its surface, but not very often. The agenda was a case in point, consisting as it did of a list of acronyms. Reading between the lines, Rex could see that the meeting would go something like this: what has been leaked, who has leaked it, and what are we going to do about it? But he also knew that nothing was ever so simple in policing, and that each team would necessarily have their own take on – and their own stake in – what any of that might actually mean.

One of the suits – Rex had already forgotten the name – was from the Cyber Crime Unit, or CCU, sometimes known as 'CU Jimmy', itself a subdivision of the Fraud and Online Crime division that shared a name – in their case, an anagrammatic near-acronym – with the block of flats where Rex lived: FALCON.

Part of CU Jimmy's remit related to computer and network intrusions, whatever the motives and objectives for those intrusions might be, and that included network intrusions into police systems. He gave a short briefing on the overall network security position and compliance with the government's National Cyber Security Programme, or NCSP, then showed various graphs of incoming malware attacks suffered by police networks in the UK over a ten-year period, before outlining an audit they had initiated in response to the current breach, which had—

'Should we save that for "Next Steps"?' asked Churchill. 'Can I ask, though, do we know if this Tennyson leak was the result of a network intrusion?'

They didn't.

'And I believe you were going to share preliminary findings,' she said. 'Can we do that now, please?'

CU Jimmy scrolled through several PowerPoint slides, until he reached one that showed a document that Rex immediately recognised as a typed copy of the statement that had been made by one of the Dodos – the Dedicated Detention Officers – who had been acquitted of Trevor Tennyson's murder.

'This will be familiar to most of you,' he said. 'The majority of assets in the leak in question, fifty documents altogether, are digital copies of assets that are already in the public domain. Like this one. Pending a more detailed analysis, it would seem that there's nothing here that we, or the public, don't already know, but that doesn't mean that this is just a **bluff**.'

Rex knew the statements well. This went far beyond his own remit as SD lead, but during both the Tennyson inquest and the trial there had been much discussion of the Dodos' written accounts of the death. The prosecution had focused on two key issues. Firstly that the Detention Officers had been allowed to converse following the incident, and secondly that all four sets of notes and written statements used near-identical phrasing and vocabulary in describing what had happened, from the moment Tennyson was **had up** until the incident itself, and this in a way that went far beyond any statistical expectation. The prosecution's argument, much publicised in trial coverage during their summing-up, had been that this demonstrated 'blatant collusion' by the officers, which, together with their demonstrable lack of **remorse**, should have given serious doubts about the credibility or otherwise of their versions – or version – of events.

'All debate about the contents aside,' CU Jimmy said, turning to the slide, 'those of you who are familiar with these forms may **observe** that there is something unusual about . . .'

And here, as CU Jimmy began to explain the technical background – in terms of coding and servers – and the ramifications of the leak, Rex slumped in his chair: this gobbledegook was going straight over his head.

Luckily Rex was not the only one.

Lollo caught his eye. 'Did you switch it off and on again?' the Detective Chief Inspector asked with a wink, speaking for all of them. 'No, but seriously, what does that mean in layman's terms?' He corrected himself: 'Layperson's terms.'

The technical explanation of autosaves and caches and metadata that followed had Lollo scratching his head. 'In other words, you can't say precisely which drive these versions of the documents came from, is that it?'

It was.

'Well, bloody say so, then!'

That was the cue for a coffee break, and opening a few more windows to get some fresh air in. After that, there was talk of openness and transparency, presentations about past employment tribunal cases involving PIDA – the Public Interest Disclosure Act 1998 – and an update on current claims against the force by staff and the small percentage of these that involved whistle-blowers. All of this was about looking for someone with a grievance.

Later the lawyers gave their opinion, and this is where it got more interesting for DS Rex King. A QC from another chambers had been brought in overnight to give a fresh pair of eyes and to report in addition to the summary of the defence team.

'Yes, a big sigh of relief all round,' he said, 'but I agree with what my FALCON colleague said earlier. Just because there doesn't seem to be anything new here, doesn't mean that whoever is behind this is bluffing. We'll discuss this later, but I think we should plan a spectrum response, anticipating that more of this material will enter the public domain, and that it may be more prejudicial to yourselves next time. Yes, of course we need to shine a **torch** on current employees with a grudge. Possible whistle-blowers and recent tribunal cases is as good a place to start as any. But my feeling is that this may be bigger than that. What we may be seeing the beginnings of here, and what we should prepare for, could be nothing less than an attempt to force the CPS to reopen the case, on the grounds, for example, that the acquittal was unsound.'

A murmur of alarm went around the room, and the Chief raised her hand. 'Steady on, everyone. Francis, do you want to explain that?'

The QC continued. 'Certainly, Chief Superintendent. In our view, and I should stress this is only a view, the **gravamen** of— I'm sorry, the *burden* of the charge was murder, and that should be irrespective of where the death happened, and' – here he slowed down for emphasis – 'irrespective of whether Tennyson had taken any steps to avoid the risk of death from other causes or not.

'That's the important bit. Do you follow me?'

It looked as if they didn't.

'Okay,' he continued. 'Let's say – I mean, God forbid – but let's

48

say Patient X forgot to take his heart medicine on the morning that he is killed by a suicide bomber on the tube. That's simple murder. Do you see? It's not somehow Patient X's fault that he died because he'd forgotten to take his tablets that day.' The QC paused to allow a murmur of understanding to pass around the table, then: 'There seems to be no suggestion that this leak comes from the family or the immediate campaign group—'

'Well, we'd know about it if it did,' said Lollo, and everyone laughed. Rex felt a few eyes land on him, but he ignored them and laughed too. Press coverage of a few high-profile 'spy-cops' cases from the 1990s did not mean that the Met wasn't still infiltrating protest groups of various kinds, but if you'd been in the Special Demonstration Squad or the National Public Order Intelligence Unit, you didn't exactly put it at the top of your CV.

'Very well, then,' said the QC. 'But my point is that, on reflection, and with a bit of distance, we wonder whether the acquittal didn't rest a little too heavily upon Tennyson himself rather than upon the accused, specifically upon any prophylactic measure that Tennyson may or may not have taken vis-à-vis his asthma; that is, whether or not he happened to have a Ventolin inhaler on his person.

'Putting ourselves in their shoes, if we were putting together an appeal, we think that this might be a place to start. It is certainly a pressure point.' Warming to his subject, Francis allowed a little hyperbole to creep in, suggesting that they shouldn't let today's lack of content lead to complacency about further leaks, and that not to prepare for such an eventuality would be 'the **acme** of corporate **hara-kiri**'.

King took little comfort from the emerging consensus view – which seemed to be 'We've got away with it this time' – and even less from Francis Bland's doom-mongering suggestion that this was somehow the harbinger of a likely retrial, but for now he didn't want to stand out from the crowd and ruin everybody's buzz by saying so.

Tabitha Churchill turned to the Met's Head of External Relations. 'Evelyn,' she said. 'Two things. One, what are the early indications from the press? I assume no one's making much of a splash, is that right? And two, are there any bigger announcements on standby, please? What about that ACPO work on police pensions? Is that ready? Let's soft-launch that. Throw them a bone. I want us to make bloody certain this gets knocked off the six-and-tens, and *Newsnight*.'

4: ÉPINARD (SPINACH)

Like any cop, Rex King knew that most murder investigations were more or less straightforward, with either 'domestic' or 'confrontation' homicides accounting for the majority of all cases. Where homicide occurred between spouses, there would usually be a history of domestic violence; the offender would almost always be male and the victim female. Whether the offence had been committed in a **vicarage** or a tower block, however carefully it had been planned, whatever attempts had been made to clean up afterwards, it was generally relatively simple to assemble an information profile – as it was known in the trade – that would be sufficient to identify the suspect, make an arrest and prepare a prosecution. Even unplanned confrontations usually had an audience, and the spontaneous nature of these homicides, not to say their frequently drunken nature, would often mean the offender had little control over the amount of evidence left at the scene: eyewitness accounts, CCTV footage, bodily fluids, items of clothing, you name it. Not so much a **song** as a **symphony** of incriminating material.

Even where this wasn't the case, and often against their own best interests, an offender could easily **negate** the scantest information profile by whatever conspicuous actions they might take in the hours and days following the incident. Leaving home suddenly or confiding in others, or their behaviour at press conferences and public appeals. The oversolicitous witness was another, though more contemporary, giveaway. Someone constantly pushing themselves forward to help the police, or especially the media. Once upon a time, that kind of behaviour might have seemed harmless, merely the exercising of some civic duty, but now it stood out like a **platypus** in a porn film. The notorious British double child-killer Ian Huntley's name had become a **byword** for such fantasist limelight-chasing. 'Doing a Huntley' was what they called it, and there could scarcely be a greater **slur** on anyone's name than that. Rex was frequently amazed at the way offenders couldn't seem to **stop** drawing suspicion upon themselves, but he was glad they did, because he also knew that such compulsive behaviour was often the detective's closest **ally**.

Rex was getting the feeling that, as Deputy SIO on the case, DS Eddie Webster was not going to have such an easy job. This investigation was different. **Save** for the obvious forensics on the scene, there was nothing much to go on – not yet, anyway. House-to-house enquiries had not turned up anything, nor had the first wave of interviews of theatre staff and contractors. There was nothing on camera either. The theatre's own CCTV archives had inevitably yielded a number of celebrity sightings, as well as glimpses of dressing-room **sprawl** and several nipples – cue much prurient **laughter** among the uniforms – not to mention one **playwright** tantrum, but little else, and the stage-door camera had been on the blink for months, they said. Outside was not much better. The local authority and Transport for London cameras had just shown the area's undifferentiated twenty-four-hour tourist throng; wave after wave of shuffling crowds on Aldwych and Russell Street, Drury Lane and Catherine Street. Coach parties and country **mice**, newly-weds and **in-laws**, **old folks** all out for their *Mamma Mia*s and *Matilda*s, their *Billy Elliot*s or *Bend It*s.

The trawl would go on, of course. The attempt to identify any evidence-based line of enquiry. Tracing the main suspect would be a start, whether Terry Hobbs had done this or not. If only to put him out of the picture. The problem was that no one had seen Terry for **dust**, that much was clear. And no one, it seemed, had seen or heard anything out of the ordinary in the days or weeks running up to the discovery of the body in the paint frame.

From where Rex King and Eddie Webster stood, it did not look good. Rex joked that he was already starting to feel that they could take this one apart with the avidity of **safari park** baboons on a banana-flavoured BMW and still not find anything. The investigation team that Webster was managing, and to which Rex was now attached, could be **hard at work** on this one for months. At the best of times, police work could feel never-ending. In that respect, he sometimes thought, it felt akin to painting the Forth Bridge, but instead of some immense iron **cantilever**, some engineering marvel to admire, all there was was an endless parade of grim and seedy crimes, their perpetrators and victims, that seemed to stretch from here to **oblivion**. Faced with that, when all you had was the manual and your training, you sometimes felt about as powerless as Popeye without his spinach. It was like turning up at some slow-motion genocide, armed only with a **first aid** kit.

That was when his phone rang.

'King,' he said.

'Hello. Detective Sergeant King? This is **Gertrude** Bisika, from this morning. Is this a good time to call?'

'Yup. No problem at all,' he said, picking up the remote with his other hand to turn down *Newsnight*. 'What can I do for you, Mrs Bisika?'

'Well, you said that I should phone you any time if I thought of anything else.'

She had his full attention. 'Absolutely,' he said. 'Thank you for getting back to me. What is it?'

'Well, **Iris**, one of the other cleaners, who lives here too, but on the third floor, she said—' She paused. 'Oh, I don't know. You'll think we are being silly.'

'Not at all, Mrs Bisika,' said King, clicking a biro and opening his notebook. 'Anything could help; really.'

5: DORONIC (LEOPARD'S BANE)

As he walked towards Rex along the sixth-floor corridor, DS Eddie **Webster** lifted a hand in greeting, then thumbed back at the swing doors he had just come through. 'You, me, **coffee?**'

'Sid's?' asked Rex.

'Nah. Downstairs,' said Webster. 'Shop talk.'

'Yeah, go on, then,' said Rex, pushing through the doors, their footsteps on the polished concrete suddenly amplified by the space and height of the stairwell. Might as well take the bull by the horns, he thought: 'How's it going, Eddie? Helen and the kids?'

Through all of their day-to-day dealings, Detective Sergeants Rex King and Eddie Webster had somehow managed to studiously avoid the subject of Helen for a decade or more, possibly nearer two, but Rex was no longer sure what had been the point. Pride? Possibly. It wasn't what you'd choose to happen, was it – your girlfriend having a whirlwind romance with your workmate and getting married six months later. It was not ideal, especially in a work situation. It had been complicated too. Certainly more complicated than Eddie knew. Lately, though, Rex had found himself sometimes wondering what all the fuss had been about. Helen and Eddie had found each other and realised that they both wanted a particular kind of life that Rex didn't; not at the time, anyway. Why wouldn't she grab that with both hands? They would have been fools not to. If you looked at it another way, Eddie had done them both a favour. He'd saved Rex and Helen's so-called relationship from a painful and lingering death.

He was still a twat, though.

'Everyone's good, thanks, mate,' said Eddie. 'Helen's gone back to teaching—'

Rex, turned, surprised. 'Really? I thought she'd—'

'Yeah, I know. But primary this time. She prefers it. Wanstead Church, if that means anything to you; over Snaresbrook way.'

'...'

'Well, it's the best primary school in the borough by a long fucking chalk. Loving it, she says. The girls are both at the Beal now too, so she can drop them off on her way to work.' Webster shook his head. 'Fuck me! This time last year it was looking as if Rachel would have to go to Chadwell Heath, which is closer to fucking Romford than Woodford, but luckily—' He stopped himself. 'Anyway, Rex, mate, you don't want to hear what we had to do to swing it, but what a bloody relief. You'd think it'd get less fucking stressful the older they get, but it's the other bloody way round.'

'How old are they now?' Rex asked

'Jennifer's coming up for GCSEs next year.'

'You're joking!' said Rex, but of course she was. Fifteen! Bloody hell. That had gone quick.

'It's not bloody **Eton**,' said Eddie, 'but it's second in the old league tables, and it's got a good sixth form, so Rachel will have her older sister there for a few more years, which is good.'

'Nice one,' said Rex. 'Good for them. Give Helen my best.'

'Yeah, course I will,' said Eddie, but Rex knew he wouldn't.

'No, it's my treat,' said Rex, a few moments later, as he paid for both of their coffees. 'Glad I bumped into you, Eddie. Lollo probably told you I was in that Tennyson briefing all day, so I missed your meeting. How'd it go?'

'Well, if I tell you that we've got fuck-all, and we're drawing a blank every-fucking-where we look, you can probably imagine the rest. You don't need me to spell it out,' said Webster, before taking a slurp of coffee. 'Bunch of clueless wankers, honestly!'

'That bad?'

'For fuck's sake. Please tell me that you and me were smarter than those fucking uniform-carriers when we started out, Rex. Talk about **plod**! I don't even want to **glorify** the twats by calling them police-men, some of them.'

Rex laughed. It was good to see a glimpse of the old Eddie.

'It's only been a couple of days, though, Eddie,' said Rex. 'Par for the course, mate.'

'S'pose so,' said Webster. 'Anyway, how was Tennyson? Not much in it after all, I suppose, since it wasn't on the news. Nothing in the papers this morning either.'

'No, they brought forward publication of that ACPO thing; keep *Newsnight* busy, just in case. But no, whoever it was, this was prob-ably just a shot across the bows. Nothing new in there at all, they reckon. Nothing that's not already in the public domain.'

'No clue?'

'No. Lawyers think it's someone angling for a retrial, and this was just their first move, just to let us know they're there. Whoever "they" are. Not the family or the usual campaigners, far as we know. Whatever it is, it makes me uncomfortable.'

'Understandable,' said Webster. 'Listen. About your mate.'

'Terry?'

'Yeah.'

'What about him?'

'Well, I don't know. You probably think he's been right **set up**, no? **Onus** on you to exonerate or whatever?'

Rex nodded. 'Tel wouldn't hurt a fly, far as I know.'

There was a pause.

'Yeah, but it wasn't a fucking fly that we found with his fucking nose cut off and hung up to dry in Terence Hobbs's studio, was it, though, eh?' said Webster. 'And now the sudden, unexplained absence. I don't want to paint a picture, but it's pretty fucking classic, isn't it?'

'You reckon it was him, then?' Rex asked.

'Unless you've got a better idea, mate.'

Rex shrugged. 'Maybe you're right.'

'Well, I don't know,' said Eddie. 'He's your pal. Where would he be likely to go? Boyfriend in the country or something?'

'Eh? No, Tel's not gay, Eddie. I don't think he is, anyway.'

'Maybe that's just because he didn't fancy you? Can't say I blame him.'

'Never came up, I suppose, but I'm pretty sure.'

'Well, we're looking at that as a possibility. That our Terence picked his victim up somewhere and took him back to the studio for a bit of S and M that went badly wrong.'

'No, I can't see it,' said Rex. 'Have you even got any—'

'"DNA"?' laughed Webster. 'Not yet, no. Putrefaction might be too far gone. No evidence of penetration neither.'

Rex shook his head. 'See? I think you're barking up the wrong—'

'Well, fuck's sake, mate,' said Webster. 'It's the best we've got at the moment, that Terence was a bum **pilot** on the pull. I mean, you know what they fucking say. If it looks like a duck and quacks like a duck, chances are it is a fucking duck.' Webster seemed pleased with this prejudice masquerading as common-sense analysis, but then he noticed the expression on Rex's face. 'Oh, come on, Kingsy! You know what these theatrical types are like. **Powder puff** country, innit.'

'Eh? No, I fucking don't know.'

King was incredulous. He knew that Webster was a twat, but every time he proved it – like with this homophobic outburst – was still a shock, an anachronism. Is that what living out in the sticks did for you? Christ, this wasn't a 1970s school playground. And suspect or not, this was Rex's friend that Eddie was talking about. The theatre world might well be a significantly more tolerant community than the average police force, but that wasn't hard, and even Rex knew that it didn't mean everyone working in the dramatic arts was gay – but then again, so what if it did! What business was that of an old git like Webbo?

'Christ, Eddie!' Rex continued. 'D'you miss out on diversity train-ing or something? Off sick that week, were we? Jesus! You can't fuck-ing go around making sweeping statements like that in this day and age!' He looked over his shoulder as if to check for eavesdroppers, 'Fucking hell! The wrong person hears you and you're out. Besides, all that showbiz magic and stardust is smoke and mirrors. You do know that, don't you? Most of the crew are big fucking hairy-arsed technicians: gaffers and sparks, chippies. Fuck's sake! Tinkerbell's not really a fairy, you know! She's a fat biker up at the back with a fucking half-ton shuttered followspot.'

Rex had discovered the rough-hewn realities of backstage life as – *duh* – a moronic seventeen- or eighteen-year-old. He had learned this lesson in shabbier venues – if you could even call them that – than the Royal Palace Theatre, Drury Lane, but the same principle had applied: the trapeze artist's apparently gossamer wings were made of coarsest hessian stiffened with coat hangers and glue, the leotard from smelly old velvet padded with horse hair.

Detective Sergeant or not, Rex King can't have been the only man of his age whose teenage years seemed not only more than a single lifetime ago, but the province of another person altogether. And yet, despite this distance, or perhaps because of it, he occasionally found himself reflecting upon the unlikely consequences of some of the unthinking decisions he had made at that time. It was only with the benefit of hindsight that he could even begin to see how little he had understood just what had been at stake, or to see quite how narrow some of his escapes had been.

It wasn't the most traditional of educations for a career in the police, and certainly not something that he bragged about these days, for obvious reasons, but in his teens the boy-who-would-be-Detective Sergeant Rex King had had a bad case of festival **fever** – a kind of Glastonbury romance. In 1984, he and a sixth-form mate called Andy had hitch-hiked up to Wiltshire for what they had had no way of knowing would be the last ever Stonehenge Free Festival, not to mention possibly the last truly free music festival of its kind ever to be held in the UK. It was, then, not so much an opening of the doors of perception, as a close the door on your way out, please. Less a brave new world, more the end of an era.

In both concept and reality, a free festival was so far beyond either of their till then severely limited life experiences that neither of them had had much of a clue what to expect. Although, once they had got there and been faced with a familiar-looking **fly-blown** field of khaki tents, ramshackle old coaches and burned-out cars, with red distress flares going off, police helicopters hovering low above the crowd, and wah-wah waves of psychedelic music being carried on the wind from all directions, King had realised – if not in quite so many words – that he and his friends' enthusiastic multiple viewings of a VHS of *Apocalypse Now* had laid a certain amount of the visual groundwork.

Together with a hitherto half-baked interest in the idea of an anar-chistic, temporary and spontaneously self-regulating community – a place where nothing was true and everything was **permissible**, to paraphrase a popular catchphrase of the time – it was a burgeoning fascination with psychedelics that had been the dominant reason for their going to Stonehenge in the first place, but the teenagers had still been amazed by the open selling of recreational drugs. One of the first things they'd seen had been a tent advertising 'hot knives' – a particularly lung-punishing way to take a hit of hash – as well as numerous painted signs for LSD and 'Afghan black', or ten-pound deals of cocaine. Having little or no interest in the produce of **Bolivia**, they had bought some 'Smiley Mushrooms' LSD, and a bag of sensimilla, which in those pre-'skunk' days was the name generally given to strong and supposedly Jamaican marijuana, especially when the weed comprised mainly seedless buds.

If the vibes had not exactly been – in the words of the great reggae singer Sugar Minott – 'level', but had seemed, in the event, a little heavier than expected, what the adult Rex knew now, both from police intelligence and from more recently published anecdotal reports, was that 1984 had also seen the emergence of a fairly heavy crew from Bristol who'd been dealing a substantial amount of heroin at Stonehenge on the quiet. Supposedly it was this crew's cars that had been overturned and burned out. **Alas** for our pals, who were completely oblivious to any heroin scene, even the sensi had been much stronger than anything they'd smoked before, and had quickly overwhelmed young Master King's limited tolerance. He had grown pale and faint, felt both nauseous and anxious, and knew above all that he needed to assume some roughly horizontal position as soon as might be humanly possible. Which is what he had done.

He was near a small stage, that was obvious, but, disorientated and struck with the horrors as he was, he'd had absolutely no idea which band was playing behind the sparkly strip-blind curtain that was hung between two tent poles at the back of the stage. There was almost nothing about the music – whether the rhythms or the sounds that the instruments were making – that he'd recognised.

Propping himself up on his elbows, once he'd been able, and looking around, he'd found himself lying on duckboards behind some speaker stacks, surrounded by cabling and crates of electrics, painted flats, and buckets. The whole place had seemed like a big dressing-up box, with piles of old clothes lying around, assorted costumes and props strewn everywhere, jumble sale-stylee. If anything, the strangeness of the music had made him feel even more baked.

It was in this still slightly disembodied state that he had suddenly seen a vision of beauty parting the curtain, and she – making eye contact and smiling – had evidently seen him. Glittering under the lights as she waded through the dry ice and stepped off the stage was a posi-punk princess, if that wasn't a contradiction in terms, in **purple lipstick** and sparkling face paint. Sporting a grown-out Mohican and wearing torn fishnet tights under some sort of sequinned **tutu**, she had seemed the epitome of cool and glamour, and not only that, but she was now making a beeline towards him. She appeared to be holding a giant violin.

King had wondered if he might be in love. 'That looks like a giant violin,' he'd said, awkwardly.

'It's a **viol**,' she'd said, puzzled – the word had sounded like 'vile' – 'or viola da gamba! Weren't you just watching our gig? I just saw you out front, didn't I? You and your mate? I only play on a couple of songs. That's me done. They'll be on for hours yet. What are you doing?'

'. . .'

Kneeling at his side, she had put her lips to his ear and half-sung, half-whispered a couple of verses of 'I Wish' by The Mob. Seconds stretched out into minutes as this became the most erotic chat-up that King had ever heard. The combination of the earnestly nihilistic lyrics, the smell of her skin – sweat, with a slight chemical note – and the feather-light percussion of her breath on his cheek was electrifying. It made his skin tingle and his cock hard. Almost as delirious with desire as he was stoned, but not quite, the young King had turned his face and kissed her, and as they'd kissed she had slipped a hand into his pocket to find and caress his knob.

Oh, yes.

Oh, no! He had moved too quickly. With a wave of nausea, the THC reasserted its control of his bodily systems. 'Sorry, I—' he'd spluttered. 'Stoned.'

If he even had been 'on a **promise**', as the saying went, he certainly wasn't any more. The spell had been broken.

'Not interested?' she'd said, taking her hand from his pocket. 'Oh well. See ya!' Standing up, she'd quickly located her things, put the viol back into a flight case, then picked up a tatty-looking leopard-skin-patterned jacket and left.

Half an hour or so later, covered in **midge** bites and with the sensi rush finally subsiding, King had got to his feet. The band were still playing, the music now recognisable as a kind of synthy, bluesy, space-rock jam. The backstage area was a mess. He'd looked out front, but where was Andy? More importantly, where could he get some food? Perhaps a beanburger or something.

It was then that the young King had put his hand in his pocket. Where earlier there had been a ten-pound note, which had been most of his budget for the few days they'd been planning to stay, there was now precisely nothing. His pocket was empty. He'd looked on the floor where he'd been lying. There was nothing there either, so it hadn't simply fallen out.

Oh, no.

Oh, yes. He couldn't say for sure, but – face burning with embarrassment – he'd not been able to help wondering if he'd just been played. He had thought she liked him, but perhaps, like some latter-day **Becky Sharp**, the viol player had just been out for herself. Or perhaps, disappointed, she had found a way to **penalise** him for his apparent lack of motivation. Mortified, King had quickly decided that he wouldn't tell Andy, and if pressed he'd just say he must have lost it. At least he'd still had a fiver and the two tabs of 'Smiley Mushrooms' in his other pocket. Maybe, he'd reasoned, he should go to the stones – the stones! – their rendezvous point, and find Andy, and they should just drop the acid.

Pleasantly stoned now, and with a pressing case of the munchies, King had stepped off the duckboards and out into the crowd. The early-evening sun had begun to lend a golden cast to everything it touched. There would be a beautiful sunset in a couple of hours, and at least if they were tripping, he'd figured, they wouldn't need much money for a day or so—

'Jesus!' said DS Webster. 'Keep your fucking hair on! It's just a theory, Kingsy. If you don't fucking like it, Mr fucking Political Correctness, you come up with something better.'

'Alright, I will,' said Rex, remembering again why he'd always thought Webster was a prat.

It was nothing to do with Helen, though how she couldn't see it, Rex had no idea. Webster was simply, first and foremost, an unreconstructed pillock of the old school: sexist, racist and homophobic. No wonder the police service couldn't **innovate** or progress. Twat.

'Do that,' said Eddie.

'Hang on. Did you get my email?'

'What?'

Rex took his phone out of his pocket, tapped it a few times, then held it up sideways. 'It's on the back of the paint frame door. None of us noticed it at the time, but the photographer caught it. What do you reckon?'

'At the scene? What's that?' said Eddie, reaching out to steady the phone. 'Trudi what?'

'Trudi B Ventox,' said Rex slowly. 'Something like that.'

'What the fuck is that?' said Eddie. 'Cough mixture or something?'

Rex shrugged. 'No idea, mate. I just saw it on one of the photos, and went back to take a closer look.'

'Well, log it,' said Eddie, 'and let's just keep trawling, eh.' He drained his coffee. 'Keep all lines of enquiry open.'

'Absolutely,' said King, but he decided that, for the moment, he wouldn't share Gertrude Bisika's call with Webster. He would pursue it a bit more first. No sense going off half-cocked. If Webbo wanted a theory, he would fucking get one. In the meantime, Rex said, he needed to check out a few leads and track down one or two old pals regarding the whereabouts of a certain Terry Hobbs, whom he still emphatically refused to believe was a murderer. 'It just doesn't seem like the Terry I know. I might go back to the scene, Eddie. Dig around a bit more. See if there's anything else we've missed. Okay with you?'

'Be my fucking guest, Kingsy,' was DS Webster's considered response.

6: MOURON (PIMPERNEL)

Waiting for Andy half an hour or so and one beanburger later, the young King had felt dwarfed by the **enormous** standing stones that ranged around him, the twenty-ton lintel **over** his head. He'd rolled a small joint to smoke while he waited, a one-skinner with just a few tiny crumbs, this time, of sensi. It wasn't the actual solstice but there had still been quite a crowd at the stones. Beside him a bushily bearded biker type – wearing his leather cut-off over an olive-green MA1 – had also been leaning back against the stone, gazing into the middle distance and beaming. Perhaps he had been tripping. King had taken out his Everyman and lit the small joint. At the sound of the striking flint, Beardy had turned around.

'**Hesperides**, look!' he'd said.

'Vesper-what?'

'Hesperides! Can you see them?'

'Um . . .'

'The ancient Greeks called them that. The nymphs of the golden evening light. Hesperides. Oh, you're not tripping, then.'

'Not yet, no,' King had said.

'Do you want some acid?' Beardy'd asked.

'. . .'

'Hundred quid for a thousand?'

King had nearly fallen over at this – a thousand tabs! – but had simply said, 'Ah, no. Got some, thanks.'

'Which ones have you got?'

'Smiley Mushrooms.'

'They're okay. Pyramid are better, if you ask me.' He'd looked at the joint in King's hand. 'Are you going to hog that or what?'

'Not much in it, to be honest,' King had shrugged, handing it over. 'Just a taste. Overdid the last one.'

'Well, I don't need to get any more stoned,' Beardy had grinned. 'I think I'm practically **immune**.' He'd drawn what turned out to be the last toke and a half, then flicked the roach on to the grass and ground it out beneath the heel of a heavy black army boot. Then he'd taken a packet of Old Holborn out of the pocket of his jacket and rolled a cigarette. 'Want one?' he'd offered. Then: 'Got a **match**?'

After a few puffs, he'd turned and said, 'Don't do the **horse**, though. I hear it's pretty strong. Practically **neat**. Supposedly someone left a **hypodermic** over in the kids' play area. Fucking evil bastards.'

There'd been a smell of woodsmoke in the air. It had been curling out of cone-topped flues on converted ambulances, camper vans and coaches across the site, and from fire pits – even though the information sheet had clearly said not to dig them – all of it contributing to a slightly unseasonal mist.

'If you ignore the people, though,' Beardy'd said, 'and the fucking helicopters, and just look at the landscape, you could be some – I don't know – peasant farmer, **husbandman**, whatever, getting high on the rye. It wouldn't have looked any different a thousand years ago, know what I mean?'

King must have looked puzzled.

'Ergot, mate! St **Vitus**'s Dance!'

Nope, none the wiser.

'Fuck's sake. LSD! Albert Hofmann, the guy who invented acid in 1938, was researching ergot. Hallucinogenic fungus that attacked damp rye grains, weren' it. Course, back in the Middle Ages they didn't know that, and they must have been eating that mouldy rye all the fucking time, so they called it St Vitus's Dance. Crazy, ain' it? Imagine all these medieval geezers tripping off their faces.' He had put the cigarette in his mouth, narrowed his eyes against the smoke, which now curled up his face, and placed both palms flat on the stones at around waist height.

'*Cogito* ergot *sum*, mate. I think I'm tripping, therefore I am. Can you feel them vibrating?'

King had tried it too. Not yet, he couldn't. Maybe later.

'These things were fucking ancient then,' Beardy had continued. 'They called them sarsens because they thought they were un-Christian, otherworldly, like Saracens, which was their name for Arab or Muslim soldiers. This was the time of the Crusades, yeah? So they called them "Saracen stones". Go on, say it with a West Country accent!'

King had obliged. It had sounded like 'sarrrsen'.

'See? Fuck me! As comparisons go, that was about as extreme as it got to your average medieval peasant. Saracens were the only thing in their known universe that was far-out enough to compare this place to.' He grinned broadly. 'I love all that shit.'

Beardy had taken a small apple out of his jacket pocket with one hand and slid a huge curved knife out of his boot with the other. He'd used the outsized blade to carve off a slice that he'd then offered to King, held between thumb and blade.

'Nice one, thanks. Fucking hell, is that knife big enough?'

'It's a *kukri*,' Beardy had said, carving himself a slice. '**Gurkha** knife. Good, ain' it. This is just a small one. Usually they're like that—' He could have been describing the fish that got away. 'Got it off a mate in Belfast when I was in the Paras.'

When they had eaten the apple, Beardy had wiped the blade on his jeans and slid it back into his boot, out of sight. That was when Andy had turned up, with a bottle of rum and coke he'd got from a stall.

'Alright?' he'd said by way of a greeting, offering around the bottle. 'It's flat, but it tastes okay.'

'Sun's over the **yard-arm**,' Beardy had said, taking a swig before holding out his hand, which King had shaken. 'I'm Pete, by the way. See you later. Gonna go and find my old lady. Have a good one, mush.'

'Yeah, cheers, thanks, Pete. You too.'

Pete had started walking away, but then turned as if he'd just remembered something. 'Oh, here's a tip for you,' he'd said. 'You'll like this. You'll be into this. If you freak out at all – I mean, I'm not saying you will, but just in case you do – ask someone where the awfully nice tea rooms are.'

They both laughed. It had sounded funny, the way Pete said 'awfully nice'.

'No, serious! I promise you, I'm not joking.'

'Tea rooms?'

'No, not just tea rooms – the *awfully nice* tea rooms. Remember that. You'll see. Cheers, lads.'

And later they would.

'Nice bloke,' Andy had said.

'Yeah,' King had agreed. 'Size of that fucking knife, though.'

'What knife?'

The acid had come on quite quickly, and not at all gently. The young King had been looking at some festival posters on a **bookshop** and **handicraft** stall. There were posters of the Hindu god Shiva emblazoned with the legend 'Stonehenge Free Festival'.

'What's that?' Andy had said.

'Um, it's like a poster of a poster, with a picture of a poster on it,' had been the teenaged King's enigmatic answer. There had followed a vertiginous recalibration of his visual sensoria. Everything had demanded a second look. It had no longer been possible to make assumptions based on visual sensation alone. Fits of giggles were interspersed with gutfuls of anxiety, waves of euphoria.

Wandering around, they had come across a two-seater sofa, the incongruity of which had seemed hilarious, but 'any port in a storm', as the saying went. Occupying this, sitting down, had helped to **anchor** them for a while, but it had felt as if they were sitting on a boat. The ground beneath them seeming to rise and fall gently, or to **inflate** and deflate, as if the very earth had been breathing beneath them. Back at home in the days and weeks ahead, our pals would swear that later on they had found an old Bedford bus that had been converted into a mobile cinema, or perhaps been purpose-built as one. There had been what seemed like lasers firing out of a great glass dome above its cab, while inside they had found a couple of dozen actual cinema seats and a screen. It had been parked in the area of the festival known as Tibet. The young King was convinced that they had watched *Carry On: Don't Lose Your Head*, laughing uproariously at Sid James cavorting around Revolutionary-era France as a Scarlet Pimpernel-type character, fighting duels and saving aristocrats from the guillotine; posing as a lisping fop for cover one minute, swash-buckling lech the next.

Beyond 'Let them eat cake!' and the 'storming of the Bastille', whatever that was, the French Revolution per se had been about as meaningless to King at that time as more or less any other random historical event: the American War of Independence, say, or the Siege of **Mafeking**! He hadn't known a flintlock from a **fetlock**, but lack of knowledge hadn't seemed to impede the *Carry On* crew either. The whole seismic episode in French and global history was being played purely for puns and double entendres, as a vehicle for arse or tit jokes.

Later, Andy confessed that he thought they'd been watching *Zulu*.

Then it had been as if the whole thing, the bus, the air, had suddenly **aged**. The film had become a dusty irrelevance. The jump cuts had become too jarring and seemed to have spilled out into the world of time and space. It was as if some **editor** had been cutting and splicing – in those pre-**Avid**, analogue days – wildly contrasting levels of resolution from one second to the next: from the molecular to the global, from micro to macro, and back again; cosmic **crash**-edits. It had all started happening too quickly, as if time had begun to speed up. There had been hair in the gate and smoke in the beams of light. It had been suffocating, dizzying, impossible to concentrate or to sit still. King had stood up and rushed off the bus, and Andy had followed.

Stepping outside had helped a bit; seeing the by then night-time sky and feeling the breeze against his skin. It had certainly felt something of a relief to have both feet on the ground as well, to walk around in the fresh air, dodging other people, as if this whole festival site had become nothing more than a three-dimensional game of *Asteroids*. But when an oncoming rock had turned to them and asked, in the nicest possible way, if they'd wanted to buy any hash, Andy had managed only to gulp and to stammer, 'I . . . I . . . I . . . I . . . I—'

Oh, no, a freak-out!

There had only been one thing for it. 'Excuse me,' King had asked the dealer, forming the words as slowly and deliberately as he'd been able, and hoping they would be more intelligible than they sounded to him. 'Do you know where the awfully nice tea rooms are?'

The hash dealer hadn't, but incredibly, some immeasurable period of time, many other requests for directions, and several UFO sightings later, they had found themselves sitting at a dining table in a 1930s living room, or amid living-room scenery at least – were they on a stage? it wasn't entirely clear – and having their orders taken by a vicar in a panama hat.

'**High tea**,' Andy had said, shaking with laughter as he'd tried to sip Earl Grey from a rattling bone-china cup and saucer. Then some vestigial memory of his mother's antique-collecting had kicked in and he'd turned the saucer over, looking, he'd said, for the 're-mark'.

'Is that like a resit?'

'No: **remarque**.'

'. . .'

'R-E-M-A-R-Q-whatever-whatever. Like some sort of maker's mark or something. Fuck knows. Oh, yeah. There it is. Anyway, look—' Andy had turned the saucer back the right way over and tipped some tea into it. He had slurped it noisily as if for comic effect, before sighing with a mixture of savour and delight. 'That is actually really nice. Cools it down. My grandad used to do that.'

In fact, by this time, the acid had started to level off nicely, enough that the young King had actually been able to roll a joint without the chintz tablecloth writhing around too much. 'A drink's too wet without one,' he'd said, quoting the strapline from a then current McVitie's Rich Tea biscuit television advert, while holding the resulting doobie up like a conductor's baton. Lighting it, he had taken a drag or two before passing it to his friend. Then, as was obviously expected, if not positively encouraged, he had turned to the waiter and asked, 'More tea, vicar?'

7: CERFEUIL (CHERVIL)

Detective Sergeant Rex King had certainly – to borrow one of Detective Chief Inspector Jethro Lawrence's phrases – 'been giving it plenty of bloody shoe leather'. He and DS Eddie Webster had drawn up a list of Terence Hobbs's usual haunts on the whiteboard: his house by the Regent's Canal in Hackney and his lock-up in the arches on Bocking Street, the Coach & Horses, The Rock & Sole Plaice. After a couple of uniforms had made some unsuccessful trips to Hackney, Rex had been following up, working his way down the list and gradually ticking them off, but without any joy. Added to that, mobile phone trace had drawn a big fat zilch. There was no sign of Tel.

The curtains of Terry's house on Andrews Road had been drawn and the windows dark. It was a handsome house looking over the Regent's Canal, a tall and narrow-fronted Victorian terrace. Terry had once told Rex that, when he'd bought the place, it'd had no roof. The windows had been rotten, and huge buddleias were growing out of cracks in the render. Slowly renovating the place, doing it properly, had been one of the pleasures of Terence's life, and it showed. Looking through the now gleaming brass letterbox on the beautifully restored original Victorian front door, Rex had seen post building up on the hallway floor.

If he was going back to the paint frame, Rex figured he could tick another one off the list by dropping in at the chippy while he was in the area. And maybe squeeze in a second visit to the Coach while he was at it. See if any of the Friday-lunchtime bar staff had heard anything.

Crossing over near a glossy redevelopment on New Oxford Street, where Museum Street joined High Holborn, Rex remembered when this place had been the West Central Royal Mail sorting office instead of this generic block of retail spaces and expensive flats. When Rex had first lived in the area it was thriving – there would be postal vans and lorries driving in and out constantly, at all times of the day and night, fluorescent lights blazing from the windows on all floors, hundreds of blue-shirted postal workers crowding the nearby pubs at break times and at the starts and ends of shifts.

The old sorting office had closed down a couple of decades ago, and in more recent years had been the subject of occasional police visits only when it was being used as a film location, or as the venue for an illegal rave. Then the inevitable had happened and the developers had moved in. It was happening all over. The sorting office in Rathbone Place had been converted into flats too. Where was all that work being done now, and where were the families it had supported?

Some parts of Covent Garden didn't really change. People still lived in the council blocks down the side streets, the flats around Stukeley Street and Neal Street, or the tiered balconies that crowded around the Oasis swimming pool. Children still grew up around here.

Once you got off the main drag and into the side streets, there were still glimpses too of the older two- or three-storey red-brick London. Smaller shops were somehow clinging on in the face of the unstoppable chains. The same could probably be said of almost every high street in London. And presumably for some of these smaller independents it would only be a matter of time before some faceless corporate entity flying whichever flag of fiscal convenience would find a way to acquire them, along with as many other adjacent plots as possible, to force dereliction and evict the tenants, to blag their way through planning and to leverage the larger plot into yet another multi-storey money pit that might bring thousand-fold returns, but at the cost of blocking the light in neighbouring streets and killing off another local community.

As Rex crossed over Drury Lane towards Russell Street, he could hear the primary-school children of St Clement Danes playing high above. Terry had once told him that the school itself dated back to at least 1666, the year of the Great Fire, but this building was obviously Victorian and, like many London schools of that era, had a playground on the roof. King wasn't entirely sure, but he wondered whether, above the otherwise undifferentiated screams and laughter, he could hear some of the children playing a clapping game: 'A sailor went to sea, sea, sea. To see what he could see, see, see', or something like it. Did kids still even play those games? Had Jennifer done that? Helen's girls: Jennifer and Rachel? Weren't they all just looking at their phones all the time now?

Street-sweepers were wheeling their barrows out of the depot next to the school. A group of smokers huddled, chatting outside Philomena's, and a woman in the black polo shirt and polyester-slacked uniform of the bar worker was using an extendable hose to water the countless plants that bedecked the Sarastro Restaurant. A board outside listed the specials: 'Slow-cooked calamari. Green salad with chervil and yoghurt dressing.' A man in a suit was reading a newspaper in the morning sun, another in shirtsleeves talking on his mobile, a briefcase propped against one leg between his black, polished shoes. Someone had left a can of 7-Up on the windowsill of number 44, and a woman studied the tourist information map near the cycle-hire docks. High above his head, another familiar and evocative sound: a teacher ringing a handbell to signal the end of morning playtime.

Rex crossed over Russell Street and pressed the button to ring another bell.

'Hello, it's Detective Sergeant King,' he said. 'Is that Jane? Oh, hi. Yup, me again.'

The door buzzed open. Rex pushed it and stepped inside. He was going back to Terry's paint frame to take another look. To see – in the words of the clapping song – 'what he could see, chop, knee'.

8: CORDEAU (TWINE)

At least mooching around the paint frame took Rex King's mind off Tennyson for a bit. The consensus seemed to be that the latest scare might have been baseless, the apparent leak being 'content-free', or a shot across the bows, as Francis Bland QC had put it, but as Rex had told Lollo, he felt little or no sense of relief. He knew that there was more to emerge, and so did the four officers who had been acquitted. It was probably only a matter of time before the shit hit the fan.

The smell in the paint frame and the wider backstage area was almost gone. It would have been a lot harder to get rid of if the still unidentified body had hung undiscovered for even just a day or two longer. Estimates were putting time of death around forty-eight hours before discovery, so sometime on the Sunday, with decomposition having been sped up by early-summer warmth, but now the crime-scene clean-up team had been in, both to the paint frame and the basement drop beneath. Ozone machines, now gone off to some other job, had been left switched on in the space for a couple of days, and while the whole place now smelled of disinfectant, it was at least comfortable enough that Rex was able to have a closer look around.

He didn't know what he was expecting to find. Socks and Co. would have hoovered up all or most artefacts and oddments that weren't merely paint-related, to be logged and sorted, pored over for occulted patterns. Besides that there were plenty of receipts, phone numbers scribbled on Post-its, photos, and various kinds of bumf. Plus the more general tat that anyone accumulates in a workplace;

the stuff that gets stuck in a drawer for later, and is never returned to. In this case, some old birthday cards, **corn** plasters, a copy of *The New Avengers Annual 1977*, and an envelope marked 'Slow-worm **moult**? Alfriston, Sussex', which contained just a section of translucent reptilian skin.

All – or any – of this could tell a story, if you could only look at it in a particular order, or a certain way. Whether it was the right story was another matter altogether. But right now, what Rex needed to do, and he and Webster were in agreement on this, was find a thread to follow. And frankly, any thread would do.

At the far right-hand corner of the paint frame and mounted against the wall was a large sink made of thick white ceramic. Rex remembered from days poring over the Aston Matthews catalogue with Helen that this was called a Belfast or butler sink, and this one was big enough to use for washing out paint buckets and brushes of all kinds. A single copper pipe with an odd tap on the end of it projected a few inches out of the wall above the sink. Next to this, with the lower end of its slightly sloping top overlapping the sink above a weir-type overflow, stood a floor-mounted stainless steel draining unit on which were ranged a white plastic kettle, a box of Sainsbury's Red Label teabags, a jar of Nescafé and a semi-solidified bag of Tate & Lyle granulated sugar, accompanied by the requisite collection of paint-spattered mugs of varying design and similarly diverse and stained teaspoons. It was all very familiar. 'Oi, Rex,' Terry used to say. 'Put the fucking kettle on, mate. That tea isn't gonna make itself.'

Rex ached for a bit of that kind of normality and bonhomie now.

Above all this, hanging by its handle from a large iron hook that had been driven into the bare brick wall, and with a flex that trailed to the two-gang socket it shared with the kettle, was a big old-fashioned Roberts radio, in wood and chrome with leatherette panelling, but so paint-spattered that its dial was all but illegible. Rex reached over the kettle and flicked one of the socket's power switches. A loud burst of static quickly subsided and Rex was pleased to hear the Roberts' wooden construction contributing to a rich and bass-heavy sound that perfectly suited the classical **music** station to which it was permanently tuned: BBC Radio 3. Whatever it was that was being played, Rex immediately sensed that he was coming to it late, since both orchestra and choir seemed to be building and ascending through wave after ever-louder wave of orgasmic blare. It was hard to differentiate individual instruments, but it sounded like a choir singing at the tops of their voices in an escalating game of call and response with fanfares of woodwind, brass and percussion, and everyone playing just as loudly as they could.

Next to the Roberts, and fixed to the wall with two torn-off strips of masking tape, was a page torn from a book or a catalogue. It was a reproduction of a print depicting a staged tableau that looked vaguely familiar to Rex. Night-time in the Holy Land, and eleven disciples are ranged across the stage in positions of repose, they are sleeping, while on the left, higher than the rest, Christ kneels at the feet of an angel. Picked out in hand-drawn white letters above the cypress trees in a dark greenish sky were the words '*Christus am Ölberge*' – Christ on the Mount of Olives, perhaps? – while beneath the image, but still part of the print per se, were the words 'Passionsspiele Oberammergau. – Christus am Oelberg.' The whole thing looked slightly off-register, as if it had been cheaply printed at the time. Perhaps it had been an illustration in a ha'penny programme, or was a souvenir postcard, rather than an artwork produced for exhibition. Across the image someone – Terry, presumably – had ruled a pencil grid, dividing the picture into equal squares, and up the right-hand side of the page they had scribbled 'Beethoven Op: 85', also in pencil.

Classical music wasn't really Rex's cup of tea. If it could be thought of as a club, then it was one of which he had no particular desire to be a **member**. **Occasionally** these days he might listen to Radio 3, or someone in the office might put on Classic FM of an afternoon, but there'd been sod-all in the way of music at school and the only record they'd had at home when Rex was a child was the 'original motion picture soundtrack recording' of *Fiddler on the Roof* that a family friend had given his parents one Christmas. They hadn't even had a record player at the time.

Hearing some classical music now cheered Rex up no end. This was what the paint frame had sounded like whenever he had visited, at least when the stage was dark. The radio would always be blaring out something or other, when there was no performance going on next door. If there were two jobs on and a couple of people painting on each gauze, it could be a **mad-house**. It was sad that those days seemed to have suddenly gone, in more ways than one. When was it that the business had started to **spiral**? And when it did, as Eddie Webster had rather tactlessly put it, had Terry Hobbs simply spiralled with it?

At last, after several great staccato stabs of noise, the music reached its stuttering climax, and then silence.

'That was *Scène héroïque: La Révolution grecque* by Hector Berlioz,' said the female continuity announcer after a second or so, and Rex almost expected to hear Terry burst out laughing at the contrast between the extravagant romance of the crescendo and the announcer's hushed and reverential tones.

'Taken,' the broadcaster continued, 'from the 2004 EMI recording of the Toulouse Capitole Orchestra and Les Éléments Chamber Choir featuring the soloists Laurent Naouri (bass) and Nicolas Rivenq (baritone), conducted by Michel Plasson. And isn't it wonderful to hear these lesser-known and early works by Berlioz. I'll be playing some more of those recordings on tomorrow's programme, including his *Mélodies irlandaises*, Opus Two: number three, "Chant guerrier", and number six, "Chant sacré", both of which also feature as soloist a certain young French pianist named David **Bismuth**' – she pronounced it 'Da-veed Biss-moot' – 'who is now, of course, something of a star in his own right. And I'll also be playing a more recent **release**, some "remixed" Berlioz from 2012's *Opera Riparata* by the **prolific** Italian avant-garde turntablist **Okapi** and the Aldo Kapi Orchestra—'

That's enough of that, thought Rex, as he turned the power switch back to 'Off'.

As if in response, but obviously coincidentally, he heard **loud applause** in some far part of the building. Perhaps there was a rehearsal going on, or a leaving party. Closer to the Piazza and it could have been tourists applauding some **mime**, or one of the many other genres of busker that played there.

He continued to mooch. Looking under paint pots, a glass jar in which the white spirits had not quite completely evaporated, a ball of twine, just on the off-chance that something had been missed. There were fan heaters and multi-gang extension leads, scraps of canvas and bundles of lath, a **sledge-hammer**, and enough bulk packs of masking tape to open a shop. After this, he was still planning to go up to The Rock & Sole Plaice for lunch; eat in. It wouldn't be the same without his mate, of course, but he could just fancy a portion of their cod and chips with mushy peas, plus the chance to have a quick chat with Ali or Ahmet, whoever was on, to see if they'd seen Terry any more recently than Rex had, or if they had noticed anything odd last time he'd been in.

The Ziyaeddin family had been running that place since 1980. Salt of the earth, they were, Ali and Ahmet. Well, salt and vinegar.

Rex had almost come around to Terry's position on mushy peas, which was that you could tell the quality of the establishment by the attention they paid to their humblest dish, in this case the **pease-pudding**. Rex had eaten in some supposedly higher-class establishments where an order of mushy peas had been answered with what appeared to be about a dessertspoonful, no more, of tinned garden peas hastily mashed with a fork and garnished with butter and a piece of mint leaf. Disgraceful. The Rock & Sole Plaice made the real thing in the traditional way, with dried marrowfat peas that were soaked overnight then simmered to a pulp. And they served them **red-hot** too.

Terry Hobbs was fond of limericks, and Rex had been pleased but not surprised to see a book of Edward Lear's on the table in the studio. It was not a collection of Lear's nonsense verse, however, but a glossy coffee-table book of the vivid and rather accomplished Levantine watercolours Lear had made during his mid-nineteenth-century tour of Albania, Greece and Turkey. Whether this had been left here as research for a commission or simply as reading for pleasure, Rex couldn't say without checking Terry's bible, his Job Book, an enormous binder, which – since it functioned as contacts book, billing system and diary of sorts – had been logged and was now at the station.

Terry knew a lot of Lear's limericks off by heart. He was also especially fond of the rather odder and more diffuse poetic form known as the **clerihew**: four-line biographical poems of irregular metre and length, and playfully derogatory in content. He'd nailed King in a clerihew years earlier, one evening after a particularly fine 'rock and chips times two'. They'd both been trying to decide between the jam sponge and the spotted dick on The Rock & Sole Plaice's dessert menu. This was sheer greed, and would have been before King's self-imposed elevator ban had begun to pay off. When he could ill afford to indulge.

'A clerihew!' Terry had announced, after a bit of furtive scribbling.

> When old Rexy King
> Ate too much pudding,
> His belly would tend
> To swell or **distend**.

True enough, and Rex still had the napkin that it had been written on, somewhere. His friend had illustrated the verse with a passable caricature.

In the paint frame there was no space that was not used to **stow** something. The volume beneath the sink and drainer was stuffed with countless jars and pots, stacks of cut-off milk cartons, one- and two-gallon cans, and buckets: vessels all for the mixing of paint. The size and shape of container being determined, of course, by the brush to be used. There were paint-smudged bottles of bleach and cleaning fluids; a plunger and scrubbing brushes. Set into the floor in front and to one side of this sink unit was a stone well the size of a large paving slab, which was so shallowly inclined on its four sides that the inverted-pyramid-like void it created was almost imperceptible. Into the centre of this recess was set a slatted iron drain cover. Every surface of this assembly was covered with what looked like a couple of centuries of paint slops, some of which had merely coloured the iron or stone, while in other places it had thickened into enamel-hard ridges and nodules that looked like puckered skin, drips upon drips. The drain looked as if it had been here for longer than the building in which it now found itself, and Rex imagined this pipe would probably once – in the days before Bazalgette's Embankment – have discharged directly or indirectly into the river. God knows where it led now.

Near the sink at the back of the room was an exceedingly shabby leather **sofa**, which had clearly once been white or off-white. Its soft cushions were covered in paint too, of course, with torn and open seams, and the whole was propped up **under** one corner with a thick-ish paperback book where a castor was missing, something that Rex had never noticed on his many previous visits. He knew that Socks had looked under the cushions. He'd seen them do so, and find all sorts of crap in the process. Pieces of change had been retrieved, a travel card or two, and a cigarette lighter that had presumably been there since before the workplace smoking ban, but he wasn't sure if they had taken any notice of the book.

Remembering his training, and the mantra 'Don't discount any-thing!', Rex decided to take a look for himself.

'Don't discount anything!' was not an emphatic admonition to shopkeepers keen to maximise their margins, but the title of an exercise in the Grade 4 'Supervise investigations and investigators' module that had been part of Rex King and Eddie Webster's PIPs training a few years back. It was good advice too. In that particu-lar role-playing exercise, during training, the phrase had reinforced a particular learning outcome, which in this case had been 'Ensure all the material gathered as part of an investigation is recorded, retained and revealed in line with current legislation and policy', which seemed fair enough. But in the real world it was also a useful reminder to always be ready to turn over one more stone; to not take things for granted; to keep going and not give up.

Kneeling with as straight a back as he could manage, and bracing himself as he reached down to lift the sofa slightly so that he could slip the book out from underneath it, Rex's attention was instead diverted by something else. His gloved fingertips had brushed an object of some kind. Forgetting the book, he stood up and went back over to the narrow workbenches that ran down the centre of the space to retrieve a large paint tin that he thought he might be able to use as a kind of jack.

Kneeling again, he lifted the sofa and slid the paint can beneath its front edge, then took his phone out of his pocket, set the flash and took a photograph of whatever it was, in situ. Then, reaching in, he first tried to estimate the extent and weight of the object before taking hold of it firmly with both hands to slide it out from under the couch, where he photographed it again. Later he told Webster that at first he'd thought it was a folded blanket or duvet cover that had been left here for the occasional sleepover. When demand was high, perhaps, or delivery deadlines were pressing, and work would continue around the clock. But this felt heavier than bedding, and the weave far coarser to the touch. It was a gauze, a large piece of scrim that even without unfolding he could see from the staple holes along one edge had been stretched for painting.

Looking at the folded gauze, then the frame, Rex figured that it must have been rolled up as it was taken off the frame, from the bottom, a little at a time, like a long flat sausage. You'd have to lower the frame a little, free a few more staples on each side, then gently roll the gauze – effectively, flop it over – from both ends at once, the pull created by this flopping or rolling motion across the width of the fabric possibly drawing the frame down a little more each time too. Difficult but not impossible for one person to do; easier for two.

The resulting flattish roll of fabric, some two feet wide by thirty feet or whatever it was, had then been folded over a couple of times from each end to create the bundle that had been placed beneath the sofa. Curious about both any image that it might bear and what possible reason there might have been to hide it, if hidden it had been, Rex decided that he would first need to unfold the gauze. In the restricted space of the paint frame, there was only one way to do this: vertically. He dragged it across to the main part of the room, positioning it on the floor in front of one of the frames – the one that remained unsullied – between the lip of the drop and the line of narrow workbenches, then unfolded first this side and then the other until the whole roll was laid out a couple of feet in front of the drop.

Grasping the wood, he pulled the huge frame down so that its upper horizontal was positioned at roughly shoulder height. Again, this would have been easier with two people, and it took a while, going back and forth, but Rex un-flopped first one end of the roll then the other, then one end, then the middle, and so on, until he had given himself a few feet of free scrim to play with. He took one corner of this with one hand, the staple gun in the other, and fastened it to the horizontal wooden beam. He repeated this along the length of the gauze, stapling it to the wood every foot or so, being extremely careful not to fall down the drop himself, then continued in this vein – unrolling, stapling, raising the frame a foot or two at a time – until enough of the image was exposed that he could see it had been copied from the print that was taped up over the sink. The sleeping disciples – minus Judas, of course – were hidden as yet, but Christ and the angel were clearly visible. The cypress trees and the night-time sky. Even though it was obviously unfinished, Rex could see that Terry, presumably, had been trying to reproduce the slightly off-register colouration of the original by masking areas out and overlaying what looked like flat washes – however these might have been applied – of transparent colour. The lighter, angel-lit areas of the image were raw scrim; it was the darkness that was being painted on, layer by layer.

Before going any further, Rex went and took a few photos of the sink and the print, then thought he had better photograph the gauze itself in this half-unrolled state. Of course, it was far too big to fit into a single static shot – at least, it would have been impossible without the widest of wide-angle lenses – so he switched the camera on his phone to panorama and took a steady horizontal scan as best he could. He'd upload them later.

Rex couldn't really remember the story, so he googled the text from the print, 'christus am olberge', without the umlaut. It was 'Christ on the Mount of Olives', a part of the Passion – the events of Christ's final days – that he remembered from primary school, although, in the versions he had been taught, the location had usually been referred to as the Garden of Gethsemane, rather than the Mount. It was where Christ was betrayed by Judas. That was why only eleven disciples were present, sleeping among the rocks and trees, because Judas was away somewhere cutting his deal with the Romans. Probably at this very moment the traitor would be leading them up the hill to betray his master with a kiss.

So why had this particular scrim had been abandoned?

Scrolling down, he also found a whole lot of detailed exegesis about Beethoven's oratorio on the subject (though Rex wasn't sure what an oratorio was); his Opus 85. It was all a bit specialist. Talk of non-Lucan this and recitative that, but one thing leaped out at Rex from the page: it wasn't an angel that Christ was talking to that night while his apostles slept and while he waited to be betrayed by Judas Iscariot – at least, not in Ludwig van Beethoven's scheme of things. Not an angel, but a **seraph**.

Unsure of the difference, Rex returned to more earthly matters.

Figured that, since he'd have to write this up, he'd better dot the 'i's and cross the 't's, see if there was anything else under the sofa. He got down on all fours and shone his torch in there just to make sure. The only other thing under the sofa was another rat-bait station, no different from the other couple he'd seen, lined up along the skirting. While you're down here, he thought to himself, and crawled around, cheek to the filthy floor, shining his light under this and that and finally into the dark recess beneath the lowest shelf of the nearest workbench.

9: MANDRAGORE (MANDRAKE)

'Your mate must have some **wedge**, then,' said DS Eddie Webster.

'Eh?'

Rex hadn't really been listening to his colleague; he'd been watching the photographer, making sure he got everything: the half-finished painting of Christ on the Mount of Olives that had been folded up and stashed under the sofa, and the weapon that he had found under the workbench. The sofa propped up on a paint pot.

The gangly photographer had been getting into position to take a shot of the knife, craning his neck to get the right angle, and for a moment Rex thought that he had looked a bit like a **heron** – or some other long-legged **fowl** – trying to figure out the best angle to spear a fish.

Truth be told, before that, while he'd been waiting for everyone to arrive, Rex had also been thinking about Trevor **Tennyson**, running through the official version of events for the umpteenth time, but there would be plenty of time to think about Tennyson later. The obvious problem was that Rex was not necessarily going to be in control of exactly when that might be.

He had radioed in this find immediately, and asked for a couple of bodies to help resecure the workshop. Webster had sent a uniform, a couple of Socks and the same photographer who had been here a few days earlier, all of whom had arrived within the hour, DS Eddie Webster himself following shortly after. Far from being in a good mood at this potential upturn in the investigation, Webbo had been furious.

'Your man, Hobbs. Must be minted,' Webster continued. 'I mean, supposedly no one's seen him for months, but the money for this place still gets paid, regular as. Plus the million-pound gaff in Hackney. I mean, he must be **worth** a fucking bob or two.'

'I doubt the house *cost* him a million pounds, Eddie,' said Rex. 'Far as I know, he's been in the same place since the late eighties, and you couldn't raffle a terraced house in Hackney in those days. Probably bought it for thirty or forty grand, tops. Back then that would have seemed like a lot. I don't know.'

'All paid off, though,' said Webster.

'Yeah, but he could have done that yonks ago, Ed. What's your point?'

Webster ignored the question and then got down on all fours to take a closer look for himself. 'Nasty!' he said. 'D'you think that's sharp enough to cut off someone's nose?'

Rex shrugged. 'Any idea yet if that was pre- or post-?'

'Mortem?' said Webster. '"Consistent with time of death" was the best they could do. "Thanks for nothing," I said. "So we don't know if we're looking for a torturer or a souvenir-hunter. That narrows it down." Wankers. What kind of knife is that, anyway?'

It was something of an **oddity**, and Webster was right. It did look nasty. Blade and handle combined described a shallow but serpentine 'S'. The curved wooden handle was so shaped to follow the line of the blade when it was folded, not that this particular knife ever would be folded again. An **evil**-looking blade; razor-sharp. The brand name 'Mandragore' was burned into the handle on one side. Once it had been photographed where it lay, it would be taken out from under the workbench and then bagged up and logged, and swabs would be taken of what looked like dried blood that appeared to have coagulated in and around the collar and handle, pooling on the cobbled floor.

'French brand, isn't it, Mandragore?' said Rex. 'Some kind of bill-hook? I don't know. A gardening knife? Looks like the kind of thing my grandad used to keep in his potting **shed**.'

There was a pause, then: 'You haven't been doing a bit of garden-ing yourself, Rex, have you?' Webster asked. 'Try and divert atten-tion from your mate?'

It took Rex a second or two to process the question, to register precisely what was being asked. Gardening? Then he nearly blew his top. 'You fucking think I fucking planted it? Are you fucking joking, Webbo?'

'Just trying to cover the bases,' said Webster. 'Wouldn't be the first—'

'It bloody would for me, mate,' said Rex, interrupting. 'What are you trying to say?'

'Would it? **Spotless** record, have we?'

'I'm not even going to dignify that with an answer, Webbo. Fuck's sake! What's got into you?'

'It's a **valid** fucking question! All I'm saying, Rex, is if you've got someone in mind for this, at least give me the fucking nod before you slap on the **darbies**, eh?'

Webster was cross, that much was clear, but he was walking a nar-row line here; **wafer-thin**. Policing should be about **light and shade**, and no one was perfect. Of course, if it was your job to uphold the law, you occasionally found yourself acting somewhere between the two, between the light and the dark, but Webbo had no grounds for suggesting that Rex was about to set someone up, that he'd – what was it? – 'got someone in mind'! What did he think? That Rex would identify some random local **ruffian** or oddball just to get his pal off the hook? It was a ridiculous suggestion and they both knew it.

So what was this about? Had Webster found out somehow? There was only one thing for it, and that was to push his colleague a bit further; touch a nerve.

'What's the matter?' asked Rex. 'Argue with the Mrs this morning, did we?'

On the surface, it was an innocuous bit of banter, but Rex knew full well that if Webster did know the truth about Jennifer, then having a pop about Helen would have been enough to tip him over the edge. It was not the most subtle thing that he could have said in the circumstances, admittedly, but he wasn't going to let Webster get away with questioning his integrity. That was about all you had in this job. Wave **farewell** to that – or let someone get away with questioning it so casually – and your self-respect might end up going **with it**. Rex had seen it happen, but he didn't have to take shit like that from fucking Webster. They were the same rank, for one thing.

Webster said nothing, but continued to **glower** in Rex's general direction.

'Look, Webbo,' said Rex eventually, lowering his voice. 'Think about it for a sec, eh? I haven't trodden on your fucking toes and I wasn't trying to fast-track anything. I told you yesterday that I was going to come down and have another look around. I wasn't expecting—'

'Trying to make me look bad, or something?' Webster said, suddenly. 'Suggesting I'm not doing my fucking job?'

'Course I'm not!'

'**My eye!**'

So that was the problem, was it? Rex got it now. Webbo had been CSM on this – Crime Scene Manager – and now he was Deputy

SIO, in effect running the case for Lollo, who was nominal SIO on all major investigations, and yet he had missed this potentially crucial piece of evidence: not exactly *the* murder weapon, but *a* weapon used in the commission of one, no less! No wonder he had the hump. But Rex was confident he hadn't put the investigation at risk. There had been no risk of loss or contamination. He might have been mooching around, but it was mooching by the book.

'Always the same with you, isn't it, Rex. Always got to go one better, always so fucking superior.'

Oh, it gets better, thought Rex. Not just touchy, but chippy too. It was a while since he'd been slagged off for having a degree. Hang on, though.

'"Always"? What exactly are we talking about here, Eddie?'

'You fucking know what I mean. Not being funny, but weren't you gonna do some asking around about Hobbs too, Kingsy?' Webster obviously wasn't about to drop it. 'Or have you been too busy trying to stitch me up?'

Webster paused, and in that second or two – presumably realising that he had gone too far – he reined it back in a bit, or **loosened** his grip at least, which was just as well, since he was in no position to be giving Rex orders. 'Anyway,' he offered. 'Nice find, Kingsy. Anything else under there?'

Rex didn't need to rub it in. 'Don't know. I just called it in as soon as. I took a couple of pictures of under the sofa and all, but I haven't looked at them yet. Wasn't gonna touch anything else once this turned up. So did you get a chance to check if this' – he nodded at the half-completed biblical scene – 'was listed in Terry's Job Book? Like I said on the phone, it could either have been listed as Beethoven Eighty-Five, Christus—'

'I did, as it happens, Rex,' said Webster. 'Looks like it was for the

Redgrave Theatre in Farnham, got cancelled when the place closed down.'

'What was the last job, out of interest?'

'*Electra*?' Webster didn't sound very sure, but then he was the kind of man who thought it manly not to know certain things. 'Or *Electric*. Something like that. For some festival up in Manchester. I gave 'em a bell. Bit **timid** at first, but I warmed them up. It was delivered back in March, apparently. Everyone very happy, blah blah. It was all, "We love Terry, anything we can do", et cetera. "Tell him to give me a bell if you see him," I said. And before that it was something about **Galileo** for the Barbican or whatnot. Wasn't he the bloke who decided the earth was—?'

'A **sphere**? Well, he was persecuted for it, anyway,' said Rex. 'Even if he didn't make the actual discovery. That was the ancient Greeks, speaking of Sophocles. In Galileo's day, most people just took the path of least resistance and agreed with the Church, but I guess he couldn't hack it.'

'Alright, Prof,' said Webster, flapping a hand in front of his open mouth as if stifling a yawn. 'Jesus fucking Christ! You still on the quiz team?'

'No.'

'Pity. Come on, then, let's have a look.'

Between them, the two Socks were lifting the sofa by its arms, and gently easing the paint tin out from under it. One of them slid it out of the way with his foot, so they could move the sofa forward three or four feet. As it turned out, there was nothing else on the floor except the bait station, but there was something on the wall, drawn in white chalk. Perhaps even the same white chalk that the strange note on the door had been written with.

This wasn't writing, though. It was a scrappily drawn but instantly recognisable cartoon of a bald-headed man with a big nose looking over a wall. Simple enough that anyone could draw it. An image that had circumnavigated the globe during the Second World War, been scribbled on every **pontoon bridge** and aeroplane, every ammo box and jeep, across the **Reich** and around the world. It had spread rapidly, appearing pretty much anywhere that US army personnel had set foot, from Oswestry to Okinawa. What would that be called now – a 'meme'?

'Well, fuck me!' said Webster.

'Kilroy was here,' said Rex.

10: PERSIL (PARSLEY)

Instead of some **top-drawer** lunch at The Rock & Sole Plaice with a possible side order of useful intelligence on any recent sightings of Terence Hobbs, Rex had ended up working right through. He'd have to go and talk to Ali and Ahmet tomorrow. He'd been offered and had accepted a lift back to the station from Webster, who obviously wanted to use Rex as a sounding board, since that is what he did for the forty-five minutes plus that they had sat in the car outside the Royal Palace before setting off. Webster gave Rex the full benefit of his opinion on the current status of the investigation: the ins and outs of particular resource-allocation decisions he'd taken, how hard it was not to become immersed in the management functions even when you knew it meant you were losing sight of your investigative role, and why this wasn't yet a case in need of an MIR, or Major Incident Room. He followed this with a blow-by-blow enumeration of known and as yet unknown features of both victim and offender, working through the standard profiling checklist. It was like old times. Christ, Webster was certainly blowing hot and cold.

'Motivation? We've knocked out "Gain" since there's fuck-all to nick,' Webster had said. 'How about "Jealousy"?' Then: 'I hear what you say, Rex, but I'm leaving "Sex" on the table.'

'Thanks, Ed,' Rex had said, seizing an opportunity to lighten the mood, 'but no thanks.'

'Far as I can see' – Webster had brushed Rex's joke aside in favour of restating the obvious – 'we're really only left with "Revenge" or

"Elimination", but all we've got is the where and the how, Kingsy. It's the who and the why I'm interested in.'

As well as hypothesis-building, all of this had also seemed like Webbo's way of testing in his own mind whether today's 'new material' – a bloodstained knife and a Kilroy cartoon! – was going to force a strategic shift in the direction of the investigation. Luckily, and for all of his faults, Eddie Webster was not ultimately the kind of policeman who would see such a change in direction as an admission of personal failure.

Rex's contribution to all this, other than nodding or saying, 'Yeah, right', and occasionally doing both at the same time, had been to introduce the idea that the offender may not have been acting alone. Terry Hobbs was still suspect number one – Webbo wasn't about to concede that – but might he have had help? There was the small matter of self-preservation on the part of the deceased. 'You've got to assume, Eddie,' Rex had said, 'that if he was conscious, our victim might have had reason to **execrate** the prospect of being garrotted and having his nose cut off with a fucking pruning knife. Might have, I don't know, tried to defend himself a bit. You're not going to go willingly into that one, are you? You know, "Would you mind awfully just stopping still while I tie this around your neck—"'

'Fucking hell, Rex,' Webster had said. 'This morning I had one fucking missing offender to find. Are you telling me that now I've got two? Thanks a fucking bunch.'

As they had turned down into the garage, Webster hadn't exactly apologised, but he did offer a bridge-building 'That was useful, mate', followed by a 'Thanks for listening' and finally a 'You coming to the team meeting?'

Rex had nodded. Yes, he was. And then, unless otherwise directed, he was going to write up this morning's mooch, then – while they waited for the DNA – go through the paperwork thus far and try to get a handle on where both knife and Kilroy might fit into all of this, if they did. Either way, these two new pieces of the puzzle did materially change things. How could they not? For one thing, the team would be checking for any other uses of the Kilroy image as a 'calling card' – if indeed that is what it was being used for here – and cross-referencing against all murders where knives had been left at the scene, whether hidden or not. Finally, the possibility of an accomplice gave a new impetus both to the house-to-house enquiries and to the CCTV trawl, which would have to be started again. Cue much groaning at the team debrief. Now they weren't simply looking for sightings of Terry Hobbs in the thousands of hours of footage, but for linked behaviours between any two or three people.

After all that, by the time Rex got home there was no choice but to throw together a late pot-luck supper with whatever he'd had in the way of dwindling grocery supplies. What this turned out to be was an unlikely-sounding combination of chips, **black pudding** and a supermarket own-brand boil-in-the-bag cod steak in parsley sauce. Classy. It was a far cry from The Rock & Sole Plaice – and any self-respecting **restaurateur** might have died of shame – but, eaten in front of a rerun of *Star Trek: The Next Generation*, it actually wasn't so bad. He'd even chucked a few frozen peas into the water while the fish was boiling, which was at least a small step in the right direction. Although, five-a-day-wise, the bottle of Australian Shiraz that he washed it down with would have to do for the other four, unless oven chips counted as a fresh vegetable.

Rex was a long-time fan of Jean-Luc **Picard** and the crew of this later Starship *Enterprise*. Not that he was a 'Trekkie' by any means, but if nothing else he did at least retain a kind of semi-nostalgic loyalty to the show. When *TNG* had first come out, watching it every week had been a feature of student life, so he practically knew the early episodes off by heart. Captain Picard's commanding catchphrase (and corresponding Royal Shakespeare Company pronunciation) had become a phrase of general utility among Rex and his fellow student housemates, to the extent that almost any question – 'Cup of tea?' – would almost inevitably bring the answer 'Make it so.'

If only managing the moods of Eddie Webster were so easy. Today's paranoid outburst being a particular case in point. Of course this was a strange investigation, and Rex's declared 'interest' in it – his friendship with Terry Hobbs – complicated that further, but what exactly did Webster have to be fucked off with him about, let alone to justify what had come close to an outright accusation of corruption, or to think that Rex might be out to undermine him?

Obviously they had had their differences, and how, but for the purposes of getting on and getting on with the job, Detective Sergeants Rex King and Eddie Webster had until now built a fairly effective 'Chinese wall' between the personal and the professional parts of their lives. Yet for some reason Webster had come close to breaking right through that today. Perhaps a wall was not the right metaphor here, and it would be more accurate to say that, by studious omission and a process of incremental avoidance, they had tacitly created a metaphorical no-man's-land, like some bleak **Aral** basin, a vast and inhospitable region to which they tacitly agreed not to go, boldly or otherwise. Until today, that is, when Webster had practically turned up at the border with his **visa** stamped, demanding entry. So what on earth had changed Webster's mind, turned him into some sort of delayed-action **sabre-rattler**?

For a long time it had been Rex who felt justifiably aggrieved at his colleague, not the other way around. But he had decided to make like **Gandhi** and pursue a strategy of non-violence as far as Webster

99

was concerned. He certainly hadn't let it interfere with his or the department's work. And besides, this had all been yonks ago, back in the early noughties.

Rex and Eddie had been good mates at the time, or so Rex had thought, anyway. They had been in the middle of an afternoon's **walkie-talkie training** – so that dated it – when his friend and colleague had received a phone call from the hospital to say that his father had died, Webster being next of kin and the only surviving relative. The death of a **parent** is tough enough news for anyone to receive at the best of times, and people respond to grief in strange ways, but God only knew why Eddie Webster, supposedly Rex's mate, had then gone and used it as an excuse to behave the way that he did.

It certainly wasn't as if Rex had been unsympathetic. Having lost both of his parents as a teenager, back when he'd still lived in **Exeter**, Rex had at least been through some of this before, albeit at an earlier age than most. **Charles** and **Geraldine** King had **rear**-ended an articulated lorry at speed on the M5 near Taunton following his father's suffering a **coronary** at the wheel. Mercifully, they had at least been killed instantly.

Having thus some inkling of what his then mate might be going through, Rex had actually gone and spoken with the trainer – and with Lollo – so that Webster was able to go home and deal with whatever funeral and estate stuff needed doing. Little had Rex known how his mate would repay him for this small kindness, but he soon found out: with all the gratitude and finesse of an **ill-bred llama**.

A few days after the death, Webster, who was still on compassionate leave, had come round to visit, ostensibly to see Rex. That was the story, anyway, but in fact he would have known that Rex was on **duty**. They were still on the same two-two-twos at the time, so his later protestations hadn't really washed. Oblivious to any of this, Rex had got home around 6 o'clock in the morning and found Helen already up and doing the washing up, and moreover seemingly furious with him.

Understandably confused by this reception, Rex had asked Helen what he had done. He had not been in the least bit prepared for her response, which was – broadly – that she was in love with someone else and was leaving him. Where the fuck had that come from? At first, Helen wouldn't say who it was that she was now in love with, but once Webster had been revealed as **Lancelot** to her Guinevere, King had felt no choice but to bid **adieu** to the friendship with his fellow officer.

Within a week, Helen had gone too. It transpired that Webster had not only turned to her for sympathy and a shoulder to cry on – and oh, how he had cried – but that he had used the excuse of the parental death to make a 'life's too short'-style declaration of his love for Helen. And as if all of that hadn't been bad enough, she had bought it. The fact that he'd done all this on Rex's own fucking sofa – and in the process knocked off the best part of a bottle of his whisky to boot – had only rubbed it in.

11: COCHLÉARIA (SCURVY GRASS)

It had got worse too. By the time Webster had returned from the two weeks of compassionate **leave** that he'd arranged – with Rex's help! – he'd not only buried his father but become engaged to Helen, who for her part had not cut Rex off cold; not completely. At least, not until she'd broken the news that she and Eddie were getting married. Before that particular bombshell there'd been a farewell fuck or two, preceded and followed by the **usual** long and emotionally draining 'It's not you, it's me' conversations, but Rex had quickly sensed that these were following a certain script. It had been as if she were looking for new and ever more convincing ways to illustrate a **policy** decision that had already been made. He had quickly become convinced that the conversations were pointless. It was obvious that they would by definition never have a good outcome for him, **owing** primarily to the fact that it really wasn't him, after all. It *was* her. And Helen's mind had clearly been made up. To make matters even worse, the change had suited Hel, and **overtly** so. She'd had a bit of a makeover and swapped her familiar 'Rachel' haircut for a short bob, and she looked great in a new **crimson** floral-print **dress**. For a few darker days, Rex had entertained **Macduff**-like fantasies of confronting the **witless** Webster, but in reality he'd decided to just leave them to it. **Big deal** though this was, Rex had quickly sobered up and, **reading** between the lines, faced up to the fact that, whether he liked it or not, there was **not a lot** he could do about it.

Beside this life-changing romantic shock, the lesser adjustment in

Rex's new reality had been that a good friendship and one forged on the Hendon **parade ground** was now also fucked. Personal history and camaraderie were supposed to mean something in the force, but still it wasn't that which had really **grated**, but rather the **monstrous** way his former pal had gone about it, scurvy knave that he was. It was more complicated than that, obviously, but for Webster now – after all these years – to have the nerve to get shirty with Rex, lashing out like a horse with **colic**, was surely some kind of joke.

Before the Shiraz sent him to sleep, Rex wondered whether Webbo had got it all out of his system for now. He hoped he had, because the kind of performance he had had to put up with earlier on, and in front of colleagues, was totally out of order. It had better have been the last of it, otherwise – God forbid – Rex might need to have a word with Lollo. If that didn't work, he wondered if he might not need to have some kind of **powwow** with Helen, use her as a **go-between** to find out what was really going on.

Rex did not sleep well that night.

Perhaps this was because of the sodium and carbohydrate rush from his unusually unhealthy later supper, or because of the old emotions that had been stirred up by Webster's lashing out. Or maybe it was just the pressure of work, in an occupation where bad dreams seemed to be par for the course.

King had read a bit of Freud in his college days, so he was familiar with the idea that dreams are a form of work through which the thoughts of the unconscious are made manifest to the conscious mind. Although he was also aware of the ways in which such ideas were widely misunderstood. He could remember Helen once saying, in all seriousness, that to dream about teeth – whether of a single loose **molar**, or of all the teeth falling out – was an expression of sexual anxiety, while any cheap dream dictionary might equally and authoritatively state that a dream about flying could be seen as illustrating *inter alia* a personal sense of power and accomplishment in real life, as if you have literally 'risen above' a situation.

Rex King's dreams were nothing like this. They contained no clichéd symbolism, although there was one familiar, recurring nightmare.

It was, of course, a recurring dream about work. Just as a CEO might dream of her company, a postman of sorting mail, or – in some *Merrie Melodies* cartoon – Bugs Bunny of being chased by **Elmer** Fudd, so the dreams of a policeman or -woman might well focus on the finer points of police procedure. Certainly, Rex's unconscious seemed always to **recycle** the same content.

The nightmare always started with dream-Rex running to the cells. The overhead fluorescent lights are flickering, as if there were a persistent electrical fault, before going off altogether; not a fault, then, but a power cut. In the dream he is running because he has found out by chance that no IS91R was issued to a detainee brought in by an Immigration Officer, or IO. Every policeman knew that migrants contravening UK immigration law were first detained using the IS81, granting authority to hold for examination or further examination, but as soon as the 'passenger' (or the '81', as they were sometimes known) was handed over to another body – whether that was the police, Prison Service personnel or an escorting or removal-agency contractor – then an IS91 'full authority to detain' had to be issued by the IO within four hours. This form then accompanied the passenger for an indefinite period of detention, irrespective of holding agency or transfer from one agency to another, until the point of deportation itself. The IS91 was meant to be accompanied by an IS91R, which had to be issued to the detainee him- or herself within the same time frame.

The IS91R was called different things by different people. No one had asked what the detainees called them, but IOs often referred to them as the 'Reasons', since it was easier to say than 'IS91R' and that is what it enumerated: the reasons for deportation. 'Have you given him his Reasons?' the detaining officer might be asked.

Dream-Rex hands over the Reasons, but as he does so he realises that there is no interpreter present, so he is not able to ensure that the detainee understands the contents of the form. This is an omission that may make the detaining agency vulnerable to a successful legal challenge under Article 5(2) of the Human Rights Act, namely, 'Everyone who is arrested shall be informed promptly, in a language which he understands, of the reasons for his arrest and of any charge against him.'

Even within the logic and experience of the dream-state, dream-Rex knew this stuff. He also knew that the detention of migrants in police custody was a joke, not least because it created in effect a **hybrid** institution that had to be run on two different regimes, and to address the needs of differing client and user groups. Where previously it had answered merely to various Home Office directorates, in recent years this had come to mean working to the sometimes conflicting directives of two entirely separate government departments, namely the new Ministry of Justice and the slimmed-down Home Office that the hiving-off of the former had created. It was not surprising – indeed it was sometimes understandable (although not justifiable) – that Immigration Service paperwork might occasionally not be administered correctly.

Such was the stuff of Rex's dreams, and in this case dream-Rex appears to have been left holding the ball, as it were.

What always happened next in this particular nightmare was that, at the very moment dream-Rex realises he has no interpreter, he is distracted by a commotion around the corner in the corridor. Going to investigate, he is surprised to see a pair of splayed legs emerging from beneath a pile of four officers. Later they will say that they were merely administering first aid, but it reminds dream-Rex of nothing so much as the scrum in a game of rugby.

His attention is drawn to odd details: the brown corduroy fabric of the trousers, say, or the fact that the man at the base of the heap of people is only wearing a shoe on his left foot, and that there is a hole on the underside of the navy-blue sock that he is wearing on his right.

In dream after dream, noticing his approach, the officers dismount, as it were, and dream-Rex is always surprised to see that the man being thus administered to – a black man of around thirty, smartly dressed in corduroy trousers and what looks from the back like a grey long-sleeved Fred Perry – is not lying back or leaning back against the wall, as dream-Rex had expected to see, but instead is doubled over so that his head is lolling above his knees. There is a pool of vomit or saliva on the carpet between his legs.

'Fucker resisted, didn't he,' one of the officers says. 'Said he was having an asthma attack. Strong guy. Took all of us to hold him down.'

'Didn't you know he had asthma?' dream-Rex asks.

'No.'

'He's been booked, I take it. Gnat's Piss, the lot?'

The officer nods.

'Did he mention it then?'

'No.'

'Where's he headed?'

'In there,' one of the officers says, nodding at the open cell.

'Well, get him bloody well in there, and put him in the recovery position now,' dream-Rex says. 'Do what you can to bring him around. And for Christ's sake call an ambulance.'

Then he finds himself driving home, and even though the dream-home appears to have more in common with the family home in Exeter that he grew up in than the flat in Falcon where he actually lives, the overwhelming sensation is one of being flooded with elation and relief. Next thing, he is being woken up by the **warble** of his mobile phone alarm.

This time, however, there was a slight, topical variation from the usual. In the moments before he woke up, just as dream-Rex was pulling up outside his childhood home, he saw that someone had chosen to **deface** the front wall of the house. In this new version of the dream, next to the front door was a large, spray-painted cartoon of a bald man with a big nose looking over a wall.

Kilroy was here.

12: PÂQUERETTE (DAISY)

Just before he opened his eyes, Rex felt slightly disorientated to remember that he was in his bedroom on the sixth floor at Falcon, and not in the back bedroom of the 1930s red-brick semi on the Burnthouse Lane Estate that he had grown up in.

When he thought of it, Rex recalled his childhood fondly. It seemed idyllic now, as if it were the product of another age, but perhaps that was merely because it had all ended so abruptly. If he thought of those years now, it might be the Devon **seascape** that his mind would turn to – the view from a train window travelling south to Torquay by Dawlish – or memories closer to his former family home, such as walking to the Dolphin Fish & Chip Shop, watching **tom-tits** on the bird feeder, or the smell of the ground after a **frost**. **Convolvulus** flowers hanging from their slender summer vines. A **coot** nesting in the reeds down by the river beyond the Priory Girls' School playing fields. Drawing diagrams of an **anode** or a diode in O-level chemistry lessons at Hele's School – the local comprehensive – or the whole class walking en masse over the footbridge to the annexe. He could remember the Latin teacher trying and failing to explain the differences between the Gregorian and the Roman Calendars. The latter supposedly relied at least partly on some kind of backwards calculation of the **kalends**, which were not only the first days of each month – pinch, punch-style – but also stood for something utterly unfathomable to do with the number of days remaining at the close of a month, plus two, which he had not understood at all, though he had been fascinated by the etymological lesson that it imparted. There had even been a mnemonic rhyme on the subject that they learned by rote, a Latin equivalent of 'Thirty days hath September', but Rex had long since forgotten it. These were innocent pleasures all, and memories that he supposed were not so different from those of many other people of his age and background.

All of that had changed, of course, and childhood been brought to an abrupt end, once **Dame Fortune** had come knocking on the door at Spenser Avenue in the shape of an unknown policeman with a concerned expression and some terrible news. Peaked cap tucked under his arm out of respect, while his colleague was sat in the patrol car eating a Twix.

In certain circles, the death of your parents might lead to a family home being sold, or an inheritance. Small consolation for such a great loss, but a **balm** of sorts. For the young King, an only child, it meant having to effect an **expeditious cull** of his parents' possessions. There had been two small life insurance payments due, of which he was the beneficiary, and which he would somehow manage to parlay into a deposit when it came to buying the flat in Falcon a few years later. Of his parents' things, King managed to save only a few papers – their marriage certificate and the like – some talismanic photographs, his mother's wedding ring and his father's best watch, an inexpensive gold Seiko with a black strap, and these he would **enshrine** with the other treasures that he kept in a small charity-shop-bought suitcase of his most valued possessions, along with his passport, O-level certificates, and sundry official documents.

Thankfully all of the other familial and funereal obligations, from house-clearance to bill payments, had been taken care of briskly and uncomplainingly by his maternal grandmother, who had also offered him the spare room in her two-bedroom house on the other side of

Exeter. He might technically have been an orphan, then, but there had been no danger of his **starving**.

He had always got on well with his grandmother, and in many ways her place had felt like a home from home. Once they had cleared out Spenser Avenue, he had never visited the Burnthouse Lane Estate again, preferring to make a clean break and get on with it.

'You don't have to call me "Granny" any more,' she'd once offered. 'Call me Daisy. Everybody else does. Your mum did.'

He had carried on with his A-levels. Everyone had thought that was for the best. Often he and his grandmother would do the *Guardian* crossword together – the quick one. Rex remembered how he used to enjoy folding the paper inside out, bringing the back cover around to meet the front in order to expose the inside back page, home of the classifieds, of cartoons by Garry Trudeau and Steve Bell, and of the two daily crosswords; then folding it in half and in half again. Taking turns to fill it in, or to ask the other when they got stuck.

'Eleven across,' he might say. 'Chauvinist; five letters?'

'**Bigot**,' she might say.

By the time they'd finished, the Quick Crossword and all the white space around it would be covered in a biro scrawl of answers and workings-out.

Or they might eat an early dinner on trays on their laps while watching the *BBC News* at twenty to six when he got back from sixth form. That way he could do more revision in the evenings. This was the summer of 1984, so the programme would have been dominated by the UK Miners' Strike, the discovery of a cache of IRA weapons, or the Iran–Iraq War and the latest attack on international shipping in the Persian Gulf. It would not be unusual for them to be sitting in her living room, eating sausage and mash or macaroni cheese, while staring at footage of the aftermath of an IRA bomb explosion in London or Belfast, or while some **imam**, or perhaps the de facto Iranian commander-in-chief, Hashemi Rafsanjani, commented upon the latest atrocity in the Gulf.

Once the exams were finished, if he wasn't going to Andy's house to hang out and listen to records after dinner, he might stay and continue to watch the television at his grandmother's for another couple of hours. There was usually a cartoon – *Tom and Jerry* or *Droopy* – on before the main evening's programming, which might kick off with *Top of the Pops* or a film, or with *Star Trek* followed by *Only Fools and Horses*.

Looking back on it later, it would seem obvious that his grandmother had indulged him somewhat, treating him like a convalescent through that period of mourning. He had almost certainly been more traumatised by the double bereavement than he was aware. Selfishly, he had not at the time considered his grandmother's own grief, her loss of a daughter, as particularly significant. Perhaps it had simply been that he needed more looking after, spoiling even. She would bring him breakfast in bed, for example, and **forgive** him the odd tantrum. But she was a good sport too, so would enjoy winding him up when the football was on by pretending that she didn't understand the **off-side** rule, or – ever the **drama critic** – by rubbishing his favourite vintage American comedy programmes, *The Phil Silvers Show* or *Get Smart*, which were being rerun on a still young Channel 4.

During the first couple of years of college that followed – his new life in London – he had often thought of how his grandmother had helped him out when he really needed it. He had phoned a couple of times early on, but she had seemed— what was it: confused? distracted? Perhaps her daughter's death had taken it out of her after all.

He had thought of going back to see his grandmother, but had never done so, couldn't face it. Wasn't that why you moved to London: to make a clean break and start again? And it was only a matter of time, of course, before she too would **croak**. Had he been able to keep in touch, he might have gone to her funeral, might have given a **succinct** but heartfelt address – she would have liked that – but apart from that, he'd felt no desire ever to return to Exeter.

13: THON (TUNA)

Detective Sergeant Rex King could not quite believe that it was still only Saturday, so not even a week had gone by since his old Covent Garden drinking buddy, the painter, raconteur and bon-viveur-about-town Terence Hobbs, had been put squarely in the spotlight for the bizarre murder of an as yet unidentified male whose noseless body had been discovered in his studio, the so-called paint frame of the Royal Palace Theatre on Drury Lane. It was still just a few days, then, since it had become apparent to all that Hobbs might actually be on the run from the consequences of said murder. A few days that had also seen the resurrection of some ancient **beef** between Rex and his old colleague and the now husband of Rex's ex-girlfriend Helen, DS Eddie Webster, who was touchy at the best of times, and who now just happened to also be leading the investigation into the murder at Terry's place, and thus the hunt for Terry himself.

Added to this, the possible resurrection, as it were, of the Tennyson case, whether as a shot across the Met's bows or not and on the eve of an SiC inspection, was the icing on the bloody cake. Having been a witness at the trial of the four officers who were acquitted of Trevor Tennyson's murder following his death in custody, Rex was only too aware that there were those who considered the Met to be as institutionally racist as ever it was pre-Macpherson, and the deaths in custody or following other contact with the police of BAME clients as evidence of what amounted to racist murder; a policy of shoot to kill.

To a detective, the word 'policy' meant only one thing. It was the name of the file that you used to keep a record of a major investigation, to document strategic and other decisions made, and which might then be referred to in the construction of a case. This was a different thing entirely. Deaths in custody? Speaking from the inside, Rex could honestly say that there was no underlying conspiracy and no such policy, in the sense of a documented principle being publicly adopted, but was it so straightforward? The crossword fiend in Rex knew full well that a 'policy' could also mean a course of action adopted, a sequence of events ratified by default. There may well be á **gulf** – if not a whole world of difference – between decisions publicly stated and actions taken, but what was it someone had once said about a conspiracy? That it only needed two people to *think* the same; no actual collusion was necessary.

It was long before his time on the force, but Rex could remember watching television at his grandmother's house around the time that a previous conspiracy to murder had been uncovered: the 'Stalker Inquiry' (named after its lead, Deputy Chief Constable John Stalker of the Manchester Police) into an alleged shoot-to-kill policy by security forces including the Royal **Ulster** Constabulary against members of the IRA and other republican paramilitary groups during the so-called 'Troubles' in Northern Ireland. Even in the Irish Republic in 1972, troops guarding **Leinster** House in Dublin had been given orders to shoot to kill civilians protesting against the Dáil's erosion of civil liberties relating to the Troubles. It was a policy that had been put into deadly and state-sanctioned practice, with executions across the six counties of the so-called 'province' – in **Armagh** and **Antrim**, in **Tyrone** and **Fermanagh**, in Derry and **Down** – and beyond; as far away as Gibraltar. There were those who said that the uncovering of that particular policy had also betrayed the hypocrisy of an establishment at war with itself too. Stalker himself was simultaneously briefed against, in what had seemed like a sustained attempt both to undermine the inquiry and to ruin his professional reputation.

Could the same happen now? Perhaps things had improved, or a similar campaign of vilification might have been visited upon Sir William Macpherson in the 1990s. But no, Macpherson had been a judge, not a policeman. If the shoot-to-kill inquiry had been led by a judge instead of a senior policeman, might the outcome have been different? Was that *why* it had been given to a policeman? Were policemen always the patsy, always destined to be shot – as it were – by both sides? It sometimes seemed so.

Rex King well remembered how the protestors who had crowded the public galleries during the trial of the 'Tennyson Four' had certainly seemed to believe that Trevor Tennyson's death had been just a further tragic outcome of a de facto policy, one that had resulted in many deaths and which itself needed to be investigated. He wondered if the protestors' calls for an overarching inquiry into deaths in custody such as Tennyson's might ever be met. If so, it seemed to Rex that the measure of the sincerity of such an inquiry might be whether it were headed by a senior policeman or a judge.

And on, and on.

And such were the Tennyson-inspired thoughts that went through Rex's mind that Saturday morning, as he pulled the front door to behind him at Falcon and jogged down the stairs. It was fair to say that he was in a bad mood.

At least a weekend slogging around on the investigation and trying to put Terry in the clear would take his mind off the SiC briefing that was coming up on Monday, and which heralded a far longer period of turmoil once the inspection itself got going. But after a night like he'd just had, and with the team meeting about to kick off at 10 o'clock, the only thing for it was to get a decent breakfast inside him, something to keep him going. A bacon sandwich wasn't going to cut it today, nor his now usual 'healthy' poached-egg alternative. It would have to be the all-day breakfast – sausage, bacon, fried egg, mushrooms, beans and brown toast, 'no tomato' – plus some extra hash browns.

Perhaps because it was a bit later than usual – eight forty-five to his usual seven – or because it was a Saturday, Sid's was busy, and taking his double espresso outside, Rex found he was going to have to share a table. The choice was between a bunch of belching builders in hi-vis and hard hats who were studying the *Sun* and the *Racing Post*, and a smartly dressed, professional-looking black woman who was eating a croissant and reading – what else? – the Saturday-morning edition of the *Guardian*. It was no contest. He'd hear enough about the racing once he got to work, it being **Derby Day**. No doubt there would be a sweepstake too.

'Do you mind?' he asked, pointing at the empty chairs with his own paper and doing his best to smile. 'Are these ones taken?'

'Not at all. Please,' she said, then returned to her reading, but not for long.

'**Madame?**' said the waitress, setting a cappuccino down in front of her.

It was not long before his breakfast arrived too, and Rex set steadily about cleaning the plate, working his way in from the outside, saving the best – the egg yolk and the crispiest piece of bacon – for last. Sid's all-day breakfast was as good as he remembered. He should do this more often. No, perhaps he shouldn't. It was fine as a rare treat, though; better that way. He could still remember what it was like having a gut, lugging those extra two or three stone around, shirt buttons straining, and he didn't miss it at all. He mopped up the bacon grease and the tomato sauce with the last piece of toast, accidentally catching the eye of his inadvertent companion. Shrugged, as if he'd been caught out.

'You look as if you enjoyed that,' she said, smiling.

'Enjoyed it a bit too much, I think,' he said. 'That obvious, was it? They do good breakfasts here.'

'So I see,' she said, smiling, then: 'I'll have to come here more often.'

She went back to her paper, Rex to his coffee, though as he did so he snuck another look at her. Slim and with a pretty face and a short black bob, she was wearing a beige trouser suit and white open-necked blouse, which, together with the tasteful gold jewellery – a locket, perhaps, a bracelet and earrings – looked good against her dark skin. Then the penny dropped. Perhaps she hadn't just been talking about the breakfast. Well, it was early, so he could be forgiven for being a bit slow. He put down his pen. The crossword wasn't going anywhere.

'Yes, you should,' he said, smiling. 'I'm Rex, by the way.'

'Susan,' she said.

'So what brings you here, Susan?'

It turned out that she had just arrived in town because her niece was scheduled for an operation.

'Oh dear,' said Rex. 'I'm sorry to hear that. Great Ormond Street?' She nodded.

'Oh well. Couldn't be in better hands, then, I suppose.'

'Thanks, yes, I know,' said Susan. 'So they say. Anyway, I thought I should try and stay nearby for a few days. It's a bit easier for me to take the time off at this time of year than it is for her mum. My sister. Lend a bit of moral support and some glossy magazines, you know. I'm not sure how long she'll need to stay. Yesterday they said they're not sure if she's well enough to undergo the actual op. We'll find out later.'

'Fingers crossed, then,' said Rex. 'I hope it works out okay for you all.'

'Thank you. Yes, I hope so too,' she said. 'Anyway, how about you?'

'Oh, I live just around the corner and I work down the road,' he said, wondering if he should leave it there, but then deciding it was better to get it out in the open. 'Police.'

He paused to see if that would scare her off, like it sometimes did. It didn't, so he continued: 'CID.'

'I'm sorry, Rex,' said Susan. 'I probably should, but I'm not sure I even know what that stands for.'

'Criminal Investigation Department,' said Rex. 'Detective Sergeant Rex King at your service.'

'Detective, eh?'

'Pays the **mortgage**. You know.'

'That's a great name,' she said. 'Rex King.'

'Thanks. Yes, I know,' said Rex. 'My parents' little joke.'

She could pay him all the compliments she wanted.

Susan lived in York – where she taught at the university – and had got the early train. 'It's cheaper if you leave before six.'

'So you must get tired of everyone telling you that you don't have a Yorkshire accent?'

Susan hadn't grown up there, she told him, but they had moved there for her husband's work. Rex was disappointed, though he did his best to maintain a neutral expression at this news of her marital status. Well, of course she would be married. It was Sod's Law.

'Then, after we divorced,' she continued – while Rex cheered inwardly – 'he moved away, but I found that all my friends were there, and I liked my job, so I stayed on.'

They chatted amiably for a while, but Rex was having to keep an eye on the time.

Susan's *Guardian* was open at a feature plugging some forthcoming television documentary series about the seventeenth-century Dutch painter Johannes Vermeer, which was to be fronted by the popular young TV presenter and Fogarty family scion Tom.

'Nepotism is alive and well, I see,' said Rex.

'Nepotism? It's practically **dynastic**,' said Susan, laughing. 'These TV families: the Dimblebys, the Fogartys and the Snows! I mean, I suppose you could be charitable and say that of course it's the world you grow up in. Not falling far from the tree, chip off the old block or whatever; but, I don't know, it reminds me of— what was that line of Brian Sewell's? Do you remember? When Alan Titchmarsh or someone – yes, it was – was presenting the Proms on the BBC, and Sewell sneered and said Titchmarsh was telling us everything he doesn't know about classical music! Something like that. Funny. Though, in his defence, at least Titchmarsh had worked for it; didn't have it handed to him on a plate.'

The puff piece included a reproduction of Vermeer's 'A Young Woman Seated at the **Virginals**'. It was one of several in the painter's limited oeuvre that depicted this bulky, early keyboard, a kind of proto-piano.

'Lovely painting, though,' said Rex. 'I've seen it, as it happens. Seen most of them. Remember there was that Vermeer blockbuster show in The Hague? Christ! Must be twenty-odd years ago now.'

'Lucky you,' said Susan. 'I would have loved to have seen that. Well, you've got hidden depths. I bet not many of your CID colleagues could say as much.'

'Well, you know. My girlfriend at the time, my ex, was an art teacher. Still is, as it goes. An art teacher, I mean. It was a romantic weekend in Amsterdam, you know. The Anne Frank House and a double-decker train to "Den Haag". She'd booked it months ahead. Tiny paintings. There's one at Kenwood,' he said. '"The Guitar Player". Do you know it?'

'Really? No.'

'That's up the Highgate end of Hampstead Heath – Kenwood House. Worth a trip if you have time.'

'Well, if not this visit, maybe next,' said Susan.

As she picked the paper up to have a closer look at the image, a small **spider** fell out on to the table, then scurried off and dropped off the edge.

'Money spider,' said Rex. 'We used to say that at school. Didn't you? You were supposed to pick up the thread and spin it around your head and you'd—'

'Be rich?' said Susan, laughing again.

'Something like that. Didn't you use to do that?'

'D'you think I'd still be a university lecturer if I had?' she said. 'With all that money?'

They paused for a beat or two. The brief lapse in conversation was filled with the rhythmic rumble of **bass** from the sound system in a passing car, which made their cups rattle lightly.

Rex smiled, shook his head. 'Very funny,' he said.

'Thank you,' she said, smiling back.

It was getting on for ten. Reluctantly, Rex took a last swig of the now cold coffee.

'That was a nice surprise,' he said. 'Meeting you.' Then, raising the empty cup, he added, 'I'd love to have another one' – and he wished he really could – 'but there's a team meeting I have to be at which starts in about five minutes.' He found himself reaching for the wallet in his back pocket, and handing her a card. 'It was great to meet you,' he said. 'Listen, I don't normally do this, and I don't know how your visit is going to pan out, but if you do wind up being down here for a couple of days and you fancy getting a drink or dinner – or even just downloading – I'd love to continue our chat. That's my mobile.'

She took the card, and put it in her own purse. 'Thank you, Rex,' she said, then handed him hers. 'Swap you. If you're ever in York, give me a call.'

'Thanks, Susan **Hollander**,' he said, reading her name from the card. 'Good luck with your niece.'

As he picked up his newspaper, Rex wanted to say, 'Please ring me – please!', but resisted, figuring it was obvious. Though perhaps he should put a bet on the Derby after all, whistle around the corner to the bookies on Southampton Row, because it was starting to feel like his lucky day.

In other respects, Saturday or not, it was business as usual, and back at the station Webster's investigation-team meeting was to be held in the same tenth-floor conference room that had played host to the Tennyson crisis meeting earlier in the week. Although, since this time there were significantly fewer high-ranking officers in attendance – just Lollo – the venetian blinds were raised. There was a pleasant breeze. He could hear the traffic a few floors below. It was better than all being crammed into the office with the phones ringing every five seconds. It also meant that, even if it didn't qualify for Major Incident Room status, the investigation was being taken seriously. All of the senior team was there: Socks, Fuck Me, the house-to-house co-ordinator, investigative team members and more. Everyone was chatting. A couple of uniforms were offering around one of their caps – and the remaining scrunched-up pieces of paper it contained – and inviting a last few takers for the Derby sweepstake: 'Fiver,' he said to Rex. 'You in?'

'Oi, Bill and Ben,' said Webster loudly before Rex could respond, and brandishing a twenty as he did so. 'Have you two quite fucking finished? I'll take the last however-many-the-fuck you've got left. So fucking sit down, eh?' He turned his attention to the rest of the room: 'Okay, everyone, mobiles off, please. We've got a lot to get through . . .'

Webster was right: they did. There was obviously some pressure to move the investigation along, because Lollo not only kicked things off by offering some opening comments – and a generalised bollocking – but he even stayed on to chair the meeting, where normally this would be deputised, particularly on a Saturday.

The gist of Lollo's overview was that low-information investigations were a fact of life, so stop moping: get used to it and get on with it. He reminded everyone that here was not only an as yet unidentified victim, but also a credible suspect who was a missing person. 'No wonder it's low-bloody-info!'

Everyone laughed. But then they stopped laughing, because they'd noticed that Lollo wasn't joking any more. He'd gone serious on them. What was not acceptable, he went on – and this was where it turned into the generalised bollocking – was if or when that lack of information was due to police failures, and material being missed first time around. And this was what had happened here. He was surprised at them for this, disappointed even. He'd thought this was a good team, he said; don't prove him wrong. He looked them each in the eye. It was time to pull their fucking socks up. He didn't need to remind everyone that, if the community or the media suddenly decided to take more of an interest in the case than they had to date, then they'd be getting it from all sides, and at this rate they wouldn't have a pot to piss in. It was time, in other words, to bloody well get on with it.

Rex was relieved that the bollocking seemed to have been directed at everyone except him and Webster. More than this, Lollo had actually singled them out for their teamwork, and for their tenacity in going back to the scene and finding new evidence. The fact that they hadn't let the lack of progress get them down. And if that was not quite how Rex remembered it happening, he was happy to share the credit with Webster. After all, it could have gone the other way. And Rex had been a policeman for long enough to know that it was better to be commended as part of a group than to be singled out and criticised for flying solo. Rex figured that being patted on the head by the DCI might also get Eddie off his back for a bit.

As to the content of the various briefings, house-to-house had turned up precisely nothing new, ditto CCTV. Rex's suggestion that there might have been two offenders was merely referenced by both teams as a point of action to be followed up. It had not been implemented in either line of enquiry yet. The tickets database threw up a good few criminal records, but none in this bracket.

Webster gave a quick rundown of the discovery of the knife, and the Kilroy cartoon; the suggestion that this latter might be connected with the mysterious chalk writing on the door.

Most interesting of all was Fuck Me. They were the only team that had acted upon the new material. More than that, they were already running with it, so the effect of Dr Sue **Stanza**'s presentation on the room was palpable. It was as if the sun had come out, and as if all those cups of bitter filter coffee from Building Services that everyone had been chucking down all morning had suddenly started working. The atmosphere changed, and it gave the team a bit of a lift. Suddenly it felt as if, instead of merely treading water, the investigation was actually rolling again, progress was being made, and all of this without Fuck Me even really **trying**, but rather just doing their job.

They had got a blood-type match on both knife and floor residue, and were hoping for a usable DNA sample within forty-eight hours, after which they would begin the process of searching and comparing with the National DNA Database, hoping for a cold hit and or a match with other samples from the scene that were already in train. If they had no joy with that, they'd go out to ENFSI partners, the European Network of Forensic Science Institutes, as well as CODIS, the United States's Combined DNA Index System, and Interpol's DNA Gateway. As to the knife, they said, if you had to choose a weapon that was ideally suited to lopping off someone's nose, you could do a lot worse than a Mandragore billhook—

'I say, I say, I say,' said one of the uniforms, interrupting.

'Oi, Bill and Ben,' said Webster. 'Have I got to tell you two again?'

'Thank you, Eddie,' said Lollo. 'Now, where were we, Sue?'

'Thank you, Detective Chief Inspector,' she said. 'I was just saying that our analysis suggests an ante-mortem wound, that the victim was alive when his nose was cut off—'

The collective reflex response to this further grisly detail was an audible cringe.

'—even if he may not have been conscious.'

The obvious general disgust at the mere thought of nasal mutilation turned out to be the cue for everyone – not just 'Bill and Ben' – to drag out any nose jokes that they could remember: 'That's not to be sniffed at', etc.

Once this brief diversionary buzz had worn off, and the laughter had died down, Sue Stanza turned to Webster and said, 'That writing – forget whether it's relevant or not for a second. Do we have any idea what it means?'

'One thing, while we're here,' Rex put in. 'I had a call from Mrs Bisika. You know, the cleaner? The woman who discovered the body? I spoke to her the other day. My interview notes are already up, but she called me again quite late—'

'Aye-aye!' said Ben, nudging Bill, as if he'd been woken up by the sudden, sexist realisation that there was only one possible reason for a woman to phone a man.

Rex ignored the provocation, '—I don't know, couple of nights ago? And I was going to follow up today.'

'Anything good?' Lollo asked.

Rex took out his notebook and flipped back through the pages until he found it. 'Ah, Wednesday night it was. One of her neighbours in the Peabody flats – lady called Iris? – apparently told her that she had heard male voices in the street that weekend. Late at night. Early hours. She'd been awake tending to her husband. Foreign accent, she said.'

'Argument, was it? What'd they say?'

'According to Gertrude – Mrs Bisika – this Iris couldn't make it out, but she could at least tell they weren't British.'

Lollo turned to the house-to-house team. 'How did you fucking idiots miss that? Didn't you do the Peabody Estate?'

'It's a date!' Sue said, looking up from her phone.

'What?'

'The writing on the door. It's French. It's a date. Not "Trudi", but *Tridi*—'

'Tree-what?' said Rex.

'3D?' said Bill. 'Like Irish IMAX, innit?'

'*Tridi treize Ventôse* – with a circumflex,' she said. 'CXCIII. It's a date in the French Republican Calendar. Didn't any of you knobs think to google it?'

'*Tridi*? I thought it was *lundi, mardi, mercredi*, and so on?' said Rex.

'Republican-do-what?' said Lollo, echoing the thoughts of many in the room: Republicans were Irish terrorists, weren't they? 'What's that when it's at home? Just assume I don't have my phone on me, eh.'

'So, *Ventôse* – I'm not sure how to pronounce it – is the name of a month in something called the French Republican Calendar?' said Sue, a rising note of uncertainty in her voice. 'It was adopted during the French Revolution, it says here. Ten-day weeks. *Primidi, Duodi, Tridi*, et cetera were their new names for the days of the week. Three-week months. Religious and royal holidays abolished, blah blah.'

'Wot no Christmas?' said Webster. 'I'm not having that.'

'No Sundays either,' said Stanza.

'I know the fucking feeling,' said Lollo. 'So what's that in old money?'

'Sorry, chief?' said Stanza.

'You said it was a date. Tweedledee something Ventilator, I don't bloody know.'

'Yeah, *Tridi, treize* – that's thirteen – *Ventôse*, CXCIII, and presumably the Roman numerals are the year. C's a hundred, isn't it? Anyone remember from school?'

'What date is that, then?' said Lollo. 'Any way of telling? Some obscure historical reference, is it? Or a tip-off, a date for our diaries. Are they making an appointment?'

DS Webster made the mistake of looking at the Detective Chief Inspector blankly.

'When he, she or it might strike again!' said Lollo, in a tone of voice that suggested he was talking to a particularly stupid child. 'Fuck's sake! Wake up! Two hours ago you were moaning that you had nothing.'

'Hang on,' said Stanza, still looking at her phone. 'There's a link to a converter here. Okay, so the year is a hundred and ninety three of the Revolution.' She fiddled with some drop-down menus on her screen, then: 'Well, depending on the method used to calculate the leap years—' She looked at Lollo. He shook his head, rolled his eyes. '—according to this, it looks like *Tridi treize Ventôse* one-nine-three is Monday the fourth of March 1985.'

'Mean anything to anyone?' asked Lollo.

No one said anything.

'Okay, well,' said Lollo, 'if you could circulate the link, Sue, that'd be great, thanks.'

As they were wrapping up the meeting, the DCI told everyone to stick around after lunch, at least until they'd spoken to Rex. He said that he wanted the DS to spend the rest of the day following up with each of the teams individually, working with them to review progress, to put any questions he hadn't had time to ask in the meeting – he'd emailed Rex a list – and to help them prioritise and plot next steps. Ideally this would mean that, once he'd fed back to the DCI and Webster, they could make sure to try to avoid ordering low-quality follow-up actions and thereby make the most of the next few days – the calm before the SiC storm – and get some results in the bag while they weren't under the microscope. It was the **perpetual** challenge: to mobilise the collective mind in order to turn a slim information profile, a few vague wisps of material, half a lead and a hunch or two, into a solid case that might actually stand a chance of getting to court.

This all took most of the afternoon, but before shutting down for the day, Rex had forced himself to call Iris. She didn't tell him much more than her near-neighbour Gertrude Bisika had done already, except for one thing: the argument, the foreign accent. No, she couldn't hear much of what they were saying, she told him, but she thought they sounded French.

Was that the sound of a piece of the jigsaw falling into place?

As he walked along Great Ormond Street, past the hospital porters smoking under the old carriage-works arch, his phone rang. It was Susan Hollander.

'Hi, is that Rex?' she said. 'It's Susan from earlier. I don't normally do this, but I am going to be here for a day or two, as it turns out, so I was wondering if you meant it about meeting up? It's been a really rough day, so I'd love to see a friendly face, and have a glass of wine and a chat. If you're not too tired, that is.' She paused for a second or two. 'I enjoyed our chat this morning, Rex. I was thinking about it this afternoon, in the hospital cafe. There was something I'd meant to ask you earlier.'

'Fire away,' said Rex.

'I hope you don't mind me asking, but: do you have any children?'

The question came out of the blue, but despite his surprise – or perhaps because of it – Rex answered truthfully, which was something that, when it came to this subject, he never, ever did. 'Yes, one,' he said. 'But that's a long story, and she doesn't live with me. Why d'you ask?'

'Just getting to know you, I suppose,' she said. 'We're all grownups, aren't we. I don't. Have any children, I mean. Sorry, I didn't mean to get all serious. Listen to me! I didn't think to check, are you still at work?'

'No,' said Rex. 'That's alright. I like you, Susan, if you don't mind me saying so. I'm just on my way home right now. I'm pretty tired too, to be honest—'

'Oh, well, of course. If you'd rather—'

'No, no, that's not what I was going to say. I'd love to meet up. Can you give me an hour or so? No, but I was just thinking, I could make us a simple supper at home. Do you eat fish?' he asked. Then:

'Oh, great. Why don't I go and pick up a couple of tuna steaks, and a nice bottle of—' He was going to say 'red', but paused and adjusted his course slightly: 'What kind of wine do you like?'

And suddenly, as he hung up, Rex had an idea of where Terry Hobbs might have gone.

II

14: PISSENLIT (DANDELION)

'But JJ, your badge,' Pea-tag said, as they trudged up the rocky path, between gnarled olive trees and prickly pear cacti, passing aloes, the radial form and fleshy spiked leaves of which he recognised from the ones his mother had kept in pots on the kitchen windowsill at home, although these ones – the first he had seen 'in the wild', as it were – were about the size of a car. 'The strike. It's over, yes?' said Pea-tag. 'Milo 'eard it on the radio. The strike, it finish yesterday, *non*?'

Up ahead, JJ noticed a large standing stone next to the path. 'Wow.'

'It is our *menhir*,' said Pea-tag, proudly. 'It is *néolithique*. Which means that our village is also *néolithique*.'

At this point, JJ had absolutely no idea of what he was walking into.

Pea-tag was a French punk, or maybe a hippy, or perhaps something in between. Of indeterminate age, with his tanned and weather-beaten skin, tatty combat trousers and a grown-out Mohican that was bleached by sun and salt, he could have been about thirty, JJ thought. Give or take five years either way. Impossible to say. To JJ, who was nineteen, anyone over the age of about twenty-five seemed old. They had only met an hour or two earlier. Pea-tag had been begging on the seafront near the Hippodrome at Cagnes-sur-Mer when JJ, fresh off the train and looking for somewhere to sleep for the night, had bumped into him.

Though he generally liked to give a bit of change to beggars, JJ had been down to his last few centimes by the time he'd arrived in Cagnes, so he had nothing to give. He would need to find somewhere to cash one of the twenty-pound American Express travellers' cheques that constituted his spending budget for the trip, and which he'd kept safely with his passport in a canvas money belt tied around his waist. What he had had to offer, though, was a filterless Gauloise cigarette from the second-to-last of the dozen packets he had bought in the duty-free shop on the ferry from England a few days earlier. He had thought that two hundred pounds would be enough money, just as he'd thought the cigarettes would last him for months. JJ had thought lots of things, but perhaps he hadn't thought very deeply, and the few French francs that he had allowed himself to cash had seemed to evaporate like smoke.

As he took a light, Pea-tag had admired the badges on JJ's denim jacket. 'Killing Joke,' he'd said, pointing at the crouching silhouette figure taken from the stark cover of the band's first LP. 'I have this.' Another badge featuring yet more silhouetted figures on a white background was for The Stranglers' 1978 LP *Black and White*, and there was one with the hand-drawn Young Marble Giants logo from the cover of *Colossal Youth*. These were the kind of cheap badges you could buy for 20p or so from most record shops. They displayed them on boards by the counter in both Left Bank and Caterpillar Records. Most of the badges on sale had the logo of a band on them, or of a record label like Stiff or 2 Tone. Others, like JJ's Stranglers badge, might feature just a reproduction of the actual record sleeve, however bad the quality could be once the image was reduced to an inch or so across. JJ also had a slightly more expensive enamel badge that said 'US out of El Salvador and Nicaragua', which he had bought – without necessarily fully understanding the United States's involvement in Central America, beyond that it was not good – at the merchandise stall outside a benefit gig at the university.

The last of JJ's badges said COAL NOT DOLE in black capital letters on a yellow ground. Firemen and other local trades unions had been out on the High Street near Princesshay one Saturday before Christmas collecting money to support the striking miners, and JJ had thrown a scrumpled pound note into the bucket. It had been cold enough in Exeter that winter, and they had good food and warm clothes, and paraffin for the heater in the hallway, and they could afford gas for the fire in the front room. Up north, there were miners and their families – whole villages – going without food, and with no money for bills or heating. Putting a pound in a bucket had seemed like the least JJ could do, and he had been proud to wear the badge ever since, and to contribute money or tins of food every now and then, whenever he saw that other collections were taking place.

They had chatted as they smoked. Pea-tag's well-practised pidgin English proved a more effective means of communication than JJ's rusty CSE French. 'Ah,' Pea-tag had nodded, when JJ had introduced himself. 'JJ, like the Frenchman in The Stranglers, *non?*'

'*Oui*,' JJ had said. '*Peut-être.*' There was a pause. '*Mais. Aussi. Mon. Nom. Je suis* Joseph Jonathan, so JJ for short.'

Pea-tag had found JJ's plans highly amusing. The idea that anyone might think they'd be able to find some secluded beach upon which to pitch a tent on the Côte d'Azur! In Northern Greece, perhaps, Pea-tag had said, in his broken English, or Turkey, yes, there were plenty of deserted beaches like that over there – 'I 'ave seen them' – but not here, *pas ici*. Come and look, he said. Also, he had a little marijuana they could maybe smoke on the beach.

This had been music to JJ's ears. He didn't need to be asked twice. If this Pea-tag bloke liked Killing Joke and he smoked dope, then he was exactly the kind of person – both hip and worldly – that JJ had hoped he would meet on his travels. Pea-tag told JJ that his family was from the deep south-west, near the border with Spain. A small rural town in the Pyrénées-Atlantiques, Basque Country, that was famous for making just two things: a particular kind of knife and a particular kind of cheese. The kind of place you have to escape from or die. 'I think to myself,' he told JJ, 'That there must be more to life than this!'

JJ had never been to France before; never been abroad at all until now. A couple of children in his class who were from wealthier families than his went on camping trips to France every year. One of their dads wore unusual navy-blue sailing jumpers and drove a big Volvo estate. The others had a Citroën 2CV and baked their own bread; canvassed for the Liberal Party in local government elections.

In fact, JJ had been the recipient of a small travel bursary, one of a couple of regular prizes that were awarded to students by the college during the A-level year. The modest prize monies were drawn from a bequest that had been made to honour the memory of a past sixth-former who had died from a sudden illness midway through her studies, and JJ had initially been delighted to learn that he had won the college travel prize, but then he had let the whole thing slide a bit. Until, that is, he'd received a note from the school office after Christmas, enquiring after his plans, and reminding him that the two-hundred-and-fifty-pound prize needed to be spent by the end of the financial year in which it had been awarded or it would have to be given back. The sudden urgency that this news imparted was the reason he was travelling in the early spring. It was also why he had perhaps not planned his trip as carefully as he otherwise might. His choice of destination had been influenced by vague ideas about the Impressionists, and a desire to come and draw and paint in the South of France, forgetting that a century had passed in the meantime. He had chosen Cagnes-sur-Mer because it was by the sea and because he remembered from A-level art history lessons that it had been the final home of the painter Pierre-Auguste Renoir, who was JJ's favourite Impressionist. Naively expecting to find exquisite pastoral scenes and fields of lavender at every turn, he'd instead found himself in the middle of a major infrastructural construction site: the soon-to-be-completed easterly section of the A8 motorway, which, once finished, would link Nice with Aix-en-Provence, just north of Marseille one hundred and fifty-odd miles to the west, and home town of another painter of the period, Paul Cézanne. JJ had planned to end his trip at Aix-en-Provence. Just to see Mont Sainte-Victoire, much less to paint it, seemed to JJ to promise an almost mystical connection with those revolutionary nineteenth-century artists. In anticipation of this, JJ's return rail ticket to London Victoria was already booked in advance from Aix.

They had crossed the road, ducking between the cars that were parked diagonally to the carriageway along the perimeter fence of the Hippodrome – Cagnes-sur-Mer's buggy racing track – and dodging the traffic that sped in both directions, to reach the narrow beach that ran along the other side of the road, more or less uninterrupted from Nice to Antibes. JJ had still not quite got used to the cars driving on the right, rather than the left as they did back at home, and had to keep reminding himself to look both ways. He had been surprised to see that there was no sand on the beach, just large grey pebbles interspersed with the occasional boulder. Peatag had still been talking about camping, and he told JJ that there had used to be campsites a couple of miles further on, but now? He shrugged and pointed along the coast to the west, where JJ could see cranes and another construction site where it looked as if some huge and futuristic ziggurat was emerging beyond the trees.

It was only March, but there had been a warm wind blowing in from the sea, and the air was clear enough that, as they smoked the spliff, JJ had been able to pick out individual buildings, rooftops and spires in what Pea-tag told him was the port of Antibes far off to their right, where the westernmost part of the bay curved around to Cap d'Antibes. When Pea-tag told him that the bay was called Baie des Anges, JJ thought he said *Singes*, and though he couldn't remember if that meant monkeys or goats, it seemed hysterically funny either way.

'You can come to La Fontaine,' Pea-tag had announced, as they'd walked back through Cagnes, after stopping at a Crédit Lyonnais bank, where JJ had cashed one of his travellers' cheques. 'It's cool.'

'Have you got a tent?' JJ asked. With nearly two hundred and fifty francs in his pocket, he was feeling rich again.

'*Non*,' said Pea-tag, matter-of-factly. 'We have a village. Come, we get the bus, but first, *du pain*.'

And that is how JJ found himself climbing a rocky track that zig-zagged its way up a steep slope somewhere off the Route de Grasse in the mountains above Nice, between the olive trees and the prickly pears, through air that was richly scented with aromatic herbs, batting away horseflies with one hand and trying to hold a bundle of baguettes together with the other.

Hanging from the frame of JJ's rucksack was a large knotted bag of what looked to him very much like the kind of young dandelion shoots his parents used to give the family budgerigar as a treat, fixing the leaves to the bars of the bird's cage with a wooden clothes peg. In fact that is exactly what they were, but here they were eaten as salad greens, and they came into season at just this time every year. Pea-tag had been excited to see them in a basket outside a small, side-street greengrocer's.

'I am excited to see the *pissenlit*, because they are two weeks early,' he'd said, as he paid for the leaves.

JJ hadn't really understood what Pea-tag had meant by this pro-
nouncement, but found it funny nonetheless. '*Pissenlit?*' he'd asked.

'*Oui!* It means the same in English, *non*? You must soak them in
cold water before you eat, or you will piss your bed.'

Back down on the road, a few yards from where the bus had
dropped them off, they stopped at what looked like an animal
trough. A stone receptacle with a curved front, like a bathroom
basin, but set at about shin level, a foot or so back from the kerb.
Rising from the rear of the basin stood a cleanly faced rectangular
slab of stone. Protruding from this at around chest height was a battered bronze pipe, from which flowed a continuous stream of clear
water, filling the basin below before draining away through an aper-
ture beneath the rim at the back. Across the centre of the basin and
set into the stone six inches apart were two flat iron bars, running
parallel. Bars upon which you might stand a bucket to fill it, and
probably strong enough to take the weight of a good-sized horse.
There was enough space on either side of these central bars for any
animal to drink from the basin. The drop between spigot and basin
rim was sufficient that Pea-tag was able to kneel on the stone edge
and – by bowing his head slightly, as if in prayer – lean in beneath
the pipe, so that the cold water cascaded over him, drenching his
hair and clothes. Standing up, he shook himself off, pushing the wet
hair off his face with his hands. Then he leaned in again to wash his
face, before cupping hands to drink the water.

JJ followed suit and doused himself too, but thirsty though he was
he felt reluctant to actually drink. Being English, he had grown up
with a mistrustful 'Don't drink the water' attitude to foreign coun-
tries, which might have had some historical basis in medical fact, but
in highly developed late-twentieth-century mainland Europe was

more like a prejudice, xenophobia masquerading as common sense. Pea-tag guessed the reason for JJ's reticence and soon dispelled this apprehension by telling him that it was spring water from the mountains, and that that he could personally guarantee its quality because they had laid the pipes themselves, or made them. JJ didn't quite understand. 'This is 'ow we survive,' Pea-tag said, and JJ wasn't sure if he was referring to the life-giving properties of the water itself, or to the money that might be made by laying – or making – pipes.

Just beyond this trough, the road curved into the beginning of a deep cutting, the pale stone faces of which still bore the traces of the dynamite that had been used to blast it out: shot holes still visible, regularly spaced across the surface. They ducked off the side of the road and scrambled up a steep, scrubby slope, which eventually gave on to a gentler stony track, and continued its zigzagging climb for perhaps half a mile as the crow flew, but it may perhaps have been three or four times longer than that on foot.

At the brow of the hill was a standing stone, a menhir, the track beyond it leading off into the trees, and beyond that, looming in the distance, was a great pale cliff formed of what JJ could see – remembering school geography lessons – was an inverted 'V' of exposed sedimentary rocks. Before continuing along this path as it dropped down to La Fontaine-en-Forêt, they stopped and turned around to look back the way they had come. Far, far below, beyond the rolling and forested hills that gradually fell away to the south, lay Antibes. From this distant vantage point, the warm stone walls and terracotta rooftops of the ancient port town seemed to be bathed in a kind of crystal clarity that may have had something to do with the light or with the dry atmospheric conditions, but could also have been a product of Pea-tag's very strong grass, which they had smoked back on the beach, and the effects of which JJ was still feeling. Somewhere down there, closer than Antibes, but hidden by the crest of these hills, was the huge construction site, a broad scar cutting through the landscape, where work continued – they could hear it – on the massive concrete viaduct that would carry the new *autoroute* above the streets of Cagnes-sur-Mer, connecting Nice and the Italian border to the east with Aix-en-Provence far to the west.

Standing here, the contrast between the two epochs felt almost palpable. The menhir marking not just the entrance to Pea-tag's village, to La Fontaine-en-Forêt, but also – it seemed to JJ – a path to an earlier age of humankind. It was a way-marker in both space and time. JJ had read about ley lines, so he knew that this stone was just a nodal point on some royal road that linked it to the next menhir, wherever that was, or to a whole network of stones, but it was also a means of travelling back through the eyes of anyone who had ever gazed upon it, or reached out and touched it, as Pea-tag was now doing, and as thousands must have done since whoever it was had put it here for whatever unknowable reason. Stoned as he was, JJ found it incredible almost beyond belief to think that people would have walked this very path ten or more thousand years earlier. How many generations was that? His maths wasn't good enough to work it out. He wondered if those *hommes néolithiques* – or *hommes et femmes* – had already learned to soak the new season's leaves that they were able to gather for food at this time of year, and, if so, from whom might they have learned it?

Tapering slightly towards its apex, the menhir looked rather like the ones that Obelix threw in *Asterix* comics.

Pea-tag laid both hands flat against the stone. 'Come, try it, man,' he said. 'You can feel the vibrations, *non*?'

'Hang on,' said JJ. 'What was that you were just saying about the Miners' Strike?'

The bag of dandelion leaves, the *pissenlit*, that they had bought down in Cagnes-sur-Mer were destined to form part of a large supper for at least some of La Fontaine-en-Forêt's current residents. A communal dining table was set upon a broad, stone-flagged and low-walled veranda, which was raised slightly above street level like a simple **dais** or stage. It could well once have been the ground floor of a house. On one side this veranda opened on to – and looked over – the small, cobbled square that formed the centre of the village, while at the back it gave on to a gorge, the depths of which were largely obscured by dense, deciduous forest. Above them, at one end of the village, towered the great cliff. The warm air was filled with hundreds or perhaps thousands of swooping, darting swifts, which feasted on the insects rising up from the forest below, following the insect swarms in a continuously unfolding and almost infinitely complex aerobatic display, screaming, clucking and screeching as they went. The noise created by so many birds was intense, and as JJ would discover it continued until dusk, when it would be replaced by the cries of more earthly, nocturnal creatures. Later, as JJ leaned on the veranda's waist-high parapet to watch this incredible display, one of the small brown birds would seem to hang in the air next to him for a second or two, almost close enough to touch, certainly close enough to make a kind of inter-species eye contact, before suddenly plummeting down towards the treetops far below.

Beside the veranda, a steep set of steps led from the square down to some perilously narrow-looking terraces. One of these was the familiar dusty *pétanque* terrain that he'd seen from the train, for playing the French game of *boules*; the rest seemed to be under cultivation. Perhaps this was the source of Pea-tag's home-grown. Sheltering the veranda in all weathers was a terracotta-tiled lean-to roof that projected over the steps and was supported along that side by three rough-hewn and age-blackened tree-trunk pillars, and by similarly ancient-looking joists that were set at their other ends into the stone wall of the adjacent two-storey building. Sockets and angles of various shapes and sizes that had been cut into the wood spoke of previous structural uses for each of these timbers.

Access to the veranda from the square was gained by a small stone step that led through a single open gateway – it looked like the original doorway – the threshold of which was just as worn as the doorsteps of all the other houses. Above this entrance, such as it was, a wooden board bearing the stencilled letters NOS RESTO had recently been attached to one of the beams.

Pea-tag bowed extravagantly, showing JJ through with a courtly flourish, as if to parody the actions of a waiter or a maître d' in some more salubrious establishment: '*Bienvenue, monsieur.*'

A blackboard was fixed up on the one complete stone wall in Nos Resto, as if for a menu, or a list of the day's specials. Instead it bore the mysterious phrase '*Tridi 13 Ventôse CXCIII: Fumeterre*'. Perhaps noticing JJ's puzzlement, Pea-tag took a tatty almanac from one of his pockets and explained that it was today's date, and something about living the revolution. He said that *fumeterre* was the particular type of herb that today's date celebrated, and that the calendar was republican. It reduced everything to the same level by honouring the *quotidien* – the prosaic, or the everyday – instead of kings and queens and gods. JJ didn't really understand, but then he had grown up in the UK, where the word 'republican' was little more than convenient political shorthand for the IRA, so he simply shrugged and nodded as if that might cover the range of likely responses.

So Pea-tag and his friends had the whole place? Wow! But what kind of place was it? JJ wasn't entirely sure about the naming conventions for human settlements, but as he was shown around he wondered whether La Fontaine-en-Forêt might be more hamlet than village, with its maybe twenty or so houses, several of which were ranged around this small central square, while the rest clustered along both sides of a narrow alley, La Petite Rue, which looped behind the single larger house that lay directly opposite the veranda. Unlike the other buildings, which were made of rough and rustic stone, this larger house was faced in smooth ashlar, its light-blue-shuttered windows surrounding a larger set of wood-panelled double doors that were more ornately constructed and embellished than the 'Z'-braced, barn-style front doors gracing most of the other buildings.

In the centre of the square, and seemingly out of proportion to all of the other buildings, apart from what JJ was already thinking of as 'the posh house', was a large baroque-style fountain. A straight-sided pedestal of smooth stone that stood some ten feet high was topped with an ornate stone urn. Around the base of the pedestal, at the foot of each of its four faces, was a semicircular pool or bath, hip-high and with raised rims broad enough to sit on, the tops of which were polished smooth with use. Above each pool a continuous stream of clear, cold water gushed from one of four pewter-coloured swan-necked pipes, which reminded JJ of the spouts of some extravagant teapot. The pools themselves appeared to be drained by means of crescent-shaped overflows that were cut into the stone at the rear of each, perhaps joining beneath the central pedestal. Two of the baths were bisected, front to back, by parallel pairs of stout iron strips upon which buckets and other vessels might be placed to be filled, just like the smaller, more functional trough in which JJ and Peatag had bathed down on the Route de Grasse. From the base of the frontmost trough, a shallow gully crossed the square, and beneath the grilles that covered it JJ could see the restless reflections of light twisting on the surface of the rushing black water as it ran away to who knew where.

An older sign that was fixed above the door of the building to which the veranda was adjoined spelled out the words '*bar-tabac*' in lower-case joined-up writing that appeared to have been wrought from a single, ribbon-like length of grey **zinc**, set sideways on, which may once have been painted but was now bare metal. To the left of this sign, fixed to a stone corner piece upon which one of the veranda's great roof joists also rested, was a red-painted metal object, an elongated diamond. JJ had seen many of these signs since arriving in France – on streets and stations and from train windows – and he remembered from French lessons at school that these were displayed outside government-licensed tobacconists. Whatever this building was now, it was not an officially licensed *bar-tabac*.

Inside, and dark behind its shuttered windows, the ground floors of two houses had evidently been hollowed out. Any internal, structural and party walls had been replaced by two centrally placed and elegantly proportioned iron pillars – shallow pedestals at their bases and with cast frieze and cornices where they supported a single mighty wooden beam above – to create a large room some twenty feet square. But if this had indeed been a bar, all other vestiges of that function had long disappeared. Where once there would presumably have been a scattering of tables and chairs, and a bar counter behind which would have been displayed a glittering array of spirits and liqueurs and the various specialised means of dispensing and imbibing them, all that now remained were several layers of worn linoleum on the floor. A rectangular gap in this linoleum, running roughly parallel to the back wall, near the rear of the room, traced the former location of the bar counter itself, perhaps, but behind this were no longer any lights or mirrors, no glittering bottles, jugs and glasses, no ashtrays, and no stacked packs of cigarettes and matches. Just a filthy-looking metal sink and drainer above the former of which two ill-matched taps had been soldered – slightly askew, as if by an amateur plumber – to some old pipes of a dull bronze colour. It looked as if thick layers of paint had been burned off each pipe to give enough clean metal that the taps might be affixed, but beyond this the pipes were encrusted with layer upon layer of the same thick, green paint that covered walls and joinery indiscriminately. To the right of the sink, and set into a broad, stone chimney breast that took up the right-hand third of the back wall, was a rusting iron kitchen range – a wood-fired oven – which might also presumably have been the primary source of heat in winter. Now the range evidently wasn't even used for cooking, but for storage, as various large and battered cooking pots, fish steamers, saucepans, wire crates, cardboard boxes and plastic barrels were stacked from hob to chimney around the flue. To the left of this and more or less in the centre of the back wall stood a single four-burner gas cooker, of relatively modern design, that was attached to a blue butane cylinder by means of an orange rubber hose. Two further cylinders, either spares or empties, had been placed between cooker and sink. On the other side of the cooker, beneath a single casement window that overlooked the gorge beyond, was a wooden kitchen table upon which were stacked more pots and pans, knives, chopping boards and an old olive-oil can filled with wooden spoons, spatulas and whisks; plus pepper grinder, salt cellar and another gallon-can of the same brand of olive oil. The table itself had presumably been so placed that whoever was preparing food might also look out at the ever-changing play of light and weather over the ravine and the hills beyond to the west. Beneath the table was an old-fashioned suitcase-style portable record player, along with some LPs by Jacques Brel, The Rolling Stones and reggae bands like Culture, The Congos and The Royal Rasses.

There were scatterings of some type of blue **pellet** on the floor, along the skirting boards and in the corners of the room, which JJ guessed might be a rudimentary form of pest **control**.

JJ had the distinct impression that Béatrice and Pea-tag might be girlfriend and boyfriend, but did not want to ask. He wasn't sure if a presumption on his part of their adherence to such traditional romantic concepts would be approved of, or not. Of slim build, with long red hair tied back in a loose ponytail, Béatrice wore a flowing cotton skirt in a dark paisley print and a loose cut-off T-shirt that continually fell off one or other shoulder.

'This is JJ,' Pea-tag said in English, as much for JJ's benefit as Béatrice's. 'He is a punk from England.'

A few doors down from Nos Resto, on the northern side of the square, was a house where several rooms were kept made up for guests, and Béatrice showed JJ around. A tour of the amenities did not take long. There was an old-fashioned hole-in-the-ground-style toilet downstairs, with two raised platforms to stand upon and a tap for flushing or cleaning. Flies buzzed over the hole. There was no kitchen, just a stone sink set into an alcove next to a large fireplace. At the centre of this, set on the large, flat hearthstone, the grate was a complex wrought-iron affair. It looked as though cooking pots might once variously have been placed upon the flat iron plates on either side, or hung from the hooks and chains above it. The wall behind this grate, which disappeared up into the chimney piece above, was black with soot, as was the underside of the chimney piece itself.

Béatrice showed him upstairs to a first-floor room that over-looked the square. Instead of a bed, there was a Japanese-looking flat mattress laid on to some wooden pallets. There were terracotta tiles on the floor, and the walls were covered in a dingy wallpaper.

'You 'ave futon in England?' she asked, then added, 'They are so comfortable.'

There were no pillows or bedclothes, but a paisley-patterned throw had been folded up and laid at the foot of the bed, and there was a knotted piece of calico hanging in the window. A tin candlestick on the windowsill reminded JJ of the illustration in a childhood book of nursery rhymes, of Wee Willie Winkie running through the town. Apart from this, the room was empty.

'*Vous pouvez laisser votre sac*,' she said. 'Your rucksack, it will be safe here. Come and find us when you are ready.'

JJ was relieved to shrug off the heavy pack, and even more so that he wouldn't need to pitch a tent tonight. Unable to believe his luck, he unlaced his DMs and lay down on the futon for a while, kicking his boots off on to the tiled floor and gazing up at the two massive wooden beams that ran across the ceiling, and which presumably held up the roof. Attached to the plaster in a nook where one of these beams met the wall were what looked like a couple of insect **pupae** or chrysalis casings, reddish-brown in colour and each about an inch and a half long. JJ wondered what kind of creature might emerge from these; perhaps a type of moth.

From what JJ had seen so far, the entire village seemed like the insect accretion of found materials, in this case tree trunks and stone, that had been, if not exactly chewed and regurgitated, then worked and fashioned into some repeating pattern of habitable units. A spiralling growth of variations on a theme that was informed by the characteristics of the local materials, and certainly had not been curtailed by any lack of these, but perhaps only by the amount of space available to its creators, the people who had once lived on this narrow rocky buttress beneath the cliff, with its deep gorges on either side. Where had those people gone, JJ wondered, that Pea-tag and his friends could simply move in? He had been to a couple of squats back at home in Exeter, mainly to buy dope from a small-time dealer and student ne'er-do-well named Phil, who had been living in one of them, or to go to a party, but the idea of squatting a whole village – if that was even what was happening here – seemed extraordinary. Perhaps he was still slightly stoned, but JJ felt as if his expectations of this trip were undergoing some sort of **kaleidoscopic** shift. 'We're not **in Toto** any more, Kansas!' he said to no one in particular.

'Hey, **lazybones**,' Béatrice said, when he went back down to Nos Resto an hour or so later to see what was happening. 'Why not do something? You could fry the **pork**.' She pointed at a ceramic bowl heaped with what looked like cubes of bacon.

'What—?'

JJ had barely formed the question when Béatrice pointed at the olive oil and a stack of frying pans on the table and said, 'Do you need me to show you?'

The answer to that was an unspoken 'No', so, while she peeled some boiled eggs at the table, JJ chose a heavy pan and splashed in some olive oil from the can. He used his cigarette lighter to ignite the cooker flame and once the oil was spitting a little he threw in the bacon, stirring it occasionally as the pieces began to turn pink, so that it would cook evenly.

Once she had peeled the eggs and cut them into halves, Béatrice drained the dandelion leaves into a large colander over the sink, rinsed them through once more and then tipped them out on to a tea towel, which she gathered into a tight bundle, Dick Whittington-style, and took outside, where she swung it around her head to force off any remaining water in a kind of centrifugal spray.

While JJ continued to fry the bacon, he watched Béatrice mix Dijon mustard and vinegar to a sloppy paste in a small bowl before gradually stirring in drop after drop of olive oil to make a glisteningly consistent greeny-brown goop.

'What are you staring at?' she asked. 'Don't you 'ave this in England?'

JJ shook his head. He didn't really know what 'this' was.

'It is *vinaigrette*,' she said, incredulous. 'For the *salade*?'

The bacon was browning nicely, and where it had once been merely coated in olive oil, it now swam in its own hot fat. Béatrice motioned for JJ to stand aside, and then she took the pan, using the spatula to hold the bacon in place while she poured this hot fat into the bowl of vinaigrette, before tipping cooked bacon pieces and boiled egg halves on to the pile of dandelion leaves. Finally she stirred the vinaigrette and bacon fat mixture then poured it over the salad, and put some wooden salad servers into the bowl.

JJ followed Béatrice outside, and was surprised to see several people sitting around the table, which someone had evidently laid in the meantime. 'Hello,' he said, to everyone at once, then sat down at the end of a bench and tore himself a piece of the nearest baguette.

'Maybe we should speak English for our guest,' said Pea-tag as he tossed the salad, and took some, then passed it on.

The man sitting to JJ's left turned to shake his hand. Skinny and very suntanned, perhaps in his mid-twenties, with short brown hair, he had shaved the sides of his head and was possessed of what JJ thought of as a very French look, which was mainly to do with his aquiline nose. 'I am Milo,' he said – pronouncing it 'Me-lo' – then poured some red wine into JJ's glass from an earthenware jug.

'In English?' said a bearded and barrel-chested dark-haired man in work-stained overalls. 'Okay, then. I was saying to Milo that the problem with **Mondale** was that 'e could not offer a better story than Ronald Reagan. No wonder 'e lost. What do you think, Englishman? If you are a punk, then you must be the anarchist, *oui*?'

Pea-tag raised his glass and proposed a toast: 'To the revolution-ary *pissenlit*! Tonight we piss the bed!'

JJ tore himself more bread and used it to wipe the dressing from the plate between mouthfuls of the salad, which was delicious. More than that, it might have been the best meal he had ever had in his life.

'Better than the usual **pea soup**,' said Milo.

'Better than eating them by the roots, *non*?' said the bearded man, to much laughter.

'Victor was making the joke,' said Milo to JJ. 'Eating them by the roots means you are dead and buried, *comprends-tu*? Is from *Les Misérables*, do you know this? Is a novel by Victor 'ugo. For some reason it is Victor's favourite book.'

'The potter cannot read,' said Pea-tag. ''e just recognise the name on the front because it is the same as 'is—'

'Why. You. Little . . . **Pip-squeak!**' retorted Victor in a kind of exaggerated upper-class English accent that sounded like an even more clipped James Mason. 'If I cannot read, then what is this?' He took a book out of his overall pocket and threw it on to the table.

'Would you like me to read it to you?' said Pea-tag.

'Oh, it's so boring,' said Béatrice, then to JJ: 'Do you know this one? *The Iceman Cometh*. Is by Eugene O'Neill?' She pronounced it 'You-zhen', with the emphasis on the second syllable. 'Such dull, you know, political *explication*. *C'est trop didactique, non*? So unrealistic.'

'Yes, how unrealistic,' said Victor. 'As if a bunch of losers would meet every night and talk politics around some shitty table! All representative of their particular stereotype, and each with 'is predictable **quotient** of motivation, prejudice and opinion. Yes, that is so . . . unrealistic, Béatrice.' He sighed and gestured around the table. 'I cannot even begin to imagine such a thing.' He looked around, pointing first at Milo then at each of them in turn: 'The green, the 'istorian, the artist, the potter, the anarchist—' He gave up with a shrug. 'It is not . . . like us . . . at all! Not at all! *Salut, mes amis!*'

With a gruff laugh, Victor held up his glass and then drained it. 'So,' he said, turning to JJ, 'which one are you? The anarchist or the idiot?'

'I am happy to be the idiot,' said JJ, laughing. 'It's my favourite Iggy Pop LP; side two, anyway.'

Conversation around the table was agile and lively. Full of convivial **vim**, it jumped from topic to topic, and was accompanied by much of what JJ would call piss-taking, good-natured ribbing, to which no one seemed immune, himself included. One moment he was being tutored in his French by Milo, who said that he should conjugate the **main verb**, but that a second is infinitive. 'Like in English: you have to breathe,' he said by way of illustration, 'but I live to fuck.' The next moment, Victor – whose family were Polish Jews only some of whom had survived the Holocaust by hiding out in the Pyrenees during the Nazi occupation – might be holding court, telling terrifying stories of his travels in Eastern Europe or Latin America: some narrow escape in **La Paz** involving the **vice-principal** of Bolivia's leading Catholic boarding school, a crooked cop and a cocaine dealer, perhaps, or some disastrous farce in Mexico City involving a prostitute, a taxi driver and Victor's ex-wife.

At times the conversation touched on those generic subjects that greeted any young man travelling at that time, such as whether there was national service in whichever country. Then Pea-tag, rolling another joint, might explain, for example, why Milo's Moroccan double-zero hash – fragrant and strong as it was, and imported by a friend in the French Aéronavale who was stationed along the coast at Fréjus – was an instrument of **colonial** oppression, while his own home-grown grass – cross-pollinated over the years from strong and favoured strains – was not.

JJ found himself talking at length to Élise, a dark-haired woman whom he kept mistakenly calling **Elsie**, and who may or may not have been Milo's 'significant other'. Of all of them, she seemed to be the repository of historical knowledge about La Fontaine-en-Forêt, which she told JJ had been settled, in common with other promontories in the region, by Celts and so-called Ligurians – including, supposedly, some tribe called the Nerusii – more than ten thousand years earlier.

To JJ this was not only fascinating, but topical. One of the books that he had been reading on his travels was a second-hand copy of the 1969 English-language edition of Peter Vilhelm Glob's book *The Bog People*, which told of Iron Age and Celtic peoples who had been found eerily well preserved in **peat** bogs across Northern Europe, the theory being that they may have been human sacrifices to some ancient goddess of fertility. The idea that he was now sitting and eating local produce on the site of a Celtic settlement reminded him of the strange feeling of timelessness that he had experienced at the menhir earlier that day.

'Yes! I 'ave seen this, but we 'ave no peat bog in this part of France,' said Élise, sadly. 'So I guess there is no chance of finding any such body 'ere. But Milo found a *néolithique* arrow'ead one time. Look, 'e keep it round 'is neck.'

Élise told him that while what was now La Fontaine-en-Forêt had not offered quite the strategic advantage of other settlements nearby – such as Vence, Tourrettes-sur-Loup, Saint-Paul de Vence or their nearest neighbouring village, La Fontaine-lès-Vence, with their uninterrupted observation points – its position between the two gorges and its relative inaccessibility, plus the presence of two very reliable springs in caves at the foot of the *baou* – the local word for any huge cliff, like the one behind the village – meant that the site had been further occupied, developed and fortified, first by the Romans, who valued it primarily as a source of drinking water, even laying lead pipes that had intermittently supplied nearby villages. The settlement had then been subject to further waves of invasion and subjugation from about the fifth century onwards, including by Huns, Visigoths and Franks, until the tenth century, when Élise said it had been occupied by Saracens and further fortified, again being valued primarily as a source of water. These Arabic settlers were masters of hydraulic engineering, and according to one medieval engraving they created an animal- or more likely slave-powered hydraulic pump, probably on the site of today's largely eighteenth-century fountain. While it lasted, the Saracens' engine ensured that water from La Fontaine-en-Forêt provided a more secure supply, even forcing it to flow uphill to more elevated nearby villages.

Plague and other diseases, including the manifestations of lead and other heavy metal poisoning caused by the continued use of the Roman pipes and cisterns, and those sicknesses of the rural poor such as **beri-beri** and scurvy that are caused by what we now know to be vitamin and mineral deficiencies, saw the village abandoned for more than two centuries during the early medieval period. This was only reversed when Marie of Brittany awarded the site to the Villeneuve family in the late fourteenth century as part of her gift of lands surrounding the nearby La Fontaine-lès-Vence.

Was she boring him?

JJ assured her not. He found it fascinating.

Guichard de Villeneuve had, of course, restored the square, removing the remains of the Moorish pumping engine and converting the few stables, byres and pigsties that surrounded it into small houses – 'Like this used to be,' Élise said, gesturing at where they sat – and finally laying the foundations for what was nowadays known as 'chez Sylvie' – she pointed at the blue-shuttered house on the opposite side of the square – for the Master of the Water. Villeneuve had primarily seen La Fontaine-en-Forêt as a reliable source of water for its larger namesake and its hinterland, which stretched as far down the mountains as Villeneuve-Loubet. The last descendants of those same Villeneuves, Élise said, were put to death at Ventimiglia as they attempted to escape the Revolution by fleeing across the Var towards the then Kingdom of Sardinia, in what is now Northern Italy. They surely could not have known, she said, that, by relying so heavily upon the water from La Fontaine-en-Forêt, they had been systematically poisoning their own populace, but this was in fact the case, and so it continued. The legacy of this long-term lead poisoning had apparently caused the area to become infamous, indeed a byword, for the various forms of cretinism it produced, a reputation that – incredibly – had continued into the beginning of the twentieth century.

Ironically, the pipelines serving Villeneuve-Loubet, Tourrettes, Saint-Paul and Vence itself were sabotaged in 1792 by Sardinian counter-revolutionaries and royalist 'Feuillants' funded and emboldened by support from the Spanish royal family and the Knights of Malta. By laying siege and cutting the water supply, these royalist militia were seeking to starve out the 'patriots' and revolutionists in those two towns, but in fact they achieved the reverse. By inadvertently cutting the supply of poison to the polis, the counter-revolutionaries unwittingly did much to improve – with almost immediate effect – the long-term health and vigour of these communes. However, what was good for *les Vençois* may not have suited those living closer to the source, for the supply of contaminated water to both Fontaines (-en-Forêt, and -lès-Vence) remained unaffected by these skirmishes. Thus was created an isolated pocket of backwardness, a place that superstitious travellers – little understanding the symptoms of lead poisoning – might hurry through, nosegays clamped to their faces, fearful of the region's **ominous** reputation and what might **happen** to the traveller who tarried too long.

Élise told how nineteenth- and twentieth-century developments such as the cutting of the railways or the building of the modern Route de Grasse had more or less passed La Fontaine-en-Forêt by. The surveyors responsible for the latter had in fact compounded the village's isolation by blasting a steep cutting right across the old donkey track that remained the only means of access to the village. Hence the steep climb, she said, from the road to the track proper. Similarly, the Nice-to-Draguignan railway, which climbed from the coast to Vence, would bring no benefits to La Fontaine-en-Forêt, instead passing several hundred metres lower and to the south of Tourrettes-sur-Loup and La Fontaine-lès-Vence, on its way to Grasse and beyond that to Draguignan, some fifty kilometres to the west.

'There is more,' Élise said with a smile. 'Always more! But maybe I tell you tomorrow.'

On his way to bed, JJ took an empty wine bottle to the fountain and rinsed it out in the running water a few times, before filling it from the spout and stoppering it to take to his room in case he needed a drink of water in the night. As he did this, he realised that he could hear a bird singing somewhere above him. He couldn't see it, but it was close. Perhaps it was on the roof of the large house. It sounded a bit like a blackbird, which had a song that he recognised. Blackbirds often used to perch on the television aerial on their chimney back at home in the evenings, where they would sing for what seemed like hours.

Hearing the rasp of a cigarette lighter, JJ realised that he wasn't the only one enjoying this avian soloist. He looked up to see that at least one set of blue shutters on the front of the large house were now open. A woman was leaning out of the darkened first-floor window, smoking a cigarette. Perhaps she had also been attracted by the bird's song. He wondered if this was the Sylvie that he had heard about from Milo. He couldn't really see her very clearly, as there was hardly any moon, and no street lighting apart from what spilled out from Nos Resto.

'Hello,' JJ said, pointing up at the bird on the roof. '*C'est joli, oui?*' he asked, before – unable to form any more meaningful sentence in French – reverting to English. 'Is it a blackbird?' he asked. 'Do you know?' He was suddenly aware of the collective sound of thousands of frogs croaking in the gorge far below the village. He couldn't understand how he had not noticed this before. When, he wondered, had the more ethereal cries of the darting swifts been replaced by this amphibian babble? He could barely hear himself think. Suddenly he felt a bit like a frog himself, rather than the handsome, prince-like figure he had hoped to strike.

'*C'est un ousel,*' she said. 'Ah, okay, in English. Yes, he is maybe like the blackbird, *son cousin*, but with the white . . . *sais pas* . . . collar? They spend the winter 'ere.'

'I don't blame them,' said JJ. 'It's beautiful.' He suddenly felt a bit shy and struggled to remember some, any, French. '*D'accord,*' he said, finally. Then a flash of inspiration: *'Bonne nuit,* Juliet.'

It took a moment or two for the joke to sink in. Then, *'Bonne nuit, Roméo,'* Sylvie said, before laughing and closing the shutter.

Opening the guest-house door and climbing the stairs, JJ reflected that he had only arrived in Cagnes earlier on today, but now, thanks mainly to Pea-tag, he had a bed for the night – or perhaps for as long as he wanted? – in some kind of extraordinary bohemian commune in the mountains. He had eaten and drunk well, and perhaps made some new friends. He'd felt slightly intimidated by Milo, and particularly Victor at first. Béatrice and Élise, less so, but Victor had seemed the most macho and competitive, albeit in a good-natured way. Did they have anything in common, he wondered, apart from the fact that they all lived here together? Certainly, they were all artists or artisans of some sort, and each of them had their own kind of openness – or generosity, perhaps – in both word and deed. He had found this directness incredibly refreshing, and looked forward to getting to know them all a bit better in the coming days. But JJ wasn't stupid. He also realised that, if he was going to stay, he had better make himself useful. Otherwise he would become a burden pretty quickly. He couldn't just hang around like a spare part and expect the incredible hospitality he had received tonight to continue indefinitely. He would have to sort something out. In the meantime, a far lesser yet still uncomfortable truth: JJ didn't know it yet, but this would be the best night's sleep he would ever have on a futon.

And, despite the dandelion supper, he didn't piss the bed.

16: CAPILLAIRE (MAIDENHAIR FERN)

Having slept soundly, JJ awoke to the sound of cockerels crowing and beyond that some man-made music, perhaps from a flute or pipe, a series of simple riffs, scales and arpeggios that lifted and fell, repeated and reversed, echoing lightly around the ravine like a musical **orison**. JJ lifted the rough **calico** drape and knotted it, then opened the window, but there was no sign of any piper. And because of the way that the sound bounced around the ravine, it was impossible to locate the source.

The village square looked picturesque and quaint from the upstairs room. Apart from the oversized and anachronistic-looking fountain, it reminded JJ of the illustrations in those **Jackdaw** activity packs that had sometimes been brought out on special occasions for history classes at his primary school. These had been wallets full of stylishly illustrated handouts – in woodcut, perhaps, or pen and ink – together with facsimiles of historical documents relevant to the period, event or person in question. He could just imagine a wood-cut of a medieval village like this one, but if so it would be populated by well-dressed peasants with clean faces and 1970s haircuts who seemed happy to live **cheek by jowl** with their oxen, pigs and geese.

Where La Fontaine-en-Forêt's main square was set upon the flat-tish saddle of this odd spur of rock, the western part of the hamlet was built on a lower level, along a broad ledge. It was this that was accessed by La Petite Rue – a narrow street, little more than an alley – which emerged again via some stone steps that brought you back up to a point just inside a plain village gate. The dozen or so houses thus accessed were built amongst, or out of, the rocks along the edge of the ravine, where they formed a kind of habitable fortification. Picturesque on the inside, street-side, but forbidding and inaccessible from the ravine below.

Leaning a little further out on to the windowsill, JJ looked out to the left across a Cubist terrain of terracotta rooftops and stuccoed chimneys; trapezoid planes angled this way and that. These were the rooftops of La Petite Rue. Pea-tag had said that their place – so he and Béatrice *were* a couple – was down there. Number eighteen, overlooking the ravine. JJ decided that he would have to go and take a look later on. From this vantage point, he couldn't see the eastern gorge at all, just the misty tops of the wooded hills on its far side. Beyond these treetops the first **tinge** of dawn was already brightening a vermillion sky that could have been squeezed straight from the tube, and which faded into oranges and yellows as bright as the pigment washes on the cover of *Sextet* by A Certain Ratio.

A few doors along La Petite Rue – Pea-tag had shown him – was an arched gateway that led out, under one of the houses, to some old olive groves on narrow terraces that ran along the ridge behind the village at the foot of the Baou La Fontaine, the immense dolomitic limestone cliff, with its caves and its springs, from which the settlement had grown.

Now that it was starting to get light, JJ decided to go and take a look at this for himself. He pulled on combat trousers and a T-shirt, and was about to get into socks and lace up his DMs, but had a second thought and pulled some flat-soled, black kung fu slippers from the pocket of his rucksack. Moments later he was outside and washing his face in the water of the fountain. He took the cork out of his bottle, to **rinse** and refill it.

A bleary-looking Victor was doing t'ai chi on the ridge, and behind him, above the olive trees, JJ could clearly see the inverted 'V' of stratified sedimentary limestone. It was as if someone had draped, well, a pile of futon over a sharp ridge. In her potted history of the night before, Élise had said these rocks – the lip of which stretched above the whole Côte d'Azur – were once the seabed, but that pressure from the African plate against the European had caused this great fold belt, which was now exposed by erosion. 'That little spring, he made these ravine, *non?*'

She'd told him that the Baou La Fontaine – it was an old Provençal word for 'boulder' – dramatic though it was, was dwarfed by the great *baous* of Vence and Saint-Jeannet to the east. Well, maybe so, but now the *baou* looked beautiful, brightened by scattered golden smears and reflections of the just-risen sun, which was also throwing shadows across the vast and irregular surface.

JJ hadn't seen anyone else up and about, so presumably it had been Victor playing the pipes. Perhaps it got him in the right frame of mind to do t'ai chi. He was wearing the same dirty blue overalls as yesterday. JJ watched him for a while, unsure whether he'd be able to **pass by** without disturbing Victor's meditation, but he decided that he probably could, and in the event he got a wink in confirmation of this as he walked between the trees towards the foot of the cliff.

Pea-tag had told JJ that Victor had a factory down at Pont-du-Loup, a mile or two further along the Route de Grasse, and that most of the money that it made was used to keep the commune going at La Fontaine-en-Forêt, slowly paying for restorations as and when they were needed or could be afforded. Victor was a trained potter. He had grown up on the **Rhine** near Strasbourg, and studied ceramics at the famous art school there. He was now in his late thirties, but didn't look it. He had a small studio, complete with pedal-operated potter's wheel, here in the village, in an outhouse round the back of Sylvie's, and he'd built a wood-fired kiln on one of the derelict plots on La Petite Rue. Victor made strong but surprisingly delicate earthenware coffee bowls and rather narrow, straight-sided beakers. There were some seconds put out for general use in the kitchen at Nos Resto. The style that he had developed over the years was for austere-looking salt-glazed vessels in mottled browns, with a slightly flared lip that made them more pleasant to drink from. There would be a little initial 'V' stamped into the body near the base, and a simple scratched hoop three quarters of the way up. When Milo had brought out a tray of after-dinner coffees, he told JJ that he was drinking from one of Victor's beakers. It felt good in JJ's hand, and he had said so.

'*Merci*,' Victor had said graciously. 'I 'ad the good teachers. In the sixties and seventies, everyone at l'École Supérieure was the fan of Bernard Leach.'

He'd told JJ that his pots were sold in higher-end arts-and-crafts shops in Nice, Saint-Tropez and Saint-Paul, as well as more locally in Vence and La Fontaine-lès-Vence. 'Is okay,' he'd said, gesturing around them, 'but selling a few pieces every week is not enough to keep all this.'

The way that Victor told the bigger story was that, when they'd discovered La Fontaine-en-Forêt and occupied the place, the first thing that he and an archaeologist friend of his had done was survey the old pipes and cisterns that had been servicing the spring – in some cases – for more than fifteen hundred years. His plan was to replace these with a new system up at the spring and then to reroute the pipeline rather than replace it, using new ceramic pipes, the priority, of course, being to supply the village itself without destroying the archaeology, but also to use natural earthenware pipes instead of shorter-term **plastic** ones. This was partly because he was a potter and he understood the material, but also because it was 'more safer, *pour l'eau potable, non?*'

He'd bought imported pipes from a supplier down in Biot, which were fine for the first batch, to finally get pure and uncontaminated water to La Fontaine-en-Forêt, but he did the maths on what he'd paid for the pipes versus what they'd cost to produce, scaled it up to include potentially supplying several new-builds a year, and then the factory at Pont-du-Loup had come up for sale.

Victor had shrugged. 'And I thought, why not?'

He had started off by leasing in the extrusion and moulding plant, but investing in three shuttle kilns. When it took seventy hours to actually fire the pipes, he'd told JJ, from cold to cold, kiln capacity was the priority; you couldn't afford not to have another couple of kilns running on different cycles. Now they produced everything from water and sewerage pipes to high-end salt-glazed kitchen sinks and bathroom ware ('Toilet, *bidet*' – he mimed washing his hands – '*lavabo*. Very nice. Sylvie 'as, in 'er place.') that were supplied to just a few of the more exclusive retailers. The terracotta **shingle** business was not worth it, he had decided, so they'd contracted that out. As a result, not only did they now have good drinking water in La Fontaine-en-Forêt and a steady flow of money to support its gradual restoration, they also employed ten local people at the factory, plus they were one of the preferred suppliers of ceramic water pipe to public projects across the whole Alpes-Maritimes region.

'Wow,' JJ had said, sincerely impressed. Without quite having the words to express it, he admired Victor's opportunism, and his agency, his ability to act quickly. JJ could sense that perhaps age had something to do with this, but he had no insight whatsoever into the way that, through your twenties and thirties and onwards, you might work to accumulate sufficient breadth and intensity of skills and experience, knowledge and behaviour, to transform a simple talent into a *métier* or profession. That success didn't simply happen by magic or by talent alone.

Victor's story had also reminded him of one that his sixth-form pottery teacher, Miss **Larwood**, had once told the class, about a friend of hers from art school days in Leeds, who had a pottery studio in an old warehouse on the River **Aire** in the city centre. It was a kind of parable about being open to life's opportunities, or something.

JJ had enjoyed pottery classes. At the end of the first year of sixth form, he had won the art prize – a **book token** that he had then used to buy the paperback of a science-fiction novel called *Nova Express* by William S. Burroughs – and Miss Larwood had bought two of the pottery figures that he had liked to make, which were little cartoonish punk rockers with Mohicans and tartan trousers. JJ couldn't quite remember every word of Miss Larwood's story now, but it had been to do with her friend, **Edward** something, who was a good potter but had been trying to find a more commercial product, something that would bring in more money than simply doing children's pottery lessons on a Saturday morning. Then, one day, while he'd been waiting for his tandoori chicken at the **Rajah** on Woodhouse Lane, the nice waiter had apologised for the delay and told him that one of their tandoor ovens, the large fired-clay vessels that were used for cooking tandoori dishes and breads, had broken. They were having to ship one over from Pakistan because – and here was the killer – at that time there had been no UK manufacturer.

'So do you know what my friend did the very next day?' Miss Larwood had asked.

(And they had all guessed, of course, although the class joker had been quicker off the mark: 'Did he have fish and chips instead, miss?' he'd asked.)

'*Exactement,*' Victor had said, when JJ had told him the story about the tandoor ovens. 'He go into production? *C'est un génie*; a genius! Is exactly what I would have do.'

At the *baou*, meanwhile, JJ quickly realised that he must have gone into the wrong cave. Outside he had seen clusters of bright-green fern growing directly out of cracks in the rock here and there, presumably because they liked the moisture from the spring. He had opened an iron gate set into the rock and gone inside, expecting to see some sort of modern waterworks, whatever that might look like: a water filtration unit, perhaps, the hum of motors, shiny stainless steel pipes and cisterns, a ceramic water main? There was nothing like that. Instead there were faded plastic flowers and unlit lanterns stuck to the uneven walls, crates of old bottles stacked up next to a filthy fridge, speaker cabinets and large spools of electric cabling. There was also – for some reason – a canoe, as well as a couple of black plastic dustbins and a tatty wooden bar that might have been the one that had been taken out of the old *bar-tabac* building at Nos Resto. A couple of rusting barbecues and some ice buckets were stacked up against an old chest of drawers. Everything was covered in a thick layer of something non-specific but nasty-looking, as if no one had been in here for a few years. JJ couldn't tell if the muck was predominantly bird shit or bat shit, but either way it made him feel a bit sick. There was a large mural on one of the walls, which appeared to have been applied directly on to the stone. Much of the paint had flaked off in the damp atmosphere, but JJ recognised the style and the theme from a school trip to see the *Picasso's Picassos* exhibition at the Hayward Gallery in London.

Here, then, was a Picasso parody, an image of an **infernal**, flaming bullring in which a satyr-like *toreador* with a huge erection fought not just any bull, but the Minotaur.

As he stepped back into the light, JJ saw that Victor was walking towards him holding something with both hands that looked a bit like a largish lemon with holes in it, and which JJ guessed must be the musical instrument he had heard.

'*Ciao*, man,' he said. 'I go to the factory. I just want to say don't go too close the edge, uh? And be careful of the falling rock. You see the yellow . . . places?'

JJ looked up at the yellow streaks that earlier he had thought were sunlight falling on to the rock. Up closer and now Victor had pointed it out, he realised that these were scars that showed where, in some cases, quite large sections of the rock had recently sheered off, and come to think of it, there were some hefty boulders scattered around in the scrub near where they were standing.

'That yellow is typical of *le calcaire dolomitique*,' said Victor, 'because the rock contain lots of the magnesium, which react with the air.' He shrugged. 'We potters must know such things.'

'I loved that music you were playing earlier,' said JJ, changing the subject and moving more quickly now, away from the foot of the *baou*, 'but what kind of instrument is that, exactly?'

It was an **ocarina**, a type of Central American flute. Victor demonstrated. He had tried making them once, but they didn't sell. 'I 'ave many, many,' he said. 'You can 'ave if you like.'

JJ took it, and thought he may as well walk back to the village with Victor, who told him that the spring was on the other side. 'That one used to be a nightclub, for many years,' said Victor, and he told JJ that when they'd first moved here the club had still opened up every now and then. It was called Labyrinth, there was a sign, and it would usually be busy too, he said. 'But not everyone could get the **ticket**, if you know what I mean.'

It must have looked as if JJ didn't.

'It was the gay club,' said Victor, 'but from the day when that must be kept secret, *non*?'

As they walked up La Petite Rue, they approached an elderly man with a bucket who was mopping the cobbles. He had filled what looked like a dog bowl under a tap on the street, and at least a dozen cats were sitting nearby on windowsills and doorsteps, keeping their distance and pretending disinterest, but all within a radius of about twelve feet or so.

'*Regarde!*' whispered Victor. 'This is Monsieur Houlette. I tell you about 'im in a minute.'

'*Bonjour, monsieur*,' said JJ politely as they went past, and Victor nodded a silent greeting, but the old man seemed content – or discontent – merely to watch them pass, eyes following them as they did so. If he had acknowledged them in any way, it had been imperceptible.

When they got around the corner, Victor said, 'You know, 'e was the last person living 'ere when we came. 'Im an' 'is cats. 'Is was the one 'ouse that still 'ave someone live in it.'

The thought of anyone living in isolation amid such dereliction gave JJ the creeps.

'For ages,' Victor continued, 'I thought 'e was mute, you know, but 'e can speak. But if you ask 'im about those days after the war, or the nightclub, 'e pretend 'e don't know what you are talking about.' Victor paused for a second, then: 'Anyway, *ciao*.'

And with that he turned left, out through the village gate and up towards the ridge and the menhir; JJ's '**royal road**'. That idea – and JJ's half-arsed talk of ley lines over dinner the previous evening – had greatly amused everyone. '*Non!*' Milo had said, '*Pas vrai! C'est une route de régicides!*'

This morning, instead of travelling some ancient mystic song line to the next menhir, Victor would only be taking the track as far as the blasted cutting, where he would scramble down the bank and on to the Route de Grasse by the little fountain. From there, it was about a half-mile walk to the factory, where today, among other things, he would be supervising the loading and dispatch of a lorry-load of salt-glazed earthenware urinals, lavatories and handbasins that were headed for some lavish new international arts centre in one of the United Arab Emirates.

Behind them, watched as ever by his cats, Monsieur Houlette continued mopping the smooth cobbles of La Petite Rue, as he did every morning. He was a small, wiry man, and JJ thought he looked a bit like a much older version of Dustin **Hoffman**. Turning back into the village square, JJ found himself humming 'The Message' by Grandmaster Flash & the Furious Five, and trying to remember how the words went: a **zircon** something, a freak show, trying to get away, but not getting far, not being able to do it on your own.

Talking of princesses – zircon or not – Sylvie came out of her front door at exactly that moment, carrying a long-necked salt-glazed jug – one of Victor's, presumably – which she began to fill from the fountain. With her long and tousled bleached-blonde hair, and wearing a **stag**-print **kimono** and dusty espadrilles, she may have been the most beautiful woman that JJ had ever seen in his life.

'*Bonjour,*' he said. '*Vous êtes Sylvie? Je suis* JJ, from last night. The blackbird, or—'

'*Ousel,*' she said. '*Oui, je sais. Mon "Roméo"!*'

They both laughed.

'*Mais, Roméo,*' she said. '*Je déteste les Stranglers. Ce sont des*

168

phallocrates, n' penses pas? What does it stand for, your JJ? Not "Jean-Jacques", I presume.'

JJ laughed and shook his head. He was a fan of the band, and had even sent off postal orders for several issues of their *Strangled* fanzine, but he wasn't about to admit that now. 'No. It's Joseph Jonathan,' he said. 'But I don't like the name Joseph.'

She thought for a moment. '*Alors*,' she said. '*Je vais t'appeller "Joe"*, OK?'

'*Oui, OK*,' he said, inwardly delighted and probably showing it too. Sylvie could call him anything she liked.

'*Bon. Salut, Joe.*'

'*Salut, Sylvie.*'

He was **hungry**. 'Um,' he said, remembering some rudimentary conversational French from school. '*Y a-t-il une boulangerie ici?*' He hadn't seen one, but you never knew.

'*Oui*,' said Sylvie, '*bien sûr*. But it is a great mystery. You cannot buy bread there. Do you want me to show you?'

JJ nodded, pleased of any chance to prolong the encounter. '*Oui, s'il vous plaît.*'

'*D'accord*,' she said. 'But first I must 'ave coffee. Do you want coffee, Joe?'

Sitting at Sylvie's dining table, drinking the coffee she had made and smoking a cigarette while he waited for her to get ready, tapping off a flake of ash in his saucer, JJ had a moment to **revel** both in the casual intimacy of the encounter – her immediate charm – and in the relative luxury of the room itself, if luxury was the right word. It was sparsely furnished, with its white-painted stone walls and flagstone floor, but compared to the other variously ramshackle and dilapidated houses that JJ had seen since he'd arrived in La Fontaine-en-Forêt – even with the larger communal space of Nos Resto – it felt spacious, light and airy. It also felt clean and dry, although it was unlike any room that JJ had ever been in. As if, rather than having been decorated, the room had been subjected to a **brutal** process of stripping away, so that only bare wood and stone remained. It felt more like a church than a house, but, whatever the reason for this austere aesthetic, it seemed to suit the place. So much so, in fact, that JJ couldn't tell if this room was even particularly bare, or if it was just that all the other rooms in the world were unbearably cluttered. Here were no carpets or curtains, no wallpaper, and no knick-knacks or ornaments, no record player, no records and no books. The structure of the room itself provided its own kind of anti-decor, and yet it felt stylish and appropriately chic – beautiful, even. An iron range that filled the space beneath a stone chimney piece even more magnificent than the one in the communal kitchen opposite had been restored; certainly it was working. After disappearing into the kitchen next door to fill the pot, Sylvie had made coffee on one of its hobs, and JJ could feel the mellow warmth of its fire. Outside it had started spitting with a light rain just as they'd come in. A breeze now lightly shook the catkins on some budding **alder** branches that had been arranged in a large, old terracotta olive jar – clearly not one of Victor's reproductions – that was set on the floor in front of one of the open windows, bringing with it the smell of rain on the stones outside. From the fresh putty and clean glass, JJ could see that both windows had recently been repaired and reglazed. The wood of the window frames had been stripped of paint and sanded down; it felt waxy to the touch.

The whole place seemed as impossibly glamorous as Sylvie herself, and JJ couldn't help wondering why she was living here alone. Partly in the sense of 'How had she managed to bagsy it?' and partly wondering if she had a boyfriend; hoping that she didn't.

If Sylvie had been **Norma** Jean herself, or if she had emerged from the sea and been borne, **Venus**-like – naked, and barely protecting her **modesty** – by fragrant winds on a great vulval shell to some Arcadian shore, she could scarcely have appeared more beautiful to JJ than she already did. Nor could the connection between her beauty and his desire have been more profound. What was a nineteen-year-old English boy with a **hyperactive** imagination who had been mistaken for a punk to do in this world of adults and – he wished – sexual possibility?

In JJ's **brain**, as with many nineteen-year-olds, a constant battle was being fought between sexual desire and a kind of priggishly self-righteous need to be politically sound – or was it to not be thought unsound? This sometimes manifested itself as a feeling that he was required to have an **answer** – possibly even the correct one – to any given challenge or situation. Not that he had been in many situations at all, whether ethically challenging or otherwise. This was also part of an unspoken and usually self-defeating compulsion on JJ's part to give an impression of effortless maturity, as if he had been born fully formed, and – to borrow a phrase from his *Marxism Today*-reading college friend **Heather** back at home – 'always-already' cool. More often than not, the tension between these two states, between desire and being politically sound, would result in a kind of all-pervading psychic paralysis, particularly at times of romantic tension. Luckily for him, or not, what went around came around, and the casual observer might easily mistake the resulting state of self-induced catatonia for a kind of cool after all.

The night before, once conversation had again turned to politics after they had seen that JJ was reading *Nineteen Eighty-Four* by George **Orwell**, Élise and Pea-tag had spoken at length about the Miners' Strike in the UK, and JJ had found – to his slight shame – that they knew far more about it than he did. He hadn't realised that so much had been at stake.

'So Maggie,' Pea-tag had said, 'succeed to portray this as a **wild-cat** strike because the miners make the tactical error over the ballot at the beginning, *non*? But even if they 'ad 'ad the ballot, the state could never let them win, you understand?'

Élise had changed the subject with a mischievous grin: 'So if you like the Killing Joke but you don't like the Angelic **Upstart**, then maybe you are not a punk but a **Lollard**.'

So-called 'Oi!' music was a branch on the evolutionary tree of punk that was also sometimes associated with the skinhead movement, and JJ had confessed that he found the boisterousness of bands like Angelic Upstarts and Cockney Rejects, or their audiences, a bit scary. That they were able to have a conversation like this at all was because punk, like the atom bomb, was a kind of shared concern of the young around Europe and beyond. Music was more of a **lingua franca** than the 'franglais' that JJ's poor French was forcing everyone to adopt. Punk or new wave was both a proxy and a crucible in and of itself: both a means to an end, and the end itself, if that end was the discussion of ideas. Back at home, even relatively recently, JJ and his friends had still liked to **toddle** off to Left Bank Records on a Saturday, and then to sit on one of the benches in the Cathedral Precinct, or on the low stone walls if it was sunny, where they might pore over the covers and inner sleeves of the records they had just bought, searching for information and ideas, for clues.

When it came to Oi!, JJ found the whole scene problematical, as his Marxist friend Heather might have said. He still associated the skinhead movement with its racist, National Front-supporting **nadir**, rather than its reggae-loving multicultural origins. Consequently, of the newer bands, he preferred the more positive critical and political messages of bands like Crass, Flux of Pink Indians or Killing Joke, of whom he was a badge-wearing fan, after all, or The Mob, with their anti-nuclear **lament**, 'No Doves Fly Here.'

He'd been to Crass's second Exeter gig back in the autumn, and his favourite of their records was *The Feeding of the 5000*. As far as JJ was concerned, the habit of the organised Church to gain wealth and influence, to lavish riches, decoration and power upon itself, was the height of hypocrisy, a contradiction in terms, and he had said so.

Oui, the Lollards thought this too, Élise had said. They were medieval English heretics, she'd explained, *comme un socialisme prototypique*. They wanted to *redistribuer la richesse*, to redistribute the wealth. These were dangerous ideas for which men – '*bien sûr*, because they think women do not 'ave political ideas, *oui*?' – might be burned alive.

'But look around,' she'd said. 'Don't you notice something strange about this place?'

JJ had still been so overwhelmed by La Fontaine-en-Forêt and its inhabitants, on so many levels, that he didn't know where to start.

'*Il n'y a pas d'église!*' Élise had said. 'No church!'

Not quite getting her point, JJ had wondered if there was some kind of equivalence here to the rule – as he understood it – that it was only towns with cathedrals that qualified as cities. 'Does that mean this is a hamlet and not a village?' he'd asked. But then, perhaps it was neither, he thought to himself. Perhaps it was just a glorified waterworks.

Élise had laughed at this display of naivety, and said she thought that the fact that there was no church meant La Fontaine-en-Forêt had always been a place for outsiders, even more so since the one road and sole means of access to the hamlet, village, whatever it was, had effectively been cut off. You couldn't get any kind of **vehicle** up here. Without a road, and with the spring at La Fontaine-en-Forêt being replaced as the main water source for the area with the laying of the Aqueduc du Foulon and the **Canal** du Loup – initially a stone-and-concrete channel, later a huge iron pipe – from a source higher up the mountain in Gréolières, the village had ceased to be useful. Already depopulated by the First World War, and safely out of sight, it had been allowed to wither.

When Sylvie reappeared, she was wearing jeans and a white cotton man's shirt, which she had tied in a knot at the waist. JJ couldn't help noticing the silver medallion that she wore on a chain around her neck. '*C'est mon **ducat**,*' she said, smiling. '*Tu l'aimes? Regarde.*'

Leaning forward with an elbow on the table, she held the necklace up as far as the chain would let her, so that he might see. The medallion itself was ornately cast but looked exceptionally old. Framed within a vertically aligned beadwork **ellipse** was a crude image of what he guessed from the halo was Jesus, surrounded by stars. It was impossible to read the embossed lettering around this central device. Gazing as he was at both the coin and the smooth, golden skin of Sylvie's breast, breathing in the smell of her perfume, JJ could do little more than nod.

'It look like nothing,' she said, 'but is real. I find it when we first move 'ere. Inside the—' She gestured at the flagstoned floor. '—stones, *oui*? In the crack. It look like nothing, but the *joaillier* tell me is a ducat *vénitien* from the Napoleonic era, when France invade Venice. 'Ow it got 'ere, I don't know.' She stood and allowed the coin to gently fall back against the skin between her breasts, where it was framed by the open neck of the white shirt. 'I think the gold ducat is worth a lot of money. This one not so much because he is only silver, but he is beautiful, no?'

'*Oui*,' said JJ, relieved and distraught in equal measure. And whether actions spoke louder than words or not, he was momentarily lost for both. 'Shall we go and see this bakery, then?' he said eventually.

As they stepped outside, and with no warning, Sylvie slipped on the wet cobbles, grabbing JJ's shoulder and arm with both hands as she did so. That he had managed to stand fast and prevent her from falling would be the source of considerable moral satisfaction for the nineteen-year-old for the rest of the day, while the memory of the touch and the weight of her body against his, combined with this sense of having been chivalrous, would become highly erotically charged. In his fantasies, this moment would be returned to again and again, and in that imaginary realm it became the prelude to their rushing back into the house in a fantasy of sensual abandon that presented itself as a series of transitionless vignettes; a Kama Sutra of sexual positions and endless erotic possibilities. Of course, it didn't happen quite like that, but even in spite of the events that followed, this accidental touch – Sylvie grabbing his arm as she momentarily lost her footing on the wet cobbles – remained the fulcrum of an erotic fantasy that would sustain JJ for many years.

'Are you okay?' he asked.

'*Oui, merci*,' she said, dusting herself off slightly, then leading the way around to a small overgrown yard off La Petite Rue, not twenty paces from her front door. It was densely packed with brambles, and Sylvie pointed across the vegetation to the small and windowless building with its arched double door. It looked like a stone shed, really, or an outhouse, and it fronted on to this yard. '*Voici*,' she said, '*la boulangerie!*'

There was a familiar, funny face painted across the double doors in faded violet paint: a big-nosed cartoon character peering over a wall.

'Kilroy was here?' JJ asked.

'Ah, *oui*, American soldiers must have stay 'ere at the end of the war to make R and R,' said Sylvie. 'When we arrive, he was everywhere. *Et aussi*, we found some **slot machine**, you know? A pinball and some **ninepin**? *Abandonné*, yes? In one of the 'ouses. They must have 'ad to leave very quick, but you know they would 'ave 'ad to bring the pinball machine up 'ere on the back of a donkey!'

This **two-bit** shed wasn't at all what JJ had been expecting the bakery to look like. Hungry as he was, in his mind's eye he'd seen a magical-looking shop-window display of baguettes and tarts, nameless sweets and savouries, croissants and doughnuts, the works. Instead Sylvie was showing him the padlocked door of a shed. '*Je ne comprends pas*,' he said, and not for the first time. 'This doesn't look like a bakery. Is that the mystery?'

'Oh, it's a terrible story, Joe. Monsieur Houlette tell it to Victor one time. This was the bakery. Look, there is the chimney. During *la Seconde* there were still a few people living here. Those who were too old to fight, some widows with children whose fathers were never coming back. The baker, he had remained here only out of loyalty to the commune, because he felt useful, and he knew that he could help to feed the ones who were left. But when the Italian occupation collapse, the Nazis move in and occupy this whole region. And when he hears that they 'ave reached Grasse, that they will be here in less than thirty minutes, he decides that he 'as 'ad enough: he will never bake bread for the Nazis. He just stop what he was doing, right there. He switch off the oven, hang up his apron and close the bakery, locking the door behind him when he go, just like you see it now. No one has been in there ever since. They have just let them grow. What do you call this in English?'

'Brambles,' said JJ. They were chest-high. 'Or blackberries.'

'*Oui*, "black berry". So now it is like a memorial.'

'Didn't he come back after the war?' JJ asked.

'No, so maybe he go home and get his gun, the one he use to hunt the wild boar when he was young, but he realise he is too old to go up into the mountain, you know, and fight *avec la Résistance*, so he turn the gun on himself instead and blow his brains out.'

18: PLANTOIR (DIBBLE)

Gradually JJ got to know the various members of the small community at La Fontaine-en-Forêt a little better. Milo was a Parisian and of indeterminate age – though obviously a few years older than JJ, perhaps twenty-five? – handsome, and with the **ruddy**, outdoorsy face of a farmer, and that great Roman nose, but skinny, tanned and perpetually filthy. He had a **mini-van** – a **rust**-bucket of a Citroën, bought for a **snip**, a farmer's box van with a roof rack, the kind you'd see selling produce by the side of the road – which he kept in the village car park at La Fontaine-lès-Vence. Whenever anything or anyone needed **running** down to Nice or Antibes, or if **paraffin** or butane cylinders needed collecting, Milo was the one to do it. And with JJ staying at La Fontaine-en-Forêt, Milo now had an assistant to hand, more or less whenever he needed one. JJ considered helping Milo out in this way to be a form of rent, payment in kind to the commune.

There was always something that needed fetching and carrying: whether it was picking up sacks of clay down in Nice for the potters in Tourrettes or La Fontaine-lès-Vence, collecting a job lot of gardening tools – spades and trowels, dibbles, rakes, that kind of thing – from Mme Valériane at the hardware store in La Fontaine-lès-Vence, or delivering the special day-old cheeses to all the local shops on behalf of whichever goat farm up in the mountains. Later, Élise would tell him that Mme Valériane had once been a famous model for the painter Amedeo Modigliani.

Milo enjoyed the work, and thus made it enjoyable for everyone else. He told JJ that the variety – of load and destination – made up for the **monotony** of driving. He could probably have made a living at this too, if he stayed here for long enough or if he ever considered the **notion** of actually charging people anywhere near the going **rates** for these jobs. It wasn't that they didn't want to pay him, nor that he lacked financial nous, rather that the whole concept of business was **anathema** to him. He made enough to simply treat this as a **spare time job**, something he could do just for pocket money when he was here, a way to keep the van in **juice**.

JJ enjoyed sitting in the passenger seat, ears popping from the descent, as they criss-crossed the Sud, from Biot to Grasse, from Cannes to the Cap, which was French for '**Cape**' – as in the coastal feature, rather than, as back home, JJ and his friends' parent-defying **rhyming slang** for marijuana: Cape of Good Hope – but by which Milo might variously mean the Caps d'Antibes, d'Ail, Bénat or Ferrat.

But Milo was a bit of a stoner too, and a couple of times they went along to Fréjus, two hours' drive along the coast. On those occasions, Milo told his English helper, '*Désolé*' – sorry – but these were heavy people that JJ would not like to meet, and who would most likely not want to meet him either. He was a stranger, after all. JJ was cool with this; he didn't mind. He was happy enough to sit and have a cigarette and a coffee in the sun for as long as it took, while his mate drove off to meet his connection from the airbase and take delivery of whatever had just come in fresh from Algiers.

In dirty overalls and carrying his trusty socket set, Milo could have passed for a mechanic stopping by to repair a tractor. But later he opened the toolbox with a grin to show JJ the massive slab of hash – a fine, blonde double-zero – that fitted beneath the moulded plastic interior. That day they took a detour to Roquebrun, a mountain near Fréjus that was as red as the cliffs on the South Devon coast, if mountain was the right word for a single outcrop of this kind. Victor the potter would have a chemical and geological explanation – JJ made a note to ask him later – but seeing this great red rock also gave JJ a twinge of nostalgia for home, driving down to **Padstow** in his parents' old forest-green **Rover** 2000 TC. He could practically smell the sun on the cream leather upholstery.

Milo seemed to know people wherever they went. Once, as JJ had been unloading clay outside one of the little potteries in La Fontaine-lès-Vence, Milo had said hello to a woman passer-by before disappearing with her into a neighbouring house for half an hour, leaving JJ to finish the unloading. 'That is my ex, Frédérique,' he shrugged later, by way of explanation, as they walked up the track towards La Fontaine-en-Forêt. 'But don't tell Élise, *oui*?'

JJ shook his head.

'I try to give her up, but I cannot. Frédérique, she give the best **oral**, you know?'

Another time, on the way to a job in Saint-Paul, a sudden torrential downpour that had rolled noisily in from the sea meant they had to pull up and shelter in the lee of the old stone church in Tourrettes-sur-Loup for half an hour. There had been little they could do but roll up the windows and laugh at the severity of the fusillade pounding on the Citroën's thin tin roof. From his passenger-side window, JJ had watched the rain dissolve the **tracing-paper confetti** that had been left from the previous Saturday's wedding. The storm stopped as suddenly as it had started, the heavy artillery on the roof dwindling to a gentle **pit-a-pat**, and then sunshine, but roads had briefly turned to rivers, and they had had to drive carefully through the mud that had been left along the old Route de Provence.

Milo was not just useful with his hands, he was good company, and JJ enjoyed bouncing around the mountain roads talking politics as they went, denouncing this **bigwig** or that **tyrant**. Milo talking about the work he did on Greenpeace expeditions – 'They need the mechanic as much as the biologist or the oceanographer, *non?*' – or extolling the virtues of Petra Kelly and the Greens in Germany, with their creed of non-violence, social justice, ecological awareness and grassroots democracy, talking about the artist Joseph Beuys and his Damascene conversion from fighter pilot to activist, or listening to Brecht and Weill on the van's tinny radio and cassette player.

Until Milo had introduced him to it, JJ had never heard of *The Threepenny Opera*, nor even *The Beggar's Opera* on which it was based. But he knew his Bowie. And although The Doors' version had not been collected on the one *Greatest Hits* record of theirs in his collection, he knew their version of the 'Alabama Song' too. So there was at least one track that he could join in on. These were carefree times: he and Milo, the van's sliding doors open to the warm spring air, singing along at the tops of their voices as they barrelled down the mountain towards Cagnes-sur-Mer. Even knowing the politics – once Milo had explained that these were left-wing songs – it felt subversive and punky to be driving around the South of France listening to songs like 'Mack the Knife' in the original. Older people would turn in shock, some deep-seated **animus** aroused, unsurprisingly, by the sound of the raucous German voices. Even at a distance of forty years, the Second World War and the Nazi occupation still felt very close: just a Place de la Libération, a derelict bakery or a bomb site away.

19: PRIMEVÈRE (PRIMROSE)

Milo and JJ stopped in Vence on their way back up the mountain. Parking up on the steep slope outside the Auberge des Seigneurs, they first bought some lemons and a huge, flat lettuce from a stall by the side of the road.

Milo went to the fishmonger in the old walled town to see what was fresh in, sending JJ over the road to get the bread.

As he queued to buy baguettes to take back to La Fontaine-en-Forêt for the communal supper, JJ thought again of that terrible story of the village bakehouse that had been locked and deserted since the occupation – the story of suicide rather than surrender – and of the abandoned oven **within**. He had been trying to visualise this, imagining great **hemispherical** steel bowls for mixing the dough, proving and drying racks, the oven; he didn't have much of a clue. But what if they could clean it up and get it working again? JJ couldn't act unilaterally, that much was clear. He would have to get the approval of the commune, but why not? They could be self-sufficient in bread, sell the surplus from Milo's van by the roadside, as seemed to be the way around here. He would raise the subject on the way back to the village and see what Milo thought.

'*Blanchaille!*' said Milo, handing JJ a large plastic bag of small fish as they got in the van. Then: 'Hey, do you like Elvis Costello? You know, one time I 'ad the ticket to see Elvis Costello playing in Nice. I really love 'im at that point. And it was the strangest thing, you know, because on the day of the concert I was quite excited, yes, and then suddenly I bump into him by Les Pêcheurs in Antibes, eating a plate of *blanchaille* and singing in front of the camera. And I am, like, "*What?* This is crazy, man!" And then maybe one hour later, I am right 'ere in Vence, and I cannot believe but I see 'im and 'is band again! This time they are dancing over there by *le point de vue*, with the Baou de Vence in the background. I realise a year later when I see it on TV that they were filming the pop video for that song 'I Can't Stand Up for Falling Down', do you know it? Man, it was so funny. Like I could not escape from Elvis Costello!'

As Milo started the engine, JJ punched the 'Play' button on the cassette player in the dashboard. They had been listening not to Elvis Costello, but to 'Reel 1' of *Sandinista!* – the other cassette box set in Milo's glove compartment – which against all the odds was fast becoming JJ's favourite album by The Clash. Now, leaving Vence on a road that followed the old railway line, they turned it up and sang along to the chorus of '**Ivan** Meets G.I. Joe'.

It would all depend upon who you asked, Élise said later, spearing the last few **whitebait** with her fork, then wiping a hunk of bread around her bowl to catch the last crisp and oily golden crumbs, the lemon juice. 'You 'ave seen the ruins at Pont-du-Loup,' she asked, 'above Victor's factory? *Incroyable!*'

They had been having a **chinwag** over supper, although JJ hadn't quite got around to discussing his plan for the bakery. Victor and Pea-tag had been locked in some intense and heated conversation about French politics for what seemed like hours. Some names JJ recognised: Mitterrand, or Giscard d'Estaing. Unable to really join in, JJ had instead asked about the bombed viaducts, relics of the same railway whose route out of Vence they had traced earlier, and which from the 1890s and for sixty-odd years had meandered between Nice and Meyrargues, a couple of hundred kilometres to the west. Milo had pointed out some of these ruins – a cutting here, signal gantry there – on their travels to one **errand** or another. At Pont-du-Loup, all that remained of a once spectacular stone viaduct was a line of great broken-topped pillars that towered high above Victor's factory, dwarfing his brick chimney. The viaduct's delicate and elegant arches had been pulverised into several thousand tons of rubble – or building materials, depending on your point of view – that had been strewn across the valley floor far below.

'Victor might say differently,' said Élise, before telling JJ that, supposedly, when the Allies had retaken Grasse at the end of the Second World War, a small Nazi commando unit had escaped along the railway line under cover of **night**. Planting explosives as they went, they had destroyed the line behind them at several key points in an attempt to stymie the Allies' advance. First of all here at Pont-du-Loup, then further down the mountain at Pascaressa, below La Fontaine-lès-Vence, then nearer the coast at Siagne.

In an impoverished post-war France – the story went – the cost of rebuilding these masterpieces of civil engineering was prohibitive, besides which the railway had never been particularly profitable, so the ruins were left where they stood. Some local stretches of the line had remained operational for a year or two, but by 1949 it was clear that it would never be worth rebuilding, and in 1950 the line finally closed for good, with some of the remaining staff redeployed to road construction or to working in the various local administrations. The former Ligne Central-Var, which had once carried Her Imperial Majesty the Queen-Empress Victoria to Grasse, was no more.

Victor joined in and took up the story. Others maintained, he said, that this had been the work of a local Resistance **hero** who had in fact been trying to delay the fleeing Nazis, to hamper their retreat rather than the Allies' advance. But there was another theory too.

The distinctly minority view, with not an **iota** of proof to back it up, was that it had actually been a home-grown **Gunpowder Plot**, a business-minded blitzkrieg carried out by some petit-bourgeois **Baader-Meinhof**, perhaps – an unlikely-sounding coalition of industrialists, the Resistance and organised crime – which had merely used the end of the occupation as cover to further the region's and their own ends, cementing their own positions of power that had been acquired within the wartime status quo. The railway had been bombed, adherents to this particular conspiracy theory might whisper, as Victor was doing now, because it had been thought that, by doing so, more post-war investment could be forced into the area. Now, with the railway irreparably destroyed, the argument went, roads would have to be built, which would in turn lift land values and property prices, bring money and development opportunities to an area that had after all known more than its share of **hard times**. It sounded unlikely, Victor went on, but just because all of these things had subsequently happened, it didn't mean the conveniently retrofitted conspiracy theory *wasn't* true!

'Really?' asked JJ, incredulously.

'You cannot really be such a **choir-boy**!' said Victor, impatiently. 'Who knows if it is true or not, but such things cannot be a complete surprise? It is so **basic**, *non*? Or I suppose you don't 'ave corruption *en Angleterre*?'

JJ pushed his empty bowl away and shrugged his reluctant agreement in classroom French: '*Oui, peut-être.*' He wondered if this might be a good time to bring up his idea to revive the bakery?

By now quite pissed, Victor was warming to his subject like some bar-room **sot**. 'You English like so much being spanked by your Maggie Thatcher, but isn't the real *technique anglaise* how you can appear to be both reasonable *et supérieur*: your fucking royal family!

At least in France we see through that **ethereal** bullshit long ago! While behind the scenes you are in the gutter making deals with the devil, *non*? And fuck anyone who gets in your way, whether that is the colonies in your glorious British Empire or to sell out your own working class!'

JJ was shaking his head, pointing at his badge. '*I* didn't sell out the working class! I supported the strike—'

But Victor was having none of it. 'Listen,' he said, interrupting. 'We were just talking about **Chirac**, you know 'im? Ah, there is no reason why you would. He was Prime Minister of France a decade ago, and maybe he will be again – what do you English say about the bad penny? – but at least 'e 'as got one thing right, and maybe for 'im it is nothing more than a slogan, but it is true what he say, that economic *laissez-faire* is the lie, a cover for the terrible *ultralibéralisme* beneath. But you know, sometimes I feel it right 'ere' – he pounded his broad chest – '*ici, dans mes os* – in my **marrow** – that perhaps all we Europeans are just the same kind of 'ypocrite. We are all just so many **cog** in the same imperialistic machine, *non*? Yes, even we in La Fontaine-en-Forêt! We think we are revolutionaries, but we are just petit-bourgeois Europeans! What are we doing that is any different? Look at the Norwegians. They are what? A superpower, but in the field of the peace and *les droits de l'homme*? That is their story! But is just a story, *non*? Do you think these politicians and oilmen in **Oslo** would not do anything, sell out anyone, to protect their export interests with whichever **authoritarian** regime it is, whether in China or anywhere? So, yes, certainly your miners are great heroes, and anyone but a fool would support them, so congratulations, *mon ami*, at least you are not a fool, but even they, the most powerful union, they could not vanquish *l'ultralibéralisme*.'

JJ could do little more than nod. Maybe it was time to change the subject. 'I was thinking earlier—'

Victor cut him off: 'Anyway, it is true what Élise say, that these towns were so depopulated after the war. But do you know what they really did? How they really rebuild? These towns are prisons!'

'Ah,' said Milo, laughing, 'now you will hear something that is not in the tourist guidebooks. It has nothing to do with the bombing of railways, but—'

Victor reached for his glass, but knocked it over. 'Ah, fuck you all,' he said as he got unsteadily to his feet. 'It can wait. I have to piss.'

A fan of light was briefly unfurled across the cobbled square, then disappeared as Sylvie pulled her front door shut behind her. As she walked over to join them, JJ thought that she looked like a **film star**. He remembered a story that Milo had told him on their travels: how Sylvie and Victor had met, perhaps six years earlier. She and her girl-friends were down from Paris. They were young and beautiful, and they had been hanging out with some rich sailors, round-the-world racers on these incredible boats – **trimaran**, catamaran – state-of-the-art ocean-goers that had just done 30,000 miles in the most difficult waters, but were now simply hopping from port to port along the Riviera, from one victory party to another.

Sailing from Saint-Tropez to Nice, Sylvie and her friends had been sunbathing on the deck when a sudden mistral had caught the team unawares. Everything was fine, except that all of Sylvie's clothes, which had been rolled up on the deck beside her, were suddenly plucked up by the wind to **festoon** the rigging for a second or two, before blowing away entirely. Stopping off in Antibes, she had had no alternative but to walk around the town like this – practically bursting out of her tiny primrose-yellow bikini – much to the amusement of the sailor friends who may have been enjoying her humiliation rather too much. In any case, the story went, none of them had thought to help.

Victor, who had been sitting on the corner outside Chez Félix drinking a pastis when this group had walked through the city gate, had heard and seen enough to clock this power play, and without a word – instead of joining the rest of the male population of Antibes, it seemed, in leering at the beautiful young woman – he had simply stood up, undone his belt, taken off his Levi's, unbuttoned his shirt, and given the clothes to Sylvie. So that it was he who was standing there in very skimpy swimwear instead of her.

One of the sailors had apparently made the mistake of laughing at the sight of the hairy, barrel-chested potter standing outside Chez Félix in a tiny pair of Speedos, but he hadn't laughed for long.

If the insouciant Sylvie had been surprised by this glorious act of chivalry, she hadn't shown it. Instead she had just turned up the legs of his jeans, pulled the belt tight, rolled up the shirtsleeves and knotted the tails around her midriff. Then, sitting down at Victor's table as if it were the most natural thing in the world, she had turned to order '*Un grand café crème, s'il vous plaît*', taken one of his cigarettes out of the packet, and before it was lit, or so they used to say, Victor and Sylvie had fallen in love.

20: PLATANE (PLANE TREE)

In a gesture of faith in the longevity and security of Il Duce and of the grand Italian imperial project that only weeks later would seem laughable if it were not so tragic, Oreste Bonomi – the short-lived Minister for Trade and Foreign Currency in Mussolini's final cabinet – had called, upon his appointment in February 1943, for the establishment of an annual trade fair that could, in a **fraternal** spirit of international exchange and in the most convivial surroundings, demonstrate to the world the industrial and scientific advances that had been made possible by Italian fascism, and to **emphasise** Italian superiority. Inspired by his own superficial understanding and vicarious, picture-postcard impressions of the New York World's Fair of 1939 in Flushing Meadows, Bonomi called for an *Esposizione La Prima Internazionale di Eccellenza Tecnologica e Architettonica Italiana* to be held in Nizza's stunning Palais de la Jetée and environs throughout August of that year.

Designed by certain *Niçois* Anglophiles as a belle-époque tribute both to Joseph Paxton's Crystal Palace and the Brighton Pavilion, and in an attempt to emulate the then current British craze for pleasure piers, the Palais de la Jetée had opened to the public in the early 1880s, and now at last its great crystal domes had been restored to their former glory, the building having spent much of the Great War doing service as an army hospital.

It would not have been **facetious** or too far wide of the mark to suggest that career fascist Bonomi – proud veteran of the Milanese

Squads (that tight-**knit** band!) and the March on Rome, the Founding President of the Fascist Merchants' Syndicate and a former Director of Propaganda at the Ministry of Popular Culture under both Alessandro Pavolini and Gaetano Polverelli, who had just replaced the rather more suave and worldly Raffaello Riccardi at the Trade Ministry in Mussolini's eighth cabinet reshuffle – needed to make a bravura gesture to cement his position, one that owed more to his long acquaintance with Il Duce, perhaps, than to his expertise in matters of national or international commerce. A grand technological trade fair in that most Italian of occasionally French cities seemed an opportunity to do just that. The picture that surviving records tell us Bonomi painted to that cabinet – of jazz-playing military bands and flying boats, of a motor racing circuit weaving between the plane trees and the palms on the Promenade des Anglais – the intoxication of petroleum and victor's **wreath!** – of *la bella gente e titani dell'industria*, each Cinecittà starlet and every **giant** of Italian commerce, drinking champagne and flirting before the sparkling azure waters of the Côte – was perhaps at least an appealing enough fantasy and a distraction from the political and military realities of those last days that it was simply waved through. Where the naive but powerful Bonomi might have seen strategic development and further opportunities for flag-waving and, no doubt, for personal aggrandisement, others merely conceded the possibility of a last hurrah.

Of course, it is a matter of historical record that Bonomi's lavish vision never came to pass. Before July was out, the decades-long dream that had been Italian fascism would be **over**. Total defeat in North Africa would be followed by the Allies' invasion of Sicily. Il Duce himself would be arrested and imprisoned. Sure, only to be freed – briefly – by the Germans, but still, the jig was up! That was all in the future, however, and no international trade fair can spring up overnight, much less an event of the prestige and calibre of the *Esposizione La Prima Internazionale di Eccellenza Tecnologica e Architettonica Italiana*, and understandably certain preparations were already well underway. Contemporary photographs show the Promenade and the public gardens littered with half-built pavilions and grandstands, as well as Fiat L6/40 light tanks, and requisitioned French 75mm guns in their improvised sandbag emplacements. Torino's finest had begun work on the motor racing circuit, while other manufacturers and enterprises had of necessity been 'setting out their stalls' from at least the end of May, even if the backdrop against which they were doing so was one of Allied bombings, deportations and the ever bolder assassinations of Italian soldiers, rather than the pop of corks and the ringing of crystal glasses and laughter. It was an increasingly unsafe atmosphere in which the troops of the ragtag occupying army could not know whether even the nanny or the pedicab rider might suddenly turn and **kill** them!

So it was that the engineers of the Conforti group – celebrated **safe**-makers of Verona – had found themselves among the first wave of exhibitors, and they had quickly set to work crowbarring open and unpacking their numerous crates, and assembling their prototype within the opulent surroundings of the Palais de la Jetée itself. But the engineers from Porta Palio were not exhibiting their finest walnut-cased and silk-lined, two-lock, multi-compartment, free-standing domestic safes, nor the usual exhibition cutaway model of one of the 12,000kg monsters they had made for the Bank of Italy. In fact, Conforti was planning to use the *Esposizione* to launch a new line entirely. The company was branching out from its usual security-based repertoire, and it was another species of behemoth that was being painstakingly assembled and tested there in the Palais. Some young Turk in the engineering department – it is not recorded who, or perhaps those papers were destroyed in the bombing raids of the time – had evidently realised that there was perhaps not so much difference between a metal box designed to safeguard its contents and one designed to **cook** them. Moreover, they might have reasoned, if Conforti's skill in the production of luxuriously designed high-end safes could be brought to bear on what had hitherto been thought of by most commercial oven manufacturers as a purely functional device, then it might result in a bread oven that looked more like the ballroom of an ocean liner, let's say, than the engine room of a tramp steamer. The *prototipo* Conforti MkI was the result, heralding a new concept in bakery ovens, and sporting sleek art-deco stylings that included a marble-effect enamel shell with chromium detailing and cast-aluminium switch gear. The MkI was one hundred per cent electrically powered, rather than the more usual steam-tube-based hybrid (a design that had been little updated since the 1850s), and was capable of processing fifty kilograms of dough per load.

The plan had been that, once this beauty was installed – a painstaking process in itself – the Conforti engineers would be joined by a team of Italian master bakers who would begin around-the-clock production in an attempt to fulfil if not all then a respectable portion of the not inconsiderable appetites of the *Esposizione*. Instead, stranded and increasingly desperate, the engineers had resorted to selling their valuable stocks of sugar and government-grade high-quality flours and semolinas to the black market in order to buy cheap **liquor**.

It was not only Mussolini's government and military leaders who needed some distraction. The food shortages in both Italy and the occupied zone, the activities of both the Resistance and organised crime, and the erratic use of sanctions against the civilian population were taking their toll on morale even away from the combat zones near coast and border. But for the baker Monsieur **Anselm** Juneau it had not been a need for distraction that had seen him rising early on that July morning in order to walk down the mountain to Vence and buy a return ticket to Nice, but a genuine spirit of scientific enquiry. He had been looking forward to the *Esposizione* since he had first read about it – and Conforti's technological breakthrough – in a copy of Nice rag *L'Éclaireur* back in the spring. And even if Bonomi's ill-fated fête – his *Esposizione La PIETA Italiana* – was no longer happening, Monsieur Juneau had already gone to such great lengths to get the necessary travel papers signed by the relevant authorities that, when he had heard from André his 'insurance man' and black-market flour supplier that the great electric bread oven and its accompanying team of increasingly anxious engineers were somehow still resident in the Palais, he had determined to continue as planned and to go and see it for himself, little realising, of course, what he might be letting himself in for. But go he did, and it was there, beneath the great crystal dome of the Palais de la Jetée, that Monsieur Juneau, **avuncular** owner of the Boulangerie **Juno** in La Fontaine-en-Forêt, had first caught sight of the great *prototipo* Conforti MkI.

Juneau had been working all his life with a traditional open-fronted and stone-built wood-fired oven that had almost certainly changed but little since before the Revolution. The heat distribution was poor, it was hard to clean, and even by setting the fire long before midnight and starting to bake at 3 a.m. he would be lucky if his daily production exceeded a single sack's worth of bread. A keen reader, when he had the time, and a devotee of science and industrialisation despite the scant **schooling** he had received during his childhood in *fin-de-siècle* Vence, Juneau had been particularly interested in those developments in baking technology that had seemed to emanate from what he considered the industrial source and well-spring of the world: the city of Manchester, England. Being possessed of a modest inheritance, and wanting to keep up with such advances, he had been able to subscribe – in those far-off, pre-war years – to Manchester's *Bakery Journal*, and from a small ad in that organ had even obtained a rare copy – in English – of Claude Dumbleton's autobiographical gem *The Oven Game*, of which he had been an avid, if necessarily slow, reader. For a while he had entertained correspondences with other bakers and bakery enthusiasts around the world. There was the **Walton** bakery in Stoke-on-**Trent**, England, and a Welsh couple whose family-run Newport factory supplied a chain of bakery shops across South Wales, although he had not heard from **Mervyn** or **Morag** since the outbreak of war. Not to mention the nationalist in **Ankara**, Turkey, who wrote long letters arguing for – or was it against – the supposed Ottoman origins and inspirations of that very symbol of French baking, the croissant.

Inspiring though they were, the industrial advances that were described in the pages of *The Bakery Journal* were as far removed from Anselm Juneau's own craft – his mechanical dough-mixer and wood-fired oven, his great, square, stone kneading block – as the life of an *Antibois* urchin fisherman might be from the submarine adventures of Captain Nemo in one of Jules Verne's scientific romances. But that didn't stop him dreaming of Swinging Tray Simplex Ovens, flour-improvers and biscuit-cutting machines; of 'tin bread', cyclotherms and oil-fired uniflows! Twelve-sack combined oven and prover plants! Twelve sacks! Oh, but what he could do with such wonders! By the same token, he had read of Baker and Newby's experiments with electrically heated band ovens, so was familiar with the principles of their system, in which wires of varying resistance would be wound on to cylindrical ceramic cores, these being contained in steel tubes that were then clustered – much in the manner of the closed-end steam-tube ovens – in such a way as to offer a range of controllable heating zones. As he swept out the ash each night and built another fire, as he scraped the oven deck clear of crumbs each week with the long wooden peel, such matters were never far from Monsieur Juneau's mind. If there wasn't quite such a thing as an avant-garde of international baking, here – in the collective pursuit and furthering of the engineering and the bread-making arts that were gathered within the pages of *The Bakery Journal* – was the likeness of one!

The great city of Nice, as he still called it, was as beautiful as ever in the glorious July sunshine, despite the abandoned pavilions on the Promenade, the gun emplacements and the scruffy and ill-disciplined Italian troops, most of whom were barely in uniform, but when he arrived at the Palais de la Jetée he was not prepared for the wretched scene that greeted him. It was as if a valuable racehorse had been entrusted to the clumsy care of random, disinterested vagrants. For there, like a great streamlined locomotive, stranded, was what could only be the Conforti MkI. While milling around it, some sitting on upturned crates to play cards, was a dishevelled and filthy bunch of miscreants, mostly tramps, it would appear, who stank of cooking brandy and rancid *saucisson*.

Juneau reached forward to stroke the marble-effect enamel panelling, patting the oven's flank, awestruck at the cleanness of the lines, then stepping back to admire the nameplate – Conforti MkI – which was spelled out in stylish art-deco chromium. He marvelled at the simple three-levered switching array – well understanding the numerous heat combinations that could be thus controlled – at the elegantly counterweighted peel doors and the broad expanse of baking deck within. Looking more closely, he could see that the smooth enamelled flanks of the machine concealed drawers and doors, means of storage or of access to the cavernous chambers around the oven itself, to the machinery and workings – the transformers and the heating elements – for cleaning and repair. Everything had been thought of! It was as if the wildest of his *Bakery Journal*-inspired dreams had suddenly come to life. Being in the presence of the great machine was a profoundly moving experience for Anselm Juneau. He felt awed by the human achievement that was represented by the future of beauty and plenty that the *prototipo* seemed to betoken. More than merely an oven, it seemed to represent – no, to *embody* – a new bond, a statement of faith in humanity's quest for survival and betterment that was diametrically opposed to the terrible and murderous urges of the time, this never-ending war. Transported, Juneau felt that he was in the presence of some great maternal principle. These perfectly counterweighted peel doors opened into a baking chamber that was as mystically charged as the life-giving womb, and which stood in opposition to war's gaping maw, the jaws of hell into which were being shovelled the bodies of the countless millions of dead. And yet – he looked at the ruffians, who had now stopped their card game and were looking back at him – how could the high ideals that were represented by Signore Conforti's great *prototipo* have fallen so low, so quickly?

'Gentlemen,' he offered, without condescension. 'An amazing feat of engineering. Thank you for your time. I am most grateful. But now I must bid you good day, and I suppose you will be needing to take her back to Italy *tout de suite?*'

'*Il mio cappello, ci sarà!*' – '**My hat**, we will!' – said one of the Italians. '*Abbiamo appena avuto un telegramma dal capo ci dice di restare. Anche se ad essere onesti, non mi dispiacerebbe uscire di qui!*'*

---

* 'We just had a telegram from the chief telling us to stay put. Although, to be honest, I wouldn't mind getting out of here!'

'*On leur a dit de rester ici*,' translated one of the *Niçois*, a smooth-talking chap, but with the weather-beaten face of a street drinker. '*Mais il veut retourner en Italie*.'* This Frenchman then gestured to a doorway leading off the exhibition hall into a service area or corridor. 'We have more materials back here, if you would like to see. Manuals and so forth, some specialist tools and spare parts, which I think Sir may find of interest.'

He may have been a peasant baker, but Monsieur Juneau was not a fool. It had not entirely escaped his attention that, of these unfortunates, the French contingent at least had been eyeing him up as if he rather than the Conforti MkI were the prize. Something about the oversolicitousness of the invitation and the fleeting sideways glance that had preceded it, perhaps, or a barely perceptible **chameleon**-like **lick** of the lips, betrayed them, told Juneau that, if he went to look, he'd just as likely be shivved or coshed on the back of the head for the contents of his wallet, then dumped in the sea. And who would notice another body in the current chaos? No, that would not do. And yet, drunk as they were, he knew that he could not outrun them.

'What are you playing?' Juneau enquired, far more quick-wittedly than the average day-tripping villager might manage in such straits, before sitting down and to all intents and purposes offering them a face-saving opportunity to rob him fair and square without the need for violence. The smooth-talking tramp and the chief engineer were not to know that Juneau was no ordinary bumpkin. They could not believe their luck, and readily joined him, although before long he had given them a lesson in poker that they would not quickly forget. He took his time, playing into the game slowly, concealing his skill behind some corny old feints that he was sure they would see through and could scarcely believe they fell for, in which he

---

* 'They have been told to stay in Nice, but he wants to go home.'

appeared to lose a couple of hundred francs. In fact it was money well spent and, watching the Italian engineer gratefully pocketing the notes, he preferred to think of this bribe, for that is what it was, as a gift: a ticket back to Porta Palio, offered in a spirit of fraternal exchange that reflected – as the sparkling waters outside reflected the sun – the altogether grander ethos of Oreste Bonomi's original vision for the *Esposizione*.

The day was far exceeding Juneau's expectations. In less than two hours, he found himself the owner of the Conforti MkI, although he managed to play-act every bit as outraged as if they had swindled him out of his life's savings, convincing them that their prize had been to be rid of it! As if they were having the last laugh by landing him with this '**Greek gift**', this Trojan Horse; such a beauty and yet such an enormous and fatally compromising liability. He played the part well too, as if his life had depended upon it, which in a way it had.

'And what do you expect me to do with this white elephant?' he screamed, to the drunk Italians' backs. 'Hoy! Come back! I want my money, you swindlers!'

Once the coast was clear, and with the various requisite Italian transit papers and bills of lading safely in his pocket, Anselm Juneau found a small officers' cafe off the Promenade – well, the Conforti MkI wasn't going anywhere – where he ate a cheap lunch of duck's liver and plain macaroni, which, seasoned by victory in those days of rationing, and in as far as it made a change from the baker's usual staple, seemed like an epicurean feast.

With André's help, Juneau cooked up a plan. It was clear that, with the Conforti MkI up and running, he would be able to increase production considerably, perhaps by as much as several hundred per cent. Of this, in addition to paying André a one-off tax, Juneau agreed to supply the Resistance a certain percentage – two sacks? – as well as to increase the protection money that he paid to André each week, while in return they would run a line to connect him to the local power supply. It was a good deal all round, and had Oreste Bonomi known of this, or indeed of the myriad other exchanges – trades and barters, inventiveness of all kinds – that he had unwittingly set in train among the ruins of his ill-fated *Esposizione*, the Italian Minister for Trade and Foreign Currency himself might even have learned something.

Juneau and André shook on it, and early the next morning a team of mechanics descended upon the Palais to help the one remaining Italian – Juneau had insisted upon this – to carefully dismantle and crate up the great oven.

André pulled some strings with the stationmaster at Colomars – with whom he enjoyed a **rental** arrangement for some disused coal cellars that were occasionally needed for his illicit distribution networks – and had the crates loaded on to an empty wagon that was then hitched to the back of an evening passenger train. An unscheduled stop was made to unhitch the wagon in the siding between the viaducts in the scrubby and rock-strewn pastures at Pascaressa, where the various constituent parts of the great Conforti MkI were quickly unloaded in order to be transported by donkey, piece by piece, up and down, time and again, to **heehaw** and scuff their way up that scented track, past fragrant thyme and **sage**, past prickly pear, and up and through the arch and into the village of La Fontaine-lès-Vence and thence on to the smaller village of La Fontaine-en-Forêt. By late morning it was done, and the work of knocking out the ancient oven and installing the immense *prototipo* in Monsieur Juneau's tiny bakehouse could begin.

Job done and spending Monsieur Juneau's money in Vence on

their way back down the mountain several days later, André's men laughed at this funny peasant baker with his hundred-year-old mechanical dough-mixer and his grand ideas; at the huge modern oven that was now crammed into his tiny village bakehouse. And if they had indeed looked twice at the mezuzah that had been fixed to the bakehouse doorjamb, they didn't show it or let on.

For his part, with a crowbar in his hand and Sylvie by his side, and having spent two or three days hacking through the brambles to finally prise the ancient padlock from its hasp and open the door of the abandoned bakery for the first time since it had been locked up those forty-odd years earlier, JJ didn't notice the tiny plaque. And even if he had, he wouldn't have known what it meant.

But maybe Monsieur Juneau should have been more careful with whom he made friends, for less than a month later, in September 1943, after the Italian surrender to the Allies and the German invasion of the former Italian zone of occupation that followed, two of André's men were stopped at Cagnes-sur-Mer railway station by SS officers from Hauptsturmführer Alois Brunner's notorious Department of Jewish Affairs who had commandeered the Hotel Excelsior on Avenue Durante, perhaps more for its convenient location near Nice railway station than for its splendid nineteenth-century architecture and decor. Whether to save their own skins, or simply seeking to ingratiate themselves, to parlay one life for the greater good of the Resistance and of France, they told the Nazis about the baker who lived up in the mountains. And that is how Monsieur Anselm Juneau – his grandparents were Polish Jews who had Gallicised their name from Janowsky – of the Boulangerie Juno in the village of La Fontaine-en-Forêt found himself suddenly bruised and penniless, under arrest, and travelling first by rail to the internment camp at Drancy near Paris, and then, within days, from there to a certain death in – or en route to – an unknown extermination camp in the east, most likely Auschwitz.

And if it may not have happened exactly like that, there was more truth in this story than in the myth of the romantic suicide of a baker who had abandoned his oven because he refused to feed Nazis but was too old to be a Resistance fighter, a story that JJ had heard from Sylvie, Sylvie from Victor, and which Victor had heard from Monsieur Houlette, who had heard it in turn from who knew where, but which had grown up in the intervening years like the brambles in the bakehouse yard. For here, after all, beyond incongruity in the tiny rustic interior that could barely contain it, was the *prototipo* Conforti MkI, which swam into focus as JJ's eyes adjusted to the darkness of the interior. Its great marble-effect enamel flanks and sleek art-deco styling dwarfing the other pieces of equipment, the stone kneading block and— Was that really a *clockwork* mixer?

Running his hands along the oven's enamel panelling, JJ wondered how on earth anyone could have managed to squeeze such an enormous oven into so small a space, and how such a beautiful machine could have lain here unused for so long. But he was already excited. He could see that the chrome might polish up nicely.

21: ASPERGES (ASPARAGUS)

'Wow,' said Élise, admiring the newly revealed yard. Then, as Pea-tag ceremonially opened the double doors – splitting the old 'Kilroy' graffito in half as he did so – and she peered into the gloom, 'My God! What is that?'

The contrast was extraordinary. It was as if the room were part hovel and part art-deco spaceship. Yes, that was it. As if the great oven was bigger than the building. As if a gleaming spaceship had somehow dropped through the roof and forced itself – propelled itself – into the very fabric of the tiny building, or a streamlined locomotive had been driven cleanly through the walls.

It had been a tough few days' work to clear the bakehouse yard of brambles. Pea-tag and JJ had taken turns at cutting and scything, digging out roots where they could, then pitchforking the vicious briars over the precipice into the gorge. Deep in one of the thickets, in a nest made of newspaper and an old knitted woollen hat, they had found a writhing nest of tiny, pink rat pups, which Pea-tag pushed on to his shovel with the side of his boot, then unsentimentally drowned in a bucket of water from the fountain. There was no sign of the parents.

Sluicing down the yard with bucketfuls of water and brooms, they noted its gentle slope and cleared the outflow that led out on to La Petite Rue, whilst taking care not to further dislodge or move any of the cobbles that had already been displaced by bramble roots, but which could relatively simply be reinstated.

They had chatted while they'd worked, about records, mostly, or comparing notes on favourite gigs they'd been to; discovering, for example, a shared interest in the output and politics of the band Crass. Pea-tag had been into them from the beginning, he had said, because his friend Simon (he pronounced it more like the name Seymour) worked in a record-pressing plant near Paris and had sent him a copy of the 'Reality Asylum' 7″ that the band had been forced to produce in France back in 1978, a pattern that continued as pressing plants in the UK and Ireland rejected their politically controversial or blasphemous content. When Pea-tag talked about Crass as revolutionary outsiders, operating as they did from an isolated farmhouse commune in Essex, practising what they preached – a non-hierarchical, communal and oppositional life of self-sufficiency, apart from society – it had been obvious to JJ that he was drawing a comparison with their own lives here in the abandoned village of La Fontaine-en-Forêt.

And what Élise had explained when she'd joined them in the middle of this conversation – bringing a bottle of cold wine and three glasses so they could toast their handiwork – was that this also drew on a tradition of *les primitifs*: experiments in art and in radical living that went back hundreds of years.

'David's pupil,' she said – pronouncing it 'Dah-veed' – 'you know, the painter David? His pupil, they would dress up as ancient *Grecs* and speak out for simplicity in art and life!'

'Really? They'd have liked it here,' said JJ, gesturing at their surroundings.

With its roughly whitewashed unfaced stone walls, flagstone floor below and age- and smoke-blackened beams supporting its roof above, the bakehouse was certainly simple, and typical of the rustic architecture of the region. Fairly typical, that was, apart from the massive technological anachronism that practically filled it. The other equipment – if that wasn't too grand a term for the collection of artefacts that still stood exactly as they had been left – appeared simple and functional, and of random design; a hodgepodge. Apart from the extraordinary oven, the bakehouse could have been a sparsely and disparately fitted reconstruction in some impoverished 'museum of rural life'. A few shelves were cluttered with this and that – a mortar and pestle; thermometers, perhaps; bowls, vessels and utensils of one kind or another – while built into a recess at one end of the room was a stone trough, somewhere between a church's baptismal font and something that cattle might drink from. Above it was a spigot and a smaller, similarly recessed stone sink in which was placed a large galvanised metal – steel or zinc – measuring jug.

'Either this was the animal shed before it was a bakery, or perhaps this would be for mixing the dough by 'and, *oui*?' said Pea-tag, running his hand along the crudely rounded rim.

Next to it stood a strange three-legged wrought-iron machine – almost chair-like, but with a large, wood-staved, zinc-lined bowl or half-barrel for its seat – which appeared to be part-hinged so that its prongs, for want of a better word, and their accompanying array of geared cogs and cranks, could either be raised – the position it was left in – or lowered into the bowl. Pea-tag took the handle and made as if to heft it from this resting position, but then thought better of it. It was not clockwork, JJ realised, but hand-cranked, and following the pattern of cast-iron cogs and wheels he could see that cranking the handle not only turned the prongs, but rotated the bowl as well. There was a kind of mangle, and some shelving; some pleated cloths. Nozzles, knives and spatulas of various kinds were hung from hooks over the stone sink. None of it was here by accident. All had something to do with the baking of bread, but quite how this ramshackle assortment of machinery and implements might actually be brought into service to that end remained a mystery.

In the centre of the room was a large rectangular block of stone, hip-high and altar-like, almost big enough that the whole place could have been built around it – 'For kneading the dough?' JJ asked, leaning over the stone as if to push at an invisible pillow – while in the other corner was a small dusty pile that looked like the tattered remnants of cloth and paper sacks. If so, they had been shredded, reminiscent of the way Milo would pick the labels off a bottle of beer. JJ scuffed then prodded at the dusty pile with his toe, then stepped back in alarm when this action uncovered the fossil-like remains of a mummified rat, still curled in its death throes as if it had been suffocated long ago by the contents of one of the sacks that had once been piled there. Any grain or flour that might have remained was of course long gone. Pea-tag was not squeamish. He picked the petrified creature up and took it outside; put it on top of the stone gatepost. Turning back, he suddenly stooped to look at something growing at the base of the sunlit wall, poking and stroking it with his finger.

'There is *asperges*: wild asparagus,' he announced, returning to the bakehouse. 'I never notice it.'

Élise was standing in the doorway, face flushed and with tears in her eyes, running her finger up and down the jamb. She had seen the mezuzah. 'It is tragic, you know. Look! That is why this place has been locked up, because of shame!'

She stepped back to lean against the baker's stone, and looking through the doorway she gestured at the yard and the world of light and life beyond it. 'Whoever he was, all of that beauty must have seemed like the past; so ugly and primitive,' she said, using anger to suppress her tears. Then, turning to look at the oven: 'And this way

– *this!* – this was the future? Or it must have seemed. An oven, of all things—' Her sentence ended in a kind of strangled sob.

Unseen against a blackened beam in the roof above the doorway was the papery accretion of an abandoned wasp nest. Beneath it, the three of them stood in silence, looking at the oven.

'*Les primitifs*,' said Élise later, standing in the gateway, 'were looking for a more lyrical way of life that expressed self-evident and timeless truths – equality, for example – at all times, here and now, rather than wanting those things in the future, or even registering the difference between past and present.

'After the Revolution,' she went on, 'there was a great popularity in France for a way of living that emulated the Pythagorean sects of antiquity. As if by simply dressing up as Pythagore they could achieve what the Revolution had failed to by politics and terror alone.'

JJ was trying to follow, but had no idea what she was talking about. Fair enough, he knew *which* revolution she meant, but not much more than that. Hang on: the *what* sex?

'Pee-tah-gore,' she seemed to be saying. 'The Pee-tah-gorian sect.'

He shook his head. '*Quoi?*'

'The ancient *Grec*?' she said. 'You must 'ave 'eard of 'im: Pee-tah-gore!'

JJ shrugged helplessly.

'*Peh*,' Élise said, spelling it out. '*Ee-grecque, teh, ahsh, ah, jheh, oh, err, euh*: Pee-tah-gore!'

It sounded to JJ like the Dada nonsense poem that was used for the lyric in the Talking Heads song 'I Zimbra'.

It wasn't until Élise took a stick and spelled it out in the dust – P-Y-T-H-A-G-O-R-E – that he understood.

'Oh! We say "Pythagoras"!' he said, pronouncing it 'Pie-thag-gerus'. It had finally clicked, but all that JJ knew about Pythagoras was from doing maths CSE at school. It had not been his strongest subject.

By now Élise and Pea-tag were laughing their heads off, but JJ still didn't understand what right-angled triangles or the square of the hypotenuse had to do with anything, let alone the Revolution.

'Because the Pythagoreans cut themself off from society,' said Pea-tag. 'They dress up and they give up their possession to live the simple life in the small group.' He looked around at his two friends as if he was indeed surveying some self-evident and eternal truth: 'It is like the punks, *oui*? Like us?'

Well, this much JJ could understand.

'Why else did you think,' said Élise at last, through tears of laughter, as she took her turn to point out the obvious, 'that my brother here is called Pythag?'

22: TULIPE (TULIP)

It was amazing, JJ reflected, as he watched Monsieur Previn dextrously manipulating the unproven dough into shape, what you could do with a **limp rag** folded into pleats, some yeast and some flour. Milo sometimes did deliveries for Monsieur Previn, the baker in La Fontaine-lès-Vence, so he had asked if JJ could come and help out, and thereby learn the ropes or at least pick up a few bread-making tips, promising faithfully that he would not get in the way. So for the **last** few days – or nights – that is what he had been doing: acting as a skivvy and doing exactly what Monsieur Previn told him to. One minute he might be using the flat wooden peel or paddle to slide the *flûtes* and *pains de campagne* out of the oven and into the wire baskets that were used to ferry them between bakehouse and shop, the next pouring a **splash** of milk into the croissant dough, or beating the sugar, butter and egg mix ready for Monsieur Previn to fold in the **almond** flour for a frangipane.

On the first night, JJ had simply had to sit still and say nothing, just **watching** and making notes, as if to demonstrate that he was **sincere**. It was only on the second night that he had been given jobs to do. At first the baker had thought him a **half-wit**, although that was simply because he didn't speak much French, and it had seemed for a while that they were working at **cross purposes**, getting in each other's way, but JJ was a fast learner and had impressed the old man with his application, quickly earning a grudging kind of **respect** from him even over just these few **brief** nights that he had been helping out.

The equipment might have been electrically powered here, most of it, but as he fed the balls of risen dough into the rollers to be flattened and then rolled into long sausage-like lengths for the baguettes, JJ was at **least** beginning to understand how the more primitive versions of the same machinery might be used, although he could see that each job would take ten times longer if done the old-fashioned way. He had been wondering what the **twelve**-pleated cloths in the bakehouse at La Fontaine-en-Forêt were for, and it was mystery solved as he first watched and then copied Monsieur Previn, carefully laying each thin *flûte* into its own pleat before gathering up the next, and so on, in order that each loaf could prove in the racks for an hour or so – holding its shape and not sticking to its neighbour – before being quickly scored with a series of diagonal scratches and going into the oven.

JJ would need to serve a much longer apprenticeship than this before Monsieur Previn would trust him to actually make any croissants – which was something of a relief – but on the third night he handed JJ a jug of beaten egg and a large pastry brush, pointing at the tray of pains au chocolat and miming the action of painting them with egg wash.

Star-gazer that he was, JJ didn't mind going to bed at 8 o'clock in the evening for a few more hours of sleep before rising at midnight to walk down to the next village. In fact he enjoyed it and found that he was **incapable** of making the journey without stopping to sit on one of the large flat boulders by the road, to smoke a cigarette or two and stare in wonder at the vast brilliance of the night sky, or to watch the slow, rhythmic pulse of what he had learned was the Phare de la Garoupe, the lighthouse on the Cap between Antibes and Juan-les-Pins far below. Once he started work, of course, he would not have time to look again until he was wheeling the last of the *pains de campagne* along the cobbled road to the shop, and by then it would be getting light. Or – last job of the night – delivering two dozen baguettes to the cafe on the square, where each morning, covered in flour, he would stop for a small coffee and a large brandy on the house, before staggering back to La Fontaine-en-Forêt and a few more hours of sleep.

It was all a means to an end, of course. Now that he and Pythag had cleared the yard and opened the place up, now that he and Sylvie and Élise had cleaned it, JJ's ambition was to revive the bakehouse in La Fontaine-en-Forêt.

JJ had begun to **hatch** this plan not long after Sylvie had first shown him the building, and it had been playing on his mind in the weeks since then. The date of his return ticket from Aix had come and gone, and he had been looking both for a way to earn his keep – over and above hanging out with Milo and helping him out on the occasional driving job – and to learn something. He wanted to actually live here rather than just be a guest, or a tourist. Reviving the bakehouse had seemed to offer a way to do all of these things, but it had taken a while for him to muster the courage to raise it with the others. Even as a relative newcomer he had sat in on one or two village meetings, so had witnessed their consensus-based decision-making first-hand. An outsider might think it was a wonder that they got anything done, but JJ understood what was at stake here, and that it could be taken away any minute, especially if it were not well managed. JJ's plan would obviously need everyone's approval, since it used the resources of the village, so he had finally spoken up the previous week, and been amazed that his idea had not been laughed out of consideration. On the contrary. It and he had been taken very seriously.

Élise had responded first, reminding everyone that, in the days of the Paris Commune, employees were allowed to take over any abandoned business. Here, quite clearly, there were no surviving employees, so perhaps that should be extended to any resident who was willing to put in the time, provided that any profits were ploughed back into the commune, and that there were no objections.

There hadn't been. Or perhaps it was just that kind of night. Wine had already been flowing and with it some trivial chat comparing notes on the TV cop show *Starsky and **Hutch***, and whether Christopher **Reeve** was any good in *Superman III*. Then the conversation had taken a darker turn, with the friends telling of their closest brushes with death. JJ told of the time he'd once absent-mindedly put a live wire in his mouth, and of how he was sure he had felt his heart stop for a few beats after he'd accidentally-on-purpose snorted a whole gram of speed at once.

Élise's **aunt** in Toulon had died of carbon monoxide poisoning from the water heater in their bathroom just a week after the young Élise and Tobie – Pythag – had been to stay with her for the holidays, each taking turns to bathe nightly in water from that same heater.

Victor had found himself on a street corner in **Zagreb** during a sudden storm, and the street lamp next to him had been struck by lightning!

Béatrice's story was about how a friend of hers who worked driving a **tractor** on the **tarmac** at the Aérodrome de Niort-Souché during the **air show** there a couple of years earlier had narrowly missed being hit with flying debris when two PAF jets had collided midmanoeuvre, killing one of the pilots.

'PAF are the official aerobatic team of the French Air Force,' she explained to JJ, 'the *Patrouille*; like your "Red Arrow".'

The only one who didn't join in was Sylvie, who – sitting next to JJ with sketchbook on lap – drew in silence throughout the whole discussion. Watching as the tentative and feathery scratching of her pencil somehow achieved the illusion of chiaroscuro and of form and mass on the page – a **cherub**! – JJ felt as if he couldn't possibly love her more. Motionless though he was, trying not to put her off, it felt to JJ as if his soul was reaching out toward Sylvie. He wanted nothing more than to fall at her feet then and there, to beg and to **beseech**, or whatever it would take – he had no clue – for her to love him back.

It had been a warm spring evening and with all this talk of death, when a sudden **mistral** had slammed an upstairs window shut with a crash of broken glass on to the cobbles below, it had broken the spell. Laughing, they had been glad to be spooked, and it was partly to change the morbid direction of the conversation that JJ had plucked up the courage to share his idea for the bakehouse. Perhaps they could be self-sufficient in bread?

JJ had felt thrilled and honoured that the consensus around the table had been, '*Pourquoi pas?*' Although this had come with a caveat: that he should somehow learn as much as he could about it first.

That was where this idea of learning on the job from Monsieur Previn had come up.

'*Bon!* Then it is agreed,' Victor had said.

'Okay, I will ask 'im,' said Milo, who had evidently been hatching some plans of his own too, which he was now keen to share.

'I 'ave always wanted to go to Stonehenge,' he said. 'Maybe this year, *non*? Before I go to New Zealand?' He was flying in July. The ticket was booked. He had a stopover in **Perth** in Western Australia, and would be flying from there to Sydney and then on to join his Greenpeace friends in Auckland when their ship, the *Rainbow Warrior*, was due to come into dock.

'Why Stonehenge?' asked Pythag.

'Why not?'

'But we 'ave our own *menhir*,' Pythag countered. 'And many stone circle *ici*. You should take JJ to Carnac!' He turned and punched JJ's shoulder. 'Man, you would not believe Carnac! It is immense! What is so special about the Stonehenge?'

'*Pas seulement les pierres*,' Milo said, then corrected himself: '*Mais oui*, of course the stones. Why not? They are a wonder of the ancient world, *non*? But not just that. I mean the festival. I 'ave always wanted to go to the Stonehenge Festival.' He turned to JJ. 'How would we get there?'

'Um, **hitch**?' suggested JJ.

'Or we drive? Maybe we should take the van.'

'*Regardez, mes amis: le boulanger et le druide!*' cried Victor, sensing the opportunity for some dinner-table ceremonial. '*Apportez les tulipes et le cognac!* Where are the brandy glasses, Béatrice? We need to drink a toast!'

Whether or not he featured in Sylvie's dreams, JJ had no way of knowing, but she certainly featured in his. How would it go? With Sylvie's almost imperceptible double take preceding her inviting him in for coffee? With a knowing glance and a sudden recognition of **expectant** complicity and suddenly they'd be fucking? With a rush of sensations? With her gently touching his **erect** cock? Or the arching of her back? Oh, Christ! Fantasies about Sylvie had dominated JJ's waking and sleeping hours since the first time he had seen her. Sylvie leaning out of her first-floor window. Sylvie showing him her silver ducat. Sylvie grabbing his arm when she slipped on the wet cobbles. He would come to look back on those few weeks at La Fontaine-en-Forêt as a kind of idyll, a golden age when anything seemed possible. He had barely questioned his own unthinking assumption that it might last for ever.

And yet—

And yet somehow all of it, from Nos Resto to the rats' nest, from driving around with Milo to feeding the chickens with Pythag, from t'ai chi with Victor to learning to bake in neighbouring La Fontaine-lès-Vence, to his endless crush on Sylvie – *trop, trop belle Sylvie!* – hadn't all of it seemed a bit unlikely from the very beginning? Too good to be true? Too perfect not to have a dark side? But then, unlikely does not mean impossible! The good is not always masking the bad!

The first that JJ had heard of La Fontaine-lès-Vence's annual

Festival d'Eau – so infamous now – was when he went to take a closer look at a rainbow-adorned poster near the bus stop while walking back with a bag of his usual edible wages from another night's work with Monsieur Previn. He realised that he'd noticed this poster out of the corner of his eye a few days before, but hadn't quite taken it in. Looking more closely, he could see that the festival was not on until the first of June, but he was curious nonetheless.

Right now, as he walked home, La Fontaine-lès-Vence smelled of a mixture of disinfectant and of summer rain on dry ground, but it wasn't quite summer and it wasn't raining. Rather, a pair of street-sweepers in baggy blue cotton uniforms had attached a hose to one of the fire hydrants on the square. It was early, but they carried on about their business with no attempt to be quiet. One of them swept litter and dog shit into the gullies along the sides of the road, or scraped discarded chewing **gum** from the stones, while the other splashed **Lysol** on to the cobbles from a ten-gallon drum before hosing everything down with a drenching high-pressure spray.

'Anyone planning on going along?' JJ asked later on, offering around the bag of croissants. 'What is it? Any good?'

'*Un peu nul*,' said Milo, who had made some coffee. 'It's, you know, what is the English word – naff? Water giving life, water for washing—'

'"Water, water everywhere",' said Victor, quoting Coleridge in his best English accent. '"Nor any drop to drink."'

'Yes,' continued Milo, 'and they spray water to make the rainbow and—'

'The emblem, *c'est un arc-en-ciel*,' said Béatrice, interrupting. 'A rainbow, *oui*? But with the village on the top.'

'*Oui*,' said Milo, pretending to stick his fingers down his throat to vomit, '*exactement. C'est trop nul*. Like Béatrice says, there are hearts and rainbows everywhere: rainbow postcards, rainbow face-painting, rainbow T-shirts, a stupid rainbow parade, food and drink, the usual kind of stupid fucking stalls, you know? It has nothing to do with tradition; it is more about attracting **sponsorship** and out-of-season tourists.'

'Is that so bad?' asked Béatrice. 'If it 'elps them to earn a living?'

'Well, yes, per'aps, but it is the lie,' said Pythag, indignantly, putting the battered yellow almanac and chalk back into the pocket of his tatty combats. As on every morning, he was up the stepladder writing today's revolutionary date on the blackboard – *'Tridi 23 Floréal CXCIII: Bourrache'* – as if simply continuing this practice might offer some kind of revolutionary grounding or foundation to the activities of each day.

No one else had the almanac, but even if they had, no one really understood the particular method Pythag used to calculate this. They just took his word for it, enjoying the seasonal tone and flavour of the plants and herbs, the agricultural tools and foodstuffs that were thus named. They enjoyed the way that these names harked back to a simpler, pre-industrial way of life, as well as the basically irreligious and non-hierarchical structure that this implied, in contrast to the regular calendar with its saints' days and Sabbaths, high days and holidays.

Jumping down, Pythag picked up the bag and looked inside to see if JJ might have hidden a pain au chocolat in there somewhere, but he hadn't.

'La Fontaine-lès-Vence might share the name with us but that is all!' Pythag said, speaking with his mouth full and spitting flakes of pastry. 'We are the ones with the water. If anyone should hold a *Festival d'Eau* it would be us!' Not by nature much of an **orator**, he dismissed this evident injustice with a scowl and a sweep of his hand.

Élise was dunking a croissant in her milky coffee, and she could obviously see that JJ was puzzled by the strength of feeling. 'The tourist, *par exemple*, 'e or she might **infer** that such a festival 'as been going on for the centuries,' she explained, between mouthfuls. 'But of course it is a kind of manufactured 'istory. It is completely fake, but then we are good at this in France, *non*? I agree with Béatrice. There are worse things. This is not so bad, but it does you no 'arm to know it. Just because you know that *Père Noël* does not exist that does not stop you from enjoying the present in your shoe.'

JJ must still have been looking a little blank. He may even have fallen asleep for a second.

'I mean that it can still be fun,' Élise said, before suddenly looking at him more sympathetically and waving him away, laughing. 'Ah, I forget you 'ave been up all night. *Alors*, what you have to understand is that *après la Seconde Guerre mondiale, tous ces villages*, all of these villages, they were lost' – she gestured at their surroundings – 'not just this funny place. So they had to be reinvented. It is **ingenious** what they did, but this was a generation ago and kind of an accident, so people may be forgiven for forgetting that it was not always like this. And there are plenty of others who do not want to be reminded of their true 'istory. Look, JJ, go to bed, man! I talk to you later, okay?'

She was right, and JJ didn't need to be told twice. The futon was beckoning.

Later on, after he had awoken from a strange, *Orlando*-like **nightmare** full of **intimations** of **immortality** and in which a **spell** seemed to have been cast upon him or her by a mysterious French **nun** who was perhaps not unlike the stern *Mère supérieure* JJ had seen at the Matisse chapel in Vence, Élise would tell JJ an extraordinary story. Although in years to come he would wonder if he hadn't imagined it. Perhaps it was something he had dreamed during those sleep-deprived days in La Fontaine-en-Forêt when he was working all hours with Monsieur Previn.

Maybe so, but he was pretty sure that Élise told him that these two mountain villages, La Fontaine-lès-Vence and La Fontaine-en-Forêt, had been so depopulated by two world wars that, after the second, the larger of the two villages had been used as a prison. A place where an agricultural workforce of convicted Collaborators – forced labour – might be contained, with the fortified mountain village still small and isolated enough to function as its own virtual panopticon: a village of prisoners and gaolers. Élise told JJ that a gay 'scene' had quickly developed in La Fontaine-lès-Vence – perhaps there were homosexuals among the Collaborators – with barns and cellars converted into nightclubs and speakeasies, which attracted artists and film-makers such as Jean Cocteau and later Alfred Hitchcock, who came with Cary Grant in tow while he was filming exterior location shots for *La Main au collet*,* albeit that he contrived to use the altogether more imposing dolomitic limestone cliff at Baou Saint-Jeannet as a backdrop wherever possible, in preference to the smaller Baou La Fontaine. 'This place was famous! They all come! You 'ave seen our Picasso, *oui*?' she asked a flabbergasted JJ. '*Le torero et le Minotaure? Dans la grotte?*'

Later still, visual artists moved in. As yet unknown painters and sculptors, demob draughtsmen from the art schools of Britain, and of Europe, who were drawn by the cheap accommodation and the bohemian atmosphere. And craftspeople: potters, weavers and jewellers, with all of their wheels, their looms and kilns, their workshops and their boutique window displays.

It had been this final, more practical wave of incomers, Élise would

---

* Alfred Hitchcock, *To Catch a Thief*, Paramount, 1955.

tell JJ when he awoke, that had identified the need for a tradition, some sort of rustic heritage for their adopted village community to appropriate and celebrate. An annual festival; a date to look forward to! Something that might align this strange village of La Fontaine-lès-Vence with more archaic and traditional, if not revolutionary, forms of folk art. A festival to soften the edges, and to attract tourists up from Nice, Antibes and Cannes – to catch them on their way to the perfume shops of Grasse – who might also buy locally produced jewellery and ceramics while they were here. Why not?

But what to celebrate? Nearby Tourrettes-sur-Loup already had a festival of violets, and Menton celebrated the humble lemon, while Villefranche-sur-Mer, with its sheltered bay, had an annual *Combat Naval Fleuri* – a maritime battle re-enacted by rowing boats bedecked with carnations and mimosa – so the motley villagers of La Fontaine-lès-Vence had to think of something else. The main problem being that it would have been to all intents and purposes impossible, in the political and social climate of the time (this was the early 1950s, after all), to celebrate the unique gay culture for which the village had become justly famous, and furthermore there were no local crops to speak of, unless you counted the stunted olive trees of Pascaressa; so none worth celebrating. One desperate suggestion that the village hold a festival of handmade wooden bowls and spoons was unceremoniously thrown out without a hearing.

Eventually a concord had been reached, and the more generic and inoffensive idea of a *Festival d'Eau* settled upon. No matter that all of the water in La Fontaine-lès-Vence had been piped in – historically speaking – either from the springs at La Fontaine-en-Forêt, or more recently from far away in the mountains near Gréolières! The villagers of La Fontaine-lès-Vence had all agreed that here was a theme with popular appeal, an identity worth celebrating! La Fontaine would become the village of water, and why not? Because what was a fountain without water anyway? Besides, Élise might have said, the idea had stuck, and now, some thirty-odd years later, the annual *Festival d'Eau* was still being celebrated, and more grandly than ever. And what's more, its founders had been right: the festival's parades and water slides, its artificial rainbows and its food stalls, attracted hundreds if not thousands of tourists every year, most of whom would go back down the mountain drenched but happy in their rainbow T-shirts, a few hundred francs lighter in the pocket, but with their bellies full of good, hearty food and their new handwoven baskets laden with local arts and crafts.

Could Élise really have told him this, or had JJ merely dreamed it?

He pulled on his combats and a T-shirt then went and filled his mug with cold water from the fountain in the square, before holding his head beneath the waters for as long as he could. Above him, Sylvie's first-floor studio windows were open. She was listening to a record while she worked: 'Sinnerman' by Nina Simone. It was a song that JJ knew because it was on a great old 1960s stereo LP that Pythag sometimes played in the evenings. It was also one of two records that Pythag said had lyrics based on lines from Psalm 78 in the Bible, the other being a particular favourite, the reggae song 'Johnny Too Bad' by The Slickers, which was on the soundtrack LP from the film *The Harder They Come* starring Jimmy Cliff.

Pythag loved reggae music, and one time he'd told JJ that the rock mentioned in both of these songs was taken from the Old Testament story of the Exodus. The Israelites are still in the wilderness, having been led across the Red Sea from exile in Egypt, but they are sinning and being struck down, and then they remember that God is their rock and they run to him for forgiveness, but in vain because the rock won't hide or rescue them.

After being told this and listening to the lyrics of other songs, tuning in, it had suddenly seemed to JJ that most of the reggae records in Pythag's collection had some kind of Old Testament or biblical connection. Perhaps it was understandable, too, that JJ couldn't help associating the rock in both songs – whether Nina Simone's or The Slickers' – with the immense dolomitic limestone cliff behind the village, the Baou La Fontaine. Was that what they had all been doing here, in the mountains above Nice – looking for a hiding place? Had they been running to this particular rock for rescue, and if so, was that what was even being offered, or would it be more like the lyrics of the songs: no rock and no rescue, no hiding place?

On another morning, when JJ had been sitting at the table on the veranda having some coffee, he had absently looked up at Sylvie's open window on the opposite side of the square and almost jumped out of his skin to see her sitting there looking directly back at him. Their eyes had met across the distance and it was as if both of them had been taken aback for a second, but then she had smiled and waved – it was a smile that had seemed to transform and illuminate her face – before looking down and going back to whatever it was that she had been working on.

JJ loved to watch Sylvie drawing. He had not yet been invited into her studio, a large room that occupied much of the first floor of her house, but he knew that this was where she stretched the canvases and mixed the pigments and made the paintings that she then sold during the summer season through a couple of small art galleries in Nice and Saint-Paul de Vence, making probably just enough to get by on, and to buy more paint and canvas. But even when she was out and about, Sylvie was constantly drawing. She would fill sketchbook after sketchbook, but also draw or paint on whatever materials she could get her hands on. It had taken JJ several weeks, for example, to notice that the complicated latticework designs on the table legs in Nos Resto had not been carved into the wood, but painted on to it. He loved the exploratory, feathery marks that she would make on paper, so tentative-seeming and yet so precise. It didn't matter whether she was drawing a still life composed of whatever objects were close to hand – a candlestick or a jug on the table while they ate supper, Pythag's chickens when she had thrown them the kitchen scraps – or conjuring some sort of rococo ornament or neoclassical figure from her imagination; he loved to see how an image would gradually coalesce on the page, appearing both solid and ephemeral at the same time.

Milo had offered to cut JJ's hair, so he went and knocked on his door, which was slightly ajar.

'*Oui?*' came the shout from inside. 'JJ?'

Pulling a chair out from the table, Milo gestured his friend to sit down, then picked up a pair of electric clippers and the various combs, the hair guide attachments, which he held up with a shrug. '*Quel numéro?*'

JJ merely shrugged and said, 'The shortest?'

It turned out that the clippers were a souvenir from Milo's army days, although JJ was surprised to learn that his friend hadn't done his national service in France. He considered himself a French Jew, but, because his parents had emigrated to Israel shortly before he was born, he was also an **Israeli** citizen, so had had to do the much longer national service over there: 'So thirty months instead of just twelve!'

The way Milo told it, national service was crazy. One minute you are working in a kibbutz, playing cards and drinking, picking ripe avocado pears from the tree – and the beautiful women, oh my God – and the next it was the sheer bloody terror of fighting in the Lebanon. Then – if you survived, and many didn't – you'd spend weeks

222

at a time, he said, working as a building labourer on any of the many civil-engineering projects that attempted to turn desert into **arable** land or build houses. Either that or you were stuck in the barracks for weeks on end, counting rifles for inspection.

While he gently buzzed away at JJ's hair, they spoke some more about Stonehenge. JJ couldn't tell if they were just chatting or actually making concrete plans. Did that matter? he wondered. Was there even a difference? Milo suggested that if one of Victor's lorries was delivering to the UK, maybe they could take over some cheap wine. Milo and JJ could take Milo's van on the ferry then meet up with Thomas – or whoever was driving for Victor – once they got to England. They could transfer the wine on to Milo's van and then take it to sell at Stonehenge.

Milo had clearly given at least some thought to this plan, and JJ was happy enough to go along with it. He didn't want to be the one to ruin the buzz, for example by telling Milo the truth: that he was broke, that he didn't actually have any money to contribute to buying the wine up front in the first place.

Milo's idea seemed to be that they would only be paying a few francs per bottle but selling them on for maybe two or three pounds each. That way, even giving Thomas or whoever a slice would leave them with a big profit.

'But is that allowed? Wouldn't you have to go through customs?' asked JJ, uncertain whether some kind of import duty or tax might be due on alcohol. Wasn't that why you had to buy it 'duty-free', after all?

He found it relaxing, having his hair cut; the rhythm of it, Milo gently running the clippers across his scalp with one hand and then brushing away the cut hair with the other.

'The *douane*?' said Milo. 'No way, man! Fuck them! They won't be interested in a lorry full of bidets.'

An **adroit** barber, Milo took the comb attachment off the clippers and spent a couple of minutes tidying up the edges, humming under his breath as he did it.

Then he stopped. 'Oh, but hey, not a word of this to Victor, okay?'

JJ thought about it for a second, then shrugged. 'Okay.'

Sylvie was sitting on the wide stone rim of the fountain, with her back to JJ as she filled a jug with water. Hearing his footsteps behind her, she turned and seemed visibly taken aback by the brutal crew cut, his newly shaved head. It was as if she was seeing him for the first time.

JJ enjoyed the moment of attention. 'Do you like—'

'Wow,' she said, grinning broadly. 'Come, let me . . .'

He leaned forward; so close and yet so far. Close enough to feel strands of her long, wavy blonde hair in his mouth, close enough to look down her top, close enough to nibble her ear had they been on such intimate terms. He drank in Sylvie's scent as she reached up to stroke the bristles on his scalp, to feel their nap: soft in one direction, catching like Velcro in the other. As far as JJ was concerned, she could do this all day. The proximity was electrifying.

'Where are you going?' she asked.

The feel of her breath on his cheek was making him hard. Could she tell?

'*À la cuisine*,' he said, nodding in the direction of the communal kitchen of Nos Resto.

'I 'ave food,' she said. Then got up and carried the jug into her house.

JJ didn't need any encouragement to follow her through the front room that he knew, with its bare wooden table and its olive jars, and into the smaller kitchen beyond. As Sylvie put the jug down on the side by the sink, she turned and they both exchanged a quick but knowing glance. There was a sudden recognition of mutual complicity and then they were kissing, JJ running his hands down her back and around her waist, Sylvie pushing JJ towards a kitchen chair, undoing his belt as she did so. Sitting down, he pulled her towards him, and she lifted her skirt to mount him there and then. JJ felt almost as if he was coming up, his nervous system opening up to the onrush of sensations: the smell of her hair or – seen close-up – the texture of the tiny dab of makeup that covered a small **pimple** beneath her lower lip. Looking over her shoulder, JJ could see an unframed photo that was pinned to the wall, of what could only be a teenaged Sylvie in hipster flared jeans and smock top, with a black **pug** on a leash. He was drawn back by the **gentle touch** of her hand guiding him towards her, then the arching of her back as she slipped down on to him. It seemed so **natural** that JJ couldn't help wondering how it had taken them this long. Kissing her neck, he was struck by the slightly bitter taste of her skin, her hands on his shoulders, her tits in his mouth, first one and then the other, his hands on her arse as she rode him. There was a brief moment, no more than a fraction of a second, where they both suddenly looked at each other, each remembering that the front door was still open – the fear of being caught in **flagrante delicto** – but both were so caught up in the rough joy and surprise of the moment that they just laughed and carried on anyway, too far gone to stop now.

III

24: BETTE (CHARD)

Rex had been at Sid's ordering a takeaway jacket **spud** with grilled tuna-melt topping and a beetroot coleslaw on the side when his phone rang. Pulling the mobile out of his pocket and answering, there had been the kind of two- or three-second pause that usually signals an autodialled spam call, but then he had heard that voice from, what, thirty years earlier? Rougher than he remembered, but instantly recognisable. The note of **mischief**. *'Bonjour, mon ami. Is this a bad time?'*

'Not at all,' he'd said, coolly enough not to betray the sudden lurch of something like vertigo. That was the training kicking in: an **anvil** could have landed on his toe and he wouldn't have squeaked! 'Just buying lunch.'

'So, do I gather that you remember our little **bohemia** on the Côte?'

'How could I forget it?'

'Well, you destroyed it, after all. But what surprises me is that you clearly seemed to think that you could just walk away' – he paused for dramatic effect – 'with *impunity*. Surely, you must have known someone would have been looking for you all this time, even if you didn't imagine that it might be me.'

'No, I've had you down for a copper for ages, mate. How else would you have got all that dope through customs? Besides, I saw you.'

'Ah yes, you *Anglons* have a particular **term** for this, *non*? "It takes one to know one"?'

'Oh, yeah? What took you so long, then?'

'Well, you are like one of those special London houses, *non*? The one in the tourist books, that proves to be nothing more than a *façade*' – he pronounced this last word with such French panache that Rex could practically hear the **cedilla**. 'Let's just say that you covered your tracks well, but perhaps not quite well enough. I saw a picture of you being pulled out of the tunnel at **Newbury**. Well, imagine my surprise! I recognised you even with the beard. You hadn't changed very much in ten years.'

So that was it, was it? Someone had certainly changed, though: where had this **high and mighty** attitude come from? The pompous persona seemed completely out of character. Or perhaps it had been there all **along**, and the more jovial and chatty left-wing banter had just been an act.

Of course it had.

Rex had indeed been at the 'Third Battle of Newbury' in 1995, but he'd been undercover; in deep with the protestors and the squatters at the Rickety Bridge and Quercus Circus camps. The campaigners had been trying to prevent the building of the Newbury Bypass, trying to protect ten thousand trees and several sites of special scientific interest – to 'save the snail', as some banners put it – and Rex had been doing his damnedest to prevent them from succeeding, whilst appearing not only to help, but to be central to the cause. The 'twigloos' and other tree houses – the whole aerial village – hadn't worked, so a more hardcore crew had left the Mothership, climbed down from the branches and gone underground in their determination not to let the bulldozers **pass**. He had been one of the instigators, one of the tunnellers, burrowing into Snelsmore Common like **death-watch** beetles into wood, daring the heavy plant to crush them. The then Deputy Chief Constable of the Thames Valley force – a certain Ian Blair – had gained his stripes by hiring climbers, paying them good money to get the protestors out of the trees, and pot-holers for those protestors hiding underground. Of course, he had had Rex and a few others working on the inside too, but credit where it's due, Blair had got the Queen's Medal for it. He'd also received a knighthood and been promoted to Commissioner of the Met too: a stellar career for that particular graduate cop!

Ultimately the Newbury protests had all been in **vain**, so it was mission accomplished. 'Operation Prospect' had been a success. But no invitations to become a **Mason** had landed on Rex's doormat. There were no black-tie **ballroom** dinners, nor monthly meetings in civvies with secret handshakes in the upstairs rooms of anonymous Marylebone pubs. Instead, ten thousand trees had been chopped down as casually as cutting a **hedge**. While the real swampies, the snails, a rare species named Desmoulin's whorls – amazing that Rex could remember his lines after all this time – down there in the wet-lands and the long sedge, had been transported to a new location and promptly became extinct.

'*D'accord*,' the familiar French voice continued. 'We must meet up while I am in town, eh? I'd love to catch up! I'll give you a call, okay? *Bon appétit, mon ami*.'

Fucking **wiseacre**, thought Rex, but just said, '*Merci*. Yeah, let's do that. Maybe we can catch a show.'

'*Oui*, I'd like that. *Bonne journée!*' Then he'd hung up.

Well, they'd been to the theatre, alright, although it might not have been quite the show that the Frenchman would have chosen to see.

Thanks to Terence, he'd been the show.

It would not have been the first 'bare **bodkin**' to be wielded behind the scenes at the Royal Palace, although this time it was not a prop, not a retractable stage dagger that had been so viciously and effectively deployed before being hidden under the workbench in the paint frame. Rex remembered how the knife handle had been **sticky** with blood, then thought the whole thing through **in sequence** once again, for the umpteenth time.

He had suggested they meet at 1 a.m. under the arcade in Russell Street, near the stage door. Terence had confirmed that the stage-door camera was 'on the blink', and he had long ago given Rex a spare key to the paint frame.

And suddenly, there he was, **as large as life**.

Still ruddy-faced and tanned, though bald now, with what was left of his hair close-cropped, and about Terry's height – and weight, too, funnily enough. Much heavier than he had been before, then, and altogether more smartly dressed, but that nose was one in a million. There was no mistaking him, even after thirty-odd years.

'*Bonsoir*,' said Rex, reaching out to shake his old friend's hand.

'Well,' said Milo. 'You must be joking!'

'**Go ahead**,' said Rex, gesturing towards the Long Dock door, which was unlocked.

And it was this exchange that Gertrude Bisika's friend and neighbour Iris had heard, carried by the breeze from an otherwise deserted corner of Drury Lane to her third-floor window in the Peabody flats over the road. French voices, she thought. Foreign men.

'You must be joking!'

Or that was what Iris thought she had heard the gentleman say.

At least, that was what she had told Gertrude Bisika she had heard, and that was what Gertrude had then phoned in turn to tell Rex: 'A foreign voice, a foreign gentleman saying, "You must be joking!"'

Only that isn't what the Frenchman had said.

He hadn't said, 'You must be joking!'

What he'd said was: 'You must be Joe King.'

25: BOULEAU (BIRCH)

Milo was right. Rex had changed his name, or rather JJ had. Back then it had been so easy – practically **standard** practice, in or out of the force – to send **away** a birth certificate and **attach** a new passport photo, **henceforth** to be known as whatever it was. They'd all seen or read *The Day of the Jackal*. But even if he did know about Newbury, how had Milo tracked Rex down here, and made the connection from those days to this? How had Milo managed to follow him all this way, from the junction of the A338 and the A303 in – what was it? Hampshire? Wiltshire? – to the junction of Theobalds Road and Lamb's Conduit Street in Holborn; from the Beanfield to the beat?

Rex had not thought about La Fontaine-en-Forêt for many years. For the sake of his own sanity, he'd actively suppressed the memories and got on with his new life. He'd got good at it too; compartmentalising, and unthinkingly performing whatever role was required. But now here was Milo in London – well, a bald guy in a fat suit who was still somehow unmistakably Milo – and although Rex had rehearsed some sort of confrontation with him many times in his imagination, particularly in the months and years immediately following that terrible June day, it had never been this way around. In those imaginary encounters it had always been Rex confronting Milo and dictating the terms, not Milo confronting Rex on his. Now that his old— no, his former friend was standing right in front of him, those long-buried memories came rushing back in with all the subtlety of a **scud** missile, and Rex realised that he was not as **prepared** as he'd thought he might be.

Béatrice – poor, beautiful Béatrice, it didn't bear thinking about – had said she would throw Milo and JJ a leaving party the night before they set off, and that night had arrived too suddenly. Reluctantly JJ had got up, leaving his beautiful love, Sylvie, in her rumpled bed, where they'd been enjoying a last siesta. What was he doing? When JJ had agreed to go to Stonehenge with Milo, he and Sylvie hadn't really been a thing yet. Now that they were, he was going to miss her like crazy. JJ wanted to abandon the whole thing, but naive as he was, he felt that he couldn't let his friend down, didn't want to stitch him up. He wasn't putting any money into Milo's crazy scheme, so the least he could do was lend a hand and keep him company during the long drive north. And anyway, he'd be back in less than two weeks.

'It will be fun,' Sylvie had said. 'I will miss you, but you will have fun and I 'ave to make lots of paintings for the summer.'

Milo's door was ajar, and when JJ knocked and walked into the converted **cow-house**, he found his friend packing. Milo was evidently more organised than JJ, for whom packing meant grabbing fistfuls of clothes and shoving as much seemingly random junk as possible into his rucksack. Milo's bag was about half the size of JJ's, and his approach was far more scientific. JJ watched as Milo picked a shirt up delicately by the yoke and with two hands, so that it hung there, dangling like a flag on a windless day. Then he gently shook it out to get rid of any creases before folding it in half, shoulder to shoulder, and – tucking the collar in first – deftly rolling and gathering it into a tight and space-saving sausage. Milo repeated this well-practised routine – hang, shake, tuck in and roll up – with a couple of T-shirts and a spare pair of trousers. It reminded JJ of his grandparents' asparagus-growing ex-army neighbour, long dead now, but for whom even the smallest task – lighting a pipe, or putting biscuits on a plate – was executed with military precision.

'Wow,' said JJ. 'Wanna do mine?'

'I learn this in the army. It means the clothes are straight, your uniform, when you take them out, *oui*?' said Milo, laughing. With a brief turn of the head, he lifted his chin to point: 'Help yourself.'

JJ turned and looked. There was an unlit joint in the ashtray. Next to it were two small glasses, a jug of water and an open bottle of Ricard. One glass was full of the milky liquid, and some splashes of water had begun to soak into the wooden tabletop at its base, darkening it and exposing the grain. JJ poured some of the clear and golden aniseed spirit into the empty glass and then poured in a little water to watch the chemical reaction before taking a sip and reaching over to pick up the doobie.

'A few years ago Victor would have killed you,' Milo said, matter-of-factly. 'He and Sylvie, they were inseparable. They were that kind of couple who everyone love because they are so much in love?'

'*Oui*,' said JJ, passing the joint to Milo. 'Sylvie told me, but she said that after a while it was too much. She felt as if she could not breathe.'

'*C'est vrai*,' said Milo eventually, '*et* because 'e love 'er so much 'e 'ave no choice but to let 'er go. That is when 'e move out of their place.'

Sylvie had told him more than this, in fact – much more – but JJ was not about to share those confidences with Milo. One afternoon after they had made love, she told JJ how, when they'd lived in Victor's apartment on the Avenue de la Résistance in Vence, he had been obsessed not only with her but also with watching other men's reactions to her. More than that, he got off on it. She told him that Victor was a **voyeur**. That in their erotic games he would ask

235

her to go out dressed in her shortest skirt and her highest heels, *sans* bra or knickers, with her nipples outlined in dark lipstick so that they would show through her blouse or top. She told JJ how, dressed like this, she would have to go to the market in the Place du Grand Jardin while Victor watched from the window of their flat, masturbating furiously, transfixed by her beauty even at this distance, but also aroused and tormented by everyone else's reactions, by the libidinous chaos that, thus attired, she would inevitably leave in her wake. From his second-floor vantage point, Victor could watch her every high-heeled step of the way there and back, clocking every sideways glance, every double take at her big, dark nipples, every catcall and wolf whistle, every man who crossed the street to try to say hello, every man who sped up to take another look, everyone who stared at her freely bouncing breasts, everyone who slowed down to follow her, everyone who angled themselves to see up her skirt, just for that millisecond-glimpse of buttock or bush when she bent over to pick up her basket, every kerb crawler, every driver who came around again, everyone who brushed past her or tried to grab her arse or who put their hand between her legs, everyone who reached out to grope or touch her breasts, every man who implored her to stop, who proposed marriage, who tried to lure her into an alleyway, every group of young men that swarmed around her, all of these reactions, this multiplication and proliferation of sexual energy, only magnified Victor's desire, only sped the blood-flow into his big hard-on, until the moment when, walking back, passing Monoprix and the steps up to the Chapelle des Pénitents Blancs, she would look up and catch his eye and nod, before – feeling almost bathed in his gaze – crossing the road and letting herself into their building and walking up the stairs clip-clop-clip to the open door of their flat, where, if he hadn't come already, shot his load at the moment their eyes had met,

236

she would walk over and put her hands on his shoulders and lift a leg to mount him and they would fuck for hours in every room, on the floor and against the wall and from every angle and on every item of furniture that could take the weight, and they would fuck and fuck and fuck like that until tired and sore and spent they simply could not fuck any more.

Nestled in the security of her new lover's arms, Sylvie had told JJ that she'd thought these games would stop once they found this place and moved out to La Fontaine-en-Forêt. In fact the difficulty that they now faced, living where they did, in enacting such erotic scenarios, only served to intensify Victor's voyeuristic appetites. But for Sylvie, being roughly jostled by farmers in the more **restricted** space of the crowds at the weekly Tuesday market in the square at La Fontaine-lès-Vence or Wednesdays in Tourrettes left her feeling more bruised and bewildered than aroused. The game suddenly lost its erotic charge, and with that loss she found that her relationship with Victor was also kaput. In retrospect, the attention she had received amidst the relative decorum of the Avenue de la Résistance in Vence seemed practically courtly by comparison with the groping proximity of the market crowd, where someone might roughly grab both of her breasts or lift her skirt and finger her with impunity as they squeezed past in the throng. And on top of that, to then have to walk home along the verge, dodging traffic before clambering up through the undergrowth by the side of the Route de Grasse in her high heels, batting away the horseflies, while Victor followed trying to look up her skirt. She had rolled her eyes and shrugged. 'I was tired, and I realise that I didn't love 'im any more, so I ask 'im to move out.'

Propping herself up on her elbow and pulling the sheet across her hip as if it offered some protection against the memory of those former sad times, Sylvie had told JJ that it had taken both of them, but Victor especially, a while to come to terms with what they had lost. For Victor, to have gone from prospective **bridegroom** to **bachelor** in the blink of an eye was not an easy thing to take, and for a while he had gone off the rails: drinking and fucking anything that moved, including the big-titted old whore in La Fontaine-lès-Vence who only came out at closing time in her still head-turning halter-neck tops and miniskirts, and in whom for a while at least – with his cock between her breasts, say, or pulling her tits out of her top to suck and pinch her big nipples, or watching them swing back and forth while she bent over for some toilet-stall knee-trembler – Victor had found some faint refracted glimmer of the reaction that Sylvie had inspired.

What had eventually shaken him out of this downward spiral, what had stopped Victor from ending up like every other drunken farmer in the Alpes-Maritimes region, was the death of his mother up in Strasbourg. Sylvie and the others had waved him off in the car park at La Fontaine-lès-Vence as he'd set off, solemn and red-eyed, on the long drive home for her funeral. Sylvie had told JJ that, in the boyishness of his behaviour, his bereftness in the face of such a primal loss, she had almost fallen in love with him all over again, but then he had accelerated out on to the road and with a slight squeal of brakes and a beep of the horn turned the corner and down the mountain to hop along the coast road to Genoa, then up through Switzerland and on to Strasbourg.

And even this trip had not been without event, including an inexplicable drunken detour a couple of hundred miles north into Germany on the day before the funeral, where Victor got himself arrested in a fight in some **Dortmund** *bier-keller*. Luckily he had been released without charge the next day, and with just enough time to drive back to Strasbourg.

It was the money that Victor inherited from his late mother, Sylvie had explained as she kissed JJ's belly and as he gently stroked the soft and petal-like skin of her inner thigh, that enabled Victor to start the business, to invest in the plant he needed for the factory and to begin the process of restoration here at La Fontaine-en-Forêt. By the time she had finished telling the story, JJ was hard again and all thoughts of Victor had been forgotten as he and Sylvie made love once more.

Walking over to Nos Resto, Milo and JJ were pleasantly stoned. By JJ's natural rule of thumb it was still daytime; that is, the cry of swifts in flight and the all-pervasive **cicada** chirrup that filled the sun-warmed air had not yet given way to screech of owl or the constant nocturnal croaking of the myriad frogs that lived far below along the watercourses that had carved these great tree-lined gorges.

Béatrice had baked a large, circular **loaf**, which was out on the olive-wood breadboard with a bread knife, some butter and a bowl of olives. She was in the kitchen next door, so JJ popped his head around the door and asked if there was anything he could do. He had to shout because she had the music up really loud. It was a record that she often listened to while she cooked: a box set of harpsichord concertos by Johann Sebastian **Bach**. JJ had come to love it too. Even though he knew next to nothing about classical music, there was something about the way that Bach seemed to be able to carve time itself into such impossible patterns that appealed to him. He shouted again, but Béatrice was in the middle of inspecting something in the oven and it was only as she closed the door and stood up that she saw him there.

Suddenly JJ caught a fragrant waft of whatever was cooking.

'Wow,' he said, taking a pantomime sniff. *'Qu'est-ce que c'est?'*

Looking up at Pythag's blackboard as he buttered a thick slice of

Béatrice's bread, JJ realised that the dish that smelled so good, so sweetly spiced and aromatic, was merely the appropriate fruit for the revolutionary **season**: by Pythag's reckoning, today's date – 25 May 1985 to the rest of the world – was the fifth day of *Prairial* 193, a day that was dedicated to the life-giving *canard*. Perhaps the big, red-faced ducks he'd seen in many of the farms that he and Milo had driven past, which he had grown up in the UK referring to as Muscovy ducks, but which Milo had told him were known here as *canard de Barbarie*.

Over the months that he had been staying here in La Fontaine-en-Forêt, JJ had grown to love the way that his new friends – Béatrice and Pythag, Victor, Milo, Élise and Sylvie – took great delight in observing the Republican Calendar, and taking some daily cue from the plant or animal, the tool, perhaps, or practice that each day embodied. This might mean eating an Algerian-style pigeon filo pie, or making mushroom soup on the appropriate day. It might mean something as minor as sprinkling freshly snipped chives on to their scrambled eggs, or as major as slaughtering a pig, or putting on the beekeeping suits to repair the hives, or cleaning out Pythag's beloved chicken coops in order to compost down their ammonia-smelling and nitrogen-rich manure for use on the gardens in the following spring. All of this, each of these thoughts-turned-conscious-actions, constituted a form of joyful adherence to, or a living out of, the revolutionary principles by which they had chosen to live their lives. The fact that today was a special occasion, that tomorrow JJ would set off to **ride** shotgun with Milo on their two-week road trip to Stonehenge, meant that, rather than simply feeding the ducks in the public gardens off the Promenade des Anglais in Nice or buying a big tin of *cassoulet au confit*, Béatrice was instead cooking her and Pythag's favourite: duck *à l'orange*. JJ felt really touched; honoured.

Since he had arrived in La Fontaine-en-Forêt— No, since he had got off the train at Cagnes-sur-Mer, JJ had been made to feel nothing but welcome, and it was Pythag and Béatrice who had initially made him feel most welcome of all. Pythag who had suggested that he stay, and then nominated him as a new member of the commune. JJ really appreciated that they had taken on an almost parental role with their English visitor, their pet punk, even though they were only a decade older than him at most.

Perhaps he was a little stoned, but looking out over the gorge from the terrace at Nos Resto, it almost seemed as if there was a relationship between the games that Bach's concertos were playing with time and the impossible geometries that the thousands upon thousands of swifts were carving through the air. The frills and rushes of Bach's music seemingly equal to the impossibly swift – *duh!* – choreographies of the tiny birds.

Sitting there, as he was, on the eve of a trip to Stonehenge, with forty cases of wine already on their way to England in a consignment of Victor's high-end toilet ware, with a piece of fresh bread and butter in his hand, with Béatrice cooking in the old *bar-tabac* next door, and knowing that right now Sylvie, his golden-skinned and tousle-haired lover – *trop, trop belle Sylvie!* – was still naked in her bed on the other side of the square, JJ had what he would later come to recognise as a dangerous thought: that he had never been happier.

'What's this?' Susan asked, propping herself up in Rex's bed and smoothing the sheet across her breasts.

'Bach,' said Rex, coming back in with two cups of coffee and a couple of glasses of orange juice on a tray. 'Concerto number one for harpsichord and strings, second movement. Sorry, I couldn't get back to sleep, so I thought I might as well make us some coffee.'

Rex might have woken early, but at least he had slept soundly, at least he hadn't been dreaming about Tennyson. Susan had taken his mind off that, alright.

On his bedside table was what the trendy shop on Lamb's Conduit Street had called a '**ewer**', a tall and knobbly 1970s water jug in shades of red and orange, into which Rex – making an effort once it was clear that Susan would be coming back – had stood a few birch twigs from the florist, resplendent with their young green leaves and catkins. He put the tray down next to it.

'I didn't have you down for a classical music fan,' said Susan.

'I'm not really,' said Rex, handing her a glass, 'but for some reason I've always loved this, and a few other things; bits of Mozart. Just that it's taken me years to actually buy it. I've had a real yen for it these past few days. Do you mind?'

'Not at all, I love it,' said Susan, smiling. 'I'm enjoying finding out things about you, you know.'

'Ha! Thanks,' said Rex, holding her gaze. 'Me too. Finding out what makes you tick.'

'Now, then,' said Susan, taking a long sip of juice and looking at him over the top of the glass, 'you're making me blush. But listen, Rex, you've been such **a great help** this past week or so. What with Ashley in hospital and everything, I don't know how I'd have coped without you; our time together.'

'Well, the feeling's mutual,' Rex said. And it was. More than just a romantic interest or a bit on the side, knowing that he'd be meeting Susan after work, whatever time that might be, had helped him get through what might otherwise have been an impossible time. 'I'm glad I bumped into you, you know that.'

'Me too,' she said, patting his side of the bed. 'You're glad I called you back, then?'

'Not half,' he said, putting his coffee down on the bedside table, and leaning over to kiss her upturned face, 'but if you hadn't called me, I'd have called you.'

'Are you sure?' asked Susan, laughing.

'Chance to do this?' he said, pulling the sheet down to expose her breasts. 'You bet!' He bent down to kiss them each in turn, enjoying the taste of her skin and feeling her nipples hardening to the touch of his lips and tongue, feeling Susan arching her back slightly.

'Did you grow up in London?' Susan asked later, as they drank their cups of cold coffee.

'No, Exeter,' said Rex – there was no reason to **skid** around now – 'but I came to London to go to college.'

'You've got a degree?'

Was that a note of surprise in her voice?

'I know! Graduate policemen are a figure of fun in the force, but there was this scheme—'

'Oh, I might have guessed: a quota,' said Susan, gently ribbing him.

'The "High Potential Developer Scheme", it was called, "for Graduates". A few chief constables started out that way and all.'

'A few chief constables and you?'

'Yeah, you could say that.'

'Any chance of you—'

'What, becoming a chief constable? I should coco. How about you, Susan?'

'**Classics.**'

'Oh,' said Rex, impressed. 'And how was that?'

'Well,' said Susan, 'if you think that being a graduate policeman makes you a figure of fun, try being a black woman at Oxford.'

'Ouch, I can imagine.'

'I lost count of the number of times I'd walk into a seminar room or a lecture theatre and some dozy don would make eye contact and tell me they weren't finished yet, or point at the coffee things, assuming that I was a cleaner, or from Building Services.'

Christ almighty! Rex thought to himself, and almost said out loud. He practically spat out his coffee, but didn't let on. He pretended to be surprised by what Susan was saying. 'Blimey, in this day and age? Are you kidding?'

Cleaner.

Of course! Rex knew where he had heard the surname Bisika before. As in Gertrude Bisika, the cleaner at the Royal Palace Theatre, with the little framed photo on top of the television in her Peabody flat on Drury Lane.

'I know,' said Susan. 'And these were supposed to be the clever ones. Oxford dons! Not National Front meatheads or anything.'

'Not many of *them* at Oxford, I'd guess,' said Rex.

'Not many, no,' Susan said. 'But plenty in the town.'

Rex made a mental note. The witness in the Tennyson case, the work colleague who said that he had lent Trevor Tennyson his inhaler once or twice when the younger man had forgotten his. The Post Office colleague whose testimony had unwittingly but effectively destroyed the case against the four policemen charged with Trevor Tennyson's murder, his name had been **Benedick** Bisika. He was Gertrude Bisika's late husband.

'There's a few in the force, though,' Rex said, 'unfortunately. Racist, sexist, homophobic, the works. Like you wouldn't believe.'

'Yes, I know,' said Susan. 'I'm black.'

26: JONQUILLE (JONQUIL)

It was **dusk** when JJ arrived back at his grandmother's house in Exeter. It felt as if he'd been running for days, and he had waited until it was nearly dark to make sure no one had followed him. The **snag**, as he well knew, was that he'd be easy enough to find in any case. He would have to do something about that.

JJ was no longer tripping, but it still seemed as if there were policemen lurking in every shadow, and at every turn, or just out of sight in the corner of his eye. Masked and boiler-suited, armed with axes and batons. As if at any second he might have to run for his life. Again.

A branch of May, my dear, I say, he thought, the song still going around in his head. Before your door I stand . . .

Hearing the bell, his grandmother looked up from her newspaper, glancing at the mirror above the bureau to the right of the living-room window – which was positioned just so – and recognising JJ's **profile** as he stood there in the porch. She was shocked by the appearance of her **grandson**, and if he'd been paying attention he might have been shocked, too, by how much she had aged in just the few weeks since he had last seen her. His grandmother had always teased JJ that he was a bit of a **scruff**, but suntan or not, he looked to her as if he'd been dragged through a hedge backwards; like he'd been through the wringer. He felt like it too. Like he'd seen something that he shouldn't have seen. As he **shut** the door behind him, she wondered if he might have been crying.

'Where are your things?' she'd asked. And it was only then that JJ remembered that his rucksack had been tucked behind the passenger seat in Milo's van.

'Um,' he started to say, but there was too much to explain, so he just let it hang.

'Well, there's clean clothes in your room,' she said putting a hand to his troubled forehead. 'Why not have a hot bath and I'll make us some supper. I've got something in the freezer you'll like.'

Half an hour later, JJ was sitting on his grandmother's **mauve** sofa watching TV in jeans and a T-shirt, with a **generous** helping of home-made **cottage pie** and a small tin of **beer** on a tray on his lap. There was a documentary on telly about the First World War poets. JJ had done them for his English literature O-level, so knew most of the poems by heart. Well, he usually did, although right now everything looked and sounded strange, and not least because everyone was speaking in English. It was all slogging to **Arras** with whatever it was; cheerful sods and incompetent plans. While the words were read aloud by an actor with a slightly **stuck-up** voice that JJ almost recognised but couldn't quite place, the camera showed pages from Siegfried Sassoon's notebooks, then a **galley proof** of the actual poem that was being read – 'The General', it was called – which had been corrected and annotated in Sassoon's own handwriting.

JJ ate his tea in silence while he watched, shovelling the food at a steady **pace**, stopping only to take an occasional sip of the fizzy lager. On the television there were lingering shots of the **Cenotaph** and of poppies growing, **garnet**-red, on the edges of Flanders fields, amidst the daisies and the **jonquil**. A single poppy waving on its tall **stem**. There was talk of Shelley, of poets being the 'unacknowledged legislators', and of how these poems of the Great War could be seen as an attempt to **adjudicate** between the myth of noble sacrifice and the more prosaic reality of tactical blunders and wholesale unnecessary slaughter, of warfare being conducted on a vast and industrial scale. What those poor men had been forced to **forgo** in those dismal trenches – under pain of court martial and the firing squad; the threat of the stigma of cowardice – seemingly included the luxury of life itself, a desperate waste that was epitomised by Wilfred Owen's needlessly re-enlisting only to be killed in the last weeks of the war. And if, as he watched this, JJ felt like he'd been through a battle himself, that was because he had.

When the programme finished and the *News at Ten* came on, JJ didn't move, and later his grandmother would simply put a blanket over his shoulders where he sat. He half expected to see himself on this item about 'new-age travellers' and Stonehenge. They showed footage of people sawing through a fence, the announcer saying that they had been making weapons to attack the police, and JJ didn't have the fight in him to say, 'No! They were sawing through the fence to try to escape!', but he knew that's what they'd been doing because he had been there.

The voiceover said that police had been forced to defend themselves after a considerable number of vehicles in the so-called 'Peace Convoy' had tried to run police officers down.

This was the opposite of what had happened. Who was writing this stuff?

Here was footage of the convoy bowling down the A338 from Savernake! The pink-painted army patrol vehicle! The yellow British Telecom van towing a caravan! Two coaches bouncing across a field at sunset, narrowly missing each other. There were people being calmly arrested by bobbies in old-fashioned helmets, no footage of the masked goons – squaddies? – in unnumbered black boiler suits wading in and cracking skulls. Five hundred arrests!

Later in the bulletin there was an update on the Riviera bombing.

Even more than 'the battle of Stonehenge', as they were already calling it, this was the **topic** he had not wanted to broach, the news that he hadn't wanted to see. News that he had heard first of all on the radio in the cab of the lorry that had picked him up when he'd stuck his thumb out at a **red light** in Salisbury, when he had still thought he was only running from Milo and the massed ranks of the police who had ambushed the convoy. He was still reeling from the sudden irreversible jolt of recognition and vertigo. The wave of grief and nausea had been overwhelming as the news story about ETA having 'not yet claimed responsibility for the blast' became a story about people and places that he knew. JJ had had to beg the driver to stop and let him out of the cab, and as the lorry had hissed to a halt, he had flung the door open and leaped down on to the verge, where he collapsed, sobbing and vomiting on to the dirty, litter-strewn grass: *Sylvie!*

And now on the *News at Ten*, here was Alastair Burnet saying words like 'terrorist cell' and 'high explosives' over pictures of Pythag, Béatrice and Élise. There had been a series of explosions, he said; deaths. Terrorists – Basque separatists, it seemed – had blown themselves up while attempting to bomb a simple festival in a small French tourist town. As part of what seemed to be a plan to escalate and broaden ETA's campaign on a new front, they had tried to bring death to a harmless annual celebration that was being enjoyed, as it was every year, by dozens of children and by tourists and French locals alike. Luckily the cell had been infiltrated by the French security services, and the terrorists had only succeeded in killing themselves.

There was a photo of French police cars, and of a cordon across the Route de Grasse, then footage of the great ruined viaduct at Pont-du-Loup, victim of an earlier bombing at the end of the

Second World War. An ITN correspondent was speaking to camera from the main square at La Fontaine-lès-Vence. They showed a shaky tourist video of an artificially created rainbow above the rooftops of an otherwise sun-baked French village, pictures of people in rainbow T-shirts enjoying a water slide and a parade. Then it cut with a jerk to a great cloud of dark smoke climbing above the olive groves and a menhir on the brow of some foreign hill, behind which JJ could plainly see a familiar rocky **outcrop**. This was the image that had already been on the front page of most European newspapers that day, too, if JJ had only seen them: a pall of smoke rising into the air before the unmistakable inverted 'V' shape of the dolomitic limestone cliff at Baou La Fontaine.

27: AULNE (ALDER)

Milo and JJ had arranged to meet Victor's driver **Tom** in the car park at Fleet Services on the westbound carriageway of the M3. They'd arrived a bit early, so waited in the Wimpy Bar. For JJ, the **bland** and tasteless burger with its limp iceberg lettuce and pink mayonnaise was seasoned by both hunger and nostalgia, but nothing would persuade Milo to try even a mouthful. He merely looked on with an expression somewhere between incredulity and disdain, which was only exacerbated when he tasted his coffee. It felt strange to JJ that he could understand all the conversations going on around him. A couple of blokes at the next table were talking football, and it was all Don **Revie** this, Brian Clough that, and Kevin Keegan the other. He wished he could have switched the conversation off. He wished they were back in France.

Truth be told, JJ was missing Sylvie like crazy. They had spent most of the last night before JJ's trip making love. First in her **bubble bath**, after which she'd put on a tiny **baby doll** nightie and they'd fucked like it was going out of fashion, she gripping the **bedstead** with both hands and crying out in filthy broken English like some Bloomsbury **bawd**. Holding each other after they'd made love, Sylvie had surprised him by wiping up some of his sperm with her finger and smearing it around the inside of the pearl-encrusted golden **locket** that she was wearing around her neck, before clicking it shut and lifting it to her mouth to kiss it. Then they had slept in each other's arms, neither wanting to let the other go.

That had been more than twenty-four hours ago. Right now, at Fleet Services, it was cold, and the only other people around seemed to be on two wheels. In one corner of the car park were some bikers who looked about as hardcore as you could get without being Angels. At least, they weren't wearing patches. These were ex-army types, Paras or Marines by the looks of it, with their cropped hair and MA1s, on chopped-up Kawasaki Zeds and Suzuki GS1100s, but definitely not **wardroom** material. While this lot loudly regaled each other with war stories – these were friendships forged in **combat**, after all, whether Northern Ireland or the Falklands – a handful of self-conscious teenagers on 'Fizzies', Yamaha FS1E mopeds, smoked furiously and tried to put in a **creditable** performance of not being shit-scared.

'I'd fucking kill anyone who gave an animal acid, though,' said one of the big boys, loud enough that they could hear. 'Fucking kill 'em.' And from his expression, JJ thought this sounded like an honest threat, if such a situation ever **arose**.

When the bikers eventually revved up to roll out of there, one of them swung a long loop around the car park, ignoring JJ and Milo but beckoning one of the Fizzy boys over. The youngster meekly obeyed, but probably wished he hadn't because all he got was bellowed at. Something along the lines of, 'Don't forget your **stabiliser**, you fucking pranny!'

None of them had even given JJ and Milo a second glance as they transferred the cases of wine from lorry to van, even though it had taken them fully half an hour to finish the job. Tom said that he was planning to stay the night in the lay-by here at Fleet before delivering his load of bathroom ware – toilets, washbasins and bidets – to an upmarket shop in Weybridge that catered to the St George's Hill set. These were rock stars and art collectors. The kind of people who had original Lowrys and Picassos on their walls, and who spent half the year down in their villas on the Côte, lunching at the Colombe d'Or or opening up their Ferraris for a quick **burst** from Monaco to Saint-Tropez, and who evidently wanted to bring a bit of that Gallic glamour into their Surrey en-suites. They couldn't get enough of it, which was handy for Victor. And for everyone else, since what was good for Victor was generally good for La Fontaine-en-Forêt too.

JJ's old school friend Andy lived not so far from Fleet. He was at college nearby in Farnham, so had been renting a bedsit in a shared house in Aldershot during his first year. Not too bad, he'd said, the last time they spoke, which would have been just after Christmas, as long as you can steer clear of the psycho squaddies who'd wander around **blotto** most weekends looking for a fight. JJ would have liked to have taken a detour and dropped by, kipped on Andy's floor, seen if he fancied another trip to Stonehenge, but Milo had put some feelers out and arranged to meet some of the Peace Convoy down in Savernake Forest, so they were headed down that way.

Of course they were.

Before they left, Milo gave Tom an eighth of double-zero for his trouble, enough to keep him pleasantly stoned for the duration, and promised another half-ounce when they got back to France in two weeks. Quite how he had managed to bring so much hash through customs was a mystery to JJ, but Milo had been fearless. He'd picked up a couple of cling-film-wrapped weights in Fréjus as usual, but had then simply tossed the carrier bag they were in under the driver's seat of his van. He hadn't even bothered to hide the slabs in the back of the socket set, where he usually put his dope. Talk about brazen. When they'd driven off the ferry at Dover and turned the corner to drive through the 'Nothing to Declare' lane, there were customs officials everywhere, which certainly didn't **bode** well. JJ had been terrified, certain it would **turn out** badly. They were swarming all over every vehicle, but as Milo had driven up they'd seemed to melt away. It had been as if Milo's old Citroën van was invisible. They had looked straight through them.

'How did you manage that?' JJ had asked, once they were safely out of Dover and **bowling** up the motorway. 'I was shitting it. I was sure we were going to be busted.'

'You 'ave to look so bored and so boring that they don't even see you,' said Milo with a shrug. 'Completely ordinary and boring. That's it.'

And this had seemed perfectly reasonable at the time – of course it had! – but looking back on it as he made his way to their rendezvous, Rex could only laugh, because back then Milo had looked anything but boring. Skinny and suntanned in his battered old Citroën box van, permanently bleary-eyed, with his filthy sleeveless T-shirt and wraparound shades, oversized combats and his *Taxi Driver* Mohawk – the shaved-sided crew cut – he looked like an archetypal stoner, the kind of bloke you'd think would get stopped and searched whenever he set foot in a public place. In terms that even the **layman** would understand, he stuck out like a fucking sore thumb.

It was so obvious, even then. The guy had a free pass! How could they not have seen that Milo was a copper? Rex had found out for himself, soon enough, but by then, of course, it had been too late to warn the others. Too late for anything.

It's always the guy with the van, Rex thought, and the money. The one who has a good backstory and a full wallet, but no visible means of support. The one who's super-helpful and super-friendly, but who's got to go away very suddenly and to somewhere very far away. Rex had more reason than most to know all this, since he had occasionally been that guy himself, back in the mid-nineties. But luckily

Rex hadn't needed to hide out in Australia or Argentina or wherever once that posting was over. He'd simply shaved off the 'white Rasta' dreads and the beard – with all its plaited-in beads and seashells – and had a wash, and he'd been unrecognisable. Rex had even seen Swampy and Co. in the street in London one time, and it was his proud boast that there was honestly not a flicker of recognition; not a fucking flicker.

But now another old rat had crawled back out of whichever sewer it was he'd been hiding in, only this time there was no need for a disguise. Not yet, anyway.

For a second, Rex had thought about meeting Milo in one of the anonymous cafe chains on Kingsway near the old **tramway** tunnel, losing themselves amongst the office workers, but then he'd thought better of it. He didn't know what his former friend was like these days – what he was like in real life! – and didn't want to risk him overplaying the old **hail**-fellow-well-met routine and turning them into some kind of **side-show**; to draw attention and give people something to **blab** about. Instead, Rex had figured that he'd meet him out the back of the Royal Palace Theatre. That was where he usually met his grasses, so what was the difference. He could tip Terence the wink and he'd accidentally-on-purpose flip the fuse on the stage-door CCTV camera's power supply, like he'd done a few times before. That way Rex knew that he could be doubly discreet, but also that Terry might be lurking around and have his back, just in case the **balloon** went up, which it might well do. Although, as he crossed over a deserted Drury Lane, Rex had no idea just how bad things would get. Well, not strictly true. He was ready for anything, but he didn't necessarily fully comprehend that before the night was out his old mate Milo would be just another **cadaver** – a nameless, noseless mystery to be solved; or not! – nor that he and Terence would find themselves with some pretty quick thinking to do.

Luckily, if there's one thing Rex was good at, it was thinking on his feet.

28: COUVOIR (HATCHERY)

By the time JJ and Milo had arrived in Savernake, the Peace Convoy had been there for a week or two, rolling in from their wintering place up in Leeds to set up camp. They had permission to be here too, and everyone knew that this was as close to Stonehenge as they could get without being moved on. Since then, more people had been arriving every day. Some in family cars – Escorts and Cortinas – or vintage camper vans, others on motorbikes or in brightly painted old Bedford lorries or army trucks and Land Rovers, some pulling caravans. Smoke curled out of the cone-topped flues that emerged from the roofs of converted buses and ambulances once destined for the scrapheap but now given a new lease of life as homes. There was a bus with STONEHENGE JUNE 1985 – GO FOR IT! painted on the front, a heavily laden and battered old Austin Princess with STONEHENGE HERE WE COME written on the driver's door in marker pen. One bus had been converted into a theatre, and another— Yes, there it was now, pulling in off the main track: a bit of British motoring history, a real museum piece, a labour of love! So JJ hadn't imagined it: a vintage, purpose-built mobile cinema, its projector housed in a great glass dome above the cab, and pulling what looked to be a box office cum power unit in a separate matching-liveried trailer.

Wandering around the site, JJ could readily see that this was not an army of anarchists mustering for war. It was not an evil incubator from which some antisocial new-age hydra might emerge, come to wreak destruction upon the land, but a diverse group of mostly young people, many of them with babies and young children. Living life on slender means, perhaps, but all wanting nothing more than the chance to make a decent fist of it. There were Greens and peace protestors, space rockers and druids, Greenham women, hippies, posi-punks, soul boys and casuals, you name it. People were pitching tents and building fires, playing guitars and singing. All of them intent on nothing more than continuing their chosen way of life, celebrating a psychedelic solstice, sure, some of them, but also exercising what all were convinced was their inalienable, centuries-old right to gather peacefully for a free festival, rather than be herded into the mass-produced version down the road that cost sixteen pounds to get into: half a week's dole money!

The gathering at Savernake was not so different from the commune at La Fontaine-en-Forêt. JJ could see why Milo had wanted to come, because this was what it looked like when people put into practice the revolutionary principles by which they had chosen to live their lives. Would the commune be able to survive on the road, JJ wondered, if it ever had to leave La Fontaine-en-Forêt? He supposed it was unlikely, but not impossible. What if they were ever evicted?

Savernake was almost like a festival in its own right, like a festival should be, albeit without the stages and the sound systems, and though he missed Sylvie, these were an idyllic couple of days for JJ. There were no leaders here, no anarchist generals, no lieutenants and warriors, but the plan such as it was, as far as JJ could gather from his numerous campfire conversations, was to wait here until there was a critical mass of people, and then by sheer strength of numbers to take the Stonehenge site for as much of June as possible. Not to wait for Solstice Eve, but to get there early. Hanging around here for too long would only give the police more time to prepare. This way they'd have surprise on their side. From Savernake they could be on-site in forty-five minutes, and that was nowhere near enough time for court orders or warrants to be issued.

With bunting and flags hanging from some of the buses, with the sounds of singing voices being carried on the warm May breeze, and the sour smell of the hawthorn blossom that bedecked every hedge, JJ found himself remembering school festivities in his childhood. The headmistress of his primary school in Exeter had built singing and country dancing into the timetable, incorporating traditional country celebrations into the school calendar. Many years later, accompanying Helen to a concert at Cecil Sharp House near Regent's Park in London – home of the English Folk Dance and Song Society – he would realise that this hadn't appeared from nowhere, and wonder whether as a young woman Mrs Gummer must in turn herself have been taught by exponents of that first English folk revival, with its rural romanticism and its classical arrangements of agricultural rather than urban or industrial song. Perhaps she had wanted to soften the lines of the new-build 1960s school building she found herself in charge of, by aligning it with these more archaic and traditional forms of folk art. Certainly JJ remembered May Day celebrations, on warm days just like this one. May Days that had been less to do with working-class solidarity than an excuse for maypole and morris dancing. The school choir on the playing field, singing the 'May Day Carol':

I've been a-rambling all the night,
And the best part of the day;
And now I am returning back again,
I have brought you a branch of May.

The first of June dawned bright and sunny, but JJ felt homesick for La Fontaine-en-Forêt. He missed Sylvie's bed most of all, but right about now he might ordinarily be learning t'ai chi moves from Victor, or helping Béatrice with some cooking. He missed Élise's history lessons, and her brother with his almanac and his daily calculations. JJ wondered what the revolutionary date might be today, though he knew full well what day it was here in Wiltshire.

In Wiltshire it was D-Day.

Word had gone around the night before that this was going to be it, so as soon as it had started to get light, people had begun striking tents, putting out fires and packing up, although it would take another few hours to actually get out on to the road. It was about 1 o'clock by the time that a flag-flying blue coach led the convoy out on to the A338 and turned south towards Shipton Bellinger.

The hedges alongside the road were bedecked with white and pink hawthorn blossom. JJ had bought some Spider's Web acid from a Leeds goth who had travelled down with the Peace Convoy, and this time he planned to be tripping when they arrived at Stonehenge. Milo looked at him like he was crazy, but JJ dropped one anyway. The sun was shining and the mood in the convoy was good, and if Stonehenge was only forty-five minutes away, then he'd be safe and sound on the site before it really kicked in.

That was the theory, anyway, but perhaps it didn't take account of British roads, because before they'd gone about twenty minutes the convoy slowed down to a crawl.

'*Putain merde!*' said Milo, slapping his steering wheel in frustration. He opened the flaps on the dashboard to try to stop the engine from overheating.

'Maybe we're stuck behind a tractor,' JJ said, remembering the country roads of his youth.

'*Oui, peut-être*,' said Milo. He punched the button to stop the cassette, then punched again to eject *Combat Rock*. He shuffled around in the open glove compartment and picked out another cassette. 'To remind us of 'ome,' he said. 'I tape it from Béatrice.'

It was a C90 tape's worth of Bach harpsichord concertos recorded from Béatrice's box set of LPs – music to cook by! – but it made JJ even more homesick for the commune and his beloved Sylvie. Milo turned it up so that the frills and runs of the music seemed to be in sync with the leaves of the hedge that were rippling in the breeze. It was like a soundtrack to a movie in which nothing was happening; a road movie in which no one moved, the flute and harpsichord notes floating up into the clear blue sky above their heads.

Behind them, an old-fashioned Bedford coach opened its doors with a hiss, and a few punks jumped out. One of them lit a cigarette while looking askance at the music coming from Milo's Citroën, then he laughed. They were walking faster than the traffic was moving.

'Is it a tractor?' JJ asked one of them. 'Do you know?'

But the punk only shrugged and carried on.

JJ took Milo's wooden-handled knife from the glove box. He figured he could cut some hawthorn from the hedges, and use it to garland the roof rack. Like in the 'May Day Carol':

> I've been a-rambling all the night,
> And the best part of the day . . .

There was a chalk drainage ditch along the verge. Bright white, it looked freshly cut, but was too wide to cross in one leap. JJ scrambled in and up the other side, where tall poppies and daisies were waving gently in the breeze. The convoy stretched in both directions as far as he could see – there must have been hundreds of cars and trucks, buses and horseboxes – while beyond the hedges on either side of the road were rolling green fields planted with young crops. He couldn't see Stonehenge yet. Perhaps they weren't close enough. Parked in front of them was a green Plaxton coach, like the ones that had taken his class at school to swimming lessons or for summer days out. Someone had painted an idyllic scene on the inside of the windows, of coaches and teepees pitching camp by a river beneath mountains and clouds and the dual light of a golden sun and moon. A poster stuck to the back said YOU HAVE BEEN MISINFORMED (AS USUAL) – STONEHENGE 1985 FREE FESTIVAL SHALL HAPPEN! It was decorated with yin and yang and Om symbols. JJ felt as if he'd been staring at this for hours, and yet with each second he was seeing it afresh. He was starting to feel the acid now, that was for sure: an adrenaline kick spreading out from his stomach while he listened to that not-quite-rhythmic sound in the distance, like far-off sleigh bells somewhere behind them. He thought of those school morris dancing lessons, the rattle of bottle tops nailed to broomsticks, a clamour of May Day voices carried on the warm air.

And now I am returning back again,
I have brought you a branch of May . . .

In the van, Milo was waggling his fingers as if playing an imaginary piano, and laughing, but above the Bach, JJ could still hear that occasional, nearly familiar sleigh bell sound. He wove two branches of hawthorn across the front of the roof rack, and some ivy. Then Milo told him to get in. They were moving again. Perhaps only just, but moving all the same.

A branch of May, my dear, I say,
Before your door I stand . . .

For a moment Rex had thought that it was Terence under the colonnade on Russell Street. Bald pate and closely cropped hair, what
was left of it, similar height and slightly overweight in his baggy
jacket, but then the head turned and Rex saw the silhouette: Concorde! Wow, he'd forgotten all about Milo's extraordinary aquiline
nose. As he got closer, of course, he saw that the suit was Armani-
baggy rather than ill-fitting.

Hearing footsteps, his nemesis turned, but Rex did not allow
himself to betray any of the shock that he felt at seeing those once-
familiar features instantly aged. Still tanned, but with even ruddier
cheeks and a much broader face. It was as if a fat bloke was wearing
a tiny Milo mask on the centre of his great wrinkled and jowly face.

'*Bonsoir*,' said Rex.

Then Milo spoke, and this is what Gertrude Bisika's friend Iris
heard from her window in the Peabody flats on the other side of
Drury Lane.

'Well, you must be Joe King,' he said.

'Go ahead,' said Rex, gesturing towards the Long Dock door,
which he had arranged to be left unlocked. 'Let's talk in private.
What are *you* called now, more to the point?' He paused for a beat.
'As if I didn't know.'

If the Frenchman noticed this, he didn't let on. François Couvoir
– the man Rex had known thirty years earlier only as Milo – took
great delight in telling Rex that he was Commissaire Divisionnaire
(roughly, Divisional Superintendent) of the SDAT, the French
anti-terrorist police. Did he honestly expect the Detective Sergeant
to be surprised? Rex may have been outranked, but he wasn't easily

impressed. If Milo – François! – were here on official business *and* on Rex's manor, Lollo would have known about it, and therefore so would Rex. More to the point, if that were the case, not only would Couvoir have been in uniform – even if not the No. 1 full dress – but he would certainly have brought more bodies along tonight. He'd have come mob-handed. You'd never organise a stunt on unfamiliar turf like this on your tod, with no backup. The fact that he had done precisely that suggested that this was something else, but what?

Had Milo always been a bit of a maverick back in the day, or was this something purely personal? Surely not after all this time. A diversionary tactic? Probably, in one form or another, but if so, a diversion from what? And yet, as Rex led the way down the Long Dock, civvies or not, the Frenchman still walked with all the confidence of a man who thought he was in charge. Or to be more precise, with all the confidence of a man who had a SIG Pro 2022 under his jacket, because even if he hadn't shown it yet, Rex would bet you anything that it would be there.

Truth be told, Rex had also been digging around. His search for Milo had been low-level, but relentless. Although for years it had borne no fruit. And when he had eventually found him, it had been by accident. In the run-up to the Tennyson trial, anxious to cover all angles, Rex had been tracking back through the campaigns and the conspiracy theories about French deaths in custody, as well as poring over the legal coverage of certain high-profile UK cases. He'd been half-heartedly looking for anything, any new angle that might have been useful in the then upcoming trial of the 'Tennyson Four'. He had found himself scrolling through photos from the late 1980s of a crowd that had been marching to mark the first or second anniversary of the death in custody of a French-Algerian student named Malik Oussekine, and there he was: Concorde! Bold as brass and holding up a banner reading L'ÉTAT TUE! TUE L'ÉTAT! – THE STATE KILLS! KILL THE STATE! The protest had been part of a then growing solidarity movement for the families of the *bavures*, the offensive French term meaning 'blunders' or 'errors' that at the time was used to describe victims in death-in-custody cases. In the surge of grief and rage that had engulfed him, sat there at his laptop, Rex had almost thrown up on the spot. Seeing Milo – unmistakable even in a suit and without his Mohawk – among the crowd of protestors rather than among the police lines had finally confirmed his fears.

After this, Rex had found it relatively easy, using Lollo's log-ins, to search the Detective Chief Inspector's 'Temporary' drive for emailed meeting notes and correspondence relating to ACPO – the Association of Chief Police Officers – Interpol or EU networking conferences involving senior personnel from the UK's Special Demonstration Squad, or more recently the National Public Order Intelligence Unit.

Detective Chief Inspector Jethro Lawrence never cleared his cache – he wouldn't have known a Temporary drive from a gravel one – and consequently Rex had been able to build these searches into his daily routine, although he had never really expected to find anything. But suddenly there he was: a Commissaire François Couvoir was listed as part of a Parisian operation that had infiltrated the French 'Stolen Lives' movement, specifically the Malik Oussekine campaign. More than this, Couvoir was named on the agenda for a knowledge-exchange gathering in London with the UK team who had themselves successfully infiltrated family and campaign groups during the infamously protracted inquiry into the racist murder of London teenager Stephen Lawrence.

It had been relatively straightforward after that to find ID and press images of the by now Commissaire Divisionnaire François Couvoir.

Rex had felt almost elated. So Milo had actually been to Scotland Yard, and not only that but he had given a PowerPoint presentation on lessons learned during the Malik Oussekine campaign? It was unbelievable: Milo had been right here in London only ten years ago!

And now he had been foolish enough to come here again.

As Rex turned the lights on, Couvoir looked around, taking stock; casing the joint. If he was impressed by this great room, this hidden slice of Georgian London in Theatreland, he didn't let on, but Rex knew the drill well enough to recognise somebody else doing the old six-point risk assessment, just like any policeman would: checking for vantage points and hiding places, potential assailants. Rex had done the same outside. Weaknesses? Weight. Risks? A gun, most likely. Exits? Only one, now that they were inside.

Bringing someone new here made Rex see this strange narrow space of the paint frame with fresh eyes. The height of the place, the narrow workbenches laden with tins and rags and brushes, the Jackson Pollock-like accretion of splashes and drips, the haze of sprayed paint. And that was without the frames themselves: these two enormous proscenium-sized grids of blackened and paint-spattered beams and cross-struts that hung suspended along either side of the studio. Stretched across one of them was a scrim, the painting on it already recognisable as a biblical tableau. Something from the New Testament. Eleven disciples sleeping, while to one side Christ kneels at the feet of an angel. The whole thing seemed to have been painted so as to appear slightly off-register, as if in imitation of a cheaply printed nineteenth-century handbill.

At the far right-hand corner of the paint frame and mounted

against the wall was a large butler sink, and above it, hanging by its handle from a large iron hook that had been driven into the bare brick wall, was a big old-fashioned Roberts radio. Rex walked over and turned it on, then went and stood in front of Milo, Couvoir, or whatever his name was, next to the narrow workbench.

'We won't be disturbed now,' he said. 'If the light's on, the radio's always playing when there's a job on.'

'Well,' said Couvoir, as if pleasantly surprised to see Rex. Was he trying to turn on the charm? Was he mad? 'In happier circumstances—'

'Don't bother,' said Rex. 'What I want to know is, what's rattled your cage after all this time?'

> It's nothing but a sprout, but it's well budded out,
> By the work of our Lord's hand . . .

The road sign said they could pick up the A303 at the roundabout, but JJ saw that instead the convoy was turning off down a side road to the left. He couldn't understand why, but he could see a police chopper hovering above the trees. Perhaps there had been an accident. JJ had a better view of the road ahead than Milo in this left-hand-drive Citroën, and as they drew closer he could see that the main road was blocked by what looked like a tipper truckload of gravel, and behind that were numerous coaches and police vans. It was as if they had brought their own convoy; bussed in the heavy mob. Of course they had. Standing in front of the piles of gravel were dozens of police officers, all directing the traffic down this smaller side road.

'*D'accord*,' said Milo. 'Get out.'

JJ was puzzled. 'What?'

'*Vite!*' said Milo. 'Out! *Maintenant!*' His expression suddenly turned. The laughter and the easy intimacy of the past few months was gone, replaced with what looked like pure hatred, or something even colder and more impersonal: contempt.

Bewildered, and by now tripping off his nut, JJ slid the passenger door open and stepped out on to the road. 'What?'

'*Casse-toi!*' said Milo, dead-eyed and practically spitting out the words, then, when JJ had clearly still not understood, '*Va-t'en!* Fuck off, you idiot.' And with that he leaned over and roughly slid the van door shut.

There was no time to take stock. Up ahead, JJ could see smoke rising above the trees. He could hear women screaming and engines revving, and that sound which wasn't sleigh bells after all, but breaking glass. Looking back the way they had come, half a mile away but getting closer all the time, were yet more police. They seemed to be walking casually along the line of traffic with axes and truncheons in their hands, smashing the windows of every vehicle they passed, then dragging people out through the broken windows and peeling away, only for more police to take their place. JJ wasn't about to hang around and find out what they'd do to him.

Just up ahead on the right was a gap in the hedge, and some people were sawing through the bars of a wooden fence. Once they'd broken through, they ran back into their vehicles and drove right through it, into the field beyond.

For some reason, JJ decided that right now there might not be safety in numbers. He would go the other way. He ducked around the front of the van, scrambled up the verge on the opposite side of the road and pushed through a small gap in the hedge into the relative safety of the field. He didn't move then, but simply lay there in the long grass, beneath the cover and shade afforded by the hawthorn branches.

On the other side of the hedge, dozens of vehicles managed to get off the road and through the fence before scores of police on foot and in cars and vans arrived to block the way and stem the flow. What those who had managed to get off the road didn't know was that they had driven into a trap.

> Go down in your dairy and fetch me a cup,
> A cup of your sweet cream,
> And if I should live to tarry in the town,
> I will call on you next year . . .

As he pulled the SIG Pro from his pocket, the expression on François Couvoir's face was one that Rex recognised immediately. He'd seen it before: pure contempt.

'Joseph Jonathan King,' he said, 'I am arresting you for the murders of Béatrice Serpolet, of Élise Burnet and Tobie Burnet, of Victor Peretz, André Houlette and' – here he paused – 'Sylvie Maronier. And since we are in England, old bean, I might add that you do not have to say anything, but it may 'arm your defence if you fail to mention when questioned something which you later rely on in court, and anything you do say may be given in evidence.'

Rex might have been a bit green when he'd first met Milo, but he wasn't now. If he went along with this, he'd most likely wind up dead. Commissaire Divisionnaire François Couvoir hadn't come to arrest Rex, but to kill him. He was tidying up. Rex well knew that there were greater infamies in Couvoir's past than La Fontaine-en-Forêt. Things that, if they got out, would certainly mess up any forthcoming retirement with honours.

Well, perhaps Rex had some tidying up of his own to do, but if so he'd better start thinking fast.

Luckily that was something Rex was good at.

Thinking quickly had got Rex a long way.

'Now you're really having a laugh,' said Rex, 'because we both know I was nowhere near La Fontaine-en-Forêt when whatever happened happened, because we were at the Beanfield, you and me. Weren't we, eh? Oh, and I've got a bone to pick with you about that and all. I saw you later on, and you know it. The only thing I couldn't figure out at first was why you'd be spying on Pythag and Co. – then I realised that you were there to keep an eye on André Houlette.'

'What do you know about Houlette?'

'Let's face it, I've had long enough to think about it,' said Rex, 'and to dig around. I know you wanted him out of the way. It was Houlette and his men who blew up the bridges, wasn't it? He wasn't just lying low in La Fontaine. He must have still had his cache of weapons and explosives in the bakehouse and the cellars and stayed there to keep an eye on it. Somebody – I hate to think, either Béatrice or Sylvie? – decided to test out the oven before I got back? Am I right? What I can't forgive is that you knew this, and yet you let me go ahead and open up the bakery! It's as if you were deliberately goading Houlette. You positively encouraged me to do it – "You've got to have a *métier*," you said! – even knowing that the shell of the oven was filled with enough unstable high explosives to set everything off?'

Couvoir was in no hurry. He had Rex covered, so was happy to let him talk.

'Under arrest?' said Rex. 'It should be me arresting *you*, you bastard. *You* killed them, not me. Élise too! How could you? Your mob must have had Houlette under low-level surveillance for years, he wasn't going anywhere, but they really fucked up when they sent you in. You started enjoying yourself too much, so you bought yourself a bit of time by saying you were infiltrating an ETA cell; cooking up a story that was just convincing enough. Pretty fucking tenuous, though, wasn't it? Sure, Pythag and Élise were from Basque Country, but that's about it.

'Pythag and Béatrice weren't even charged that time they were picked up for panhandling in Antibes, I remember it well, but the mugshots were there on file so why not use them, eh? They were just a convenient smokescreen, weren't they? All of us. Collateral damage! Boost that story with a bit of spectacle and you've got what to all intents and purposes looks like a terrorist act, to make it seem like you'd been a good boy and to divert attention from what's about to go down in New Zealand? They were disposable and I was just fucking cover. You might as well have killed Sylvie with your own hands! Was it because you couldn't bear that it was me she wanted and not you? Or was it just to make yourself look good?'

Rex paused for a moment. 'You forget, I saw you and Frédérique Bonlieu together! Next thing I know, her face is all over the news for the *Rainbow Warrior*. Were you her handler or was she yours? It must have been just before she got posted down to New Zealand as ship's cook or whatever her story was. How the fuck have you managed to keep your involvement in all that a secret? Jesus, the *Festival d'Eau*! All those rainbows! It was like a fucking premonition! So what then? Did you pretend to be Bonlieu's boyfriend when you turned up on the *Rainbow Warrior*, or just an old school friend on a gap year, who happened to be in New Zealand and was good with his hands?'

Neither of them spoke for a while. Rex had talked himself out.

'Ah, well, you are right, of course,' said Couvoir eventually, 'but those were different times, *non*? There was a cold war, remember? And besides, fortunately I have the gun, and it is *me* who has arrested *you*, so it is you who will be taking the blame, not me. Although, you are quite correct. I'd rather not test that in a court of law, if you know what I mean, so I'm afraid that in a minute or two there will be a struggle. You will resist arrest, my friend, and unfortunately I will have no choice—'

'I'm not your friend,' said Rex, 'and anyway, why try and save face now? No one's going to hold you to it. Everyone's happy with the official version of events. No one associates you with either bombing. Everyone's forgotten all that shit apart from you, and maybe a handful of conspiracy-theory lunatics.'

'And you, apparently,' said Couvoir.

'Well, yes, okay: and me,' said Rex.

'That's why,' said Couvoir.

There was a commotion outside, a movement on the other side of the door.

A branch of May, my dear, I say,
Before your door I stand,
It's nothing but a sprout, but it's well budded out,
By the work of our Lord's hand . . .

The sound of breaking glass and boots on tarmac.

Peering through the greenery, JJ saw the police stop at Milo's van and order, not pull, him out. So if they were in Wiltshire, why were these coppers speaking with Yorkshire accents? Bored up there since the end of the strike, were they? Got a bit too used to advancing in the old Roman-shield formation? Twiddling their thumbs now, without any heads to crack? They handcuffed Milo and led him away, but not before one of them, as if acting on an afterthought, turned back and raised his arm, bringing the baton down to smash the Citroën's windscreen. Then, putting one knee on the doorsill, he reached under the driver's seat to retrieve a plastic carrier bag: Milo's stash. JJ was stunned. It was as if he had known where it would be. Could they have been under surveillance all this time? Had someone been following them, watching everything they'd done since arriving at Dover? JJ couldn't quite tell if this paranoia was a result of the Spider's Web acid or not, but it got worse: had someone been spying on them as they had travelled up through France? Could one of Milo's dealers in Fréjus have been a plant?

> The hedges and the fields they are so green,
> As green as any leaf . . .

Was that the last time he'd seen Milo, until now?
Not quite.

> Our Heavenly Father waters them
> With his Heavenly dew so sweet . . .

The overhead fluorescent lights began to flicker as if there was a fault, before going off altogether; not a fault, then, but a power cut. Rex was running down the stairs back to the cells because he'd just found out that no Reasons had been issued to the 81 who was brought in. No one was even getting in the door at Holborn without an IS81, but as soon as the IO handed them over, an IS91 had to be issued within four hours, and an IS91R – the reasons for deportation – had to be issued to the detainee him- or herself within the same time frame. And this time, surprise surprise, that had failed to happen. The fucking idiot fucking IO hadn't torn off the fucking Reasons, so Rex was covering his back by making it right, because if it wasn't right and the 81 didn't have his Reasons, and if the shit

272

should hit the fan, then as SD lead it would be Rex standing here with this trousers down, and he wasn't having that.

Fucking IO!

So Rex was running down the stairs now, with the Reasons in his hand.

Down the stairs two at a time, back to the cells.

'Reasons,' he said to the Custody Sergeant. 'Where's that eighty-one that just came in? Fucking IO didn't give him his fucking Reasons.'

'Interpreter?' said the Custody Sergeant.

'Does he need one?' said Rex, looking for the 81's name on the sheet, then handing it over. 'Yeah, fair enough. That's your job. Give Jinksy a bell. He's got the list. Tell the eighty-one his interpreter is on the way.'

They were both distracted by the sound of a scuffle.

> When I am dead and in my grave,
> And covered with cold clay,
> The nightingale will sit and sing,
> And pass the time away . . .

How JJ found himself off his tits and sitting up a tree, he didn't know. Well, the acid he knew about, but how long had he been sitting here? The sun was getting low in the sky so it must have been hours. A police Transit pulled up and four coppers piled out to unload the cases of wine from Milo's van. Stretching away along the road in both directions were a hundred or more stationary vehicles, windows smashed in and some in flames.

From where he sat, he could see over the hedge on the other side of the road, and into the large field beyond. The last remnants of the convoy, it looked like, were still driving around the field trying to find a way out, but there wasn't one, not apart from the way they'd come in, and that was blocked by police. JJ had never seen so many police in one place. It was impossible to say how many: hundreds, certainly, or maybe more than a thousand. Some were in uniform, but many more wore unnumbered black boiler suits and visored helmets. Were they soldiers, like the rumours said had been brought in during the Miners' Strike, plus random headcases from other parts of the security services or the MoD? Ex-Paras recalled for duty at a time of need? Anyone in a vehicle seemed to be driving around for as long as they could, trying to put off the inevitable: the batons through windscreens – smash! – and being dragged out by the hair. Three or four officers piling on to each hippy. Putting the boot in: smash! Mothers and children too. Fracturing skulls: smash! Dragging them away. Children and babies separated from parents. An old yellow British Telecom van pulling a caravan: smash!

JJ watched as one coach crashed into another and the police swarmed all over both of them, axes and batons raining down: smash!

A baton under the chin and a knee in the balls.

A punch in the mouth.

A well-aimed boot in the small of the back; tried and tested techniques.

A woman pulled through the broken window of one coach – smash! – then on the floor and restrained with a knee in the back.

A flash of breasts and knickers and 'I don't fancy yours much' as she's dragged away by three officers and thrown in the van.

A couple of dozen vehicles were still moving but trapped in a dodgem dance, each one pursued by half a dozen police at least. Piling on, mob-handed. Two men pulled out of the observation turrets of a pink-painted armoured patrol vehicle with Rasta colours on its radiator grille: smash!

'Okay! Okay! Just don't hit me any more.' The traveller was buried beneath a pile of black-boiler-suited men with helmets and shields, a hail of blows. 'Okay! Please!' then a sickening crunch as the blunt end of an axe-head fractured his skull.

> Take a Bible in your hand,
> And read a chapter through,
> And when the Day of Judgement comes,
> The Lord will think on you . . .

A pair of splayed legs emerging from beneath a pile of four officers, Bill and bloody Ben among them.

'What's going on?'

'Resisted, didn't he,' said Bill.

'Well, he's not resisting now, is he?'

'No, skip,' said Ben, but they didn't move.

'So fucking get off him, then!'

Sheepishly they disentangled themselves and stood up, straightening ties, to reveal a black man of around thirty years old, smartly dressed in corduroy trousers and what looked like a grey long-sleeved Fred Perry. He was not lying back or leaning back against the wall, as Rex might have expected, but instead had been doubled over so that his head was lolling above his knees; arms handcuffed behind his back. There was a pool of vomit or saliva on the carpet between his legs.

'Fucker resisted, didn't he,' said Bill again. 'Said he was having an asthma attack. Strong guy and all. Took all of us to hold him down.'

'Didn't you know he had asthma?' Rex asked.

'Yeah, but still, I thought he was trying it on, skip.'

Rex knew he needed to start thinking fast, but thinking fast was something he was good at.

'He's been booked, I take it. Gnat's Piss, the lot?'

Ben nodded.

'Where's he headed?' asked Rex.

'In there,' Bill said, nodding at the open cell.

'Well, get him bloody well in there, then! Check his airways and put him in the recovery position now,' said Rex. 'And for Christ's sake, call an ambulance.'

> I have a bag on my right arm,
> Draws up with a silken string,
> Nothing does it want but a little silver
> To line it well within . . .

'That you, Rex?' said Terence, right on cue. 'Tea's not gonna fucking make itself, mate!'

Couvoir turned and made to cover the door to his right. Not for long – a split second – but long enough that, in the moment of distracted confusion that followed, Rex was able to grab the closest thing to hand. The heavy tin of paint hit Couvoir square in the chest. At the same moment, Terence had pulled the Frenchman's arm down and around, locking the elbow and headbutting him in the process, before knocking the gun out of his hand. Mercifully it had not gone off.

'Nifty!' said Rex, impressed by his friend's footwork. 'Where did you learn to do that? Got some chalk, Tel?'

When he'd come round, Couvoir found himself facing his own gun, a ligature around his neck.

Terence marched him across the room, where Rex forced him to write a date across the black-painted double doors. Not today's date, but the date that they had met for the first time; a date in the old French Republican Calendar.

The day after the miners had been defeated.

The day that Rex had arrived in La Fontaine-en-Forêt.

The day when everything changed.

Tridi 13 Ventôse CXCIII.

Rex was thinking on his feet. If this was Couvoir's suicide note, it was also a puzzle that there would be nobody left alive to understand: not Pythag, Béatrice or Élise, not Victor or Sylvie, and certainly not Couvoir himself.

Not even JJ, technically speaking.

JJ died in June 1985, on the day that he got a passport back in the name of his dead twin, Rex. Although, as far as anyone else knew, JJ had already been killed in the ETA blast at La Fontaine-en-Forêt. Nothing left of him to bury, poor thing. Locals had spoken of an English student who'd been staying in the village, who had been learning to bake, after all. There were no border records of JJ entering the UK because Milo's van had simply been nodded through the barrier: a French undercover colleague entering the country 'off the books' to be an active observer at some European security-services training exercise.

The only person who knew that JJ had come back to the UK was his grandmother, and when he'd told her that he was being chased by French gangsters who dressed as policemen – which was not too wide of the mark – it had played to her protective nature and to the xenophobia of her generation, and she had said nothing, even or especially when a local policeman had come knocking at the door with the sad news of her grandson's death in France. Broken as she had been in spite of appearances by the death of her daughter, Daisy had already suffered a series of small strokes and quickly succumbed to ill health. So when she'd told neighbours that she had seen JJ that same night, or said that he had phoned, they'd put it down to a visitation or the dementia, bless her. They'd read the papers, after all.

As soon as the new passport had come through, Rex – now – had got up under cover of darkness and hitched a ride to London. Started over, in the days when you could still do that. Started over like his life depended on it.

> And now my song is almost done,
> I can no longer stay,
> God bless you all both great and small,
> I wish you a joyful May . . .

'Right you are, skip.'

'But listen,' said Rex, going through the man's trouser pockets, 'he never said anything about asthma, right?'

There it was. He took the inhaler out and put it in the pocket of his Harrington.

Bill and Ben looked at him for a second, before understanding dawned on their faces.

'He didn't mention it, right?' said Rex. 'Have you all got that? Who was the booking officer?'

'Jinksy, skip.'

'Okay, recovery position now!' said Rex, running past the Custody Sergeant and up the stairs, two at a time, back to the desk.

'Interpreter's on the way,' said Jinksy, without looking up.

'Thanks, mate,' said Rex. 'You still doing Gnat's Piss on that Occupy arrest that Jimmy and Binder just took down?

'Yeah,' said Jinksy, 'doing it now. Nearly finished.'

'Hang on.'

Rex quickly scanned the screen over Jinksy's shoulder, and in passing he saw the name Trevor Tennyson, but – poet namesake aside – it didn't mean anything. No more than might a random name taken from the phonebook. 'Has it gone through yet, Jinksy?'

'Fucking Gnat's Piss, what do you think?'

'Scroll back up,' said Rex.

'Eh?'

'Scroll back up. Existing medical conditions. They made a mistake, we need to correct it.'

> I've been a-rambling all the night,
> And the best part of the day . . .

JJ watched from his vantage point as ambulance crews tended to the injured. How many ambulances: thirty? forty?

Dozens of men and women with fractured skulls and other serious injuries were stretchered off to hospital, while van after vanload of others, the lucky ones, those less badly injured, five hundred and thirty-odd, were driven off to who knew where. Families separated and sent to Basingstoke, Andover, Salisbury and more. And still the waltz of the last few vehicles: Bedford camper vans and buses, cars and army trucks, driving around the field.

Off his tree and up one, JJ could see everything. It was like a medieval battlefield. Policemen were wandering around in a daze with their shields and batons, or with axes hung loose in their hands. People – men and women – were still jumping out of buses and trying to make a run for it, still trying to get away. There were dogs running around, barking their confusion. There were pile-ups, and the smoke of the vehicles that had been set on fire cast long flickering shadows in the golden light of the low sun. And suddenly there they were: the Hesperides. The golden-skinned nymphs of the golden evening light. He could see them now!

But then JJ saw something else.

Something that he wasn't meant to see.

Someone standing behind the police lines with the press photographers.

Hadn't he been one of the first to be arrested? So how could he be standing there in a black boiler suit, helmet under his arm, chatting to one of the coppers? Was it just the acid? Surely it was just the acid! But then the black-clad figure turned so that JJ had a clear sight of his profile.

Distinguishing features? Not much. Just a nose like bloody Concorde!

From the safety of his tree, JJ watched as Milo – it was definitely Milo – took a packet of cigarettes out of his pocket and lit one; offered them around. Feeling conspicuous on his perch, JJ reached over to try to pull a nearby branch across his face, but as he did so he could have shat himself right there on the spot, because suddenly Milo turned and seemed to be looking right at him. He didn't know whether to try to stay perfectly still and hope that Milo was simply looking in this general direction or to run.

Surely he was too far away, too obscured by foliage.

Surely it was the acid.

But no, the Frenchman narrowed his eyes and looked directly at him.

Milo had seen him.

Their eyes met across the intervening space, and JJ's blood ran cold.

Now he knew what to do. He had to run.

Milo took a drag from the cigarette, then lifted his chin and squinted down his nose at JJ as if he was taking aim.

> And now I am returning back again,
> I have brought you a branch of May . . .

Kilroy. A man with a big nose peering over a wall. The cartoon image that had circumnavigated the globe during the Second World War. The face that had been drawn on to every surface, every tank and landing craft, every gun emplacement and shell casing across the European and Pacific Theatres and around the world, appearing everywhere that US armed forces personnel had set foot, from Greenham Common to Iwo Jima.

Now Rex made Couvoir draw another one, here in the paint frame, on the wall behind the sofa.

'For Pythag!' he said, remembering that day when they had cleared the brambles in front of the bakehouse and found the rats' nest.

Or one of them, anyway.

Little had they known.

Pointing out the fading Kilroy that had been painted on the bakehouse door, Pythag had gleefully commandeered the device as the revolutionary commune's regicidal mascot: 'Kill *roi*!' he'd said, enjoying the simple franglais pun. 'Kill the king!'

> A branch of May, my dear, I say,
> Before your door I stand,
> It's nothing but a sprout, but it's well budded out,
> By the work of our Lord's hand . . .

After that it didn't take the two of them long to tie Couvoir to one of the cross-struts of the paint frame by the ligature around his neck, to make it look like a knot that he could have tied himself. Without his SIG Pro, Couvoir was a pussycat, pleading and begging like a teenager. The frame wobbled at his weight, and as if suddenly seeing the huge contraption and the drop behind and beneath him for the first time, as if seeing what this was, the Frenchman panicked, standing on tiptoe with his back arched and trying to throw as much of his weight forward as he could; anything to try to hold the enormous wooden structure steady.

Now it was time for Rex to reach into his own pocket, but it was not a gun that he pulled out.

'I've been meaning to give you this back,' he said.

Wrapped in cling-film, it was a wooden-handled knife with an odd curved blade. Terence held Couvoir's arm immobile as Rex put the knife into his hand and wrapped the Frenchman's fingers around it, then loosened them and wrapped the handle back up in the cling-film.

While Terence held the frame steady, Rex pinched Couvoir's nose closed with his left hand, holding the billhook beneath it like a steel moustache, and looking straight into the Frenchman's eyes. Sharp side up, it was beginning to draw blood. With tears in his eyes, the Frenchman opened his mouth to breathe, and as he did so Rex wondered how it had happened all those years ago. Had it been Béatrice who, wanting to surprise him, had experimentally fired up the oven to test it out before they got back from Stonehenge? Certainly the two of them had been looking at the Conforti's panel of three big aluminium switches, which were more or less the same as the ones in the bakery in La Fontaine-lès-Vence, and based on what he had learned from Monsieur Previn, JJ had explained what he thought the various settings might be.

Whatever it was, this fucker had known it would happen.

This fucker, who had poked his big nose in, and dared to call a bunch of harmless punks and hippies terrorists, *etarras*, in order to save his own skin. To cover his own tracks, his liaison role with the DGSE out of Fréjus – the *Direction générale de la sécurité extérieure* – in *Opération Satanique*, the bombing of the *Rainbow Warrior* in Auckland, New Zealand, just a month later. Who had cynically used La Fontaine-en-Forêt and the young Rex for cover, and who dared to crawl out of the woodwork now!

Without breaking Milo's gaze, Rex nodded, then, at exactly the same moment his friend sent the great oak frame hurtling down, Rex pulled the blade up sharply, enjoying the terrified and agonised expression in Couvoir's eyes in the split second before he flipped and was dragged headfirst into the void.

Rex was left holding what had been Couvoir's most prominent and distinguishing feature.

Drained of blood it looked fake, like a costumier's prop.

If the Frenchman's neck wasn't broken the instant his body got dragged roughly through the slot, the drop into the void below would certainly have done it.

Rex bent down and dropped the severed nose on the floor, for long enough that he could be sure it would make a potato-print-like mark. Then he picked it up and wrapped it in a spare end of the cling-film that he was using to hold the knife. Thinking on his feet.

'Rats must have had it,' said Rex, matter-of-factly. Then he let the still opened knife fall to the floor to produce some localised spatter before using the cling-film to push it into the shadows beneath the lower shelf of the nearest workbench. 'First place I'd look,' he said. 'Could easily have fallen there.'

Meanwhile, in the huge dark space beneath where they were standing, as deep again as the paint frame was high, the now dead and noseless Frenchman's anal and urethral sphincters relaxed and the contents of his bowel and bladder began to leak out, soaking first into his clothing and then, once the fabric was saturated, dripping down on to the cobbled floor far below.

29: PERVENCHE (PERIWINKLE)

'Shall we go out and celebrate?' **Susan** asked. Her niece had been discharged and was now recovering well at home.

'That's good enough for me,' said Rex. He was standing and talking to Susan on his mobile in the station canteen. Looking down from the window, he could see an abandoned **Croc** – a child's rubber sandal – and a broken umbrella on top of the bus shelter on the other side of Theobalds Road. 'Where do you want to go?' he asked. 'Somewhere posh with a **doorman**; no **riff-raff**? Or the kind of place where your drink comes with a **straw**?'

It was great news, and the relief showed in her voice. But that wasn't all this was about.

They were both aware of what wasn't being said. They'd seen it coming: that Susan would with Ashley released from **hospital ship** out. That if her niece had gone home, Susan would be going home too, and in her case that meant going back to York. That this wasn't just a celebration.

Perhaps they had moved too fast. He hadn't expected to fall for someone quite so quickly, quite so easily, but he had. 'Hook, line and sinker', as they used to say. Part of him had hoped that she wouldn't need to leave quite so quickly, but obviously she had to go back to work. They were luckier than most, of course. Even to the extent that they had discussed their respective personal lives, which was not much, he knew that they both had good jobs and neither of them was particularly **in debt**, but even then neither of them could afford to run away, much as he might have liked to.

'I don't know, Rex,' she said. 'I fancy something simple—'

'Who are you calling simple?' he said, with mock indignation.

Susan ignored the useless joke. 'Remember that Pizza Express along the road from you? Where you used to live?'

'Coptic Street?' said Rex. 'Good idea. Yeah, why not?'

He decided not to bore her with his usual story about the Coptic Street Pizza Express being only the second branch that the chain ever opened, way back in 1967, fascinating though he found this fact, for some reason. In the 1980s, when he'd lived over the road, Pizza Express had been quite posh. A simpler menu than it was now, perhaps, but whose idea was it that the dessert menu would be improved by getting rid of the chocolate bombe? Or Rex's old usual – now long disappeared – the chilled glass of Vin Santo with *cantuccini alla mandorla* for dunking. Now that's what Rex called a dessert!

These days, although he still ate there occasionally, partly for convenience but also for old times' sake, it often seemed that Pizza Express had become a place for the nannies of upper-middle-class London families to take their charges for a kind of mass high tea. Rex wondered if it was the introduction of the UK smoking ban in 2007 that had cemented this transformation, turning the chain from a place of sophisticated adult conversation to a series of echoing playgrounds full of screaming brats.

He'd once made the mistake of bringing a date here and only then finding out that she was vegan. How had he missed that? 'Do their bases contain **whey** powder, do you know?' she'd asked him at one point. If romance was a sport, that one had been an **air shot**: missing the ball, much less the goal. Talk about killing the moment. He'd cried off mid-meal, in the end, feigned sickness. Unable to face the forensic examination of the dessert menu that he felt sure was coming. Unsure how to **seduce** someone who was that obsessed with food.

He wished he'd bought **stocks** in Pizza Express, though. He had read about it in the paper a few years ago, that when they'd first floated in 1993 you could get shares for 40p, and by 1998 they were worth an incredible 987p! It had struck Rex, though, that after that high-water mark, the sequence of franchise buybacks, international mergers and takeovers, the pre-crash real-estate expansion by franchise holders, the buyouts and disposals – culminating in a recent **purchase** of the Pizza Express chain by some Chinese private-equity firm – was probably a lesson in contemporary international finance.

He could have said all that – and perhaps at another time, to another date, he might have – but he didn't. 'Shall we say eight thirty, when all the kids will have gone?'

London trivia was good for some things, he'd long ago discovered, but it was not on the whole conducive to romance. Unless you got off with someone at a pub quiz. A few years back, Rex had been a regular at the quiz in his local, and an enthusiastic member of the inter-station quiz circuit to boot – **group-captain**, if you could call it that, of all the Holborn Police Station teams, no less – but he'd quickly found that you could have too much of a good thing.

Whereas romance, on the other hand . . . This beautiful woman, for instance, met by chance just a week or so ago and who'd been sharing his bed most nights since? He could never get enough of that. Normally he'd play it a bit careful like, take his time, make sure they check out. But Susan was different, classy, and he'd just thought 'What the hell?' and grabbed it – her – with both hands. The truth was that she had found a shortcut to his heart, and he couldn't get enough of her. From her choice of **hooch** – the off-dry Rieslings that she liked to drink – to the way that, at the end of a hard day, she liked to have both feet massaged at the same time and symmetrically – working out from **instep** to sole, then flexing her painted toes – to the way she dressed: no **fashion plate**, but 'chic as fuck', as he once put it when asked. She knew what suited her, alright, and Rex hoped that extended to him too, because she certainly suited him. His appetite for her was limitless.

'My thoughts exactly,' said Susan. 'I've had enough of kids for a while, being in that place every day.'

'I should think so. You've been a real star,' said Rex.

'Bless her heart, it was the least I could do for her,' said Susan, 'but thanks, hon. That's nice of you to say. I'll see you at eight thirty, yeah. Oh, by the way, I've been shopping.'

'Oh, yeah? Where?'

'Your favourite,' she said. 'Bye, darling.'

Rex knew what that meant.

Wow.

Susan had been the perfect antidote to the shitstorms at work. Rex was aware of his tendency – wasn't it everyone's? – to practically **canonise** any new lover or romantic interest, but right now, as far as he was concerned, Susan really could do no wrong. Whether that was their lazy breakfast in bed the Saturday lunchtime just gone, listening to a Congolese **rumba** show, of all things, that she had somehow found on the radio, or her persuading him to pop into Richer Sounds to buy a new flat-screen TV and ditch the old **cathode**-ray tube model – something that he then wished he'd done years ago – Rex didn't know what he was going to do without her. Of course there were always shitstorms at work and Rex had always weathered them, but the eager anticipation of a romantic date later on was definitely the best way to get through the most tedious or testing day.

And there was no shortage of those. At the moment it seemed every day was a total bastard. With the SiC inspection due to start tomorrow, everyone in the building from Detective Chief Superintendent Tabitha Churchill on down was now officially on tenterhooks. Everyone was twitchy, the whole place under heavy manners, and not without reason, because for the foreseeable future Holborn Police Station would have company. So – in Lollo's words – it was time to get the best china out.

If the inspections at Ealing and Paddington Green were anything to go by – and they'd all been poring over the reports – there would be a couple of team leaders from Her Majesty's Inspectorates – one from Prisons, the other Constabulary – plus three or four inspectors, again drawn from both directorates, and most likely the HMIP would be bringing along a couple of researchers and a healthcare inspector, while, not to be left out, the Care Quality Commission would probably want some bodies in there too. So that would be anything from eight to a dozen-strong team, with an agreed schedule of work – all questionnaire this, and 'intrusive dip sample' that – but also, in Lollo's memorable words, 'with absolute Cate fucking Blanchett to go anywhere and speak to anyone they bloody want to, from PC gaolers to custody sergeants to eighty-ones to convicted criminals who began their arrest journeys here.

'They'll be looking at Gnat's Piss training, custody training, risk-assessment training, UFO-incidents training, pre-release risk-management training, you name it. So if they turn up wanting to speak to you, be frank and truthful and remember, **fawn** or flatter all you like, it won't wash. So just knuckle down, speak when you're spoken to, and get used to it. 'Cause if any of you lot show me up, I'll fucking have you. **Honour bright** I will.'

He didn't need to expand. No one who had ever seen Lollo angry or been on the receiving end wanted a repeat performance. It wasn't just a **pose**. Detective Chief Inspector Jethro Lawrence made **apoplexy** an art form; made Sir Alex Ferguson look like a lightweight.

The only good thing was that there'd been no more noise on the Tennyson front. As Lollo had said, whatever that leak had been about, whether it had indeed been a shot across the bows, or something intended to do more substantial damage, they appeared to have got away with it this time. Although of course – as Rex told Lollo – just because they'd had the official all-clear from upstairs didn't mean whoever it was had gone away or wouldn't have another pop.

That much was certain, at least.

There'd always be someone wanting to have a pop.

'Aye, there will that,' said Lollo.

And they might be closer to home than you think, thought Rex.

It was six forty-five by the time he left the station, so he ran up the Falcon stairs two at a time. Quick shower and a shave and tidy the place up a bit before strolling along to meet Susan. He didn't need to think about what he was going to wear, because he'd picked up a couple of new Fred Perrys in Lamb's Conduit Street at lunchtime. When it came to buying Fred Perrys, 'white or bright' was Rex's motto. Reach a certain age, he had discovered, and if you're wearing a black Fred Perry people assume you're the staff. Black Fred Perrys were a young man's game. He'd given the ones he'd had to the charity shop and never bought another. Tonight was more **rose-red** than pastel-blue, he figured, so took that one out of the bag and laid it on the bed, along with a pair of off-white chinos and a black leather belt; navy deck shoes. He put the white wine in the fridge and a bottle of better-than-usual Australian Shiraz on the table with a couple of glasses, then he did the drying up and the putting away. He straightened the cushions, bleached the loo, and opened the smaller windows to air the place.

So when the knock on the door came, at least the flat was looking nice.

When the knock on the door came, he was having a shave.

'Hang on,' he said. 'Won't be a sec.'

They knocked again, but harder this time.

Rex splashed his face.

They knocked again.

'Coming,' said Rex from the bathroom.

He walked across to the front door drying his hands and face, and looked through the spyhole.

Strange, he thought. What were Lollo and Eddie Webster doing coming around at this time?

Didn't they know he was on a promise?

Then he saw the coat hangers on the stairs behind them.

Bill and Ben.

Why would— Oh, yeah.

Mob-handed, he thought.

Fuck.

Rex opened his front door before they could **bash** it down.

Lollo and Webster came in; the PCs stayed outside on the step.

'Cup of tea?' said Rex. 'Coffee?'

'Can I have a glass of water, please?' said Eddie Webster.

'Well, you can help yourself to that,' said Rex. 'You know where everything is.'

Webster let the cold-water tap run for a bit, and then filled a glass and took a taste. He made a face: 'Got any ice?'

'Yeah, guess where!' said Rex. 'And don't tell me that the water tastes better in fucking Essex.'

'Nowt for me, thanks,' said Lollo, looking around. Was he admiring the place or doing the old six-point? Rex couldn't tell. 'You've got it looking nice,' Lollo added, but that meant nothing. 'I like that bird **motif** on your wallpaper. What's that, then?'

'Swifts,' said Rex, remembering a sky filled with a continuously unfolding aerobatic display, the impossible geometries carved through the air by the tiny brown birds. 'Thanks. Helen chose it back in the day, but they remind me of my childhood. It's Sanderson's.'

'Eh?'

'Sanderson's, Lol. It's the make. It's 1930s, but Heal's had a reproduction. Well, you fucking asked.' He paused. 'Anyway.'

DS Eddie Webster dropped a couple of ice cubes into his glass, and then shoved the tray back in the freezer compartment. 'Expecting someone?' he said, looking at the expensive bottle of Hornbeam

Shiraz and the two glasses that were standing on a mat on Rex's dining table. 'You old fox.'

'What?' said Rex. 'Do you think I drink fucking **Buckfast** like you? Course I'm fucking expecting someone. Or they're expecting me. She. Susan, her name is. If that's okay with you.'

'Sit down, son,' said Lollo, pulling a chair out from under the table. 'We wanted a word.'

Webster put his glass of water on the table, then he picked up the Shiraz and the glasses and placed them on the side next to Rex's newspaper – which was open at the Quick Crossword as usual – before sitting down himself.

Rex noticed something on the floor next to Webster. 'I think you dropped something, Eddie,' he said.

Webster looked down. 'Oh fuck, yeah. **Ear-plug.** Thanks.'

He looked at Rex then patted his gut with both hands, like some Georgian John Bull. 'Swimming. Helen's orders.'

Rex didn't have time to respond, because Lollo cleared his throat; drew a line.

The frivolities were over.

So this wasn't a social visit, then.

But, truth be told, Rex already knew that.

Rex already feared the worst.

The only question was, what did they have?

Had they made the connection with Couvoir?

Had something come up in the pre-SiC audit?

Had he overlooked something in the Tennyson paper trail, or worse: left tracks?

Had they found his finger-prints, digital or otherwise?

Say nothing, he thought.

See what they've got.

See who would speak first.

Because if this was what he thought it was, they'd have planned how to play it.

He'd done it himself enough times.

It was a simple matter of tactics, order of play: me then you, or whatever.

If Lollo spoke next and then handed over to Eddie, this would be about Terence and the Royal Palace Theatre.

If it was the other way around, it would be Tennyson. But then, if it was Tennyson, why were Bill and Ben here?

He didn't relish either **prospect**, but the fact that it was these two – Lollo and Webster – and not a couple of plain-clothes from another station, or another service altogether, the fact that they were being polite rather than bundling him into a car, already meant that it wasn't something more serious. Or if it were, that they were biding their time.

Perhaps they hadn't got that yet. They might have, but then again, they could just be holding fire, digging around. Waiting to **itemise** a list of charges and then pounce. Don't even think about that, Rex admonished himself. You'll only invite Mr **Freud** along, and slip up. Just listen and see what they've got. Get them comfy and speak when you're spoken to.

He had a word with himself. Be **unafraid**, he thought. Be very unafraid!

'All set for tomorrow, then?' he said, taking the seat that Detective Chief Inspector Lawrence had offered.

'Are you gonna tell him, or am I?' said Lollo.

Oh shit, thought Rex. They hadn't seen through his elaborate set-dressing in the paint frame, had they? But then Webster spoke.

'We saw your window was open, so we come up on the off-chance.

Lollo thought you should know that it looks like your mate's in the clear after all.'

Rex didn't need to act relieved, but he almost had to stop himself from bursting out laughing. 'That's great!' he said. 'I knew it! I told you!'

'Aye, you did,' said Lollo. 'I wanted you to know soon as.'

'I knew it,' said Rex, more quietly this time, clenching his fist. Then: 'Hang on, what have I missed? Who was it, then?'

'You'll not believe it,' said Lollo. 'Turns out it were a copper.'

Rex shook his head in disbelief. 'What?'

'The victim,' said Eddie. 'A French copper. When Sue Stanza's mob compared the DNA with the ENFSI datasets—'

Lollo interrupted: '*Robert*,' he said (pronouncing it 'Rob-air'), 'is *votre* fucking uncle.'

'So who is he, then?' asked Rex. 'This frog?'

'Name's Francis Coyvoor,' said the Detective Chief Inspector.

'It's Couvoir, sir,' said Eddie. '*Fron*-swah *Coo*-vwah.'

'Anyroad, he's an high-up from Paris,' Lollo continued, 'or used to be, until last week. Senior anti-terror. But that's not the worst of it.'

'There's more?' Rex asked.

'Not half,' said Lollo. 'The knife—'

'The billhook? Under the workbench?' Rex asked.

'Aye, the one you found,' said Lollo. 'It's his, they reckon. Turns out to have his prints all over it. But it gets worse—'

Rex was shaking his head in disbelief. 'What?'

'Beggars belief, it does,' said Lollo.

'It looks like he cut – off – his – own – fucking – nose!' said Eddie, chiming in with the gory bit like a kid unable to hide his delight in this grotesquery. 'Can you fucking imagine how painful that would be? Oooh, it brings tears to my eyes, mate, I tell you.'

'What? To spite his face?' said Rex.

'Summat like that,' said Lollo, chuckling. 'Fuck knows. Same time as he hung himself, they reckon, give or take.'

'Jesus fuck!' said Rex. Then: 'Well, where the fuck was it, then? I didn't see any spare fucking noses knocking about in there. Did you, Webbo?'

'No, I fucking didn't,' said Eddie, laughing.

'Rats must have taken it, Fuck Me reckon,' said Lollo. 'Old Sue Stanza. That's her theory.'

'Oh, no! You are fucking *kidding*!' Eddie and Rex both recoiled in pantomime disgust, as if this vile scene were playing out on the table between them. 'Uuuuurgh!'

'We've had to bounce it up, of course,' said Lollo. 'Diplomatic channels, in't it. Turns out he'd gone AWOL from Paris a few days before. Hopped on fucking Eurostar. Some sort of breakdown, they reckon: PTSD. Gone on a bit of a spending **spree** while he's been here and all. Using his cards all over. Bond Street, **Chelsea**, you name it. We've got him on CCTV, the lot. Exemplary record otherwise.'

Like hell, thought Rex, but he just said, 'Why the Royal fucking Palace? Why not just—'

'What? Check into a cheap **motel** and blow his brains out with his standard-issue, like every other fucker?'

'Something like that, yeah,' said Rex.

'Fuck knows,' said Lollo. 'He could have gone to Pamplona and got **gored** by a fucking bull, for all I care. What a **needless** waste, eh? Maybe he were just trying every door and by chance it were this one that opened. Apparently security on that stage door's been on the blink for a bit. And it's not as if your mate has any connection with France. We've checked. He's not been there once. So it's—'

'Totally. Fucking. Random!' said Eddie, brightly.

'So you can tell your mate he's off the hook,' said Lollo. 'Without a **smudge** on his name. Not that you've any idea where he is, of course.'

'Course,' said Rex, deadpan. 'Jesus! Who'd have fucking thought it, eh?'

'Turn-up, in't it,' said Lollo, standing up. 'I thought you'd like to know.'

'Cheers, sir,' said Rex. 'Case closed, then. Hoo-fucking-ray!'

'Bright lad, that Jimmy Rattle,' said Lollo, nodding in the general direction of the coat hangers outside as Rex showed him to the door. 'Him and Binder Singh. Bloody Bill and Ben, eh? They remind me of you two. "The Likely Lads", we used to call you. D'you know that? Always mucking about, you were. Long time ago now, eh? Anyroad, I'm glad you put all that business with Helen behind you. It *is* behind you, in't it?'

Rex nodded and shrugged. 'Yeah.' And he meant it. He wasn't going to play a lovelorn Demetrius to Helen's disinterested **Hermia** any longer.

Eddie nodded too. 'Yeah, 's ancient history, sir.'

'Champion,' said Lollo. ''Cause I was thinking of asking you two to take young Rattle and Singh under your wings a bit; mentoring or whatnot. Me and Eddie were gonna take them for a pint or two up at The Queen's Larder and then have a bite of pizza to celebrate. Or Cagneys, if they're full. My treat. Plus, you know: SiC tomorrow. Condemned man, and all that. But it looks like you've got some plans of your own already, eh?'

Rex nodded.

'Well, there's no accounting for **taste**,' said Lollo. Then, with a wink: 'Lick 'er out for us, Kingsy, eh?'

'Sir?' said Rex.

'What?'

Rex gave him the finger with both hands. 'Fuck off, you Northern bastard!'

Once he'd shut the door behind them, Rex could hear Lollo singing as he walked down Falcon's stairs.

'"A dignified and potent officer", he sang, "whose functions are particularly vital!"'

It was something cheerful from *The Mikado*, one of Rex's grandmother's favourites, and he could hear Lollo's voice fading – the gradual diminuendo – as he went further down the stairs:

> Taken from the county jail,
> By a set of curious chances;
> Liberated then on bail,
> On my own **recognisances**.

He's in a good fucking mood, thought Rex, shaking his head. He wasn't the only one either. This evening's supper with Susan was turning into a double celebration. Or was it a triple? He was losing count. Fucking Lollo! Rex wanted nothing more than to **chin** the cunt, but he'd have to be a bit cleverer than that; take it slowly. And right now, Rex had more important things to think about. For one thing, thanks to his fucking DCI, he was late.

He pulled on the new Perry and gave himself a quick spray of Floris. He used the letterbox to pull the door to behind him, like he always did, and then it was down the steps two at a time.

Rats, indeed!

Rex was good at thinking on his feet, and that was one of the best. Taken by rats! Fuck me!

As he crossed over Southampton Row and walked along Bloomsbury Way towards Coptic Street – where Susan would be waiting by now – Rex knew perfectly well where Couvoir's nose was. Wasn't it an old **Spike Milligan** gag: 'I have the body of an eighteen-year-old. I keep it in the fridge'?

Rex had nearly had a heart attack when Eddie had asked for ice. Webster might have got more than he'd bargained for if he'd dug around in the freezer compartment, behind the bag of frozen peas. That would have been Rex **hoist** with his own petard right there! It would have served him right, too, for not getting shot of them sooner, but he'd got away with it, again.

Got away with it for now.

He and Terence both.

Fucking hell.

But tonight was about Susan. He was looking forward to seeing what she'd bought in Agent Provocateur. Some sort of 1950s **girdle** thing, perhaps, and some black-seamed stockings? A half-cup bra from which it would be all the easier to scoop out those beautiful breasts of hers. Rex was looking forward to a big helping of Susan's **sugar** tonight. Fuck the bread and olives. Fuck the dough balls. Fuck the Margheritas and the Napoletanas. Fuck the Four Seasons, the Formaggi and the Sloppy Giuseppe. Fuck the Fiorentinas and the Venezianas, the American Hots and the Sohos and the Giardinieras. Fuck the mixed salads and the coleslaw. Fuck the Classic and the Romana bases. Fuck all of that. Given half the chance, he would **bend** Susan over the table in her new Agent Provocateur underwear, spread her legs and fuck her right there in the **ceramic**-tiled interior of the Coptic Street Pizza Express.

Maybe after they'd eaten they could go to The Perseverance, and then walk back to his flat via Great Ormond Street, if Susan wasn't sick to the back teeth of the place. He could tell her about his twin brother who had died at birth, strangled by Rex's umbilicus.

'What was his name?' she would say. 'Did he have—'

'Oh, yes,' Rex would say. 'They used to baptise them and everything in those days. His name was Joseph King. Joseph Jonathan King.'

Then, once this was over; once tonight was over and Susan had gone back to York – not that he wished it over; he wanted to savour every minute of it – but once she'd gone home, he'd check what time the **tide** was going out and maybe walk down to the river, to Wapping or Woolwich or even further downstream. Yeah, that's what he'd do. Once she was back in York, he'd take them from the freezer compartment and walk down by the river or over one of the bridges. He'd see the water rushing back out to sea, and he would throw them as far as he could. He'd chuck them into the middle of the river. Milo's nose, whatever his name was, would sink immediately and disappear, but Trevor Tennyson's inhaler wouldn't. It would float on the surface, but it would just be one more tiny object amongst the millions of others that were churning in that turbulent and muddy water, with its freight of **lumber**, bottles and plastic bags, tree branches and traffic cones, of weeds and footballs and dead fish. And it would move fast, alright. It would be carried out to sea at a rate of knots. Churned and battered, its blue plastic casing would become brittle before eventually breaking apart and falling away, leaving just the tiny aerosol canister itself to be carried in and out by successive tides.

Rex reached for the door handle, pulled it open and stepped inside, enjoying the familiar sounds of cutlery and quiet conversation, the short scrape of wooden peels on the baking-deck floor; the warmth of the ovens, and the rich and savoury smells of yeasty dough and baking, of cooked tomatoes, herbs and toasting cheese.

Good call, he thought. He could murder a pizza.

The place was packed as always – the young couples, the work colleagues, the travellers, the birthday parties and the family treats, all tucking in – and for a second Rex couldn't see Susan, but then he did. She was sitting by the window looking at her phone. He walked over, going on to pantomime tiptoes – 'Excuse me, ladies' – as he squeezed through the gap between two tables with a wink.

'Hi, gorgeous. Sorry I'm late. Lollo, my boss. Don't even ask!'

'Hi, Rex,' she said, smiling. 'Don't worry. I was just chatting to Ashley.'

'Wow, you look amazing,' he said, lightly touching her shoulder and leaning forward to kiss her upturned lips, to touch her cheek and stroke behind her ear. 'Beautiful.'

Yeah, that's what he'd do.

AUTHOR'S NOTES

Some readers will have noted that the 'Royal Palace Theatre' depicted in this novel occupies roughly the same space and location as London's famous Theatre Royal, Drury Lane, but they should also note that any similarity ends there. This Royal Palace Theatre is completely fictional, its name a crude translation of Théâtre du Palais-Royal, after successive Parisian theatres so called.

Similarly, the Holborn Police Station depicted herein shares some external features and its location on Lamb's Conduit Street, London, with the real Holborn Police Station, but internal layouts, command structures, procedures and operations, cases, etc., are all entirely fictional.

Readers seeking information or support regarding deaths in custody are directed to the work of the UK charity INQUEST, which monitors deaths in custody and provides 'a specialist, comprehensive advice service to bereaved people, lawyers, other advice and support agencies, the media, MPs and the wider public on contentious deaths and their investigation'.*

The Fountain in the Forest and the two novels that follow are mapped against a specific period in UK history: a brief interregnum of ninety days (or nine revolutionary weeks, according to Sylvain Maréchal's decimal calendar) from the end of the UK Miners' Strike on 3 March 1985 to the Battle of the Beanfield on 1 June. Each chapter is mapped against one day in 1985, converted into the French Revo-

---

* www.inquest.org.uk/about/home

lutionary Calendar, but as well as being shot through with the daily symbols from the Revolutionary Calendar, *The Fountain in the Forest* also uses a 'mandated vocabulary', i.e. a predetermined list of words that *must* be incorporated into the text – namely, all of the solutions to the *Guardian* Quick Crossword from each of those same days in 1985.

Mandated vocabularies are of course one of several literary techniques or constraints that were proposed by Oulipo, the *Ouvroir de Littérature Potentielle*, or Workshop for Potential Literature, whose best-known exponent was the novelist Georges Perec (1936–82). Perec himself is perhaps most celebrated for a novel in which the constraint operates at the level of the individual letter rather than using a mandated vocabulary: his 1969 'lipogrammatic' novel *La Disparition*, written entirely without using the letter 'E' (which is available in Gilbert Adair's 1995 English-language translation, *A Void*). A less well-known work written using a mandated vocabulary is the late Oulipo member Harry Mathews' short story 'Their Words, for You' (published in his 1977 collection *Selected Declarations of Dependence*), which uses only the words from forty-six proverbs.

While undertaking the research for *The Fountain in the Forest* (which included writing the stand-alone novella *Dicky Star and the Garden Rule*), I studied – among other sources – the *Guardian* newspapers of the period, which are held in the newspaper collections of the British Library. Sitting at the microfiche readers, first in Colindale and more recently in Euston Road, I found myself paying particular attention to the *Guardian*'s back pages, which is perhaps not so surprising since completion of the Quick Crossword had been a daily habit of mine in 1985–86. Remembering that, in the later years of his life, Georges Perec had composed a weekly crossword for the news magazine *Le Point*, and in order to reimmerse myself in the habits of the time, I redid now those same crosswords that I had first completed thirty years earlier.

More than just an aide-memoire, I found that writing these words out again activated a kind of linguistic 'muscle memory', that this smattering of words was woven into the warp and weft of my experience of those days. Using the solutions as an Oulipian mandated vocabulary offers, then, a linguistic and historical 'time capsule' of the vocabulary of the period, as well as a pantheon of historical figures, from Hastings Banda and Walter Mondale to Spike Milligan. It also gives a meter and a measure to the prose, in counterpoint to the measure that is provided by the French Revolutionary Calendar and by the daily symbols of French rural life drawn from it. Thus chapters 1–6, 8–13, 15–20, 22–27, 29 and 30 are each written using all of the solutions to the *Guardian* Quick Crossword (adhering, with one or two exceptions, to hyphenations, etc., of the period) from the corresponding day in 1985 (*Guardian* days only, so excluding Sundays), and in order of their appearance in the text, as follows:

CHAPTER 1
henbane, cabinet, Emma, least, cavil, prosaic, indispensable, Gallup, reason, Tuesday, night-watchman, Banda, icicles, vinegar, spice, Mark Twain, Iliad, my type, aspect, wallpaper, thrill, ebb-tide, tea-shop, geyser, Eric, enemy (*solutions to Quick Crossword No. 4,649*, Guardian, *Monday 4 March 1985*.)

CHAPTER 2
old, crabby, bargain, riding, free and easy, assign, underwear, Nye, motor, bus, reredos, gaunt, apostle, often, duple, front runner, Newmarket, finger-print, forthcoming, tighten, indignant, war, banker, printable (*solutions to Quick Crossword No. 4,650*, Guardian, *Tuesday 5 March 1985*.)

CHAPTER 3
schedule, penny-farthing, ramp, sherry, she-bear, sinus, physiotherapy, discern, drudge, skyscraper, subjective, Erin, sediment, pond, bluff, had up, remorse, observe, torch, gravamen, acme, hara-kiri (*solutions to Quick Crossword No. 4,651*, Guardian, *Wednesday 6 March 1985*.)

CHAPTER 4
vicarage, song, symphony, negate, platypus, byword, slur, stop, ally, save, sprawl, laughter, playwright, mice, in-laws, old folks, dust, safari park, hard at work, cantilever, oblivion, first aid, Gertrude, Iris (*solutions to Quick Crossword No. 4,652, Guardian, Thursday 7 March 1985.*)

CHAPTER 5
Webster, coffee, Eton, plod, glorify, set-up, onus, pilot, powder puff, fever, fly-blown, permissible, Bolivia, alas, purple, lipstick, tutu, viol, promise, midge, Becky Sharp, penalise, innovate (*solutions to Quick Crossword No. 4,653, Guardian, Friday 8 March 1985.*)

CHAPTER 6
enormous, over, Hesperides, immune, match, horse, neat, hypodermic, husbandman, Vitus, Gurkha, yard-arm, book-shop, handicraft, anchor, inflate, Mafeking, fetlock, aged, editor, avid, crash, high tea, remarque (*solutions to Quick Crossword No. 4,654, Guardian, Saturday 9 March 1985.*)

CHAPTER 8
corn, Avengers, moult, music, member, occasionally, fiddler, mad-house, spiral, bismuth, release, prolific, okapi, loud applause, mime, sledge-hammer, pease-pudding, red-hot, clerihew, distend, stow, sofa, under, seraph (*solutions to Quick Crossword No. 4,655, Guardian, Monday 11 March 1985.*)

CHAPTER 9
wedge, heron, fowl, Tennyson, worth, oddity, evil, shed, spotless, valid, darbies, wafer, thin, light and shade, ruffian, farewell, with it, glower, my eye, loosened, Electra, timid, Galileo, sphere, pontoon bridge, Reich (*solutions to Quick Crossword No. 4,656, Guardian, Tuesday 12 March 1985.*)

CHAPTER 10
top drawer, execrate, black pudding, restaurateur, Picard, Aral, visa, sabre-rattler, Gandhi, walkie-talkie, training, parent, Exeter, Charles, Geraldine, rear, coronary, ill-bred, llama, duty, Lancelot, adieu (*solutions to Quick Crossword No. 4,657, Guardian, Wednesday 13 March 1985.*)

CHAPTER 11
leave, usual, policy, owing, overtly, crimson, dress, Macduff, witless, big deal, reading, not a lot, parade ground, grated, monstrous, colic, powwow, go-between, molar, inter, Elmer, recycle, hybrid, warble, deface (*solutions to Quick Crossword No. 4,658, Guardian, Thursday 14 March 1985.*)

CHAPTER 12
seascape, tom-tits, frost, convolvulus, coot, anode, kalends, Dame Fortune, balm, expeditious, cull, enshrine, starving, bigot, imam, forgive, off-side, drama critic, croak, succinct (*solutions to Quick Crossword No. 4,659, Guardian, Friday 15 March 1985.*)

CHAPTER 13
beef, gulf, Ulster, Leinster, Armagh, Antrim, Tyrone, Fermanagh, Down, Derby Day, madame, mortgage, dynastic, virginals, spider, bass, hollander, stanza, trying, perpetual (*solutions to Quick Crossword No. 4,660, Guardian, Saturday 16 March 1985.*)

CHAPTER 15
dais, zinc, pellet, control, sac, pupae, kaleidoscopic, in toto, lazybones, pork, Mondale, pea soup, pip-squeak, iceman, quotient, vim, main verb, La Paz, vice-principal, colonial, Elsie, peat, beri-beri, ominous, happen, ousel (*solutions to Quick Crossword No. 4,661, Guardian, Monday 18 March 1985.*)

CHAPTER 16
orison, calico, jackdaw, cheek by jowl, tinge, rinse, pass by, Rhine, plastic, shingle, Larwood, Aire, book token, Edward, Rajah, infernal, toreador, ocarina, ticket, royal road, Hoffman, zircon, stag, kimono, hungry (*solutions to Quick Crossword No. 4,662, Guardian, Tuesday 19 March 1985.*)

CHAPTER 17
revel, brutal, alder, Norma, Venus, modesty, hyperactive, brain, answer, Heather, Orwell, wild-cat, upstart, Lollard, lingua franca, toddle, nadir, lament, vehicle, canal, ducat, ellipse, slot machine, ninepin, two-bit (*solutions to Quick Crossword No. 4,663, Guardian, Wednesday 20 March 1985.*)

CHAPTER 18
ruddy, mini-van, rust, snip, running, paraffin, monotony, notion, rates, anathema, spare time job, juice, cape, rhyming slang, Padstow, Rover, oral, tracing paper, confetti, pit-a-pat, bigwig, tyrant, Beggar's Opera, animus (*solutions to Quick Crossword No. 4,664*, Guardian, *Thursday 21 March 1985*.)

CHAPTER 19
within, hemispherical, Ivan, whitebait, chinwag, errand, night, hero, iota, gunpowder plot, Baader-Meinhof, Hard Times, choir-boy, basic, sot, ethereal, Chirac, marrow, cog, Oslo, authoritarian, film star, trimaran, festoon (*solutions to Quick Crossword No. 4,665*, Guardian, *Friday 22 March 1985*.)

CHAPTER 20
fraternal, emphasise, facetious, knit, wreath, giant, over, kill, safe, cook, liquor, Anselm, avuncular, Juno, schooling, Walton, Trent, Mervyn, Morag, Ankara, my hat, chameleon, lick, Greek gift, rental, heehaw, sage, clockwork (*solutions to Quick Crossword No. 4,666*, Guardian, *Saturday 23 March 1985*.)

CHAPTER 22
limp rag, last, splash, almond, watching (brief), sincere, half-wit, cross purposes, respect, (watching) brief, least, twelve, star-gazer, incapable, hatch, hutch, Reeve, aunt, Zagreb, tractor, tarmac, air show, cherub, beseech, Mistral, Perth, hitch (*solutions to Quick Crossword No. 4,667*, Guardian, *Monday 25 March 1985*.)

CHAPTER 23
expectant, erect, gum, Lysol, arc, sponsorship, orator, infer, ingenious, Orlando, nightmare, intimations, immortality, spell, nun, Israeli, arable, adroit, pimple, pug, gentle touch, natural, flagrante delicto (*solutions to Quick Crossword No. 4,668*, Guardian, *Tuesday 26 March 1985*.)

CHAPTER 24
spud, mischief, anvil, Bohemia, impunity, term, cedilla, Newbury, high and mighty, along, pass, death-watch, vain, mason, ballroom, hedge, wiseacre,

bodkin, sticky, in sequence, as large as life, go-ahead (*solutions to Quick Crossword No. 4,669*, Guardian, *Wednesday 27 March 1985*.)

CHAPTER 25

standard, away, attach, henceforth, scud, prepared, Beatrice, cow-house, voyeur, restricted, bridegroom, bachelor, Dortmund, bier, cicada, loaf, Bach, season, ride, ewer, a great help, skid, classics, Benedick (*solutions to Quick Crossword No. 4,670*, Guardian, *Thursday 28 March 1985*.)

CHAPTER 26

dusk, snag, profile, grandson, scruff, shut, mauve, generous, cottage pie, beer, Arras, stuck up, galley proof, pace, cenotaph, garnet, jonquil, stem, adjudicate, forgo, topic, red light, outcrop (*solutions to Quick Crossword No. 4,671*, Guardian, *Friday 29 March 1985*.)

CHAPTER 27

Tom (Bowling), bland, Revie, bubble bath, baby doll, bedstead, bawd, locket, wardroom, combat, creditable, arose, stabiliser, burst, blotto, bode, turn out, (Tom) Bowling, layman, tramway, hail, side-show, blab, balloon, cadaver (*solutions to Quick Crossword No. 4,672*, Guardian, *Saturday 30 March 1985*.)

CHAPTER 29

Susan, croc, doorman, riff-raff, straw, hospital ship, in debt, whey, air shot, seduce, stocks, purchase, group-captain, hooch, instep, fashion plate, canonise, rumba, cathode, fawn, honour bright, pose, apoplexy, rose-red (*solutions to Quick Crossword No. 4,673*, Guardian, *Monday 1 April 1985*.)

CHAPTER 30

bash, motif, Buckfast, ear-plug, prospect, itemise, Freud, unafraid, spree, Chelsea, motel, gored, needless, smudge, Hermia, taste, recognisances, chin, Spike Milligan, hoist, girdle, sugar, bend, ceramic, tide, lumber (*solutions to Quick Crossword No. 4,674*, Guardian, *Tuesday 2 April 1985*.)

ACKNOWLEDGEMENTS

With special thanks to my incredible agent, Patrick Walsh, and assistant John Ash of PEW Literary; to my brilliant editor, Lee Brackstone; Ella Griffiths, Samantha Matthews and the rest of the great team at Faber & Faber; and to copyeditor Silvia Crompton, and proofreader Sarah Barlow.

Sincere thanks to Dr Sanja Perovic, Professor Patrick Ffrench and colleagues in the Department of French at King's College London; the artists Stuart Brisley and Maya Balcioglu; Evelyn Wilson, Suzie Leighton, Jana Riedel, Noshin Sultan and the Creativeworks London team; Alastair Brotchie and Tanya Peixoto. I would also like to thank Judith Károlyi; Forma Arts and Media Ltd; Jane and Louise Wilson; Caroline Smith; Fiona McMorrough and Diane Gray-Smith; James C. White; the Such family; Rosy and Ian Horton; Chris Dorley-Brown; French and Mottershead; Domo Baal; the late Malcolm Bennett; and the people of the Département des Alpes-Maritimes, France.

Above all, I would like to thank my wife, Sarah Such.

As noted in the Preface, readers wishing to find out more about the French Revolutionary Calendar are directed to Sanja Perovic's excellent *The Calendar in Revolutionary France: Perceptions of Time in Literature, Culture, Politics* (Cambridge University Press, 2012).

The traditional 'Bedfordshire May Day Carol' (which appears in Chapters 26 and 28) was collected by Sir Ernest Clarke for the

English folksong collector and researcher Lucy E. Broadwood's *English Traditional Songs and Carols* (Boosey & Co., 1908).

*

Tony White was creative entrepreneur in residence funded by Creativeworks London and a visiting research fellow in the Department of French at King's College London, 2013–15.